Caliburn

MERLIN'S TALE

Caliburn
MERLIN'S TALE

Virgil Renzulli

Bagwyn Books

Tempe, Arizona
2015

Published by Bagwyn Books, an imprint of the Arizona Center for Medieval and Renaissance Studies (ACMRS), Tempe, Arizona.

For Dylan and Abby

*Special thanks to Michele Peters, Kendra TerBeek, Roy Rukkila,
and Todd Halvorsen of Bagwyn Books; media maven Marshall Terrill,
Ken Lowell for the cover illustration, and most especially
Jewell Parker Rhodes, mentor and muse.*

Book One

1) The Apparition

Ahead, atop the crest of the steep hill, they were finally able to catch sight of the abandoned castle's tower. Only partially visible in the storm, it was gray stone, coated with snow on its seaward side, its top portion shrouded in a cloud. The two hunters, their bodies tilted forward against the fierce gale, made slow progress in snow that was knee-deep in places. One paused to look at their destination, but the wind intensified, driving a curtain of snow and sleet across the tower's face.

Allum, the taller of the two men, whose features — but for his eyes — were wrapped in a cloth, had three fowl hanging upside down over his back. All three were frozen through. Donal, his beard a near solid mass of snow crystals, walked with a limp a few paces behind him. Slung across his shoulders, its legs hanging over his chest, was a young deer. It, too, had begun to freeze.

Donal stood still, his eyes fixed on the castle, and shouted ahead to his companion to be heard over the storm. "Allum, I say we should turn back for home."

Allum continued to trudge forward and shouted back to Donal. "I've been in storms such as this, and we'll surely freeze to death if we don't make the shelter of that castle."

"You have!" Donal paused as a gust of wind blew across his face. "But you said there's never been a storm such as this."

"I've experienced storms *almost* as fierce as this one and know well how quickly — and painfully — they can kill a man."

"But it's a bad luck castle." Donal continued to stand still, watching Allum get farther ahead of him. "It's abandonned and ruined, isn't it? That must be bad luck if ever there was such a thing."

Allum waved dismissively at Donal. "Nonsense."

Donal adjusted the position of the deer across his shoulders and resumed walking. "They say this is likely ancient Valphain Castle. . ."

"Can't hear you."

Donal shouted louder. "Valphain Castle, that's what they say this is, and there's talk of an apparition that's been seen in the castle's tower and movin' along its walls or what's left of its walls." He looked up at the tower again. "I feel as though we are bein' watched at this very moment."

Allum turned to look back at him. "You sound like an old woman."

"More than one man has seen this. . .this specter. White as a mist and hooded so that his face cannot be seen is he. Or perhaps. . ." Donal hesitated. "Perhaps, it has no face."

The incline steepened and Allum struggled to ascend it. "I've visited many a castle and walked many a forest." He paused to take a long breath. "In all my time I have yet to encounter a specter or a demon or even an ogre." He placed his hand on the hilt of his sword. "But show me your specter, and I'll deal with it."

"Surely you know that specters can't be harmed by swords."

"No, because they don't exist."

"You believe I concoct stories, but hunters have even seen a fire burnin' in the castle tower." Allum stopped walking, looked back at his companion and waited for him to come closer. "That's right. Actual fires, they've seen."

"And what need would an apparition have for a fire?"

Donal, his eyelashes and brows caked with snow, had a quizzical look on his face. "To keep warm, of course."

Allum, shaking his head, allowed Donal to limp past him.

They began to ascend the sea cliff, which made the going even more difficult. The wind now carried more sleet than snow, and it stung their faces. Far below, the gale drove the surf with increasing violence against the rocks along the shore.

Donal was grunting and breathing uneasily as he struggled forward. "I feel as though we'll be swept over the edge and into the sea." Allum did not answer. "And I still feel we are bein' watched." The castle was within reach, but the storm continued to worsen. "You see, Allum, the storm is tryin' to keep us from reachin' the castle. It's warnin' us."

Allum remained silent.

They reached the castle's front wall. Great stones of what once must have been an imposing structure now lay like so many jagged teeth, some half buried in the ground; other stones that had toppled from the higher portions of the wall had rolled a distance from their original location.

Donal was moving slowly and straining even harder to breathe. "If this is, indeed, Valphain Castle, then the ruin of these walls was caused by the magic of the Wizard Merlin." His eyes opened wide, and he spoke in a hushed voice. "Do you suppose the specter is Merlin?"

Allum rolled his eyes and tilted his head skyward. "Merlin is long dead. Even you know that. And there is no specter. And if you don't stop this nonsense and your infernal complaining, I'll leave you out here to your fate."

The pair started to thread their way through the lowest section of the toppled rocks to the great oak door that was the entrance to the castle tower. The massive door must have been challenging to move when it was new. All these years later, the wood was warped and splintered, the hinges rusted and columns of ice and snow filled every crevice. Allum and Donal dropped their game to the ground and threw their shoulders against the door, but it did not budge. Twice more they assaulted the door, and on the fourth attempt it moved back not quite a foot.

Allum rubbed his left shoulder and shook his arms. "Your apparition must be quite narrow to pass through this opening."

"Specters don't have bodies like ours. They pass through wood and stone as we pass through the driven snow. That's why they're called specters."

"And yet, according to you, they've need of fire?"

Donal frowned and wiped some of the snow from his beard. "Damnation with specters," he said angrily. "Strike the door once again and chatter less."

They managed to open the door just enough to allow their entry. Retrieving their game from the ground, the two men hurried into the tower of what might have been the famed but now abandoned Valphain Castle. The dim exterior light streaming through the partially open door illuminated only a small portion of the tower's great hall. Allum noticed a well-worn torch tilting from its holder by the entry door and reached over to grab it. As he did, Donal drew his sword.

"Preparing to meet your apparition, Donal?"

"No, I sense somethin'." He extended his neck, trying to see in the darkness. "There may be somethin' of flesh and blood in this old tower. Somethin' menacin'."

"Then, you stay on guard," said Allum sarcastically, "while I do something useful like finding the means of starting a fire."

Allum had no sooner finished those words than the pair heard a great whooshing sound off to their left, and the great hall was suddenly lit by an enormous flame filling the height and width of the hall's fireplace.

Donal looked about anxiously. "Was that you, Allum?"

"Of course, it wasn't me." Allum drew his sword. He carefully approached the fireplace, reached out the torch in his left hand and rotated it into the flame until it was fully engaged. He turned toward the dark portions of the great hall, torch extended in one hand, sword in the other. Donal walked close beside him, his arm brushing against Allum's back. The great hall was spacious and in the limited reach of the torch light, they could see nothing at the far end.

Allum shuttered when his torch lit the face and shoulders of a very old man, a face seemingly as old as time itself, drawn, pale and hollow with a long white beard and topped by a faded, hooded cloak. At first the old man did not appear to be alive except for the reflected torch flame that burned in his black eyes.

"Welcome to Valphain Castle." The old man had a deep and vigorous voice. He looked down at the two swords pointed in his direction. "Surely two great hunters and warriors do not fear a harmless old man?" The fire behind them suddenly flared. While the two hunters were turned looking at it, the old man walked casually past them, directly between their drawn swords and toward the fire. "Come warm yourselves," he said. Then, he bellowed at them. "And close the door you have left open. You have let in the cold."

Donal and Allum sheathed their swords and went to shut the door, which was nearly as difficult to close as it had been to open. "He's a wizard," said Donal, looking back at the old man.

"First a specter; now a wizard! What next? He's just an old man, is all."

"But wizards *are* old men."

Although they had whispered, the old man heard them and addressed them in the exaggerated voice of a court crier. "That is the conundrum. Wizards are, indeed, old men. . .unless of course, they are young men. But not all old men are wizards. How is one to know which is which?"

With the tower door finally shut, the two hunters came close to the fire and began to remove their snow covered boots and outer garments, the flames causing the snow on them to melt into pools of water at their feet. The old man dragged well-worn chairs to serve as seats by the fire, and the three men sat down.

"I'm Donal," he said, thumping his chest. "He's called Allum. And what's your name?"

The old man laughed. "What matters a name? It does not alter the thing itself, does it? My name! What a question!"

"Have it your way," said Allum. "But if you won't give us a name, we'll just call you 'Old One'."

He smiled. "Yes, Old One, a description, not a name. Of course, a description too often used becomes a name. Where does that leave us?"

Allum leaned toward Donal and whispered. "He must be addled."

"Addled!"

"Sorry." Donal apologized for his companion's comment.

The Old One became animated and spoke in sharp tones. "It was not I who was caught out in the worst storm in living memory. It was not I, nearly frozen stiff, who had to take shelter wherever he could find it — in this ruin of a castle. So, let us be clear about who is — and who is not — addled." The Old One smiled, and his tone softened. "I offer you a warm fire and would also offer you a hot meal, but alas, I have no food." He glanced down at the frozen fowl by Allum's feet. "However, I see that you have the makings of just the kind of meal that will warm a man's innards while the fire warms his skin."

Donal moved closer to the fire, and Allum began to strip the feathers from the smallest of the three birds he had shot.

The Old One, meanwhile, disappeared into the darkness and returned with a spit, a pan to hold the feathers and discarded innards of the bird, and a sharp knife. "Allow me to demonstrate to you the best way to strip a fowl." The Old One displayed his technique not on one bird but rather on all three and soon had them roasting on the spit. "One for each of us."

Allum looked from the birds to the Old One. "Any one of the three would've been enough for all of us."

The Old One ignored the comment. "A feast at Valphain Castle. Just like days gone by."

"Then," said Donal, "this is actually the Valphain Castle they speak about in legend?"

The Old One sat erect in his stool and answered with indignation in his voice. "Did I not say that already? Did I not say 'welcome to Valphain Castle' in a very clear voice when first I saw you?" He raised his eyes up and looked about the darkened hall. Relaxing back into his seat, he spoke softly again. "This was the site of many a feast and more than one battle. It was a place of great men and beautiful women, of valor and treachery, of love and deceit, of victory and disgrace."

"You speak as though you were there." Allum sounded skeptical.

"I know many things and can tell you all the great tales of our people."

"We've heard them all," said Allum. "I know them at least as well as you."

"But do you? Have you heard stories or *true* stories? A tale is not like anything else. With a tale, a fish the size of a frog becomes as large as a horse with the telling and the retelling. A man who observes an archer score three successive bullseyes eventually becomes the archer. A tale about a flying cow is accepted without question by some because it seems too improbable to be a made-up tale." He leaned closer to the two hunters. "You see, there is fact, and there is legend. And there is a place where fact and legend collide."

"I suppose," said Allum, "we've no hope of avoiding hearing whatever tale you have the intention to tell."

"It will be a tale suited to men such as yourselves, experienced men, warriors certainly, a tale with fierce Saxons, Picts and Norsemen."

Allum held up his hands. "I know all I need to know about barbarous Saxons, Picts and Norsemen. I needn't hear more about them."

The Old One shook his head. "Come, come. How can there be a tale about a British warrior without an adversary or two?"

"And do you know many Saxons, Picts and Norsemen?" asked Donal.

"I knew the ones in this story. Or knew of them." He looked from Allum to Donal. "Do you know the story of the Sword in the Stone and its prophecy?"

Allum smirked. "The story of Excalibur and how Arthur became king when he drew the sword is the best known of all the Celtic stories."

"Excalibur is the Sword of Kings given to Arthur by the Lady of the Lake," the Old One said in a tone of apparent satisfaction. "It was Caliburn that was the sword in the stone, the Sword of Destiny."

"Do you mean to tell us the story of Excalibur, I mean Calibur?" asked Donal.

"Caliburn. . .burn. Exactly so. Great men do not simply spring from the ground like toadstools after a rain. No, great men before they become great must labor at it, and they require a mentor who can teach them properly. So, this is a tale about Arthur but also a tale about Merlin, for without Merlin there would have been no Arthur. Would there?"

"No, there wouldn't," said Donal.

The Old One smiled. "Of course, there would have, but he would have been a different Arthur."

2) Courage, Determination, Intensity

Arthur pulled on the chainmail tunic. Its weight felt good. It meant protection. But it would not prevent the bruises and pains from the hardest blows his fellow students would deliver with their thick wooden swords.

Especially if he had to fight Marrek again today.

Next he strapped greaves to his lower legs. They, like everything else he would use in combat training, were borrowed, and they were ill-fitting. The sores caused by his chafing greaves were more painful and persistent than any of the swellings, cuts and aching muscles he had received during nine days of sparring with wooden sword and shield.

Had it been only nine days? It seemed longer. Much longer.

Next he strapped leather bracers to his forearms.

Finally he pulled on a metal helmet, and as it came down over the sides of his face and its thin metal nose guard dropped into place, he felt — as Merlin would say — in his element. Merlin often told him he was destined to be a knight, a great one, but Arthur did not believe him, not completely. As the second son of a minor nobleman, he could hope only to be a squire to his older brother, Kaye.

Still, his most persistent dreams and his constant daydreams concerned becoming a knight. Dressed in fine armor that gleamed in the sunlight and sitting atop a black or a white or a brown stallion, he would defeat all-comers in a tournament, win it by dethroning the reigning champion, and humbly bow before a cheering crowd that had stood up at their seats in the flag-decorated grandstand.

That would be enjoyable.

Training for such a moment was not.

Arthur picked up his wooden sword and his wooden shield — one of the two leather straps that held it on his forearm was loose and in constant need of refastening. He walked past the tents where the four dozen or so students and their instructors were temporarily housed, and, as usual, he was the first student to be out on the field for late morning sparring.

The field, a level grass area a few hundred feet long and more than a few dozen feet wide, had been cleared to one side of its rough wooden and straw human figures that were used for morning sword and spear instruction and the round targets that were meant for both archery and light spear throwing practice.

Arthur found the regimentation and the repetitive nature of those training sessions tedious. He preferred the sparring. It was closer to real combat, which, after all, was why they were being trained. The problem was that sparring was painful. In addition to the sores from his ill-fitting greaves, his right shoulder was achy, his left knee slightly wobbly and there was an occasional searing pain in his back, just left of his right shoulder blade. Standing here, waiting for combat to begin was the worst part, like waiting to jump into a cold pool of water. After the first hard blow, the first hurt, he did not worry about bodily injury, only about winning.

He was ever mindful of Merlin's instruction:

Think of yourself as the best, and even if you believe you have achieved that status, strive always to improve.

He was not the best. Marrek was.

Kaye was approaching the field. He was dressed in the new helmet and chainmail armor their father, Ector, had given him for this training camp. Kaye was tall and with the new armor was imposing looking, but Arthur considered him slow and awkward, and lacking in the intensity a good warrior required. Kaye had not beaten Arthur sparring in a year, not since Arthur's fifteenth birthday when Kaye's advantage in age and size were no longer sufficient to defeat his younger brother.

Merlin warned him that Kaye had not yet accepted being second best in the family:

Your brother is intimidated by your combat skills and will be jealous of your success in the training exercises. Treat him gently. He will be your closest ally one day and you his.

Kaye walked straight toward him and was certain to ask Arthur, as he did every morning, about his chances in the day's contest. Arthur thought he had done well in his sparring but could not say so to Kaye; he could not boast that, by his own reckoning, he had beaten or stood toe-to-toe with every opponent he had faced so far, no matter how old or how big. Save one. Marrek.

Kaye reached Arthur as the field began to fill with student combatants. "Arthur, do you think you'll draw Nele again today? Does that worry you?"

Nele, tall, strong and intelligent, was considered by everyone, except Arthur, to be the best warrior among the students. Arthur had learned to move in close enough that Nele could not strike with the full extension of his arm, lessening his power. But he dare not tell Kaye that he had held his own against Nele.

"Nele is very good although he doesn't always fight at full intensity," said Arthur, "perhaps because he doesn't feel the need to constantly demonstrate his skill."

Kaye frowned. "So, you're saying you can beat him?"

Arthur shrugged his shoulders. "I'm merely giving an assessment. Warriors must assess their adversaries."

"Assessment! You sound like Merlin. He's filled your head with dreams far larger than your station in life."

Arthur paused to calm himself. He did not want to argue with Kaye, especially before a sparring session. "You asked me if I worried about Nele, and I was giving you an assessment." Arthur bowed in exaggerated fashion. "Oh, excuse me. You do not approve of that word." Kaye glared at him, but Arthur had long since ceased to be intimidated by his older brother. Attempting a conciliatory tone, he continued. "I merely wanted to explain why I don't worry about Nele. . ."

"Because you believe you can beat him."

"No, because I would have said — had I been permitted to complete the thought — that I worry far more about Marrek, who thrashes me every day."

"You say that now because I challenged you. Why not just admit you consider yourself better than everyone, including Nele?"

Arthur decided not to respond, to end the conversation here. "It's better to think that you can beat everyone than to know that you can beat no one." These were the worst words Arthur could have spoken to Kaye, and he regretted them even as they slid out of his mouth. Kaye's face flushed red; his nostrils flared. There was no point in trying to make amends now. But then, Kaye should have known not to provoke him or any warrior as he was about to be bashed, battered, bruised and bloodied on the practice field.

Arthur would try to reconcile later by complimenting Kaye during the sparring.

The combat master, an aging and overweight but once formidable warrior named Jago, was calling the group to attention, which silenced the many conversations among the students that had been taking place. Jago began to shout out names, two at time, and as he did so, each pair of warriors would take their place on the field of combat, face each other and begin to spar.

Arthur seemed to draw the most difficult opponents each day, and he believed Merlin was responsible for that.

Arthur was called and walked out to the field, hoping he could begin the morning's combat with an opponent his own size. The next name called was Gerens. He was the youth who had traveled the greatest distance to join the training and had arrived with a good reputation. Gerens was one of the larger youths here but so far had not distinguished himself. Arthur had not yet faced him and welcomed the opportunity.

The two youths crouched behind their shields and slowly circled each other. The field was alive with the sounds of wooden swords striking wooden shields and metal armor, with war cries and cries of pain. Those distractions dropped below Arthur's level of awareness, as he concentrated on Gerens. He moved in on his opponent and delivered a series of hard blows to his shield. Gerens struck several sword blows of his own, but they were more to ward off Arthur's attack than to launch one of his own. Arthur backed off to consider his next approach. They circled again, then Arthur began his second offensive, and after that, a third. Although Gerens put up a reasonable defense, it was clear to Arthur that he could take the larger youth.

They continued to spar for a time — sparring was one of the very few activities that caused Arthur to lose track of time — then Arthur unleashed an attack that caused Gerens to continually back up and essentially hide behind his shield with no hope of taking the offensive.

Arthur backed off to give his opponent an opportunity to recover. After all, this was training, not real combat. When Arthur moved in again, Gerens retreated and continued to back away and circle. Gerens no longer wanted to fight.

Never quit on a comrade in arms. Never allow a comrade to quit on you.

Arthur, deciding to teach Gerens a lesson, charged him and delivered a rapid series of forceful blows that had Gerens staggering backwards. Forehand, backhand, overhand, the blows came until Arthur's adversary teetered and fell over backwards.

As Arthur stood over Gerens catching his breath, he felt moisture on his mouth. His lip was bleeding but not badly. Gerens' sword or shield must have caught Arthur in the face as he fell backwards, but Arthur had not felt the contact. Often it was not until he was taking off his armor that he found all the bruises and cuts he had received that day.

Jago was again calling the group to attention.

Arthur stuck his sword in his belt, took off his helmet and wiped the perspiration from his forehead.

"No restin'," said Jago and Arthur put his helmet back on. "If Saxons were on the other end of the field, they wouldn't be allowin' you a rest except for the permanent rest none of you would want." Jago surveyed the group. "Next round. Arthur, take the first place."

Arthur had been feeling pleased with his sparring performance so far but had been wondering if he was being singled out for special treatment, whether as a challenge or some kind of punishment.

"Merrak. Come forward and join Arthur"

Arthur took a deep breath and rotated his right shoulder to loosen it. He adjusted his helmet, tightened the loose strap on his shield and withdrew his sword.

Merrak was not as tall as Nele but had broad shoulders and a thick chest. The blows he delivered, in Arthur's estimation, were far more powerful even than Nele's. Worst than his punishing attacks, Merrak defense was impenetrable, and Arthur in nine days had yet to land even a single good blow. Merrak's armor, narrow slats layered over one another rather than chainmail, was the best Arthur had ever seen as was Merrak's helmet, which covered everything but his eyes. His bracers were metal, and he wore leather gloves with metal insets. There was not a vulnerable place on his body.

The two squared off. Merrak struck first with a blow to Arthur's shield that caused his arm to tingle. Arthur backed off until he was certain his arm had not gone numb. Now Arthur went on the attack. Merrak deflected Arthur's sword strikes with his shield and delivered a series of hard blows that left Arthur unsteady on his feet.

Courage, determination, intensity.

Again Arthur went on the attack, and again he was beaten back. It was as though he were throwing himself against the unyielding stone of a castle wall. He caused no damage except to himself.

This time it would be different. He would hit Merrak so hard the mighty Merrak would shatter like ice dropped on a rock.

Arthur charged him. Merrak beat him back with several staggering blows, then whipped his shield into the right side of Arthur's body, sending him sprawling to the ground. Arthur lost his sword. His shield was dangling from one strap. His helmet had been knocked off center. As Merrak approached him, Arthur managed to get to his hands and knees. He lunged at his adversary and wrapped his arms around his knees with the intention of tipping him over backwards. But Merrak was too strong and had bent over Arthur for additional leverage. He drove the butt of his sword handle into Arthur's back again and again, and when Arthur refused to release him, he brought a knee up into Arthur's face, knocking him to the ground.

As Arthur staggered to his feet, someone took hold of his arm. It was Jago. "Time for a rest. You're bleedin' badly."

Arthur looked down at his blood-soaked chainmail and cupped a hand under his face to catch the blood, which was coming from his nose as well as his mouth. "I can keep fighting. I want to keep fighting."

Jago laughed, slapped Arthur's shoulder and straightened his helmet so that he was no longer looking out a single eye slot. "And so you shall. So you shall. But first let us find your sword and fix the handle on your shield."

It was not long before Arthur, his shoulder and back aching, the bleeding from his nose and mouth stopped, felt no better and no worse than he had any other day of fighting. He was allowed to rejoin the sparring and thankfully was paired with an opponent his own size.

There was a loud scream, a sound of agony so great that everyone stopped to look at its source. It was Merrak. He dropped his sword and shield, and put his hands to his helmet. Merrak pulled off his helmet, threw it to the ground, grasped the sides of his head and screamed. "My head! My head!"

While Jago and another instructor ran to him, the other students slowly gathered around. Arthur found Kaye, who had been standing closer to Merrak when he began screaming, and asked what had happened.

"It's the strangest thing, Arthur. I don't believe he was touched." Kaye gave Arthur a playful elbow. "I'll wager you are happy that you are not likely to have to battle him again today."

"There's not a mark on him. He'll be back. If not today, surely tomorrow."

Merrak did not return that day. The following morning he sat without armor or weapons watching the sparring and could be occasionally seen putting his hands to his head. By afternoon he was gone.

3) Vision in a Stream

Merlin paused at the forest edge, just beyond the clearing where Ector's manor house stood. It was a modest estate, befitting a lord of modest standing. In addition to the wooden house, there was a large barn, a fenced pasture on the far side for Ector's horses and milk cows, and beyond that fields of grain and vegetables.

The morning was already warm, and Merlin was stripped down to his sleeveless and legless undergarments, revealing his slender arms and slightly outwardly bent skinny legs. The hooded cape that he usually wore was tied in a neat bundle hanging from the end of his long staff, which was decorated at the top with a carved owl's head.

Merlin well understood the importance of *presentation*. His normal Druid-like appearance, his sometimes puzzling manner of speech, roaming the danger-filled night forest alone armed with only a staff—things such as these when coupled with his occasional ability to see the future created the widely held belief that he possessed otherworldly powers. So, before meeting Ector, he put on his cloak, pulled the hood up and over his head, and positioned his staff as though he had been using it to assist in walking, which, in fact, he had not.

Ector, who stood tending to the hind leg of a horse, was aging faster than his contemporaries. Tall, thin and awkward in movement, not unlike his son Kaye, Ector had grown a belly far out of proportion to his spindly body, and some might have difficulty believing that he was once a warrior of slightly above average ability. He had light brown hair except on the top of his head but he concealed — or attempted to conceal — his bald spot by sweeping locks of his hair from left to right as though covering it with a small blanket of hair. As usual, the blanket had slipped from its position, and a cascade of brown hair now fell over his ear and rested on his shoulder.

Had Merlin wanted Arthur, who had never been told the true circumstances of his birth, to be raised by a great battle lord, he would have chosen someone other than Ector for the task. One of Ector's assets was that he was a man of delicate heart, a necessary asset in raising a son who was not his own. And he had integrity — in most things. The primary exception was that he often had little courage in standing up to Merlin. And, of course, the man whose hair now covered his shoulder rather than the top of his head had little integrity when it came to the vanity of his appearance.

Merlin called out to Ector as he stepped out of the forest and into the clearing where Ector's land began. Ector looked up at the approaching wizard and gestured toward the sky. "A magnificent day. A truly rare day, I would say."

"Truly rare, indeed." Merlin, then, mumbled to himself. "Identical to yesterday and likely similar to tomorrow." As he approached Ector, he asked, "Have you not noticed the heat?"

Ector shrugged his shoulders. "It feels wonderful."

"And *rare*, I would imagine. And where might young Arthur might be?"

Ector nodded toward the barn. "Kaye's in the barn tending to his chores."

"Yes, of course, I am sure Kaye is well. I–ah--I assumed Kaye was in the barn. . ."

"But that Arthur was not?"

"Exactly so."

"And as for Arthur, now that I think of it, I haven't seen him since our morning meal." Ector looked around as though searching for him, and his eyes appeared to settle on a pile of partially chopped wood. "And I cannot say I see that even one of his chores has been completed."

Merlin could guess where the boy was, and as he began to walk to the other side of the estate, to the woods beyond, Ector called after him. "Tell that boy there still remains firewood to be chopped before the mid-day meal."

Without looking back, Merlin raised his right arm to indicate he would deliver the message. Working his staff with his left hand, he entered the woods and followed a narrow path that led to a stream from which Ector and all the other members of his household took their water. There resting with his back against a tree, as the wizard had foreseen, was Arthur.

The boy was unaware of his presence, and Merlin took the opportunity to admire how well his protégé had grown. With broad shoulders, a large chest, muscular arms, and large hands and feet that promised more growth, Arthur would certainly become a formidable warrior. Physical strength was important in a leader. Merlin was even more pleased with Arthur's mental growth, particularly his skills of analysis. But along with that skill he had become more challenging for Merlin. People told him a change of that sort was typical of youths Arthur's age, and Merlin did not know enough about raising children to think otherwise.

One feature that had not changed were Arthur's dark, clear, penetrating eyes — eyes not unlike those of a wizard, Merlin had to reluctantly admit. At this moment those eyes were locked in a stare, apparently witnessing things that were not actually there. Merlin noticed the lad's lips were moving silently as though speaking to the unseen, and he waved an arm as though gesturing to someone who was elsewhere rather than here.

It was time to *wake* the boy.

"What foul creature were you vanquishing, boy? What comely maiden were you rescuing?"

Arthur, startled, scurried to his feet and stood before Merlin. "I was resting for a few moments. And I believe the time has come for you to stop calling me *boy*. For twelve brutal days I did well enough sparring against a variety of opponents."

"So they told me."

"Who is *they*?"

"Do not concern yourself with *they*. Concern yourself with Ector who said you have not completed your chores."

"I wanted to rest and to clear my mind."

"You obviously did not abandon your chores to practice with your sword which I do not see, or with your bow and arrows, which also escape my sight."

Arthur looked his mentor in the eye. There was emotion in his face, exactly what the emotion was Merlin did not know, but it was directed at him. "For twelve days I practiced and sparred as long as there was light to see by and more than one day we performed battle games in the dark."

"That was yesterday. This is today."

"You sound like Jago." The emotion might be anger. "The problem, Merlin, is that yesterday's injuries still hurt today." Arthur held up a hand to keep him from interrupting. "I know: That is the cost of greatness. Think of yourself as the best, and even if you believe you have achieved that status, strive always to improve — even if it hurts."

"Do not repeat my words back to me. Try to act as if they have some value."

"I do try."

"And I never said 'even if it hurts'."

"Maybe not, but that's what you mean."

Merlin knew he was being hard on the boy — on Arthur, he had to remember to think of him — and considered relenting. But no, Arthur would face far greater challenges than this. Merlin noticed a small pile of neatly stacked wood and kindling, and gestured toward them. "Ah, over there appears to be the making of a fire. But since it is morning and there is no need of firelight, and it is warm and there is no need of heat, I can only assume that you were trying to start a fire as a test of your magical skills, of which, of course, you have none."

"I'm no longer nine years old, Merlin. I'm not trying to become a wizard. But what if that was my intention? You, yourself, told me that wizards are more powerful than knights and battle lords."

"Stop turning my own words against me."

"They can use thought and magic, you told me, instead of always relying on sword and spear. And suffering thrashings."

"I also told you that one cannot simply become a wizard. To become a tall oak, a tree must begin life as an acorn. The same holds true for growing into a wizard."

"But men are also born to knighthood. As the second son of what you call a 'minor lord,' I can aspire to be no more than a squire. Yet, you say over and over that I can become a knight one day."

"And I say it again. You can grow beyond station and expectations to full knighthood."

"But not to wizardry! Why not?"

Merlin pointed to the pile of wood. "You evade the issue. What were you doing with the wood pile?"

"I evade the issue?" Arthur shook his head. "The wood pile was an experiment."

"To see if I truly have magic or if there is some trick to my lighting a fire?" Arthur lowered his gaze and nodded. "Good. Question me as well as everything else." Arthur looked up and smiled. "I am sorry if I become excited at the suggestion of wizardry. I have become concerned that you think that magic is an easy path to follow like defeating imaginary enemies with your imaginary sword instead of practicing your drills with a real sword." Merlin held up a hand to keep Arthur from interrupting. "Do not tell me again about your twelve days of sparring. You have been alive longer than twelve days and cannot use those twelve as an excuse indefinitely." He motioned with his staff. "Follow me."

Merlin led Arthur to the bank of the stream, and the pair knelt down as the wizard plucked a handful of grass, tossed it into the stream and watched it be swept away by the current. "Answer me this. If you were a fish in this stream, in which direction should you swim?"

"I'm well beyond this, Merlin."

"Answer."

"It depends, of course, on which direction I wanted to go."

The old wizard smiled to himself. He would have to phrase his questions more carefully. "Answer this instead. In which direction is it easier to swim?"

"Downstream, of course, which is exactly why you just told me that I should not aspire to wizardry because I think it is too easy a path to take."

Merlin had trapped himself in a web of his own analogies. "That was a different lesson," he said unconvincingly. "This is a new one." He leaned close to Arthur. "Following your destiny is like floating downstream. Resisting your destiny is like struggling to go upstream. Look into the water." Arthur hesitated. "Go ahead, look and tell me what you see." Arthur leaned over the edge of the stream and looked down into the water. But he said not a word. "Go on, tell me what you see."

"I see a knight."

"A knight!" Merlin blurted out his reaction without meaning to. He leaned over the boy's shoulder and looked down into the water both left and right but saw only the boy's reflection and his own. "Yes, of course, a knight exactly as I said." The wizard gently pulled the boy back from the water before the image could change. "A knight, exactly so. And I think we have had enough...enough...well, just enough." He put his arm around Arthur, who was left characteristically silent by his vision, and led him back toward the manor. "You have some wood to chop if we are to have our midday meal."

"The image in the stream, was it real or did you conjure it, Merlin?"

"You observed it. What is your opinion?"

Arthur shrugged his shoulders. "It looked real, but you have taught me that appearances can be deceiving."

"Exactly so. We can talk more about that later. I believe our midday meal awaits us."

Before the entrance to the manor house, a large wooden table had been laid out with plates, goblets and utensils. Ector, a smile on his face and his hair blanket atop his head, came forward to greet Merlin and Arthur. "On this beautiful morning. . ."

"Beautiful and rare."

Ector smiled at Merlin. "Yes, beautiful and rare and lovely morning, I thought we should eat under the sky."

Merlin smelled, or imagined that he did, meat simmering in its own juices, but there was no food on the table. Ector caught the wizard's gaze and moved his eyes from Arthur to the woodpile and back again. Merlin nodded his approval. "But we shall delay our excellent meal until Arthur finishes with the wood that still requires chopping."

Arthur looked first at Ector, then to Merlin. "Can I have my meal first?"

"Chores come first." Ector smiled at Merlin, who gave him another approving nod. "The work will go faster if you keep your mind on the task at hand."

Arthur sighed and started for the wood pile. Then, he turned back. "First, a word with Merlin." He waited until Ector left to summon Kaye. "Something has been troubling me, Merlin. Marrek was the best fighter of any I encountered while I was away. He was invincible, untouchable. One day he gave out the worst scream I've ever heard and grabbed his head. But there was not a mark on him. They took him away, and he never returned."

"And you wonder how a fighter of such skill could be felled in such a manner? And what that means for a warrior of lesser skill?" Arthur nodded. "Like a pain the belly or a soreness in your neck where there is no external mark, the same can happen inside the head. You just did not witness the blow that caused it."

"But not a mark. . ."

"It may have been an unusual blow of one sort or another. Fate — both fortune and misfortune — play a part in combat as they do in everything else."

4) The Final Arrow

The group of five rode without speaking, the only sounds the rhythm of the hooves of their horses on the earthen trail and the noise of their bodies shifting in their leather saddles. Arthur, mounted on a brown mare, pulled back on the reins, slowing his horse so that he fell behind Merlin, Ector and Kaye, who were in the lead of their little party. Prywycke, the fifth member of their group and Ector's lifelong companion, a stoop-shouldered man whose reddish complexion carried the scars of a childhood disease, caught up to him. There was a question that had bothered Arthur during the ride, and rather than ask Merlin, who would give him a quick and firm answer, he planned to work out a conclusion on his own by talking to Prywycke.

Before speaking, Arthur looked at the three others riding single file ahead of them to assure himself that he was out of earshot. "Prywycke, do you believe Ector is intent upon winning this archery contest?"

"Oh, yes." Prywycke did not seem to think the question was unusual. "Normal practice is to wager livestock — cows, pigs, goats, chickens, sometimes bushels of grain. This time the entry fee was silver, pieces of silver."

"How many?"

Prywycke shook his head. "Oh, I'd never ask Ector that. Long as I know him, I wouldn't presume to ask."

"He equipped Kaye with a new bow for this contest."

Prywycke gave Arthur a puzzled look. "You need a bow? Use mine."

"I have Kaye's old bow."

"You think you would shoot better with mine, you're welcome to. . ."

"That isn't what concerns me." Arthur again checked to be certain they would not be overheard. "I don't wish to sound arrogant, Prywycke, but I'm a better archer than Kaye."

"Oh, you're as fine an archer as I've seen — at your age."

"Then, why equip Kaye and not me with a new bow?"

"You want a different bow, you can take mine."

Arthur pointed to the one strapped to the back of his saddle. "I have this one. But Kaye has the new one. Understand?"

"I see." Prywycke nodded. "Maybe Ector thought a new bow would help Kaye shoot better."

"And do you think a new bow would help Kaye shoot better?"

"No, but what other reason would there be?"

Arthur knew. Kaye was the older son. Arthur often felt caught between Merlin on one side and Ector and Kaye on the other. The wizard expected near perfection from him, and Arthur believed he excelled in most of the knightly skills Merlin considered important. Those skills came to him naturally with minimal effort. Kaye, however, was awkward, and the harder he tried to master such things as archery and the use of sword and spear, the more awkward he appeared. Yet, anyone listening to Ector's praise of his older son would have thought Kaye was ready to compete for the championship of the annual tournament in Londinium. And Ector hardly ever mentioned Arthur's skills. What bothered Arthur even more was that Kaye, from outwards appearances at least, had begun to believe their father's overly generous view of him. That was one reason, Kaye's false confidence — along with Arthur's natural competitiveness — that Arthur enjoyed beating his brother in contests of skills.

If Ector's unjustified praise of Kaye was one point of confusion, another was Merlin's equally unwarranted prediction that Arthur would become a knight and a great one.

"Prywycke, you have known Merlin a long time," said Arthur.

"Indeed, yes."

"As a wizard, Merlin lives outside of convention."

Prywycke took his eyes from the trail to look at him. "Con — what?"

"The way most people live."

Prywycke laughed. "Never heard that word before, but yes, anyone who sleeps in a hollow tree, eats roots, and speaks to owls lives outside of con..."

"Convention."

'Con-vention."

"His views and opinions, therefore, would also be outside of convention."

"So it would follow." Prywycke laughed again. "Not many want to live on roots and berries, sleep in a hollow tree."

"But sometimes he sees the future?"

"Sometimes. Maybe that's because he lives outside of con-vention."

They rode silently for a time until Prywycke had a question. "Know the rules? For the archery contest."

"There are four archers, and each shoots four arrows."

"Per round."

"Per round!"

"Each round, one team is eliminated."

"And how many teams are there?"

"Twelve. Fourteen. Maybe twenty."

Arthur pulled his horse to a stop; Prywycke halted with him. "I wish I'd known. I've been practicing for days. Adding twenty rounds of four arrows to what I've shot these few last days will wear out my shoulder."

"Have no concern. You'll do well."

"I appreciate your confidence, Prywycke." Arthur resumed riding, looking ahead at his father and his mentor, who were now engaged in conversation. "Still, I wish Merlin or Ector had told me."

When they arrived at the village hosting the archery contest, they stopped before the communal stable just long enough for Ector to make an announcement. "It is important for all of us joining in the contest to have a good meal so that we will have sufficient strength to pull our heavy bow strings again and again during the long afternoon."

"Skill and mutton in equal proportions," said Merlin.

Ector missed the sarcasm. "Well yes, but mutton may not be on the menu. While Merlin and Prywycke and I take ourselves to nearest inn to order a midday meal, Kaye and Arthur, you two are to take care of the horses."

Arthur and Kaye led the five horses into the stable, and while they were unsaddling the first two, Kaye made a rare confession. "I'm anxious about this competition. It's worrisome, isn't it, the manner in which Ector has been telling me that I'll do well? He even supplied me with a new bow. That places an expectation squarely on my shoulders, don't you agree? But you, Arthur, you're an excellent archer. You know that you'll do well."

Perhaps, Kaye was not always as confident as he appeared. Arthur felt more sympathetic to his brother and wanted to put him at ease. "I'm as concerned as you are." Arthur lifted the saddle from his horse and hung it on a large wooden peg. "Merlin has placed expectations on me as Ector has on you. I have never before competed in an archery tournament, and no one told me we would be shooting almost a hundred arrows today..."

"That many?"

"And I overused my bad shoulder practicing."

"The one Marrek injured?"

"Yes, but it was more from the twelve days of sparring than any one thing Marrek did."

Arthur thought he might be able to help Kaye, who in his view and that of Merlin, was *unnatural* in his approach to using a bow. "May I make a suggestion?" Kaye nodded yes. "Merlin says that good bowmanship depends upon reflexes and thought is the enemy of reflex. I pull an arrow from my quiver, load it, look at the target and shoot. You think about the position of your right hand, which means you are not thinking about the position of your left, and when you think about your left, you are ignoring the target."

As often happened when Kaye was worried or confused, he looked as if he were experiencing physical discomfort. "That may well be, Arthur, but isn't it too late for me to change my approach?"

Kaye had a point, and Arthur did not think being more natural would greatly improve Kaye's performance. He would, however, look less awkward. "It isn't necessary to change your entire approach, but you could modify it some."

"Why haven't you said this to me before now?" Kaye's expression grew more pained. "Do you want to confuse me?"

Arthur held up a hand, palm facing Kaye. "You're correct. Forgive me for mentioning this now. Let's see how we do, and we can compare approaches later."

When the two brothers finished their work, they joined the Ector and Prywycke at the inn, where their meal had already been laid out, rare beef, some green vegetables and bread. "Where is Merlin?" asked Arthur.

"He has disappeared." Ector seemed unconcerned about the wizard's absence and might even have been pleased by it. "And there was no time to await his reappearance. Merlin would not be Merlin if he was always where you would expect to find him."

Arthur knew the reason for the wizard's absence; he was to undergo this test on his own without any assistance from Merlin.

Arthur sat next to Prywycke. He tried the beef and ate most of a crust of bread, but he had no appetite. Glancing over at Kaye's plate, he saw that his brother had not eaten much either.

Ector was the first to leave the inn; he went ahead to pay the entry fee. Soon after, the other three walked to the center of the village. They passed the practice area, where more than a dozen circular practice targets had been arranged next to one another in a straight line, and each was being used by one of the competing teams.

It would be a long competition.

Beyond the practice area was the competition target area, surrounded on three sides by wooden benches, built up row upon row. Hundreds of spectators were arriving and filling the seats from the bottom row to the top. Arthur had never competed before a crowd. His eyes moved across the rows of people: men, women and children, most of whom were talking and laughing, some gesturing toward the competition area, a few eating from wicker baskets they had with them. This contest would be enjoyable for them while Arthur felt he was waiting to plunge into a pool of cold water.

Ector, sweeping his fallen hair from his shoulder back onto his head, called his little group to attention. "I just want to say to all of you that I have every confidence that we will not merely acquit ourselves well this afternoon but that we have every chance of winning this contest."

Prywycke tapped Arthur on his shoulder and pointed down at his bare forearm. "Your bracers? Want mine?"

"I must have left them at the inn."

Ector frowned when Arthur turned to leave in the middle of his speech. Prywycke pointed to his own forearm. "Left his bracers. At the inn."

Arthur ran to the inn, found his bracers on the bench where he sat during the midday meal, and started back to contest site. He paused when he heard squealing and screaming coming from around the corner behind the inn. The sounds were coming closer, and he now heard laughter as well as shrieking.

From around the side of the inn a score or more of children, boys and girls ranging in age from perhaps as young as seven to about fourteen, came running, apparently being chased. A girl with long blonde pigtails seemed to be their leader, and she shouted for the group to stop. A heavy-set boy, who was out of wind, paused next to her.

An older boy dangling at arm's length a rotting fish came running at them from behind the barn. The girl with the blonde pigtails taunted the boy with the rotting fish by putting her hands to her waist and shaking her hips at him. The boy lifted his arm up and back, and threw the fish toward her. His throw was well off the mark, and it struck, square in the face, the heavy set boy, who stood with his arms shaking, bouncing at the knees while the fish, caught above his nose, hung across his eyes. Everyone, including Arthur, was laughing at the boy with the dead fish on his face.

As the chase resumed, Arthur thought that when he was the age of these children, he was usually performing a chore for Ector, practicing one of Merlin's old lessons or learning a new one. He had never played in a game such as this, never had regular playmates other than Kaye, and never, as far as he could remember, had done anything truly silly.

By the time Arthur rejoined the others, Ector was standing at the edge of the contest area flailing his arms at him. "The contest has already begun," he shouted. "We nearly forfeited for lack of a full team. Kaye and I have already shot." He took Arthur by the arm and led him toward the straw target. "Hurry. I've had to put you fourth."

Arthur strapped on his bracers, grabbed his bow and quiver, and moved behind Prywycke, who was standing before the target. He was feeling guilty for almost losing the tournament, especially after the negative things he had thought about Kaye.

It was his turn. He toed the archer's line, drew his bow and shot — more quickly than he intended. His arrow landed off center. A three out of five. He could do better. Ector, who gave him an angry stare, apparently thought so as well.

He had mentally recovered by his second turn. His next shot was a five as were the two arrows that followed. The three consecutive fives might have drawn some cheers from the crowd or some praise from the others on the team but did not. Perhaps, no one was keeping Arthur's personal score, and indeed, he was only paying attention to his own performance and did not know the team score until a smiling Ector returned from the table where the judges sat. "Men, we have advanced to the next round. I told you all we would be competitive."

This became the pattern. Arthur, his right shoulder occasionally aching and feeling stiff, continued to shoot fours and fives with an occasional three mixed in, and Ector continued to return from the judges table to say they had advanced yet again.

Against Arthur's expectations and thanks primarily to his performance, they were one of the two teams to reach the final round. During the last match, they shot four arrows each, first Ector, followed by Kaye, then Prywycke, and finally Arthur. But Arthur did not tally the score and was surprised when Ector informed him that the contest had come down to the last shot and that it was his.

Ector no longer exuded confidence. "Arthur, no one expects you to be perfect."

Arthur looked at the other two. Kaye was wearing his pained expression and even old Prywycke appeared worried. "I don't understand. I think I've shot well."

"The score," said Ector. "Don't you know it? We trail by five points with only your lone arrow left."

Arthur stood, looked Ector in the eye, then glanced both at Kaye and Prywycke. He took his bow and his final arrow, toed the archer's line and stood before the target. He fixed an eye on the red circle at its center, drew back the bow string and let fly.

A five!

Cheers went up from the crowd, and Arthur thought he heard his name being called by some of the spectators. Prywycke was on one side of him patting his shoulder, Kaye on the other shaking his hand.

Ector rushed to the judges table and stood next to the opposing team captain. "I assume we share the prize — evenly."

"Indeed not," said the opposing captain. "It is and always has been winner takes all."

One of the judges motioned toward the crowd. "You don't want to be tellin' them that they sat in those wooden stands all day and got splinters in their arses only to witness a draw."

"Another round then?"

"We've been here long enough," said the opposing captain. "One arrow per man."

"One man, one arrow," said one of the judges. "And if there's a tie, they shoot again."

"Fair enough," said Ector. He returned to his team and explained the decision. "Everything will be decided with one arrow per team. A single shot each. Unless there is a tie. Then, there is a second arrow. And so on and so on."

Arthur started readjusting his bracers for this last shot when Ector turned to Kaye. "It is your turn, Kaye. I have every confidence you will do as well as Arthur did on his turn."

Arthur looked at Kaye, who appeared to be as surprised and unhappy with Ector's choice as he was. Turn! What did that mean? They had been shooting in sequence, true, but holding to it would have meant that it was Ector's shot. Turn! Ector was favoring Kaye and trying to conceal it. But Arthur could not dismiss the possibility that he was being punished for being late for the first round. He was disappointed and angry but also embarrassed that he had assumed he would be chosen for the last arrow. He hoped no one noticed him adjusting his bracers or saw surprise in his face when Kaye was chosen.

The opposing team was to shoot first, and their archer stood spread-legged before the target. He stood still some time before he loaded an arrow, pulled back the string but he paused. He eased the tension in the string and took a deep breath. Again he pulled the string to full draw. This time he let fly. A two. A murmur of disappointment sounded from portions of the crowd as the archer, his head bowed, returned to his team.

Kaye now took his shooting position and went through his normal routine of checks and rechecks, taking even longer this time, and giving Arthur the impression that he did not want to actually take the shot. Finally, after staring down the target, he let loose his arrow.

A four!

Ector, his hands to his face, and Prywycke, his right arm raised over his head, were shouting for joy. Arthur, too, was caught up in the moment, and approached Kaye to congratulate him, but a crowd of onlookers rushed the field and surrounded Kaye.

When Arthur turned back, he found Merlin standing behind him. "You saw the contest, Merlin?"

"All of it. I commend you, Arthur. I took note of every arrow.. ." The smiling wizard pointed to his head, ". . .in here. You had the best score of any archer and did well by your brother. I am proud." He reached out an arm and gently shook Arthur by the shoulder. "But you are unhappy because you believe Ector should have given the last arrow to you."

"You don't always know what is in my mind, Merlin."

"Am I correct or not?"

"Yes. This time."

"You think it unfair."

"I think it is convention."

"Convention!" The wizard's white eyebrows arched high.

"You don't recall the word?"

"I do not recall when I taught the word to you. Convention! Indeed. Can you see convention? Touch it?" Merlin pointed to his nose. "Smell it?"

"Neither can I touch honor, courage or intensity. Convention must be as real."

"Well, of course, it is. Who said otherwise?" Merlin leaned closer and whispered. "But convention can be broken, and it can be risen above. Is there more you wish to know about convention?"

"No." Arthur had another question, but he would not ask it of Merlin: Why, among all his emotions, was he also happy when Kaye was chosen for the final shot?

Book Two

5) The Warlord Vollo

There were things for which Theil could be thankful. The sea off the coast of Britain was calm, the wind gentle and steady. The sounds of the oarsmen moving back and forth on their benches and the gentle splashing of their oars in the water were pleasant. Even the bright late afternoon sun was cooperating for the moment; descending behind a cloud, it gave some rest to his eyes.

Theil sat in the bow of the last vessel of the five that constituted the small Saxon fleet commanded by the warlord Vollo. Never had he done so much sailing in so short a time. His hips and knees ached from being confined shipboard. The pain and stiffness disappeared when he was on land but quickly returned after a short time on this vessel, and with each reoccurrence the pain and stiffness worsened.

Young Bayn, still thin and frail looking from an illness, was approaching from the stern. Theil stood up, stretched his legs and turned to look out to sea so that his back was to the boy. Bayn came up behind him.

Theil tried to treat his son as just another Saxon warrior, but the illness had caused Bayn to appear even younger than his sixteen years. Theil thought he now looked much like he did when he was a young boy and saw in his face the features of his dead mother.

The boy spoke in a low voice. "Father, are we going home to Germania?"

Theil's tone was soft but stern. "You asked your commander this question before and received no answer. You should not ask again."

Bayn remained motionless as though waiting for Theil to say more, and when his father did not again speak, he turned, and steadying himself against a sudden rocking of the ship, headed back to the stern.

"Wait." Theil hesitated while gathering his thoughts. "It's important that the others not think you receive special treatment because you are my son."

Bayn's tone became defensive and emotional. "I ask for no special privilege and have not during the entire voyage. I just asked a question." He gestured toward the others in the boat. "It's the same question they all have."

"And it is the same question I have." He looked sympathetically at his son. "Nothing would make me happier than going home. But where we are going is a mystery to me as well as to everyone else. Vollo says nothing. When he decides, we all shall know. It's best not to think of such things. It only makes the trip that much more difficult. Just think about getting safely through the night and tomorrow about getting through the day."

The boy's expression darkened. In resignation he nodded his understanding and returned to the rear of the vessel.

Bayn, whose mother died in childbirth, was Theil's only family. Eager to prove himself an adult, Bayn convinced Theil to include him on this journey. Theil regretted that decision. He could not have anticipated that the voyage would last this long or involve as many raids as it had. He felt his son was now at great risk, as were all the men.

And Theil was almost as weary of killing and maiming British as he was of seeing Saxons being killed and maimed.

Theil looked ahead to the lead vessel, where Vollo's large frame was silhouetted against the twilight sky. Vollo was a huge man — in height, in girth, in demeanor. He was a powerful man with huge hands, thick, shoulder-length white hair and a stare that Theil described as being able to back down a pack of wolves. Vollo was not in the habit of announcing his intentions or consulting with his chief aides or answering questions. A question of any sort might be taken by him as a challenge to his authority.

But they must be going home. Even Vollo must know that the losses they had suffered in five prior raids and the hardships they endured being on campaign these many days left them ill prepared for further combat.

Theil kept watch on the lead boat. As the sun began to set, the vessel turned not west toward Germania but rather east toward the shore.

The other ships followed. One by one the five Saxon vessels were beached, and in the fading light the men were directed by Vollo to divide the loot into four piles. On the left went anything that a warrior could use, from a shield or broadsword to leggings or a heavy cloak. Other objects, including pieces of silver and copper goblets, were stacked on the right. In the third pile, also on the left, went anything that could be eaten or drunk that would last for a length of time, such as casks of grain and mead and salted meats of every kind. The fourth pile, on the right, was for food that would soon spoil. Everything on the left was then hurriedly buried before the last of the sun's light had disappeared. All the remaining goods, those things that were of little or no use in battle, were reloaded onto their boats, and portions of the perishable food were set aside for this day's supper and tomorrow's morning meal.

The Saxon force made their campfires, which provided insufficient warmth against the bitter British nights, had their supper, and slept or tried to sleep. Bayn was assigned the first watch on one side of the camp, and Theil, breaking his own rule about always keeping a distance from his son when possible, joined him sitting on a large piece of driftwood.

Vollo, awake late as usual, sat by his own campfire reviewing notes and a map by firelight. That could only mean he was planning another raid.

Theil motioned for Bayn to sit closer to him. "Do not repeat this to anyone. It could be fatal to both of us." The boy, appearing apprehensive, nodded in agreement. "A warrior should always do as he is told without questioning his warlord, but this situation concerns me. We have been moving south down the coast of Britain and have conducted five raids, each a day or two's sail farther south from the last. We have lost six good men in those raids, and more are maimed badly enough to no longer be of much value in a fight of any kind. We also have suffered through terrible weather at sea, and more than a few of our company are immobilized with illness. All this you know as do the others. And all of us, the bruised, the illness-ridden, those chilled to their core, are ready to go home — all except Vollo.

"It is a mistake to conduct another raid as he seems to be planning. The British are not fools. They will be able to discern this pattern of nightly raids at near regular intervals, always moving south along the coast. At this very moment, an alliance of British tribes may be amassing a force to attack us at our next landing. In our condition how well would we fare against an enemy force of experienced warriors?"

"If Vollo does not understand this, shouldn't someone inform him?"

"He knows." The question reflected the naivety of one so young. "Vollo knows but is willing to take the risk."

"But you said the British might be waiting for us on our next raid. Does he understand that as well?"

Vollo understands.

Bayn did not seem to realize that the issue was whether anyone had the courage to challenge, even in a cautious manner, the warlord's thinking. That task, if it was to be done at all, fell to Theil as second-in-command. One day, perhaps soon, Bayn would understand this and might consider his father a coward for not issuing that challenge. Maintaining the respect of his son was well worth incurring the displeasure of Vollo. It was also true that if Vollo had any special appreciation for Theil, it was because he had spoken out once or twice before.

Theil rose to his feet and approached Vollo, who sat with the firelight casting shadows across his face. The warlord looked up and motioned for Theil to sit next to him. A good sign.

"Thank you, Lord Vollo. May a soldier speak freely?"

Vollo looked at him, his thick white eyebrows lowered into a frown. "Meaning you have something unpleasant to say."

"Just an opinion and one hopefully that Lord Vollo does not find too unpleasant."

"Speak." Vollo turned back to his map.

"We have lost six good men and have almost twice as many injured."

"I am aware."

He had to word his next comment carefully. "Our raids have been somewhat. . .periodic."

"Periodic!" Vollo sounded annoyed but fortunately not angry. "Theil, you have more sense than the others, which is why you are my second, but you give these British too much credit. Do you think they are organized enough to link one raid to another? And why do you think we have disguised ourselves as Norsemen on these raids?"

"Norsemen raid; they do not campaign."

"And why have we been burying supplies?"

"You plan a larger invasion at a later time."

"Exactly." Vollo pointed a finger at Theil. "You speak to me of raids, of a half dozen men dead. I think of much larger issues." Theil had never before seen Vollo as intense without also being angry. "I think of campaigns of tens of thousands of men, of invasions not raids, of new territory and the movement of large numbers of people. Six or sixty men may have to die so that six thousand or sixty thousand can advance." Vollo paused and took a breath. "Expanding an empire cannot be achieved without risk and sacrifice."

Theil nodded and stood to leave.

"Wait." Vollo looked up at him. "You brought your son with you on this voyage. It was a mistake. It has made you soft."

Theil had no response to that comment, and he knew he could no longer caution Vollo about his excesses without facing the same accusation.

Theil returned to the fire by Bayn, and the boy looked eager to hear what Vollo had told him. "Lord Vollo speaks about matters that are far beyond you and me and all the men here. He speaks about the future, and the weakness of the British. So, he will have one more success before we go home." At least one. Theil forced a smile but did not think he deceived Bayn, who might also have a bad premonition about this next raid. "Son, we have won five battles. The sixth will be no different."

At first light the next day, Vollo called his five commanders, including Theil, to his tent. He unrolled a crudely drawn map and tapped his finger on the location for the next attack. "This village was scouted some time ago. The village and surrounding farms border Valphain Castle and supply Uriens with a large portion of his winter grain. If we can reach the central storehouse before the grain is transferred to Valphain Castle, Uriens will be deprived of much of the food he requires to withstand a siege. And if we can locate a safe cave to store a quantity of grain that large for future use, it will be a twofold victory." Vollo looked at each man. "Questions?" There were none. "Study the map and learn the terrain."

The wind was dead calm when they took to their ships, so they rowed their way south. At mid-afternoon, Vollo ordered the fleet ashore and told the men to rest because they would attack at night when the village was asleep.

That night, when the full moon was directly overhead, the Saxon force, with Vollo in command, moved inland. To avoid detection, they skirted footpaths and avoided bridges, forcing them twice to cross small streams that left their wet feet cold in the frigid night. By Theil's estimation they had traveled at least two leagues from their camp, where a few of the injured men had been left behind to guard their ships, their one means of escape.

The sky clouded over for a time, slowing their progress through the woods. When the sky began to clear again, there was sufficient moonlight for them to make out the outline of the village in the distance. There were several dozen cottages spread out over an expanse of flat, open ground and a large structure, a storehouse, at the far end. Vollo split his force in two, sending each portion in a half circle to surround the entire village.

The village was quiet, not a sound, not even a barking dog; nor was there the light from a hearth or even a candle. And there were no sentries that Theil could see, which caused him to wonder if they were entering a trap. He would have felt more comfortable had he seen any signs of life.

The village was completely encircled by Saxons, every third of whom was equipped with a torch. The torches were for light rather than for destruction, or at least they would first be used for light, then destruction if necessary, because their purpose was to acquire loot and not to make war on this village, not any more than was necessary.

The cry of a hoot owl sounded; this was the signal to attack. Theil, a sword in his right hand, a torch in his left, burst through a cottage door.

He sensed — he did not know how unless it was the intuition born of too many years of warfare — something moving in his direction and instinctively raised his sword arm to cover his face just as a great weight struck and broke his arm in two places. Had it hit his head, it certainly would have cracked his skull open. His first thought was that some giant villager had hurled a stone at him, and laying down his torch, he reached to recover the sword that had fallen from his hand. He would have to fight left-handed.

A large stone, dangling from a rope, struck him a second time but with far less force. That is when he realized that the villagers must have evacuated to the surrounding forest and that if they had left this trap, there were certain to be more.

A Saxon warrior entered a nearby cottage, and his skull was crushed by falling anvil.

Another stepped into animal trap hidden under straw, and his ankle was crushed.

Still another kicked in the door of a small structure, and before he could enter it, he was attacked by guard dog. The animal knocked him onto his back and leapt onto his chest. The warrior, screaming for help, needed both hands to keep the dog from tearing out his throat. A second warrior rushed in and struck the animal a sword blow across its back. The strike opened a large wound but did not kill or sufficiently incapacitate the dog. It took another blow to finally kill the animal, but not before it left its badly bitten and clawed victim soaked in his own blood.

Theil, his shield hung across his back, his sword in his left hand, his broken right arm limp, hurried toward the center of the village, where they had prearranged to stack their loot, or alternatively, to assemble for a retreat. Several injured Saxon warriors were already there, and one arrived carrying a dead comrade over his shoulder. Vollo was there as well.

Whether it was the pain in his arm or his concern about Bayn, Theil confronted the warlord. "The raid was expected." Vollo did not respond. "We could search every building and are unlikely to find anything of value. We must retreat."

More injured men were arriving at the village center, but Vollo, apparently lost in thought, remained silent.

Without thinking about the risk he was taking, Theil grabbed Vollo's arm. "A British army may be about to come down upon us."

Vollo slowly turned toward Theil. "Very well. Organize a retreat. But first check the grain storehouse."

Four Saxons, including young Bayn, had been sent to secure the grain storehouse against any attempt by the villagers to destroy its contents rather than let it fall into the enemy's possession. They battered in the building's door, and each of the four, carrying a torch and a weapon, advanced to a different corner of the structure. The ground beneath them was covered with straw and in places was slippery from scattered manure beneath. There was also thick, dark oil mixed in.

There were no signs of life in the storehouse.

"This building is secure," said one of Bayn's companions.

Bayn turned to join the others; his left foot began to slide out from under him. The boy reached out reflexively with this left arm to steady himself against some barrels of grain. He dropped his torch.

The instant the torch flame touched straw, the floor ignited, and through the layer of oil and manure beneath, the fire spread with the speed of the wind. Bayn's legs were burning. The entire floor was ablaze as were portions of the walls. Clay vessels containing more oil burst from the heat and sent tongues of flames into the air.

Theil rushed to the grain storehouse. The large structure was fully ablaze, as though the building itself had become a single great torch. A section of the flaming roof fell in and part of a wall collapsed. Theil looked about anxiously for Bayn and called his name.

Someone, Theil did not know who, took him by the good arm and said, "None got out. They're all lost." Theil turned and looked disbelievingly into the eyes of the man called Munn. Theil tried to break free of Munn's grasp, but the man held onto him. "No one has survived in there.

Your son is gone, and by now only ashes remain of his body. I am truly sorry, Theil. The only thing you can do now is exact revenge."

Revenge, thought Theil. Yes, but not on nameless, faceless villagers who were only protecting their own property. But revenge nonetheless.

He thought about killing Vollo.

Theil's spirit perished in the fire along with his son, and during the long walk back to their camp, his mind was numb. He did not even feel the pain of his broken arm.

It was a difficult journey. A handful of men were hurt badly enough to require assistance walking. Two bodies had to be carried back for ceremonial burning. Everyone, including Vollo, seemed dispirited.

They arrived back at their camp shortly before dawn. While the injured were tended to and a funeral pile was built, Vollo walked among the men. Assessing *his* losses, Theil assumed. Theil was close enough to hear Vollo ask Munn how many were lost in the storehouse fire.

How many were lost? Not who was lost?

Theil was as near to a confidant as Vollo had, and yet, the warlord never asked if Bayn was among those who died in the fire. A maddening thought entered Theil's mind. What if Vollo learned of his son's death but instead of offering condolences, again said it was a mistake to take the boy on this voyage?

He would kill Vollo then and there. He should kill the maniac anyway before more died in another disastrous raid.

But how?

Theil, his broken right arm bound in a splint and supported by a sling, would have preferred to cut the madman's throat or plunge a knife into his heart, but even with two good arms, he was no match for the brute. And there were the other men to consider. They hated Vollo but feared him even more. In an open fight, they would side with the battle lord against him. Whatever he did, he would have to be done in secret.

Theil made a pact with himself. *If* he could find a suitable means of eliminating Vollo, he would do so.

Vollo did not fear an attack by the villagers, believing that they had done their worst against the Saxons with the traps they left behind. Rather than put out to sea, he decided to keep this camp another day, wanting, uncharacteristically, to give his men time to heal physically and recover mentally.

The next afternoon as the midday meal was being prepared, Theil remembered that before leaving Germania, he had worried about a boy as young as Bayn being captured, particularly by any of the barbarous tribes of north Britain. So, he purchased Bayn a ring with a hidden compartment containing powered poison. Bayn had not always worn the ring, especially after his illness when he lost weight and the ring was loose enough to turn on his finger. The ring might be among his belongings.

Let Bayn determine whether Vollo lived or died.

Theil went to his vessel and found Bayn's sack. Just looking at it caused his eyes to tear, and he was uncertain whether he could open it. But he did open it, and he wept as he withdrew Bayn's few possessions — a goblet, a dagger, a spare tunic, some dried meat. The bag was empty. No ring. To be certain, Theil turned the bag upside down. The ring fell out and onto the ship's floor.

Vollo would die.

Theil, wearing the ring on his left hand, returned to camp and watched as the cook ladled a large portion of venison stew into a bowl. Perfect. This was Vollo's meal. He always received the first portion and always had it brought to him while the others would have to wait in a line. Theil hurried to the cook, a small and frail man better suited to a stewing pot than a sword, as he was pouring mead into Vollo's goblet.

"Cook, could I ask a favor?"

"Ask anything, good Theil."

Theil stood directly before the man, closer than he would have in other circumstances, and maneuvered himself over Vollo's goblet. "On account of this injury, could you bring me my meal and portion of mead?"

"Certainly, I'll get them now."

The cook turned toward the stew pot. Theil opened the compartment of the ring. Fool! He never checked to see if the poison powder was still in it. Too late for that now. He tilted his left hand over the goblet. A small quantity of white powder fell into Vollo's mead. He closed the ring.

"Cook, best serve Lord Vollo first. I will have my meal in my usual place."

The cook nodded as he dumped a partially filled bowl of stew back into the pot. "As you like, Theil. I'll bring you stew as well as bread and mead as soon as I finish serving Vollo."

Theil, his eyes locked on Vollo, sat by a fire. The battle lord was served his meal and not only quickly finished both his food and his mead, but asked for, or rather demanded, second portions of each. He appeared perfectly fine.

Theil now wondered if there had actually been poison in the ring. He could not distinguish white powder from poison, for one thing, and he had no reason to believe the ring's seller had been truthful about its contents, for another. Perhaps, it was poison but it had lost its potency during their long journey. More likely, a dose large enough to kill an average man was insufficient for a man of Vollo's great size.

Vollo suddenly grasped his throat with both hands. He emitted a loud wheezing, gasping sound. He seemed to be trying to cough and inhale at the same time and was accomplishing neither. His enormous body began to shake, and he keeled over onto his right side.

Theil must try to help the warlord, or it would raise suspicion. He hurried to Vollo as his massive body went into convulsions.

Munn was among the others who joined him. "What do we do?"

"It must be the fever," said Theil. "We can cover him."

"And bring water."

Theil covered Vollo with a blanket. Munn dipped a rag into a pale of water and gently wet his face.

The convulsions stopped, so did Vollo's coughing and wheezing. He lay perfectly still. Theil bent down to check his breathing and listen for his heartbeat. "Our great warlord is dead. Surely it must be from a strange disease from this strange land, and only the great lord's strength kept him from yielding to it sooner."

As Vollo's second, Theil was now in command. "Tomorrow we make a proper funeral pyre. Now and through the night, we maintain a vigil over his remains."

Vollo was laid out in his armor and helmet along with his sword and shield. Small oil lamps were lit at his head and feet and on both sides of his body forming the shape of a cross.

That night Theil, on watch while the rest of the camp slept, sat by a fire, thinking about the events of the last day and night. His entire life had changed between the space of two sunsets. His beloved son was gone. Vollo, who had dominated his life these many days, was dead. Theil, the warrior, had become Theil, the assassin.

He had no future.

Theil felt a presence behind him. He turned and in the darkness saw the leg of a large man standing over him. His eyes drifted up the massive figure to see Vollo in full battled attire. Theil was speechless and was not completely certain he was not seeing a ghost. But the large figure began to stagger and fell to his knees, supporting himself against Theil's shoulder.

Theil steadied Vollo. The large man's weight pinned him to the ground.

"What happened to me?"

"You were very ill." Theil worried that his voice betrayed his guilt. "We thought you had died."

Vollo pulled the neck of Theil's tunic so tight he thought he would choke. "I was attacked. Strangled. Stabbed in the belly. I felt it."

Theil feared that his choice of words might give him away. "No, there was no attack. You fell ill, very suddenly and very violently."

A wild look came over Vollo's eyes, and he pulled Theil's tunic so tight he thought his neck would break. "I was eating. I remember now. Eating,"

"Yes, eating."

"Poisoned. I was poisoned. I was poisoned once before. You remember that."

"No, Lord Vollo, I did not know that."

"My own brother. That is why I trust no one. We have a traitor among us. Find him." He squeezed Theil's neck tighter still. "Find the traitor so I can skin him alive, roast him and feed him to the dogs. Now get me to my tent. I do not want the men seeing me like this. You, Theil, are the only one I trust. The only one who can see me weakened as I am."

Theil helped the battle lord to his tent, assisted him into his cot and closed the tent flap for privacy. He briefly considered plunging a knife into man's throat, but he was no longer certain Vollo was only human. And if he killed him now, the others would know it was murder and either hang Theil or cut off his head.

Theil spent the night keeping a watch on Vollo, who awakened frequently and apparently was not in full possession of his senses. Each time he looked to make certain Theil was still there with him, and more than once, he thanked Theil by name for helping him.

The next morning, Vollo appeared fully recovered and ordered Theil to assemble the men. That was easy enough; most of them were standing by the cross-shaped arrangement of oil lamps wondering what happened to Vollo's body.

Vollo, still dressed in battle gear, presented himself before his astonished band of men, most of whom were too stunned to speak.

A warrior near Theil whispered to the man next to him. "Is he back from the dead?"

"Likely, never died at all."

"Did you see him? I did. He looked dead to me."

"Well, he is speaking now, and dead men do not speak."

"Men, yesterday you saw me collapse and nearly die," said Vollo. "And now you see me returned to full health. So too shall you recover from the misfortunes we suffered during our last battle. You have fought long and hard and well. We have had more than our share of victories and suffered a single defeat that was the result of cowardly trickery. Even the best warriors, such as you, need time to recover. We will take our spoils and return to Germania."

Cheering erupted everywhere among the assembled warriors; a few even embraced one another.

Vollo held out his hands to silence them. "But we will return to Britain with a vast army and conquer it."

The men also cheered this remark. Theil believed they did so because Vollo expected them to cheer. He doubted there were many who wanted to return here with Vollo to fight a long campaign. But that was not his concern for the moment. He had to worry whether he would reach Germania without Vollo suspecting that the cause of his near death was Theil's treachery.

6) Sparring

Ector leaned over his horse and pointed to a clearing in the woods just off the forest trail. "This appears to be an ideal place to camp."

"Yes, *ideal*," said Merlin.

Ector looked up at the sky. "Fortunately, there is still enough light for the boys to spar."

"Boys! If I use that term — *boy* — Arthur is quick to correct me."

Ector nodded. "True, they are hardly boys."

"*Hardly.*"

Usually optimistic, Ector suddenly appeared worried and lowered his voice. "Merlin, I. . .I'm not completely certain that Kaye is ready for the tournament."

"Not certain!" Merlin gave a sarcastic laugh. "Anyone can see he is not ready."

Ector's eyes opened wide. "But you were the one who insisted that we go to Londinium this season."

There was indignation in Merlin's tone. "Would Kaye be any more ready next season? Can the events of the world wait until we are ready?"

"Events of the world? What events are those?"

Merlin began mumbling. "I have my doubts about Arthur too."

"What has Arthur to do with it?"

"Who said Arthur has anything to do with it?"

Ector shook his head as if to clear Merlin's confusing words from his thoughts.

The rest of their party, Arthur, Kaye, and Prywycke, who trailed a pack horse, caught up to them. They all dismounted, and Ector quickly gave them assignments: Prywycke was to tend to the horses, unpack their gear and set up their tent. Arthur and Kaye were to take their swords, shields, and helmets, and practice combat while there was daylight. The task Ector gave himself was to stroll farther down the forest trail in whispered conversation with Merlin.

Arthur watched the two disappear around a bend in the road. "We all have our chores," he said, more to himself than to Kaye. "Some more difficult than others." He thought his task was the most difficult, to prepare Kaye to compete in tournament combat.

They put on their helmets, strapped their metal shields to their forearms and stood across each other on the forest path. "Kaye, take the offense." This was Arthur's strategy to build Kaye's confidence, having his brother first attack and later defend. Now that Arthur was Kaye's size, only stronger, he could withstand the best Kaye could muster with little or no consequence, and he would allow Kaye to be aggressive to build his confidence. When Kaye was assigned to defense, Arthur's attacks usually overwhelmed him. That was necessary to give Kaye a taste of what he was likely to encounter at the tournament. Confidence alone would win him little.

The two brothers withdrew their swords, held their shields at shoulder height, and began to circle each other. "Look for an opening in your opponent's defense, Kaye. Vary the pattern of your movement. Watch your opponent's entire body but focus on his eyes."

They circled and circled, but Kaye made no move. Arthur stood erect, lowered his sword and shield, and stared at his brother.

Kaye gritted his teeth and advanced on Arthur, who quickly returned to combat position and easily deflected Kaye's sword with his shield.

"Stay on the attack." Arthur slowly retreated. Kaye delivered two more sword strikes. Arthur parried the first with his sword and deflected the second with his shield. Kaye made an attack that was unbalanced, and Arthur sidestepped his wild overhead swing, almost causing Kaye to fall on his face.

"Now," Arthur said, "I'll take the offensive." Kaye crouched, his shield held high. Arthur started slowly at first, pounding Kaye's shield and driving him backwards but giving him time to adjust to the speed of the attack. "You'll need a good defense against Bryso and others of his stature." The blows now came faster and harder.

Arthur was startled by a loud crash. Against all his years of training, he turned to see the cause of the commotion and let his shield drop.

Their tent and tent poles, their cooking and eating utensils, and extra spears, everything Prywycke had loaded onto their packhorse had toppled to the ground.

He had looked away for only an instant, but when Arthur turned back toward Kaye, he saw a malicious look his brother's eyes just as Kaye's shield smashed across the side of Arthur's helmet.

It was the worst pain Arthur ever experienced. It immobilized him for a few moments, and he was not even certain what was injured until he felt the blood streaming down over his mouth and chin. He put his hand to his face and felt that the nosepiece to his helmet was dislodged to one side and his nose with it.

The pain subsided enough for him to recall the expression in Kaye's eyes. The injury was deliberate. Arthur raised his sword, charged Kaye, and unleashed a volley of blows that left dents in Kaye's shield and beat him backwards a dozen feet. Arthur gave a shout and struck the upper portion of Kaye's shield with a blow that toppled him onto his back.

Arthur, sword lowered to his side, stared down at Kaye, who was breathing heavily and looking petrified. Enough. He has learned a lesson. End it now. But Arthur could not hold his tongue. "The next time you consider a trick such as that, remember that I can put you on your back any time I please."

Ector was shouting at them. He rushed to Kaye. "Are you injured?"

"Is he injured! I am the one with a broken nose and bloody face."

Merlin was at his side. "Calm yourself, Arthur."

"I am calm. If I were not, I would still be on top of him."

Merlin led Arthur away to tend to his injury. Behind them he could hear Kaye telling Ector that the blow to Arthur's face had been accidental.

7) Maeve

On the morning of the Londinium fair, the aging knight Uriens slowly rose from his bed. His back hurt, and his arthritic right hip, which made walking difficult, caused him to wince as he slid his long, thin frame off the bed and onto the floor. Squinting against the sun filling the bedroom window, he searched for Maeve, his second wife, who was more than twenty years his junior. She was by the window in shadow, her back to him, pulling on a gown.

Walking with a pronounced limp, Uriens went around the edge of the bed, crossed the floor and came up behind Maeve. "Good Morning, dear." He wrapped his arms around her waist. She did not answer and did not turn around. "Is there a problem? You're not angry with me, are you?" Still no answer. "What have I done now?"

She turned to face him. Maeve did not have the kind of facial features that men usually found attractive, and as she had aged, her teeth had become discolored, lines had formed around the corners of her mouth, and her skin had turned a sickly grayish tone. "It's not what you did; it's what you couldn't do," she said. "I told you not to drink so much mead."

He held up his right index finger. "I had one goblet. Just one." She frowned at him. "You don't believe me, but I swear." He looked down at the floor as though searching for something. "It's just that. . .It's. . .I was tired."

Maeve put her hands on her hips. "You are tired a lot lately."

"Maeve, I'm not as young as I used to be."

"Oh, is that it?" She laughed sarcastically. "If the problem is age, I have no hope, do I?"

"Not so loud." He looked over his shoulder to the bedroom door.

"There are no servants around. Why you worry about them is beyond me. You should worry about me instead. I'm losing my patience."

"What does that mean? You are losing your patience."

"You should have become king long ago. Perhaps, you are too old now."

The remark struck him hard. "Maeve, must you speak to me so harshly?"

She walked away from him, sat at a dressing table and began to comb her long brown hair before a mirror. "Do you not want me to say what is on my mind, to think something but not to speak it?" She slammed her brush down on the dressing table and turned to face Uriens, who was now standing over her. "It has been my talking, my ideas, that have helped you immeasurably these last years. You should never tell me not to speak my mind." Her voice was getting louder. "Who proposed that Bryso represent you in the tournament last year? Me."

"Hardly a day goes by that you don't remind me of that."

Maeve raised her raised her eyebrows and shouted loud enough to be heard beyond their bedchamber. "It's still true, isn't it?"

Uriens waved his hands at her. "Not so loud."

She turned away from him, picked up her brush and resumed combing her hair. "And this year who gave you the idea about the sword? Me."

"Yes, of course." Uriens came up behind her so that he could see her face in the mirror. "Maeve, I don't mind what you say to me in private." He looked down at the floor. "Actually I do mind." He looked up again. "But what is said between husband and wife is one thing. What you say in front of others is something else." Uriens tone became forceful. "Turn around and look at me, Maeve." She did so. "Do you know what some people say? How can Uriens rule Britain when he cannot rule his own wife?"

Maeve dropped her eyes and was silent. When she finally did speak, it was in a whisper. "Of course, you are right, Uriens. I'm sorry."

Uriens wrapped his arms around Maeve, and she rested her head against him. "This is the Maeve I know and love."

"There is so much at stake with the tournament and sword. I get upset sometimes."

"I know. I understand. I feel the same way."

She was nearly sobbing. "And I always want to look nice for you, but every time I do something special, that daughter of yours. . .I know she mocks me to her friends."

"Complaining about Brenna again!"

"Don't blame me."

"You two spar like warriors and that shouldn't be. Brenna is young. Young girls laugh a lot, but that doesn't mean she is laughing at you."

She tried to pull away from him. "You always take her part."

He held her close. "You are my two girls, and I take your part as well."

"Take my part? Why? What does she say about me?"

"I didn't mean — "

"She must have said something or you would not have to defend me."

"We don't want to be late for the fair." He released her and walked toward the closet that stored his clothes.

"Don't change the subject, Uriens."

"I can't wait to show you off. You'll be the most beautiful woman at the fair."

Maeve stood and walked after him. "What does Brenna say about me?"

Uriens turned back to her and sighed. "You and I had a little argument this morning and have mended things. Let's enjoy the fair — and the tournament. You and Brenna will mend things in due time."

"I almost forgot and apparently you did as well." Maeve smiled. "You keep mentioning the fair. Is there something you want to give me?" Uriens appeared puzzled. "Don't pretend, Uriens. I saw you hide the box in your dresser."

"You did?"

"You know I love silver."

"You opened it!" Uriens looked from Maeve to the dresser and back to Maeve.

"Well?" Her tone was more of a demand than a request. Uriens, moving slowly, walked to the dresser, opened a drawer and withdrew a small box. He turned and tried to hand it to her. "No, take it out of the box and put it around my neck." He withdrew a silver necklace placed it on Maeve so that the thin vertical strands of silver lay on her chest in the shape of triangle pointing down.

She hurried to the mirror to admire the necklace. "You've done well, Uriens."

8) Girl at the Fair

The next day after Arthur and Kaye's sparring incident they ate their morning meal by a campfire. Kaye tried to conceal a smile as he glanced at Arthur, whose nose had been encased in a mud plaster by Merlin to keep it straight while it healed.

"You think my new nose is an improvement, Kaye?"

Kaye laughed. "I do. More of your face should be encased in mud."

"I'll consider doing that just for your amusement." Arthur bent his head down to get a look at himself in his metal goblet. "It is pretty funny, especially how it's distorted by the curvature of the goblet."

Prywycke smiled. "And we shall see how Kaye looks after tomorrow's tournament." Prywycke's joke caused Kaye to assume his pained expression, which, in turn, caused Merlin to elbow Ector.

"Oh yes," said Ector, his mouth full of food. "I have announcement." He paused to finish chewing.

Despite Arthur's training methods and Ector's high, but unwarranted, praise for Kaye's combat skills, Kaye had to know he was facing a good beating from the knights and other warriors in the Londinium tournament. Arthur had no desire to experience more thrashings like the ones Marrek gave him, but he was jealous of his brother. After all the years of training, ten of them by Arthur's reckoning, he would not be able to put his skill on display in a real tournament, not have the thrill of walking on the Field of Honor before a match, not have the opportunity to bow before a crowd after beating an opponent. With those possibilities denied to him his training was close to pure drudgery.

He understood his station, however. Like the last shot in the archery tournament the year before, tomorrow would be Kaye's day, not his.

Ector cleared his throat with more noise that seemed necessary. "Boys, ah, Kaye and Arthur, I mean. I do have an announcement. I think you will be delighted with Londinium, and because you have worked so hard. . ." He paused to look at Merlin. "I have a treat for you. You will have the day free in Londinium to enjoy the fair."

The news did not much bolster Kaye's spirits, but it excited Arthur, who had never been to a fair and was not sure what to expect. Whatever it was, it had to be better than sparring or performing combat drills.

It was a short ride into Londinium. To Arthur the city was a marvel, far beyond anything he anticipated. He looked about wide-eyed and sometimes opened-mouth despite Merlin's caution not to appear like a peasant who had spent his life in a barnyard. Londinium had more buildings and larger ones than he had ever seen or imagined. But what surprised him most was how far the town extended. They rode into what he thought was the town center, and passed through it only to find another town center, and a third beyond that and a fourth.

Arthur turned toward Kaye, who finally appeared relaxed. "Merlin once told me a story about a fish in pond that could not imagine how large the sea was. I feel like that fish."

Kaye pointed ahead. "Look at that."

The tournament and fair grounds were also impressive and far more colorful. The Field of Honor was large and surrounded on two sides by wooden stands, enough seats, Merlin had told him, to accommodate five thousand people, several times more people than Arthur had seen in the entirety of his life. The fair grounds, consisting of dozens of colorful tents, were to the north of the field. To the south, the various knights and noblemen had erected their personal tents, each with a flag and a shield displaying their coat of arms.

Arthur sometimes almost believed Merlin's prediction that he would become a knight and had given thought to the coat of arms he would choose for his own — if ever given the choice. When he was eleven years old, he settled on colors and an insignia, light blue and silver to represent the sky and an owl to represent wisdom. The wizard rejected that suggestion, saying that an owl would not strike terror into the heart of any adversary. If Arthur fancied a bird, Merlin suggested one that was more menacing such as an eagle, falcon or hawk. Then, no birds at all, Arthur decided. He would rather have something even more powerful instead. A bear was what he had settled on.

However, as they rode through the colorful encampment, Arthur saw that the bear insignia had already been taken. Twice. One was on a light blue and silver background, his chosen colors, and the other on a dark blue and gold background. There were even more lions than bears — a prancing lion, a lion head in full face, and a lion head in profile on a scarlet and gold background. The fiercest appearing animal was none of these but rather a wolf's head in black and dark blue. Two animals often discussed but rarely seen, a dragon and a griffin, were also represented as were Merlin's suggested birds of prey.

There were also coats of arms with weapons: a sword facing down, two swords crossed and facing up, two swords facing down crossed over a shield, a battle axe, two battle axes crossed over a shield, two spears crossed over a shield, and so on. Finally there were patterns: red and blue squares, yellow and green crosses on a white field, and silver shapes Arthur thought represented stars on a black background.

Never had Arthur anticipated that if he succeeded against all odds to become a knight, his biggest quest might be finding an insignia and colors that had not already been taken.

Having been released from their duties in setting up their tent at Londinium, Arthur and Kaye dismounted at their new campsite, tethered their horses and hurried to the fair, where there was much to see.

Arthur found himself ignoring the stalls containing goods and food for sale or barter and the entertainers who roamed through the crowd. He preferred to look at the women, especially the attractive young women. Being confined most of his life to Ector's manor and the surrounding forest, he had seen precious few girls like these. There were scores and scores of women, wearing elaborate and colorful dresses. Most of them had brown or black hair, but a few had red or blonde hair, and they wore their tresses in a variety of styles from being piled on top of their heads to hanging down below their waists. Their complexions, for the most part, were soft and unspoiled, unlike the women who spent years in the fields regardless of weather. A few had faces more beautiful than he knew a person could have, and when one yellow-haired woman walked close by him, he noticed that she smelled good.

Good smells were not common.

Arthur turned and began to walk behind her.

"Where are you going?" asked Kaye.

"Let's see what's in this direction." Arthur's eyes remained on the yellow-haired woman ahead of them. "A thought occurs to me, Kaye. How long have we been sparring?"

"As long as I can remember. But that's an odd question."

"What else have we been taught?"

Kaye hesitated, most likely puzzled by the nature and timing of these questions. "Archery, hunting, fishing..."

"Planting, harvesting, milking, skinning, wood chopping. What have we been taught about women?'

"Nothing. Not one thing that I can remember."

"And we are both of an age. . ."

"Merlin taught you nothing about women?"

Arthur laughed. "That is the one subject about which he knows the least."

Kaye tugged on Arthur's sleeve. "Look, horses."

A pen had been erected to contain horses that were for sale. Arthur noticed a stallion that was pure white and reluctantly turned from the yellow-haired girl to accompany Kaye to the horses. The white horse sauntered toward him and extended his neck over the wooden rail so that Arthur could stroke his nose.

"Beautiful," said Kaye.

"Did you notice that yellow-haired girl?"

"The one you were following?"

"She is far more beautiful." Arthur leaned toward the horse and sniffed. "And she smells much better." Kaye had success in the tournament as his goal. Arthur now set a goal for himself — to meet a girl at the fair or at least to speak to one.

They moved from the horse pen to an open area where a juggler entertained a small crowd. Arthur had heard of juggling but had never seen it performed. The juggler, who was no older than Arthur, effortlessly kept three balls in the air at one time. "Who among you would try his hand at juggling?" The performer looked at the faces in the audience and selected Kaye.

Kaye, who blushed at being the center of attention, stepped forward and was handed two balls. Kaye tossed them awkwardly at first but succeeded in maintaining a rhythm. "And now three," the juggler shouted. He threw a third ball to Kaye, and when Kaye turned to catch it, all three hit the ground.

The juggler collected the balls and withdrew three long knives from a leather pouch. He spun them into the air, one after the other, catching each by the handle. The crowd watched anxiously as he kept the knives rotating in the air and cheered him when he brought them all down and took a bow. In jest, he stepped quickly toward Arthur and offered him the three knives.

"Oh no," said Arthur. "I'd like to keep my fingers, but I'll try with just one." He took a knife by the blade and spun it into the air. It made three and half rotations before he caught it by the handle. Laughing, he took a bow as the juggler had done. Those in crowd who appreciated the humor applauded, and one man cheered.

When Arthur looked up, he noticed a beautiful, dark-haired girl. She looked him in the eye and smiled. She turned to leave but first looked back at him over her shoulder.

He had a special feeling about this woman as though there were suddenly some link between the two of them. Merlin had always taught him to assess facts, weigh alternatives, and think rationally. Lately the wizard accused him of being too rational and too thoughtful — as if there could be such a thing. Use instinct and intuition on occasion, Merlin said. Perhaps, that was what was happening with this girl. An intuition. Or more likely, an instinct.

Kaye was tugging on his sleeve again. "Do you hear that most peculiar voice? Do you think that could be an elf?"

Arthur tried again to catch sight of the dark-haired girl as Kaye led him in the direction of the strange voice.

The voice did not belong to an elf but rather something almost as fantastic, a brightly colored bird that spoke. As they approached the animal, it called out, "Good day, me lady."

"It speaks," said Kaye "but its vision is not so good, especially for a bird. What's your name?"

"Good day, me lady."

"No, your name?"

"Good day, me lady."

"His vocabulary is as small as his body," said Arthur

"I suppose owls are more intelligent."

"When I was a boy, I attempted to converse with a good many owl, and 'good day, me lady' is more than I have gotten from any owl." Arthur's attention was drawn to a group of three young women who were passing by. "These women, I cannot take my eyes from them. Their skin is so soft; I wonder how it feels to the touch. But I would be happy to simply speak to one and not be at a loss for words to say."

Kaye moved closer to Arthur and whispered, "Do you ever think about performing *the act*?"

"Today more than any other time. There is one girl, in particular, I would like to meet. She is not very tall, but I find her size very pleasing. Her hair is dark, her eyes lively, and she has a bright smile. She was in the crowd with the juggler. She looked at me and gave me a smile."

Kaye laughed. "Of course, she did. You are wearing a nose made of mud."

Arthur raised his hand to his nose and felt Merlin's mud plaster was still in place. How could he have forgotten it? He had spent a good portion of the morning trying to catch the attention of pretty young women. He thought their smiles had been flirtatious but now knew they were mocking his ridiculous appearance. While his brother continued to laugh at him, Arthur hurried off to find a bucket of water. He found one and carefully washed off the mud, very carefully for his nose was still very sore. He found a polished shield in which to check his appearance. His nose was swollen, but it looked better than it did with the mud plaster. Checking his nose several more times and combing his hair with his fingers, he went off in search of the small, dark-haired girl.

He searched the fairgrounds everywhere for her and not finding her, concluded that she and her friends had left. There was nothing to do but find Kaye.

"You look much better without the mud nose." The comment came from a soft woman's voice behind him. He turned to see the small, dark-haired girl and her friends strolling past him.

He wanted to speak to her but could not decide whether he should mention the mud cast or make reference to the injury that caused his nose to be encased in mud. He could give his name, or ask hers, or inquire as to her well-being. Perhaps, he could ask about the fair. Or the tournament. Were women even interested in such things?

His indecision caused the moment to pass. She was already out of sight, having mixed into the crowd.

Kaye was now calling to him. He was accompanied by a small man who was as close to looking elfin as Arthur had ever seen a person to appear. "Arthur, he thought I was you. He claims he must speak to you."

The man, wheezing from keeping up with Kaye's walking pace, stood a head shorter than Arthur. He spoke between wheezes. "You've lost your sword, and I can find you a new one."

The man was confused. "I have not lost my sword."

"Is your name Arthur?"

"Yes."

"Then, you've lost your sword, you have. Don't take my word for it. Look for yourself."

Arthur wondered if this were some kind of trick that was played at the fair on people who were new to Londinium, but there was no harm in checking his sword. He and Kaye, with the little man trailing a distance behind, walked to their campsite, which was on the other side of the Field of Honor. They entered their tent. Arthur saw his sword lying in a corner with his helmet, shield and armor.

"What's this?" Kaye held up his empty scabbard. "It's my sword that is missing. I would wager that little man knows where it is."

"He is likely the one who took it."

The little man, breathing heavily, had reached the tent entrance. "Am I right or am I right? You are in need of a sword, are you not?"

9) The Worlds of the Wizard

Merlin, the wind causing his robe to flap behind him, stood on the highest point of the castle wall to watch the sunrise.

Footsteps were approaching. It was King Uther Pendragon, his cloak wrapped around him against the cold morning air.

He had come here before.

"You arise early, Merlin."

Those were first the words spoken.

"It's worth rising early, Uther. There is magic in a sunrise. Or don't you see it?"

Uther stood beside the wizard but paid no attention to the rising sun. "I leave the magic to you."

"You have no choice in that," said Merlin. Then, he mumbled, "Or I'd have little magic left, wouldn't I?"

Merlin had a secret gift. It was not speaking with owls or casting spells, as people thought. Unlike other men, he sometimes lived in the past and in the future as well as in the present. And on occasion he also lived in dreams. This was not a memory; he was living the day that King Gorlois and his company arrived at Uther's castle.

"You, Uther, are also out and about early."

"I haven't slept at all."

"You need to be rested and ready to reach a peace with Gorlois when we negotiate tomorrow."

"I haven't slept well for three nights."

Merlin looked at Uther, trying to assess how tired he was, and there was, indeed, weariness in his eyes. "I assume you have finished the sleeping potion I made for you. You are a strange man, Uther, even for a king — at ease during war and ill at ease with the promise of peace. So, you have found me at here at daybreak for sleeping potion?"

"Not for now, not for this moment. For tonight. But if making more potion is troublesome, I can always consume enough mead..."

Merlin interrupted him. "You have never killed a man in your sleep, at least, not yet. I prefer you asleep to drunk. I'll make the potion but warn you, as I always do, to take heed of the quantity you use. Too much, and you'll fall into a sleep from which you won't awaken. And promise me, Uther, that you'll be cordial to Gorlois and his party, and make an honest effort to bring about a peace."

Uther put his hand over his heart. "My word on both."

The visiting delegation, King Gorlois, his young wife Igraine, and two dozen soldiers, several flying Gorlois's pennant on the shafts of their spears, appeared in the distance late that afternoon. They rode two abreast to the castle, and Uther was among those who stood at the gate to meet them.

He greeted Gorlois, who remained seated on his horse and appeared irritated. "Welcome to my castle," said Uther.

"We have ridden a long way, Uther. I hope these talks will be worth the journey."

Uther's expression turned angry momentarily, then he forced a smile. "I have no doubt your visit will be a fruitful one. Let me also welcome your lovely queen."

Igraine was young enough to be the daughter of either Uther or Gorlois. She had pure white skin, light blonde hair, dark eyes and a delicate mouth. She was shapely and was wearing a tunic that fit her tightly across the chest. Uther took her hand to assist her down from her mount, and the eyes of most of the soldiers present, both Uther's and Gorlois's, followed her as she descended from the horse.

"Welcome, Igraine. If there's anything you require during your stay, you need only ask."

She nodded to Uther without making eye contact with him and gently pulled back her hand. Merlin observed her reaction and wondered if she, like Gorlois, might be irritable from their long ride, or if she had sensed something unpleasant about Uther.

That evening Uther entertained his visitors with a banquet. He, Gorlois and Igraine sat at the head table. A place was set there for Merlin, but the wizard ate alone at the far end of the great hall, keeping a watch on the interaction between Uther and Gorlois, and between Uther and Igraine, and observing the glances exchanged among the soldiers from the two warring kingdoms who sat on opposite sides of the hall.

Servants brought jugs of mead to the head table, followed by trays of roasted meats and vegetables, and still more mead. Uther was too obvious in his attempts at charming Igraine and was having little success. He even performed a servant's task for her, taking a jug of mead from a kitchen girl's hand to fill her goblet; he filled Gorlois's as well.

Merlin was concerned that too much drink would lead to a confrontation between two of the opposing warriors if not between Uther, who was being talkative and loud, and Gorlois, who for the most part, sat quiet and sour-faced. But the evening ended peacefully.

Late that night Uther rose from his bed and walking barefoot, went down from his fourth story quarters in the castle tower to the third story room he had assigned Gorlois and Igraine. He stopped outside their room and put his ear to the door. There were the sounds of someone snoring in deep sleep. He took a key from his pocket, carefully unlocked the door and pushed it open a crack to see that both Gorlois and Igraine were asleep. Uther crept to her side of the bed, lifted Igraine into his arms and quietly left the room.

Gorlois never once stirred.

Uther carried Igraine down the hallway and started up the stairs. She gave a soft moan and repositioned her head on Uther's shoulder. She called Gorlois's name and kissed Uther gently on the neck. He paused, and when she did not move again, he carried her to his dark bed chamber.

The next morning Igraine awoke beside her husband in a panic. She tried to wake Gorlois but could not. She shook him and slapped his face hard enough to get a response. "Wake. Something happened last night."

He opened his eyes but did not appear attentive. "Something happened last night."

"What happened?"

"I'm not certain. I was with you, but you became Uther." Gorlois sat up and grew more alert. "You and Uther, you seemed to meld one into the other. He took me to his room."

Merlin was entering the tower and caught sight of Gorlois in his night clothes hurrying across the great hall toward Uther, who sat at his morning table. "Rapist, liar, cheat!" shouted Gorlois.

Merlin saw the sword in Gorlois' hand.

Gorlois ran at Uther and raised his sword. Uther grabbed a carving knife from his breakfast platter. As Gorlois tried to strike at him across the table, he lifted the table up and into Gorlois, who was thrown off balance long enough for Uther to thrust the carving knife into his belly.

Igraine shrieked. She stood frozen, her hands to her face.

"He attacked me," said Uther to Merlin. "I had no choice. Gorlois must be drunk or mad or possessed."

Merlin rushed between them to hold off another attack by Uther and bent down to assist Gorlois who had fallen to the floor. He was alive but bleeding badly. Several servants hurried into the great hall. Merlin directed one to aid Igraine, who was hysterical, and the others to help him tend to Gorlois, who was seriously and perhaps mortally wounded.

Gorlois lost consciousness. Merlin tried to stop the blood flow with a cloth, but Gorlois continued to bleed. When he had done all he could for Gorlois, Merlin confronted Uther.

"You witnessed it, Merlin. He attacked me. I had no choice. He must've been mad or possessed."

The wizard moved closer with a look in his eyes that caused Uther to retreat a step. "I see it now and dearly wish I had foreseen it yesterday. I noticed how you looked at Igraine. You lust for her. The sleeping potion was not for you but for Igraine and Gorlois. And I was the unwitting accomplice in your crime. You are unworthy!" Merlin turned and walked toward the castle door.

"Wait. I haven't told you that you may leave."

"I am leaving anyway."

It was many days later, exactly how many Merlin did not count, that Uther and a small contingent of warriors came riding through the forest looking for him. He heard them at a distance but did not answer their calls until they had stumbled their way to where he was resting against a tree.

"Merlin." Uther motioned for his men to remain where they were. He dismounted and approached the wizard. "Merlin, I need you to return. I'm dealing with great turmoil. Gorlois' allies are massing against me."

The wizard stood before him. "And who created that turmoil by killing a king who was his guest? I assume Gorlois is dead."

"He died the following day."

"And Igraine?"

"With child."

"Yours?"

"Yes."

"So you think, but you will never be sure, will you?" Uther frowned. "Imagine King Uther raising Gorlois's son."

"Enough, Merlin. I know there's a reason behind your mockery. What is it?"

"I offer you this bargain in return for my continued assistance. This child may or may not be yours. My mockery aside, you may never know. If this child is male and if — you will pardon my bluntness — if you were to die an early death, the child becomes mine. If that comes to pass, I foresee that the child will become a great king."

"Of course, my son would become a great king. I could make that prophecy myself." Uther laughed. "I accept that bargain — without hesitation. I plan to live a very long time. And when I die, I assure you, Merlin, I'll have little interest in anything you do."

─────

Merlin lay uncomfortably in his tent. He had a feeling that something was happening or about to happen. He opened the tent flap, peaked out and saw Uther sitting by the fire. The wizard wrapped his blanket around his shoulders, walked out to the fire and sat next to the king. "Uther, you have been at war for — what is it? Seven months now? I would think you'd be sleeping well."

Uther stared into the fire. "I worry about Igraine. She should have the child very soon."

"You have managed to convince yourself the child is yours." Merlin held up a hand. "No need to answer. I can sense it. But don't think you can break our bargain."

Uther looked from the fire to Merlin. "The bargain only concerns a male child, and that is yet to be known."

It is a boy.

"More important, Merlin, I'm still alive and still king."

"Even a king, Uther, must learn that a bargain is a bargain. I leave you to your thoughts."

Merlin returned to his cold tent and tried to sleep. A short time later he heard a rider approach, most unusual for the middle of the night unless it was bad news. And a short time after that, he heard a horse ride off.

Merlin was struck with a feeling of dread.

He hurried out of his tent and saw a rider unsaddling his horse. "Where is Uther?"

"I brought him news that he has a son. He's returning to the castle."

"And you allowed him! At night! Alone! Strap that saddle back on. I need your horse."

Merlin rode after Uther through the dark forest. Ahead he heard a horse whinny and thought he must be close to Uther. Soon he could make out the form of a horse. But it was facing toward him. And it was riderless.

He dismounted, took the reins of Uther's horse as well as own, and searched the ground for the body he expected to find. Uther Pendragon lay face down, two arrows in his back, one through his neck.

Gorlois had been avenged.

Merlin returned to the castle the next morning to see Igraine, who lay on her bed. Her blonde hair was disheveled, her face red, her eyes tired. When she saw Merlin approaching, her expression turned to anger. "I bring you sad news," he said, knowing that she hated her new husband and would not react to his death as she had to Gorlois'. "Uther has been killed."

She lost none of her anger. "And do you think I will grieve for him?"

"No, I understand what he did to you."

"With your assistance!"

"My unwitting assistance. I mixed a sleeping potion without knowing its purpose. If I could change the shape of people, as you believe I can, Igraine, I would not appear before you now as I am. I understand that you hate him and hate me. But you can end your torment now. You can go home to your people." This news had a greater impact on her than the word of Uther's death, and she began to cry. Merlin gave her a moment to gather herself before coming to the real reason he had delivered the news of Uther's death himself. "I know you did not want this baby, but whether you want him now or not, hate him or grow to love him, there are many men, especially among your own clan, who would like to end the bloodline of Uther Pendragon. The child, if he stays with you, will not live to see his first birthday. I will keep him safe and see that he has a good home."

Igraine, continuing to sob, did not look up at him as she spoke. "Uther told me of your bargain, but I didn't expect Uther's death so soon. The son of Uther Pendragon and the wife of Gorlois has no future. All this time I have thought myself just a part of some plot you have concocted."

There was no use in responding to that comment. Instead, he asked, "What have you called the child?"

"Uther wanted to name him in tribute to himself. Arthur."

Twenty years later, Merlin wondered whether Igraine regretted the quick decision she made when Arthur was born. He assumed she did, but he never saw her again. What began with Uther's deception and was followed by many years of planning, work and hope was about to reach its culmination.

There was, however, still one last task for Merlin to perform, to protect the integrity of the myth of Sword in the Stone, for without its legend the second son of a minor nobleman could never ascend to the throne.

The sword had long been part of his plan although it was not his creation. The very existence of Caliburn came to Merlin in a dream, the seed of which must have been planted in his mind by Queen Mab, the magical creator of dreams. In the dream he clearly saw the sword and the inscription carved into the stone beneath it, but it took him more than a year to locate the sword itself in a secluded wood in Londinium.

For the legend to have credence, many men had to try and fail to withdraw the sword. And for nearly twenty years the men who won the Londinium Tournament did try to free the sword and failed. In frustration, some who thought they should be king changed the tournament rules. Next they might seek ways of circumventing the necessity of drawing the sword from the stone.

That is what concerned Merlin now.

He found Ector wandering the fair, and together they walked to a large tent near the Field of Honor. It was here that a gathering of knights and noblemen would review and sometimes change the tournament rules. As they entered the rear of the tent, Merlin said, "If we are not careful, Ector, they will hand the crown to Uriens without holding the tournament and leave Caliburn wedged in its stone."

"And that concerns you?"

"Of course, not," said Merlin sarcastically. "The future of Britain is of no great consequence."

By the time they took seats at the rear of the gathering, Gareth, a respected leader well past his physical prime, stood to address the group. He looked from one side of the assembly to the other before speaking. "As you well know, we have held this tournament all these many years, and still we have no king."

Leaning to Ector, Merlin whispered, "If he is about to argue that we need a king, I will agree with him, but not Uriens, not now, not with both his body and memory fading."

"Last season. . ." Gareth was momentarily distracted by Merlin's conversation. "Last season, we amended our rules to allow nobles of a certain rank to pick champions to represent them in the tournament."

"That was a perversion." The man objecting was Loth, a short, broad-shouldered, red-headed man, who shouted from his seat on the right side of the tent.

"How so?" asked a Gareth. "If a new rule is applied equally to all, how is it unfair?"

"Fairness is not the issue. These changes are a perversion of a tradition that we have all embraced, although I now believe some embraced less so than others. What next? Open the competition to stable boys and milk maids?"

"Hear my proposal before you condemn it," said Gareth. "We don't propose to open the competition further but rather that the champion who has won the contest may attempt to draw the sword on behalf of his lord."

"I no longer have patience for this," said Merlin to Ector. He gave a shout that quieted the group. The wizard stood up and walked to the front of the assembly. "Have any of you examined the Sword in the Stone lately? Well, have you? Have you read the inscription? Do you know what it says? Apparently not. So, I will quote it to you, 'He so ever pulls the sword from the stone, he is rightful King of Britain.' Do you hear any mention of a tournament? No, that was an invention of this body, although not all of you were here at the time of that invention. Understand that this is not a test of combat skills nor of strength. It is a test of destiny. You could, indeed, as was suggested in jest, let a stable boy attempt to draw the sword, and if he was meant to be king, Caliburn would slide out in his hand."

Merlin's words were having the impact he expected, but he was interrupted by a commotion outside that had attracted the attention of the group.

Merlin smiled. He had an idea of what might be the cause of it.

10) The Sword in the Stone

The little man led them to the woods a short distance from the tournament field. The trees, mostly pines, were tightly spaced, and a tangle of bushes and vines wound through them. The man pointed to a narrow, barely noticeable opening in the forest. "Follow the path."

Kaye looked from the man to the path, then back to the man. "You expect that we'll be able to find a sword in a forest?"

"Shouldn't be too difficult for two bright young men such as yourselves."

Arthur thought the odd little man was suppressing a smile. If they found a sword at all, it would probably be Kaye's own sword, and the man would demand a reward for finding it.

Kaye also seemed skeptical. "You're saying there is a serviceable sword in the forest?" The man nodded. ". . .just lying on the path waiting to be picked up?"

"Didn't say it was lyin' on any path."

"Then, it's hanging from some tree, and we're supposed to find it?"

"Can't help but find it." He raised his right hand. "I swear." He waved them on with a flick of his wrist.

"Aren't you coming? Do you expect some reward?"

"Been rewarded already."

As they watched the little man walk away, Kaye asked Arthur, "Rewarded for what and by whom?"

"For making us appear foolish. Perhaps we have been marked as peasants on our first journey to Londinium, which is the truth, and this is some trick to make fools of us."

Kaye laughed. "You spent the morning smiling at girls while you had your nose covered in mud. Are you now concerned that you might appear foolish walking in the woods?" Kaye had a point. "And have you any better suggestion for getting me another sword?" Another good point.

Arthur swept his arm toward the path, and Kaye led the way. As they walked, Arthur glanced up at the trees, looking for but not expecting to see a sword dangling from a limb. Kaye's eyes moved from one side of the path to other, and when he pulled back the branches of a bush to look behind it, Arthur complained. "If this sword exists and is hidden in a bush, we could be here the entire season and not find it. It must be in a more obvious location than that."

The path turned to the left, wound back around sharply to the right, and ended in a clearing. Arthur first noticed the stone, set off as it was like a shrine or a monument, and then, he saw the sword standing atop the stone, its handle facing the sky. "There is your sword, Kaye."

Kaye, a look of distain on his face, approached the sword. "Do you think that sword would last through the tournament? It appears old and battered and rusted. "

"That's what you notice about it! Don't you see that it's plunged into the heart of a large stone?" Arthur gently pushed the sword to see if it might have a broken blade that had been balanced on the stone. "It has actually penetrated the stone. I would think the blade would break first or the stone would chip away."

"I don't think it's much of a sword, do you? Perhaps you can take this one, and I could use yours in the tournament." Kaye pulled on the sword handle, but it did not move.

"It won't come out easily, and I doubt it will come out at all. Why else would it still be here? Try rocking it back and forth to loosen the grip of the stone holding it."

Kaye tried pushing the sword with his hand and leaned his chest against it, but even the force of his whole body failed to move the sword in the slightest. "You try, Arthur. You're always bragging how strong you are. Put your strength to good use."

"I don't brag!"

"You think you're much stronger than me. Don't deny it."

"But that's not bragging."

"Just try the sword."

Arthur placed both hands on the handle of the sword and braced a leg against the stone. He took a deep breath and pulled. The sword came out so easily he almost fell over backwards. The sword felt alive, a sensation Arthur could only attribute to vibrations that must have been caused by its being released from the stone's grip.

"Look at it, Arthur. See how it appears with light running up its blade."

It certainly looked better reflecting the sunlight, but Arthur was more mindful of its vibrations.

"Let me have it." Arthur did not respond to Kaye's request. "You've held it long enough. You have a sword and wouldn't have even walked to this place if I hadn't convinced you to go." He held out his hand for the sword.

Arthur swept the sword through the air. "It has a very unusual feel to it."

"Arthur!"

He handed the sword to Kaye.

Kaye held the sword high over his head. "I feel nothing unusual." He swung the sword in a circle and made several belly-high thrusts.

Loud voices were approaching. Dozens of men hurried out of the forest and approached Arthur and Kaye. Still a distance away, a burly man shouted and shook his fist at them, but Arthur could not understand what he was saying above the voices of all the others. A second man tugged the burly man by the sleeve, turned him around and engaged him a lively discussion. A third man joined them; they appeared to be arguing with one another. The crowd seemed to be divided into groups of two, three, and four men, some appearing angry, others merely excited, all talking at once. Occasionally someone would look in their direction and point a finger at Kaye. But otherwise the men in the crowd seemed more concerned with each other than they did about the two brothers.

Arthur thought he and Kaye must have committed some offense against the sword that Kaye now held. The sword in the stone might be a shrine they unintentionally defiled or a monument they damaged.

Where was Merlin? He could explain all this and calm the crowd. Arthur searched the crowd and looked beyond it to the forest path. Merlin was approaching. His staff held high in his left hand, the wizard squeezed past people and pushed his way forward until he reached the front of the crowd. He looked first at Arthur, then at Kaye. The wizard was motionless for a few moments. He grasped his staff with two hands, and Arthur thought it appeared as if Merlin had to lean on it to keep from losing his balance. Something had shaken the wizard.

~~~

Merlin ushered them into their tent and closed the tent flap behind them. "We have left the madness out there but only for the madness of our own in here. And when I say 'our madness,' I mean you two, Arthur and Kaye." He pointed to the stools at the center of the dimly lit tent. "Sit." And all three, Arthur, Kaye and Ector, sat down on backless, folding stools. Kaye held the sword point resting on the ground, grasping its handle with two hands. Ector glanced at it and opened his mouth to speak. "Quiet, Ector." Merlin pointed to each in turn. "Quiet, all three of you." The wizard started pacing but almost instantly became too agitated even to pace. He stood before Arthur and Kaye and looked down on them. "Leave it to you two to waste the magic in an ancient legend."

Arthur did not know what the legend was, but he now realized the sword must be magical. How else could it have been in a stone? But why was magic of that sort so important? A sword trapped in a stone was of no practical use. He thought it only a little better trick than the man juggling three knives at the fair.

"Who drew Caliburn from the stone?"

"I did," said Arthur.

"And yet when the crowd gathered around, the sword was in Kaye's hands."

"He asked to see it, and I gave it to him."

"He asked to see it, and you *gave* it to him!" Merlin's tone could not have been more sarcastic.

"You make it sound that handing him the sword was sheer stupidity."

"Even worse."

Arthur had grown increasingly intolerant of Merlin's complaints and scoldings. He was not a child who had pilfered a chicken leg from the table before dinner was served. "He asked to see it; I handed to him. He needed a sword; I didn't. He is fighting in the tournament; I'm not."

Ector spoke up. "And, Merlin, Kaye is, after all, the elder son."

"Quiet, Ector. I am older than all of you, but age has no bearing on the situation."

"I was the one who wanted to find the sword. Isn't that true, Arthur?" Kaye looked at his brother, who nodded in agreement. "Arthur thought it was a fool's errand, but I said to continue, didn't I?"

Merlin leaned over Arthur the way he did when Arthur was just a young pupil of the wizard. "And didn't you feel the power in the sword, the power in Caliburn? Or are you accustomed to holding swords that feel alive?"

Arthur shrugged his shoulders. "Yes, I felt something, a vibration. I didn't know what it was. I know now there was some magic in it."

"Some magic! Didn't you understand the inscription?" Arthur was puzzled. "The inscription on the stone. Is there some other inscription of which I am unaware?"

"Merlin, I don't appreciate the sarcasm in your tone. And never have. You make me — and Kaye as well — feel guilty for committing some terrible offense. If we shouldn't have touched the sword, we are sorry. We did nothing harmful intentionally and saw no inscription on the stone or elsewhere."

"The inscription," Ector whispered, "reads he who pulls the sword is king."

Arthur looked to Merlin for verification. "Not word for word, but that is the essence of it, yes."

"Me, a king!" Arthur could not take this idea seriously, but nonetheless argued as though it was a possibility. "I'm too young. I have no royal blood. I have no training. I don't fully understand what a king does other than wear a crown and be like other knights. I could give you many more reasons why it makes no sense, sword or no sword in a stone. One moment I'm at a fair watching jugglers and young women, the next I'm supposed to be king?"

Did he even want to be a king? What obligations and responsibilities did that entail? There was probably no end to them.

"Merlin," said Kaye, "should I return the sword to Arthur?"

"No! That would only worsen the situation." Merlin addressed himself to Arthur. "Do you understand what all that arguing out there was about? One faction believes that anyone who pulls the sword has the right to be king. The other holds that only the tournament champion can even attempt to draw Caliburn. Can you imagine the argument that would ensue if we now tell them you pulled the sword, not Kaye? No, the time for that has past. I fear we are bound in this situation and must do what we can to hold even our present position in which only half the knights out there support us." Merlin started to pace and seemed to be talking to himself as though no one else was in the room. "We need a new plan. Twenty years of planning and effort, twenty years, all wasted. He just gives the sword away, doesn't even see the inscription."

Arthur, whose agitation had been mounting, was overwhelmed with anger when he realized the meaning of Merlin's words. The wizard seemed no longer a benevolent mentor but rather a manipulative plotter. "Twenty years of *your* planning and *your* effort," shouted Arthur, as he stood up to confront Merlin. "Almost all of those years were mine. Your instruction, but my effort; your expectation, but my obligation. Is that what I've been all this time, since the time I could stand on my own feet and you put a toy sword in my hand? I'm a plan!"

It was the first time he had ever seen the wizard cowed, and Merlin fumbled for words. "There are things, Arthur, certain things that are larger than you and me."

"That may well be, Merlin, but my life is of more than a little consequence to me. That may come as a surprise to you. You blame me and blame Kaye for the failure of this grand twenty-year plan of yours. But we're not the cause." Arthur pointed a finger at him. "It failed because you knew about the sword and didn't tell me, because after all the years of preparation, you didn't prepare me for this last and most important thing."

The wizard was uncharacteristically quiet, and when he did speak, it was in a soft voice. He seemed more trying to convince himself than to persuade Arthur. "I could not. It was a test."

"And did I pass?" asked Arthur sarcastically.

"You pulled the sword, didn't you?"

"But I didn't keep it."

Merlin hesitated, "Perhaps, then, you did fail."

"So, I have failed. And the time has come, as you say, for a new plan. And I'm free of the old one. I'm certain you will think of something." Arthur turned to leave. It was his intention to return to the fair although in this ill humor, it was unlikely that he could enjoy anything.

11) Beauty and Danger

The Old One carried three platters and a knife to where the fowl were roasting and pronounced them sufficiently cooked. He took a small bird and cutting it into equal portions, gave half to Donal and half to Allum. He pulled the largest bird from the spit, sliced it into two unequal portions and took the larger for himself.

He bit into the meat as though he were a half starved and took another large bite, as a trickle of hot juice ran down his beard. "Very tasty," he tried to say but the words were muffled by food. "Delicious," he tried again but it was no clearer.

Donal was also making quick work of his portion of the meal. "So, Arthur and Merlin had a fallin' out?"

"It would appear so — if you were listening to the story."

"And Kaye becomes king?" asked Allum.

"Stories must unfold in their proper sequence or they are not stories. We have not yet come to the coronation."

Donal appeared confused. "There's one part of your story I don't understand."

"Only one?" said Allum.

"About Calibur, the sword in the stone."

"Caliburn — burn, Caliburn."

"Caliburn, I meant to say. I heard that when Arthur pulled the sword from the stone two pure white eagles circled overhead and each dropped a serpent at his feet. But you made no mention of that."

"Who told you that?" Donal meekly shrugged his shoulders at the story teller's challenge. "Well, there were no eagles circling overhead." The Old One waved a finger about his head to represent a bird in flight. "Not a single eagle, not white or otherwise, not a pair of sparrows, or even a single sparrow."

"And what about the serpents?"

"How could there be serpents if there were no eagles to drop them?"

The Old One's stare caused Donal to concentrate on his meal, and they ate without further discussion. When they were finished their meal, the Old One looked about the great hall. "Listen." The only sound was that of the fire. "The storm has ended. I want to see what it has left behind."

Donal and Allum followed him to the castle entrance and looked at each other as the old man easily opened the door that they had found so difficult to budge a little while earlier. The Old One wrapped his cloak around his shoulders and stepped several paces into the night. Allum and Donal followed him.

The storm had ended; the wind was still. The land- and seascapes before them were perfectly silent. There were still some low clouds in the sky, and when they cleared sufficiently to show the moon, moonlight fell over the ocean in a line from where the waves broke gently on the shore out to the horizon. Everything on land lay under of covering of thick snow, and even some of the flaws of ruined Valphain Castle were hidden by it.

"It is on nights such as this," said the Old One, "that the world stops for an instant and takes stock of itself."

"Beautiful," said Allum.

The Old One nodded in agreement. "That which was dangerous leaves behind beauty. This is also true: that which is beautiful can bring danger." He looked from Allum's face to Donal's. "Now we have come to the next part of our story, Merlin's new plan. And that involves Uriens."

12) A Compromise

One of the wizard's unusual gifts, although it was nothing in which he took any pride, was the ability to block from his mind most of the concerns that might trouble a normal person. The accusations Arthur made against Merlin were true, he was forced to accept, and he did feel guilty about using the boy — now a man — as the centerpiece of his strategy. But the fate of Britain was at stake, and Merlin had no time or taste for self-recrimination.

He went in search of Uriens and knew he must be in the tent near the Field of Honor where the debate was continuing among the assembled knights about whether Caliburn had been drawn legitimately. Uriens was easy to spot. He was the tallest man there and one of the tallest in Britain. Whereas Merlin would once have described the aging knight as physically imposing and always with a look of keenness in his eyes, Uriens was now stoop-shouldered with eyes that most often revealed his weariness.

The old knight was too weary, Merlin saw, to directly engage in the vigorous and acrimonious debate that was taking place; he was content instead to have his proxies argue his case.

Uriens smiled when he saw the wizard approach — he must have momentarily forgotten that Merlin did not support his position in this dispute.

Merlin took him by the arm and started to lead him away. Uriens protested. "I can't leave while the debate remains unresolved."

"You are not engaged in the debate, but you and I can resolve it."

There was a spark of energy in his tired eyes. "How so?"

"Come."

Uriens, his right hip tilted forward causing him to move in an uneven gait, followed Merlin across the field to a place on the grandstand where they could sit and talk privately. It was peaceful here although in the distance they could hear muffled voices coming from the debate raging in the tent.

"You understand, Uriens, I am certain, that the sword in the stone was enchanted." Uriens nodded. "Once the enchantment is broken, it cannot be restored. Any man — or woman or child — could pull the sword now. Do you realize what that means?'

There had always been gentleness in Uriens's voice, and it had become more pronounced with age. "It means many things." Either he did not know or simply did not wish to answer.

"For twenty years, Uriens, we hoped the Sword in the Stone would bring us a king. Now it has been drawn, and if we let this opportunity slip away, it leaves war as the likely means of finding a king. These are dangerous times, Uriens, as you well know. Have you probably heard of the Norsemen raids along the coast?"

"Yes, several villages were pillaged by Norsemen, including one where my grain storehouse was burned to the ground with everything it contained."

"They were not Norsemen. They were Saxons." Uriens appeared surprised by this information. "A Saxon in an animal hide can easily pass for a Norseman during a night raid. And you must ask yourself, Uriens, why Saxons would disguise themselves as Norsemen." A look at Uriens made it clear he would not reach the conclusion on his own. "They plan an invasion. We have neither a king nor a peaceful way of selecting one. Of course, there are those who would say that you, as the wealthiest knight and the lord with the largest army, should be king."

"I wouldn't attempt to deceive you Merlin. I, too, for years have thought I should have the throne." The comment was delivered with humility rather than arrogance.

"Old friend, some of the words I will now say will injure you, and for that I am deeply sorry."

Uriens expression became troubled. "Perhaps then, you shouldn't say them at all. I'm an old man and need not be insulted any more than age has already insulted me."

"That is precisely my point. You have declined physically with the passing years."

"We all grow old, Merlin; you as well. That is why Bryso has served as my champion. But many kings are old, and once a knight becomes a king, he often retires from the battlefield. My decline in strength doesn't disqualify me from the crown." Uriens looked away and spoke more to himself than to Merlin. "Sometimes when I climb the tower stairs, I find myself with difficulty breathing, and there are days when I have aches and pains in my body and I cannot think of what I have done to cause them." He turned back toward Merlin. "That is just the price we pay for growing old."

"And your mind has aged as well." Uriens was surprised by that comment. "There is talk among your servants about your forgetfulness."

"They say that about me?"

"And what about Maeve?" The mere mention of his wife caused Uriens to become more attentive. "Do you grant every whim she has?"

Uriens lowered his eyes. "You aren't married, Merlin. You don't understand that sometimes it is simply easier to yield to a wife. Does that mean that a man cannot be husband and king?"

"If there were a King Uriens, would Queen Maeve do much of the ruling? And your daughter, who you are said to pamper, would you yield to her as well? No, Uriens, more strength than that is need. Your time to be king has sadly passed you by."

Uriens, who had the look of a defeated man, began to relent. "I have so little time left. That's why I have pressed so hard. . ."

Merlin placed a hand on Uriens shoulder as the aging knight stared down blankly at his hands. "And what if you became King Uriens for a year or two and passed on? What then? Having no sons, you would leave us with two alternatives: Either becoming subjects of Queen Maeve or needing to devise some means other than an enchanted sword to select a king. And you see where the enchanted sword has brought us."

"I must admit I hadn't considered the possibility of Maeve ruling on her own without my moderating influence."

"But there is a way, Uriens, for you to launch a line of kings who could lead Britain to a golden age." Uriens searched Merlin's face attempting to determine if the wizard was serious. "Support Kaye as king, and I will see that he takes your daughter Brenna as a queen. There will be royalty in your family now and far into the future. It is a means, Uriens, that you, without a son, can launch a dynasty."

Uriens carefully weighed the idea.

"Think of it, Uriens. Your daughter a queen; your grandsons and great grandsons kings; and you a counselor to a king. And as counselor you will have nearly the influence over the affairs of Britain as you would have had as king." Merlin paused before concluding his argument. "If not this proposal, then what is the alternative?"

It was a rhetorical question, but Uriens answered anyway. "I don't know the alternative. I see your point that there may be more chaos unless the boy Kaye is confirmed king. Merlin, I believe I may well agree to this arrangement and do so now conditionally."

"Conditioned upon what?"

"I need time to think and to discuss your proposal with Maeve. Until I do, tell no one of our discussion."

———

Uriens sat in a chair in his spacious tent; his wife, Maeve, stood over him, hands on hips, fury in her eyes.

"I expected you would be disappointed," said Uriens, "but this level of anger I don't understand."

"No? Because you are a fool, that's why. This is but another indication of the toll age has taken on you," said Maeve. "You shouldn't have agreed to anything without speaking to me first. I've been your backbone these last few years."

"I didn't agree. I agreed on condition."

"Merlin will not see it that way. He has taken advantage of you."

Uriens motioned for her to lower her voice. "The servants."

"They are not of the same station as we are, and I don't care in the least what they hear or what they think." She shook her finger at him. "You are the leading knight and lord."

Uriens mumbled to himself. "But listen to how you speak to me."

"Everyone defers to your opinion. Yet, you gave the crown to these...these peasants."

He gave her a look of defiance. "Are you more angry that I will not be king or that you will not be queen?"

"Don't pretend to me that you are indifferent to the throne." Her voice became more shrill, and she began pacing before him. "What angers me is that you and the other fool knights have fallen prey to a silly legend about a sword in a stone and have allowed a peasant to lay claim to the crown. Even accepting that this superstition has validity, you, yourself, said no one saw the boy draw the sword. Did none of you require proof? You still have influence, Uriens, or you did until today. But it may be too late. Are you naive enough to believe Merlin is telling the others that you only *conditionally* agreed to his bargain?"

"Yes, I trust him."

"Fool!"

"Your voice." He glanced at the tent entrance. "They will hear."

She waved an arm in the air. "Stop talking about the servants!"

"I haven't told you everything."

Her eyes opened wide. "There's more?"

"Yes, there's more, and this will please you." Uriens smiled. "I convinced Merlin to have Kaye take Brenna as a wife. She will be queen."

Maeve seemed unable to speak for a few moments, then she leaned toward him so their faces were only a short distance apart. "Now I understand. You favor her over me. You always do." She picked up a bowl from the table by Uriens's chair, lifted it over her head and smashed it to the ground, sending fruit and pottery shards across the floor.

The sound alarmed a nearby servant, and Bryso, Uriens' champion, came to the entrance to their tent and asked if all was well.

"Just an accident," said Uriens to Bryso, who remained outside the tent entrance. "No need to be concerned. Tell the servants that all is well and dismiss them."

Bryso dismissed the servants but remained within earshot of the argument.

Maeve lowered her voice. "Have you spoken yet to Brenna?" Uriens shook his head. "Then, don't."

"And I told Merlin to tell no one of this arrangement."

Maeve began to pace again but more slowly than when she was at the peak of her anger. "The situation may not be completely lost, but Merlin will require an incentive other than keeping his word." Maeve stopped pacing and looked at Uriens. "Tell Merlin that Brenna is headstrong. If not handled in just the correct manner, she will refuse to marry Kaye. You can also say that if Brenna does not consent to this marriage happily, she will make this Kaye an unhappy and uncontrollable wife." Maeve smiled. "Yes, an unhappy and uncontrollable wife. Merlin would not like that. It would interfere with his scheming." She pointed to the tent entrance. "Go to him now. Tell Merlin of the issue with Brenna. Make sure he understands that no one else must know about this possible marriage or it will ruin his plans."

"I don't understand what all this accomplishes."

"It gives me time to think. And let's keep Merlin, Kaye and the rest of his party close at hand. We will invite them to Valphain Castle until this entire matter is settled."

13) An Old Secret Revealed

Someone was calling Arthur's name. It sounded like Ector. Arthur, sitting on the grass behind a food stall at the fair, was still angry and regretted nothing he had said, but leaving as he did, he felt as though he had lost his family and home, and was glad someone was coming after him.

"There you are, lad." Arthur did not look up at him; so, Ector sat down beside him. "I can use a rest. Looked all over the fair for you. Legs a bit tired. Taking a bit of a rest yourself, I see."

Arthur tore a few blades of grass and absentmindedly tossed them into the breeze. "If you have come to tell me to apologize to Merlin, I won't."

"Ah, no." Ector shook his head. "No, I didn't think you would. Nor will he apologize. Best that today be forgotten."

"Forgotten!" Arthur tore a fist full of grass and slammed it back to the ground. "This matter doesn't concern only today but my entire life." He was so angry at Merlin that until this moment, he had not considered Ector's responsibility. "And what of your part in all this? I understand that you favored Kaye as Merlin favored me. I suppose that is the way of families in the sense that Merlin always seemed to be a part of the family. But as my father, you gave Merlin free rein. You allowed him to make me the center of his grand plan with the sword."

Arthur could see that his words wounded Ector, who sat with his head down. Ector took a deep breath and began to speak. "I know, Arthur, that you tell most things to Merlin."

"Not any longer. And I no longer hear his voice constantly in my thoughts giving me instructions, giving me advice, giving me warnings."

"You must promise never to tell Merlin that I told you what I am about to say." Ector's eyes were moist. "I am not your father, not your real father. You are the son of Uther Pendragon and Queen Igraine. Uther, who had many enemies, died the night you were born. You were in grave danger from those who never wanted another Pendragon on the throne of Britain. Merlin took you to protect you."

Arthur was speechless and stared wide-eyed at Ector. This news meant that he had to reevaluate every aspect of his life, and he did not know where to begin. After a long silence, he spoke in a soft voice. "Has anyone ever received two more startling revelations in a single day than

I have? First I learn I could have been king just for pulling a sword from a stone and now that I have the royal heritage to justify it."

Ector lowered his eyes; there was a slight trembling in his chin. "You must feel very confused and have many regrets. For that I'm truly sorry."

"Regrets? The world has been turned upside down. I don't know what to think or what to feel."

"I in no way mean to compare my situation to yours, but all these years Merlin has also been an issue for me. He was always interfering, disapproving and demanding."

"Is that why you always deferred to him and always consulted with him even if it was just an exchange of glances?"

Ector became more composed. "Exactly. But I understand his thinking — at least part of it. And you must try to understand it as well. Merlin has always seen his task as guiding the future of Britain — not directly but rather through a worthy king. He first tried with Uther, who didn't have sufficient self-control." He pointed an admonishing finger at Arthur. "You share some of that trait along with all of Uther's physical strength and battle skills, but are far more sensible and compassionate, two words that could hardly be applied to Uther. That is why you, born with Uther's physical abilities and raised under a wizard's guidance, were his great hope. And you must credit him with this. You have grown to be an extraordinary man."

Merlin had always told him that in addition to the five senses, there were other ways of knowing. Arthur now wondered if somehow he always had a vague understanding that the obligation he felt toward the wizard was to something far bigger.

Arthur knew it would take many days to gain perspective on all that had happened today, and there was nothing else either he or Ector could say now that would help. They sat quietly for a time, and they returned to their tent, where Uriens was just ending a conversation with Merlin and walking away.

Arthur and Merlin avoided making eye contact. They and Ector entered their tent, where a smiling Kaye sat, still clutching Caliburn. The wizard waited until Arthur and Ector were seated and stood before them. "I will tell you two what I have just explained to Kaye, but it is to remain a secret among the four of us. Uriens has tentatively agreed to support Kaye's claim to the throne. I persuaded him that he must voice that support soon to end the current turmoil, but he can and he might well withdraw that support before Kaye is crowned. In return, Kaye is to take Uriens' daughter, Brenna, as a queen." Kaye frowned. "That is the price we pay, Kaye, even if this Brenna has the face of hag and a disposition to match. But the girl is strong willed, a common trait among our youth." Merlin glanced at Arthur from the corner of his eye. "She must be approached delicately about this arrangement or Uriens says she will not agree, not that she should have any choice whatsoever in the matter. I also suspect that Maeve is somehow involved in all this since Uriens does nothing without her approval. Once Brenna gives her consent and assuming no opposition from Maeve, we four will form an inner council that will make the most important decisions during Kaye's reign. We will also announce a formal council that will include a handful of the most important knights and nobleman. Uriens will be chief advisor but in name only, lest Maeve exert her influence." He finally looked at Arthur. "As next in line to the throne, you will become a knight and a battle lord."

A third revelation! All Merlin ever predicted for him was that he would become a knight, and that is the vision he had seen years before looking into a stream. The day's momentous and perplexing events seemed to have left him in excellent circumstances, and he was more than a little happy that he was not the one who would have to marry the hag-faced Brenna.

Ector had a question. "And do you think Brenna will agree to the marriage?"

Merlin assumed his most sarcastic tone. "Yes, but then I was fool enough to think that Arthur would not only draw the sword from the stone but also manage to hold onto it."

14) Invasion Plan

The fleet sailed along the coast of Germania, Vollo's vessel in the lead, the other four ships following in single file. The cook served the warlord his midday meal and returned to his place in the rear of the ship. Vollo spooned a portion of the stew into his mouth, made a face as he chewed and spat the food out over the side. He lifted the bowl to his nose and sniffed. He raised the bowl as if to throw it overboard. Instead, he walked from the bow of the vessel to the stern, where the frail cook was cleaning his cooking gear. Vollo threw the contents of the bowl into the cook's face and smashed the bowl on the deck. "This is not fit for swine."

The cook waited for Vollo to return to his place in the bow of the vessel before wiping the cold, greasy stew from his face.

Vollo, his face and fleshy neck flushed bright red, turned back toward the cook. "Bring that man to me; yes, the cook."

The two men closest to the terrified cook grabbed the diminutive man and dragged him forward, where they held him before the warlord. Vollo wrapped one of his massive hands around the cook's throat and lifted him to the tips of his toes, causing the man to lose control of his bladder. Vollo spoke slowly, his teeth clenched in anger. "I couldn't have been poisoned without your negligence or assistance. Which was it?"

"Poison?" The cook could barely get the word out. "I know nothing…"

"Negligence or assistance, which was it?" Vollo tightened his grip. The cook did not answer.

"Your silence and the fear in your face betray your guilt. Did you have an accomplice or did you act on your own?" Vollo squeezed even tighter. The brute strength in Vollo's hand crushed the cook's throat. The man stopped moving and began to sink to the deck. Keeping the one hand on the cook's neck, the battle lord reached down with his free hand, grabbed the cook by his leg, lifted him overhead and threw him overboard.

The stunned crew watched as the cook quickly sank beneath the surface of the sea.

Theil, in command of the last vessel, saw from a distance Vollo toss a man into the sea but could not imagine why except that the warlord had been acting more temperamental since his poisoning, complaining about such things as the cleanliness of ships and the manner goods had been stored in them, matters he previously considered too trivial to warrant his attention. It was not until they reached home port and dis-embarked that Theil had a chance to ask Munn, who had been in the lead boat, what had happened.

Munn leaned close to Theil and whispered. "He didn't like his stew; that much was plain. And as far as I could tell, he thought the cook had poisoned him. I suppose he thought the stew was poisoned."

The cook's blood was on his own hands as well as Vollo's, thought Theil, and he wondered if he had he been there in the first vessel, would he have had the courage to intervene on the cook's behalf or to confess that he was culprit.

"Theil!" Vollo, approaching from behind, was shouting to him. Whenever the warlord called him, he expected this would be the time Vollo would confront him about his treachery. He turned and walked back to the warlord, who stood nearly a head taller than him. "Tomorrow I will meet with King Cergin to report on our voyage and detail my plan for future incursions into Britain. I need you to be there."

Theil nodded his acknowledgement of the order.

Ever since the night when he had helped the poisoned Vollo to his tent, Theil had become the warlord's favorite aide. Despite being in the warlord's favor, Theil still wanted to see him dead or dishonored, and that could well happen if Vollo exhibited his worsening temper during his audience with the king. At the very least, he hoped Cergin would reject Vollo's invasion plan. Theil had his fill of death and destruction, especially under Vollo's leadership.

The next day Theil waited in the ante-chamber of Saxon king's throne room. Vollo should have been there already but was late. If Theil was called into the throne room, he would have to make an excuse for Vollo's absence and might even be asked to describe Vollo's plan for another but larger and more strategic military expedition to Britain. Against that eventuality, Theil struggled to remember the few details of the plan Vollo had revealed to him. The buried caches of food and weap-ons he knew well, and Vollo seemed to be relying greatly on a well-posi-tioned traitor in the British ranks. But as for the numbers of warriors and vessels required and most other things, he had not been told.

The door to the throne room opened. A guard appeared and asked for Vollo, and when told that Vollo would be late, the guard instructed Theil to come before the king. Theil worried that he might be punished for Vollo's absence or later punished by Vollo for not adequately describing his invasion plan.

What had become of his courage?

Theil had never before seen the throne room. It was the largest chamber he had ever been in and could easily accommodate hundreds of people. The walls were decorated with colorful murals and tapestries, and the wooden floor was a rich, dark color. He always imagined that if he ever met the king it would be for some act of heroism he had performed. It was ironic that he was here indirectly because of poison in a ring.

Waiting for him across the long hall was the one man in Germania who was likely not fearful of Vollo. King Cergin, who sat on a throne with crowns carved into the armrests, was a slight built man with light hair. He was young, and some of those who had met him said of the king that his mind was as sharp as his vision was not. Theil had heard that the young king was sensitive about his size and poor vision, and disliked larger men who thought their size alone made them superior to smaller people. That would make for an interesting meeting with Vollo.

This might be Theil's one opportunity to say something to the king that would prevent him approving Vollo's invasion plan. But he could not be certain that Cergin and Vollo were not allies, rather than the rivals they were made out to be. And disloyalty of any kind was always frowned upon. Theil would be exceedingly careful.

The king was flanked by several guards, and his chief advisor, Algar, stood by the king's right shoulder within whispering distance. Theil bowed to the king.

Cergin smiled and raised an eyebrow. "Does Lord Vollo deliberately keep his king waiting?"

Theil bowed again, then realized the initial bow had been sufficient. "No, Sire. Vollo eagerly anticipates this meeting. I can only think that the meticulousness of his preparations delays him."

"And your name?"

"Theil." He inadvertently bowed yet again.

Cergin looked back over his shoulder at Algar and back to Theil. "You were with Lord Vollo on his last voyage?" Theil nodded yes. "And can attest to the events of that voyage?"

"Yes, Sire."

"Some men — Theil, is it? Some men, Theil, are given to overstatement. Of course, by that I don't imply that Lord Vollo is."

"Of course, not, Sire." But Theil knew that Vollo was not only given to overstatement, as the king phrased it, but believed many of his exaggerations to be true. The warlord would, therefore, be able to argue convincingly for his plan.

"And you would know, Theil, would you not, if certain people were engaged in overstatement?"

"Yes. Sire. I believe I might — in some cases."

There were heavy footsteps behind him.

Cergin looked past Theil and squinted at Vollo as he entered the far end of the room. The king motioned to Algar to lean closer. "Look at him. Have you ever seen a man who indulged himself in greater self-aggrandizement than Vollo?" The remark was made within earshot of Theil, but the king seemed not to care if he was overheard. And there was truth in his statement. Vollo was clad in a long, flowing white tunic, matching his finely combed, flowing white hair. "He is reminiscent of those supernatural beings depicted in Christian churches," said the king, and the advisor concealed a smile. "All Vollo lacks is a pair of large wings. Perhaps, that is what he will ask for. I wonder if the man will have the audacity to claim to his king that he returned from the dead while in Britain." Vollo was nearing the throne. "But we must be serious, Algar. "

Vollo, as though performing a ceremonial task, walked more slowly as approached, stood at attention and bowed to the king. "Your Majesty." He stood erect again.

"Lord Vollo, welcome home from Britain."

"It was a long voyage, Sire."

Cergin smiled at Algar. "A very long voyage, according to some."

"Ah, Sire, you may be referring to the story of my death and return." The king nodded. "Men at sea and freshly home from a long voyage tell fanciful tales, as I'm certain Your Majesty knows."

"Oh course. One wonders how such tales are begun. Whatever its source, the report that you were laid out for a funeral one day and completely fit the next has only added to your illustrious reputation."

"Thank you, Your Majesty. If Your Majesty pleases, I can report on my voyage."

Cergin invited Vollo to give his report and granted Vollo permission to unfurl a large map. On the map were drawn the southeast coast line of Britain, a crude drawing of a castle marked Valphain, four circles on either side representing villages, and markings for rivers, streams, roads and bridges.

The king's interest in the map was exaggerated. "You say the circles represent villages." Vollo nodded. "Then, does the size of the circle, represent the wealth or power of the village?"

Vollo could see that the king was not serious and hesitated before answering. "The markings are approximate locations only. However, I can have the map redrawn if His Majesty wishes."

"Unnecessary." Cergin delivered the remark with a dismissive wave of his hand. "And Christian churches? My advisor and I were just discussing them before you entered. Some have images of strange supernatural beings." Algar was unable to conceal a smile. "Did you encounter any Christian churches, and if so, might they be used as fortifications?"

Vollo stared at Algar as he answered, and the king's advisor stopped smiling. "No, to your first question, Sire, and what few Christian churches may exist in Britain are not likely to be formidable in terms of their construction."

Vollo proceeded to give the details of his excursion. He said he and his men attacked and looted eight villages, four north of Valphain Castle, and four south. This was untrue. As Theil well knew, they had raided only six villages, all in the north, and the last raid was a disaster. The king looked to Theil for confirmation of Vollo's story, but Theil pretended not to notice.

Vollo said they had suffered only moderate causalities in the face of fierce opposition. Another untruth. The causalities were neither moderate nor primarily from fierce combat action. Their single biggest loss was to the traps left behind by unarmed villagers. Vollo also failed to mention the toll taken on the men by sickness and the frigid nights spent outdoors in Britain during early fall. The weather, thought Theil, should be taken into account if Vollo planned to suggest a return in late fall or winter.

The bulk of Vollo's report seemed not to impress Cergin, but what Vollo had to say next did. "The British are in disarray." Vollo spoke with passion and impudently looked the king directly in the eye. "They have been so for years, but no more so than now. Many of their great lords and knights, Uriens chief among them, are aged and in decline. New leaders have not emerged to replace them. Year after year, the fools try to name a king through a superstition involving an enchanted sword. And year after year, they fail. It is unlikely that there will ever be any better time to establish a foothold there."

"And how have you acquired this information about Uriens and the others?" There was both interest and skepticism in Cergin's tone.

"I have a spy, a well-placed traitor."

Theil had some experience of this traitor although he did not know who the man was. One night he accompanied Vollo into the countryside and kept guard while the battle lord met with a mysterious man awaiting him by a well.

Cergin raised an eyebrow at Vollo. "A spy and a traitor. And why would a British knight or nobleman, particularly one, as you say, who is well placed, turn against his clan and countrymen?"

"He is wise enough to see that a Saxon conquest is inevitable and wishes to profit, rather than suffer, by it."

"And how would such a person profit?"

"Traitors never profit."

At first Vollo proposed what amounted to a full scale invasion involving many thousands of men, hundreds of vessels and shore landings at six locations.

Cergin allowed his chief advisor to voice the objections to this plan. "Such an invasion would require a vast amount of resources," Algar said, "and would take time to mount. You, yourself, Lord Vollo spoke of the importance of acting quickly while the British are in disarray. There is also the issue of whether the homeland would be left inadequately defended." Vollo, who seemed to have anticipated all these objections, did not attempt to contradict Algar. "And while I, while all of us, I can safely say, have the utmost confidence in you, Lord Vollo, in the most unlikely event that an army of ours that large would suffer a defeat, it would be one from which the crown might not recover."

Vollo was prepared with a lesser version of his plan, which he now outlined. He requested enough men, vessels, weapons, and provisions to take and hold Valphain Castle. The castle could become an impregnable Saxon stronghold and a base from which to attack other British fortifications and to raid villages. And if the British laid siege to Valphain to reclaim it, they would weaken other areas of the coast for subsequent invasions.

"Thank you, Lord Vollo," said Cergin. "You have given me much to consider. I will have any answer for your in due time." Vollo was dismissed.

15) Abduction

Theil sat in a dark corner of the inn, his supper sitting untouched before him, his goblet again empty. Several other tables were occupied by small groups of men who ate and drank in relative silence. A large, boisterous group of drinkers sat where several tables had been pulled together. He paid no attention to any of them.

After the audience with King Cergin ended and he could take his leave of Vollo, Theil came directly here, ordered a meal, and lost interest in it even before it was served. He did drink, however, and continued to drink until his capacity to both see and to think were diminished. The innkeeper came to his table, said something he could not comprehend and took the plate of cold food away. It must be time to leave.

He stood up and had to quickly brace himself on a corner of the table for balance. Walking on unsteady legs, he crossed the floor to the door, stepped outside into the night air and walked along an alley, uncertain of which way he was going and which way he should be going. Between the brisk air and the walking, he hoped his mind would begin to clear.

Theil felt a blow across the back of his head and found himself on his hands and knees with no recollection of falling. He had an intense pain in his head, and the fall aggravated his still splintered broken right arm. He felt a hand take hold of his left arm, and for an instant thought someone was helping him up. He quickly realized his hands were being pulled behind his back and tied. A sack was thrown over his head, and he was lifted to his feet. Theil was dragged along the alley and thrown onto a wooden cart. He tried to get up. He was struck across the head again, and he lost consciousness.

Theil had no idea how much time had passed until he finally regained consciousness. He sat in a straight backed wooden chair, his arms tied to the arms of the chair, his head throbbing in pain, the sack still over his head.

There was no doubt in his mind as to what had happened to him. Vollo had finally determined that Theil, his second in command, was the person who poisoned him. Theil was a dead man, that much was certain. The only question was how much torture he would have to endure before death. He was resigned to dying but not to torture.

Theil heard voices. People entered the room, and footsteps approached him. The sack was pulled from over his head. Theil's eyes could not focus immediately. He was in a dark, torch-lit room, a dungeon, and there were at least several men standing about him. That much he could discern immediately. When his vision began to sharpen, he was surprised to see standing before him not the massive Vollo but rather the diminutive King Cergin.

The king, hands on hips, stood before him. "Theil, is it not? That is your name?" Theil nodded yes, uncertain that he could find his voice. "Tell me, Theil, why are Lord Vollo's men, men like you, so loyal to him?"

"His men, they fear him." Theil spoke through parched lips.

Cergin pointed to one his guards. "Give this man some water." A cup was brought to Theil, and he took a long drink from it. " 'They,' you said. Do you fear him as well?"

Theil, his lips wet and dripping with water, nodded yes. "Most fear and hate him."

"But are still willing to die for him?" Cergin folded his arms across his chest and looked down at Theil. "You must know the precarious situation in which you find yourself."

Theil was regaining his wits but was still groggy enough to say exactly what he thought. "You have questions, Sire. Ask them, and they will be answered truthfully."

Cergin smiled. "And your lies will protect Vollo."

Theil laughed bitterly. "Protect Vollo, no!"

"That remark comes easily to you in these circumstances."

Theil struggled to focus his vision to look the king in the eye. "An experienced soldier understands the situations in which he finds himself and knows when deceit serves no purpose. Vollo has never been a lord who could inspire loyalty by any means other than fear. Yes, his men fear him but now hate him much more because on this last voyage his arrogance and enormous appetite for glory cost the life of more than a dozen men, including a mere boy on his first voyage."

"Arrogance and enormous appetite for glory. Those are words I, myself, would use to describe Vollo." Cergin moved from Theil's right to his left, his eyes locked on the captive's face. "You specifically mentioned a boy. Was this your boy, your son?" Cergin paused when he saw tears welling in Theil's eyes. "I see. I am sorry for the loss of your son." He crossed back to Theil's other side. "It is also said that Vollo, himself, had trouble near the end of your voyage. Did he, in fact, have the sudden illness he claims? The one that caused him to appear dead?" Theil nodded yes. "And what caused this illness?"

"Poison."

Algar stepped forward. "And who would want to poison Vollo?"

The king smiled. "A father with an account to settle. Untie him and bring him more water."

Once untied, Theil rubbed his hands and his damaged right arm, then the back of his neck and his head. The king took a chair and sat directly in front of him, causing Theil to believe for the first time that he might survive this encounter.

"The report Vollo gave of his exploits in Britain," said Cergin. "Was he telling the full truth?"

"No, but he believes most of what he said to be true. He sometimes has delusions." At the king's prompting Theil told in detail about the number of villages they had raided, the extent of their successes, and the losses they had suffered during their last raid. He was careful to point out where Vollo's account differed from what had actually happened. He also mentioned how the weather at sea, the cold nights and illness had also taken their toll on the men.

"The disarray among the British that Vollo described, is this accurate?" Cergin seemed most interested in this question.

Theil shrugged his shoulders. "Vollo does not tell even his most trusted aides all that he knows."

"And what of the British spy Vollo mentioned?"

"That much is true. Lord Vollo met the man one night. He went alone. And the man's name was never spoken afterwards."

"Tell me, Theil." Cergin leaned closer. "I may well authorize Vollo to lead an invasion of Britain. If he were successful, would he attempt to establish himself in Britain, become independent of the crown?"

"Sire, no one can say one way or another. Vollo rarely shares his thoughts."

Cergin stood up in a sudden burst of energy and faced Algar. "See that this man is fed and cared for." He turned back to Theil. "You will now serve your king by continuing to serve Vollo. I will arrange to send messengers to Vollo during this next expedition to Britain, but the messengers will in actuality serve for you to send reports to your king."

Theil nodded his agreement, thankful he had been spared torture. It did occur to him, however, that he now had two secrets to hide from Vollo, either one sufficient reason for the warlord to kill him.

But for the first time in many days, he was happy to be alive.

Cergin started to leave and turned back to Theil a final time. "If for king and country, you were asked to. . ." The king paused to find the correct word. "Were asked to *eliminate* Lord Vollo, would you be willing to do so?" Theil closed his eyes and nodded yes. "Good, and I trust you would make a better job of it next time."

16) The Black Hammer

Arthur strolled through the fair alone. He again saw the juggler and the bird that said "me lady" and visited the place where horses were for sale to see the white stallion, which, he was told, was fittingly named Snow Storm. He also looked for the beautiful girl with the dark hair but did not encounter her again. And all the while, he thought about Kaye, so inept at battle, becoming king; whether Arthur would, as the wizard claimed, actually become a knight; and if his relationship with his life-long mentor Merlin would ever again be what it had been. Mostly, he thought about the Sword in the Stone, whether he should have kept it, and whether he or Merlin was mostly to blame for how things turned out.

He wandered to the tents that contained weapons for sale and saw Merlin standing there as if waiting for him. They greeted each other awkwardly with slight nods. Arthur pretended to be interested in one of the swords on display and tried to think of something to say that would begin a conversation without starting an argument.

Merlin, who stood observing Arthur handling the weapon, spoke first. "Do you regret not becoming king?"

Arthur had hoped to avoid this subject. "You went to great lengths to explain that Kaye is *king-elect*, not king."

"Yes, yes," Merlin said dismissively. "King or king-elect, whichever you prefer. But answer the question."

"Yes, I have regret because being king-elect has meant people fawning over Kaye and giving him presents to curry his favor. And no, because being king is certain to become far more difficult than it has been for Kaye so far."

"Far more difficult, that is for certain." Merlin selected a sword and handed it to Arthur to test its feel. "Are you prepared up here..." Merlin pointed to his head. "...for the tournament?"

Arthur evaluated the sword's weight and balance. "There will still be a tournament? I thought it was held to pick a champion to try to free Caliburn from the stone."

"I wish you had realized that earlier."

"I wish that you had told me earlier." Arthur softened his tone. "Let's not have that discussion again."

"There are other reasons to have a tournament." Merlin waved his arm about to indicate the great assemblage of people that surrounded them at the fair. "These people traveled a great distance to see warriors bash each other, and so they shall have their spectacle. It is also good to have the best knights test each other at least once a year. It establishes a ranking of sorts."

Arthur wondered whether Merlin's question about the tournament was as casual as he had first taken it to be. He turned toward the wizard. "What did you mean, am I prepared for the tournament?"

"It has been your lifelong dream, hasn't it, to fight in the Londinium tournament and become its champion? I would think you be more excited about the opportunity."

"And when were you going to tell me that I would fight in the tournament?" There was more annoyance in his voice than he intended.

"I did inform you. Not directly. Through Prywycke." Merlin also became annoyed. "Oh, you needn't tell me. Prywycke never spoke to you. Nonetheless, the fact is you have been entered as the king-elect's champion, and you will receive new armor and weapons, which is exactly why I thought you would be here among the weapon sellers."

Arthur always wanted an opportunity to earn the recognition that would come from winning a tournament but was now anxious about the possibility of humiliating himself before thousands of people and disappointing himself and Merlin — again.

"And Kaye has even made a present to you of a horse. Now, what was that horse's name?" Merlin, rubbing his fingers down his beard, could not remember. "The word 'white' was in the name, of that I'm certain."

"A white horse!"

"Yes, Snow Storm. That's it. I knew the word 'white' was in the name. But before we collect the horse, you must select a new weapon, one that is appropriate for the tournament."

Merlin led Arthur past two tents filled mostly with swords to a third. "You understand the nature of the tournament." Arthur listened attentively to the wizard. "There is no stabbing in the belly or throat, no cutting off of limbs or heads. Two opponents sit on horseback, pummeling each other's shield until one is unhorsed and eliminated. Most combatants are comfortable with swords and therefore, use them." Merlin smiled. "But I propose a hammer."

The wizard pointed to a double-headed hammer, and the seller retrieved it for him. Merlin weighed the heavy hammer in his hands and handed it to Arthur, who did likewise. "Had you paid attention to your science lessons, Arthur, you would know that the heavier head of the hammer. . ."

Arthur completed the thought for him. "Delivers a more forceful blow to a shield than a sword."

"Very good." Merlin appeared impressed.

"But the speed of the blow also matters." Arthur returned the doubled headed hammer to the seller and asked for the one that had caught his eye. This hammer had a black head with black leather wrapped around its wooden handle. It had a single flat surface forming the front of its head, and the back and top of the head had spikes. There was a third spike on the bottom of the handle, giving the weapon four striking surfaces rather than just two. Weapons were not just a necessary aspect of life. They could also be objects of beauty, as Arthur thought this black battle hammer was. "I like this one." He whipped it around over his head, careful not strike Merlin or the seller.

"Then, take it. You must also decide on a coat of arms." Merlin chided him. "I hope you won't select an owl again."

"No owl, but every other bird of prey already resides on some knight's shield and so do most animals, except for chickens and swine and other animals that can be found in a barnyard."

"And how about a weapon as a symbol?"

"All taken."

"Even the hammer?"

Arthur smiled as he looked down at his new weapon. "A black hammer on a white or silver background would look striking."

"Worry less about how you look and more about how you will fight. It's one thing to thrash Kaye about and quite another to face the likes of Bryso and Balan on the field."

17) The Tournament

The Field of Honor was decorated with colorful flags, each representing the coat-of-arms of one of the combatants. Five thousand people — that was calculation Merlin had given Arthur — filled the stands
that lined the tournament field. King-elect Kaye sat with Ector in the
best seats, those in the center of the west stands, facing away from the
sun and high enough to observe the entire field but not too high to make
it difficult to see the nuances of the contest that was about to take place.
Every important knight and lord in the vicinity of Londinium was here,
either in the stands or as a participant; every beautiful woman Arthur
had seen during days of wandering the fair must also be present.

From the tented area where the participants kept their horses and
weapons, Arthur looked out at the arena he would soon enter and felt
uneasiness in his stomach. He went back to the stool outside his small
tent, sat there fidgeting for a short time, stood up and went over for
another look at the tournament field.

Merlin, observing all this, came up behind Arthur. "I have never
seen you so anxious. You have fought in combat drills since the time you
could stand on your own feet."

Arthur, his expression solemn, turned toward the wizard. "I haven't
fought against this quality of competition and not in front of so enormous a crowd."

"There was a crowd when you outperformed everyone at the archery
tournament."

"This crowd is many times larger than that one and is full of lords
and ladies. At the archery contest, no one knew my name; no one paid
much attention to what I did. Here I am younger brother to the king-
elect, and even have my own coat-of-arms." All this was true, but there
was another, more compelling reason why he was worried. To fail at
what Merlin expected him to become was one thing. To fail at what he
expected of himself was more serious.

Merlin frowned at him. "Is this what I taught you, to fill your mind
worry and doubt?"

"What I need least at this moment is to be vexed by you."

"Vexed! Wait until you enter the Field of Honor, and then you'll know
how it feels to be *vexed*." Merlin called to Prywycke. "We must repaint

Arthur's shield, Prywycke. Remove the hammer and replace it with an owl. No better yet a sparrow."

Arthur stared at Merlin. "Your sarcasm does not help."

"Oh no? I see anger in your eyes instead of worry." Merlin turned and walked away.

"He is insufferable. Why has it taken me until now to see that?"

Prywycke rested a hand on Arthur's shoulder. "Merlin means well."

"What has me anxious is the delay in getting onto the field. I've been ready since early this morning, and I'm still waiting. Once I can actually engage in combat, feel a sword strike against my shield, some pain, perhaps a little blood, then I'll rely on my training and reflexes."

Now it was Prywycke who appeared worried. He opened his mouth to speak, closed it again, and finally spoke. "Think you'd be more comfort with a sword."

Arthur sighed. "I'm committed mentally to the hammer. But thank you for the suggestion."

There were sixty-four combatants, half of whom would be eliminated during each of six rounds, ultimately leaving one man standing, or more accurately, one man still mounted on his horse. Three judges sat at a table with tokens representing each of the participants and arranged them in pairs for round one. In an effort to prevent the king-elect's brother, the youngest combatant entered that day, from embarrassing himself, they gave him the weakest opponent in the field and scheduled that particular match to be the last of the thirty-two in the opening round.

Finally, after waiting half the morning, Arthur was called to the ready. He put on his helmet, grabbed his shield and hammer, and mounted Snow Storm.

While it was yet to be determined if Arthur was the best warrior in the field or even a good one, he was certain this was the most imposing he had ever appeared. Astride a pure white stallion, a black and white blanket under its saddle, Arthur had a short, black cape tied behind his shoulders and one white and one black plume on his helmet. On his left arm he carried a shield decorated with a black hammer on a field of white, and in his right he carried the black hammer depicted in his coat of arms.

The first part of each contest was more ceremonial than a significant aspect of the combat. The two contestants would charge each other from opposite ends of the Field of Honor, and as their horses raced past each other, the warriors would try to strike a blow with a sword or a mace, if that was the contestant's weapon of choice. On this day, the combatants failed to deliver a blow on about half of these charges. Sometimes one or both combatants landed a blow that did little damage. On one occasion a lucky warrior succeeded in unhorsing his opponent on the opening charge. Every other contest so far that day had been settled by the two warriors moving in close, shield to shield, and pounding each other until one was toppled.

The flags representing the two contestants, Arthur's black battle hammer and the black and dark blue wolf's head of his opponent, were brought to the center of the field. The flag bearers allowed the crowd's anticipation to build for a short time and then lowered the flags.

Arthur spurred Snow Storm into a gallop. His opponent did likewise to his mount. The fast-moving horses quickly shortened the distance between the two riders. Arthur made no move until his adversary was almost upon him. He lifted his hammer back and up, and swung it in an arc that caught the wolf's head shield square in the middle and toppled the rider.

Arthur did not notice the cheering until he turned Snow Storm around and rode back to where his opponent struggled to regain his feet. It must have been a hard fall at the speed he was moving. Arthur dismounted and helped the man up, eliciting another cheer from the crowd.

In the stands, Ector was one of many who had risen to his feet to acknowledge Arthur's success, and in doing so, his hair fell from his bald spot to his shoulder. Uriens and Maeve also stood to cheer, while Kaye hesitated before following their lead.

During Arthur's second battle, he and his opponent each struck a glancing blow on the initial charge. They turned their horses around, charged again from much closer range, and again struck glancing blows. They moved in for close combat. Arthur struck three fast and powerful hammer blows and toppled his opponent backwards off his horse.

Arthur's third contest was similar to the second, another quick win. And he ended his fourth battle on his initial charge with one blow of his hammer.

After this fourth victory, a smiling and proud Prywycke leaned toward Merlin, who was an arm's length away. "Arthur's feat today will long be remembered."

The wizard did not take his eyes from the Field of Honor. "He will have to win the tournament first. Legends are not told about warriors who almost won."

Arthur was one of the last four contestants. Bryso, another one of the four and last year's champion, won his next contest and moved to the final match. Arthur had watched Bryso carefully, assessing his strengths and searching for a weakness. Bryso was of average height. He had broad shoulders and powerful arms and legs. He sat solid in the saddle and was able to take a pounding by his opponent without visible impact. Indeed, Arthur thought Bryso's major asset was his ability to take punishment until his adversary wore himself down.

Arthur was called to the ready for his contest against Sir Balan. Merlin did not want to be seen counseling Arthur out of concern that people would attribute Arthur's victory to the wizard's magic. He grabbed Prywycke by the arm. "Quick, run to Arthur and tell him that Balan is left-handed."

Arthur noticed Prywycke's approach and thought he could not possibly be coming to again suggest he use a sword instead of the hammer. Prywycke held Snow Storm's bridle as he spoke. "Balan. Left-handed."

This information was of great importance. Balan's sword and shield were on the opposite sides of the other combatants. Balan would try to position himself so that he was on Arthur's right where he would be able to use his shield but Arthur would either have to use his hammer for defense or turn awkwardly in his saddle to bring his shield around for protection.

The flags were dropped. The two men charged.

Arthur, planning how he would attack Balan, did not pay enough attention to his opponent's maneuver and allowed Balan to get on his right side. Arthur had to bring his shield across his body to deflect a blow from Balan's sword. The two wheeled their horses around and charged again. And again, Balan, an excellent horseman, got to Arthur's right. This time Arthur pulled Snow Storm off to the left and avoided contact.

They moved in for close combat. Once again Arthur was outmaneuvered and found himself with his shield away from Balan, forced to deflect Balan's sword strikes with his ax. Unable to take the offensive in this position, Arthur spurred Snow Storm and disengaged.

The two riders faced each other, moving their mounts from side to side, occasionally feigning an attack, each trying to out-position the other. Finally Arthur charged. As he had hoped, Balan turned his horse to the left, not noticing that Arthur had begun to bring his mount around to move in the same direction. They wound up racing parallel to each other, their shields almost touching. Arthur delivered a powerful hammer blow to Balan's shield, then two more in quick succession, and a fourth that toppled his opponent.

Arthur had reached the final match against Bryso.

The two finalists faced each other across the Field of Honor. Bryso saluted his opponent with his sword, and Arthur returned the salute with his hammer. The thousands of people in the stands rose to their feet for the start of the last match, many of them shouting encouragement to Arthur.

The flags were dropped. Arthur and Bryso charged.

On the first pass, each man dealt the other a glancing blow to the shield. They wheeled their horses around for a second charge and a third with neither man doing any damage to the other. Now they moved in for close combat.

The two men pummeled each other, with Arthur delivering roughly four blows for every three managed by Bryso. Arthur thought Balan a more skilled opponent than Bryso, but striking at Bryso was like hitting a boulder. Nothing seemed to have an impact on him. Arthur's hammer arm was getting tired. He doubted he could outlast Bryso and decided to try something unexpected.

Arthur turned the hammer in his hand so the spike was its striking edge. With a forceful blow, he dug the spike into the top of Bryso's shield and whipped the shield clean off the leather straps that held it to his opponent's arm. The maneuver left Briso exposed and imperfectly balanced. Not giving him an opportunity to recover, Arthur struck Bryso across the shoulder with his shield. Bryso half toppled off his mount, tried to hold onto the neck of his horse but failed and fell to the ground.

Arthur was the new champion.

As Arthur had been instructed before the final match, it was customary for the victor to salute the crowd and to be saluted by them. Holding his hammer above his head, Arthur slowly rode before the spectators, who cheered him enthusiastically. When Arthur finished riding the circuit, he went to salute the king-elect and his party. Sitting atop Snow Storm, he removed his helmet and held his hammer aloft. He first noticed Ector waving frantically at him and Kaye to his right. His eyes went to the row behind his brother, where he saw looking down at him, the petite, dark-haired girl. She smiled at him, and he smiled back.

18) Another Kind of Sparring

The afternoon sun was low in the sky when Arthur accepted congratulatory words from the last of the many well-wishers who flocked onto the Field of Honor to speak to him. He felt elevated, like an eagle gliding high in the clouds. A long-time dream had become reality although it did not always feel real, and there were moments when his mind was blank, overwhelmed by the day's events.

Certainly no one could now call him a boy or a youth. He had proven himself equal to or better than any knight in Londinium. And he was free of Merlin. Perhaps not *free* because the wizard's influence would always be with him. But he was now *independent* of Merlin as his new future unfolded.

It was twilight by the time Arthur had stabled Snow Storm, removed his armor and cleaned up. How odd it was that he felt more comfortable with a helmet over his head, a shield on one arm and a hammer in his other hand than he did now, freshly washed, his hair neatly combed and wearing a new tunic. He was uneasy about entering Uriens's large tent, where a banquet was being held in his honor — and Kaye's.

All of the guests were certain to speak to him, and he would have to say something sincere and intelligent to each and every one of them. He was already weary of hearing himself speak.

And there was a matter of the petite, dark haired girl. She had smiled at him from the grandstand, and that might have meant something, but another of the wizard's oft-repeated lessons was to be wary of appearances. Arthur had set meeting her as goal. If he did, it would make this a perfect day. If she ignored or rejected him, it would tarnish what was otherwise the greatest day of his life.

The best of all possibilities, he decided, was if she were not present at the dinner. There would be no risk and no regret.

When Arthur appeared at the tent entrance, a cheer went up and spread throughout the assembled crowd, as those with goblets in their hands raised them to salute the champion. Kaye, smiling broadly, his eyes watery from drink, was the first to greet him. Arthur thought he would never become accustomed to this, having to hear the same praise again and again, and just as often, giving the same humble response. He would prefer to sit by himself in a corner of the tent and enjoy something to eat. Such was not to be the case. There seemed always to be a small group of people around him. At first he tried to remember the names that people gave him, but he abandoned that effort after being introduced to the first dozen.

She was here. He caught a glimpse of her across the large tent, engaged in conversation with a handful of young men. Working his way toward her would require an effort, and the chances of speaking to her privately seemed dim. He would need to wait until her situation changed.

Arthur overheard someone say that Sir Balan was approaching. Arthur had never seen Balan until their match on the field and was surprised that the man did not appear formidable without armor, owing to his boyish features and lean body. Having no experience greeting men he had defeated in combat, other than Kaye, of course, he had no conception of how he would be received by the knight. Balan was more than gracious. He greeted Arthur with a slap on the shoulder, done gently, but certainly he was a man of strength despite his lack of bulk.

Finally, Arthur could give someone else a compliment. "Sir Balan, you fought well today, and I hope never again have to face you on the field."

Balan laughed and again slapped Arthur on the shoulder, this time with more force. "I believe the very opposite will occur, that you and I will challenge each other many times but that you will remain the champion for many years."

After Balan left him, Arthur found himself standing alone, which made him feel even more awkward than being the focus of attention. He searched the crowd for *her,* and when he saw that she was still in a group, he moved in the opposite direction, pretending to be paying no attention to her as he nodded and smiled at various people. After a time, he circled back for another attempt. Only two men were speaking to her now. This might be the best opportunity he would have to meet her. He walked up behind her and stood several feet off to the side, hoping she would turn and see him. She did not. He waited for a pause in the conversation that would allow him to say something without causing an interruption. There was no pause.

He must look the fool, he thought, and moved on.

Arthur noticed a woman at the far end of the tent berating a servant and was surprised by the anger in her face, a level of intensity he thought could only be appropriate on the battlefield. What could a servant do, or not do, to elicit that kind of reaction? He moved on, but a short time later, found the same woman, an older woman with an oddly gray complexion, rushing straight toward him.

"Arthur." She took his hand, shook it gently and held onto it. "Oh, Arthur, what a performance!" The change in her demeanor was remarkable. She was smiling broadly as she spoke. "It was thrilling to watch you out there on the field."

Not knowing what else to say, he introduced himself. "I'm Arthur."

"Oh!" She put her hand to the top of her chest and dipped one shoulder. "Forgive me." She laughed again. "I'm Maeve." She moved closer to him, entirely too close. "You were wonderful today."

Arthur was not only unnerved by how close she stood to him but also by the way she flung her arms about, dipped her shoulders and shook her breasts. He was naïve when he came to women and their behavior but thought she was attempting to be seductive and that the insincere laughter and the exaggerated movements were an effort to appear younger than her years.

He smiled blankly and nodded as she spoke without paying much attention to her words.

"And when you pulled off your helmet. . ." She paused and gave him a coy look. "I thought what an excellent looking young man."

He was hoping for a graceful way out of this situation, that someone would join them or that Maeve would leave him to speak to someone else, but no end to this conversation was in sight. "I must get something to drink," he said impulsively and awkwardly, and although good manners required him to offer her a drink as well, he merely bowed toward her and turned to walk away as she gave a final giggle.

To validate his comment to Maeve, Arthur went in search of a goblet of mead and found instead Bryso, the dethroned champion. Unlike Balan, Bryso was actually more formidable appearing without armor. His chest was deep, his shoulders broad and his hands large even in proportion to those features.

Bryso frowned at Arthur. "I trust you realize, sir, that you must replace my broken shield."

Arthur was about to say that he had been unaware that one combatant was responsible for the damaged equipment of another and would gladly replace the shield when Bryso broke into a smile and extended his hand to shake Arthur's. "Congratulations. I'm happy that it is to you, a fighter of consummate skill, that I lost my place as champion."

Arthur was never comfortable being praised and responded with authentic humility. "I have won but a single tournament. You have shown skill and courage in actual battle — and on more than one occasion."

Bryso laughed. "Don't apologize for your victory. The day I became champion was the day I knew I would one day no longer be champion. Enjoy the moment."

From the corner of his eye, Arthur saw someone approaching, a small woman, and he thought it was Maeve. But it was the dark-haired girl, and she placed herself between Arthur and Bryso. It was the first time he had seen her this close. She had flawless white skin that contrasted well with her brown eyes and black hair, a small but perfectly shaped mouth and teeth that were white and perfect. When she smiled, a little too much of her pink upper gum showed. But he found even that appealing.

The girl held out her right hand, palm down, to Bryso. He took her hand in his and bowed to her. She, then, held out the same hand to Arthur, who followed Bryso's example. Touching her hand had a surprising impact on him, one that he could not understand or articulate. The intensity of the experience was not near to that of pulling Caliburn from the stone, but he felt some connection to this woman.

She must have felt something too because her expression turned to surprise for an instant before she regained her composure.

He had to regain his composer as well. "I'm Arthur."

"I know well who you are." She smiled the same smile she had given him from the tournament stands. "I'm Brenna."

He felt the energy drain from his body. Brenna, of all people, the girl Merlin was attempting to wed to Kaye. Of the many young women he had seen at the fair, this was the one he could not have. Arthur thought he should find an excuse to walk away. But he did not want to leave so soon after finally meeting her. He enjoyed being close to Brenna, looking at her, and listening to her speak. After all, she and Kaye were not yet married or even betrothed. And what harm was there in having a conversation with her in a tent full of people?

As fate would have it, Bryso took his leave of them, and Arthur thought it would be impolite to leave her standing alone.

"Congratulations on your victory today," she said.

"Thank you." There was one issue he wanted to explain. He pointed to his nose. "I hope I redeemed myself for wearing a bandage of mud."

Brenna laughed. "My friends and I wondered about that." Her laugh was sweet and genuine; she was altogether charming. "They thought you wore the mud because you were an entertainer. We saw you juggle a knife. I said it must be a combat injury."

"Yes, a combat injury, from sparring, an odd injury, but that is a story that wouldn't be of much interest to you."

"No, I would be most interested." There was something in the way she glanced up at him that caused him to think she was more interested in him than in the story. "You must have practiced very hard to acquire the level of skill to win the tournament the first time you entered it and to beat Bryso, who is rarely beaten. You must tell me about that as well."

Arthur wanted to impress her but did not want to be a braggart, which was Kaye's frequent accusation against him. "I would say 'yes' that I have trained long and hard. Merlin might say I was lazy and inattentive at times."

"Are you as good with a bow as you are with your hammer?"

Arthur smiled. "If I told you how good, you would think me a braggart and not like me very much."

She looked into his eyes quietly for a moment before answering. "I will like you fine." She smiled at him coyly. "Perhaps you can give me archery instructions."

The gathering was called to dinner. Arthur briefly thought it was best if he left her now. Instead he found himself asking if he could be seated with her during dinner. She agreed.

They sat next to each other at the table and across from Maeve, who was beside Kaye, talking excitedly to him, gesturing lavishly at him and giggling as she had with Arthur.

The meal was served, and Arthur felt Brenna's leg touching his under the table. At first he thought this must be accidental and wondered if he should move his leg away. But if he felt the contact, she must have as well and therefore, the touching was deliberate.

Brenna sat quietly while a servant spooned portions of meat and vegetables onto her plate. She turned toward Arthur. "Where you there, Arthur? When the sword was drawn?'

He nodded. "It appeared to be just an old rusted sword when it was in the stone, but once withdrawn, it shone brightly and in an odd way. That might have only been a trick caused by the angle of the sun. But what was even more unusual was how it felt, as if there were energy in it, as if it were momentarily alive."

She was surprised by that comment. "You held it?"

He leaned close to her and was struck by the sweet fragrance in her hair. "Promise to tell no one." Sharing a secret with her would create an additional sense of intimacy. "Yes, I held it."

There was a disturbance across the table. Kaye toppled over his goblet, and mead spilled onto the table. Kaye thought it funny; as did Maeve. They both appeared drunk.

Brenna leaned toward Arthur and whispered. "Forgive me for being blunt, but your brother is not acting in a very kingly manner. And notice how Maeve comports herself with him. She is obsessed with being attractive to men. When she gazes in a mirror, she sees only what she wants to see and feels the equal of any woman, no matter how young and no matter how beautiful. And my father contributes to this fantasy by telling her things she wants to hear. Do you see that silver necklace she is wearing?" Arthur looked at Maeve and nodded. "My father had that necklace made for me, but somehow she got her hands on it. Look at her. She not only flirts with Kaye but throughout dinner she has kept an eye on you, Arthur."

Arthur touched Brenna's soft, warm arm, in part to signal that he wanted to say something, but more because he just wanted to touch her. "You don't mean that she was seriously flirting with me as well?"

Brenna laughed. "Of course, she was, and she wants you even more now that she sees you with me. Anything I have or might have she wants. She is obsessed with competing with me."

"Her own daughter?"

"Stepdaughter. Didn't you notice that that we aren't similar either in appearance or demeanor?"

He glanced up and down her body. "I noticed."

"I was still young when my mother died and my father married Maeve." There were tears in Brenna's eyes, but anger in her expression. "But I was old enough to know what she is. Once she became lady of the castle, everything my mother, a kind and gracious woman, did was wrong and Maeve was going to correct her mistakes in how the household was run and our banquets held. I heard this from several of the servants, but when I heard myself, I confronted her."

Brenna was interrupted by the loud laughter coming from across the table. It was Maeve and Kaye again. Brenna grimaced, then turned back toward Arthur and smiled. "Enough about her. Tonight is a celebration." She raised her goblet. "A toast to the champion."

He smiled and a raised his goblet. "And to new friends."

They avoid further discussion of Maeve and Kaye, and at the dinner's conclusion, Brenna turned toward Arthur so that their knees touched. "I trust that you know that you and your party will be staying with us at Valphain Castle." Arthur nodded yes. "I look forward to seeing you there and perhaps learning something of your archery skills."

He gave her *a look* and received one in return.

Arthur lay uncomfortably on his cot, unable to sleep, the day's events rushing through his mind like a flooding stream. There was Balan trying to outmaneuver him, and Bryso unflinching under the blows Arthur delivered with his hammer. There were all the people who congratulated him, Balan saying he would be a champion for years, Bryso saying that to be champion was to wait to be dethroned. But mostly he thought of Brenna, her laugh, her touch, her eyes when she gave him *the look*.

He felt guilty even thinking about her, but an offense was in the act, not in the thought. He began to imagine the circumstances that might lead him to physically coupling with Brenna. And based on how she reacted to him at dinner, he thought it might be only a matter of the proper circumstance.

Perhaps, they could go hunting together. Uriens or even Kaye, busy learning to be king, might suggest that Arthur accompany her on a hunt. They could ride together into the woods, stop to rest under the shade of a tree, and their legs might touch as they did under the banquet table that very night. This, he was sure, was the only spark they would need.

Or perhaps, either by accident or design, they might find themselves alone one evening in a secluded part of Valphain Castle. It would be a dark place where even a servant was unlikely to go. She would point out some object of interest, a tapestry or painting, and their shoulders and arms would touch.

Or given her apparent boldness, Brenna might secretly come to his bedroom one night and crawl into bed with him. If he could become champion of the Londinium tournament, he believed anything was possible, even Brenna being the aggressor. The vision of her doing so was as clear in his mind as a memory.

19) The Night Visitor

The grandeur and excitement of the Londinium tournament and fair were over. The stalls of the vendors and entertainers were gone. Most of the tents that housed the tournament participants and spectators were either packed away or being disassembled. A handful of people still walked the near empty fair grounds. Small groups of riders trailing pack horses were heading off in different directions.

One of the last tents still standing belonged to Uriens. Outside his tent Brenna was tending to her horse, a brown mare with white markings on her face. It had been saddled, but the saddle straps needed tightening.

Maeve, the last to rise that morning, walked slowly from the tent. Her eyes were droopy, her expression pained. Brenna glanced over her shoulder at her stepmother. "Don't look at me in that fashion," said Maeve. "Don't dare give me a disapproving look. I am your elder."

Brenna fastened her saddle straps without looking back at Maeve. "You see only your own guilt."

Maeve's eyes opened wide, her nostrils flared. "Guilt!"

Brenna turned toward Maeve. "Yes, guilt." Her tone was loud and angry. "Guilt for flirting with Kaye and Arthur last night and for drowning decorum in drink to the embarrassment of my father."

Maeve took hold of her arm and squeezed it. Brenna shook free of her hold. "Uriens is my husband and my concern. But you. . .you are disrespectful and insulting. And delight in being so. I was entertaining my guests. You are too naïve to know the difference between charm and flirtation."

"But not too naïve to know the difference between being charming and *trying* to be seductive."

Maeve put her hands on hips and stepped almost nose to nose with Brenna. "Oh, but you are naïve. A girl can flirt, but only a woman can be seductive."

Someone was calling to them. Approaching on horseback from a short distance away were Arthur and his party, who were to accompany Uriens' household to Valphain Castle.

"Uriens has failed to discipline his spoiled daughter, but you'll learn a lesson one day." Maeve composed herself and walked toward the riders, smiling and waving at them.

Brenna turned back to her horse, took its reins and prepared to mount up. She hesitated and leaned forward so that her forehead rested against the saddle.

Bryso, who was about to mount his own horse, saw Brenna propped against her horse and called to her. "Brenna, do you want a hand up." She did not answer. "Brenna." As he walked to her, she turned around. He frowned when he saw her face. "You're pale."

"Too much food. . .and drink. . .at last evening's banquet."

Bryso laughed. "You're not alone in that state. But you should rest before beginning the journey."

She shook her head. "I'm fine."

"Let me help you to your saddle."

"I can manage." She climbed into the saddle and rode toward Arthur's party.

Leaving servants behind to dismantle and pack Uriens' tent and equipment, two dozen riders began the journey to Valphain castle. Uriens and Maeve rode in the lead; Arthur and Brenna managed to pair up a distance back.

Bryso put his horse into a fast trot until he caught up to Kaye, who was riding alone. "You've taken well to being king," said Bryso.

"King-elect, Merlin is quick to point out." Kaye cast a glance back down the trail to where Arthur and Brenna were in conversation.

"You must have much on your mind."

Kaye smiled. "Yes, much, but I'm also anxious to see Valphain Castle. I'm told its design and location are near perfect. Do you share that opinion? I think I'd like to build a castle very much like it."

"Build a castle?"

Kaye's smile became a frown as he studied Bryso's expression. "Yes, a castle is, among other things, a symbol, and symbols are important, don't you think? A king, after all, must have a castle."

"Of course, a king requires a castle." Bryso shrugged his shoulders. "But castles require time and resources to construct."

"Oh, I didn't mean that it would be my first task. It was simply something I was thinking about. You asked me what was on my mind, do you recall?" Kaye smiled and now spoke with enthusiasm. "No, the very first thing I'll do is seek the advice of men like you and Uriens. Of course, there's also Merlin to give me counsel."

"Merlin, of course."

"Merlin says I must meet as many of the great knights as I can and solicit their advice and support."

Bryso continued to ask Kaye questions. A few, about his training and experience, Kaye answered with a smile. A few more, primarily about the afternoon he found Caliburn in the woods, caused him to frown and answer evasively. Bryso took his leave of Kaye and caught up to Uriens and Maeve at the head of their small column. Bryso looked back at Kaye and leaned across his saddle toward Uriens. "I'm not certain what kind of a king this boy Kaye will make." The remark drew the attention of Maeve as well as Uriens. "He doesn't present himself like a king. He certainly doesn't speak like one, not judging from the conversation we just had." Bryso again looked back at Kaye. "Perhaps, Uriens, you should withdraw your support of him."

Uriens took a deep breath. "What choice do we have? Turmoil on the one hand; hoping for another enchanted sword on the other?"

"You sound like Merlin," said Maeve sharply.

Uriens forced a smile. "I suppose I do. But he does have his arguments. "

"Arguments for Merlin's own purpose."

"Yes, Maeve, for his own purpose. That, however, doesn't necessarily make them invalid. He was correct to point out my advancing years. That was very difficult for me to accept." He looked from Maeve to Bryso. "If I can accept my aging, surely the two of you can. Would you have me wait yet another year for yet another tournament?"

"Yes," said Bryso. "Wait for the next tournament."

Uriens sighed. "But there is nothing for which to wait. Even if you were to win the tournament, Bryso, and—forgive me for saying this—you would need to beat Arthur, who is quite formidable as you well know. Even if you were to win, Kaye has the sword, which no longer has any enchantment."

"Yes, you're right." Maeve appeared deep in thought. "If the sword has failed in that it gave us Kaye as a possible king, why would anyone trust it a second time even if it still had enchantment? No, you're correct, Uriens. The sword no longer has a use."

"What then?" asked Bryso. "Simply accept this Kaye as king."

"Kaye is weak," said Maeve. "That is your belief, Bryso, although he still has Merlin. Let's see what unfolds over the coming days. Let's see how weak Kaye is and how much influence Merlin has over him. Perhaps, the best alternative for us now is to take control of a weak king rather than to fight an already lost battle to give the throne to Uriens."

———

It was another new experience for Arthur, seeing a castle as grand as Valphain. As their party approached it, Arthur appraised its location. Picturesque overlooking the sea, yes, but he was more taken with the military value of its setting. Located on a tall cliff, Valphain's defenders had the high ground against any land attack, and the height and sheerness of the sea cliff made an assault from the sea impossible. Massive stone walls, topped by stone crenelations, surrounded the castle. And although they were told that there were a number of structures of varying size and use behind those walls, from where they were only the tall and formidable tower was visible above the walls.

In late afternoon they rode through Valphain's gates, were shown where in the castle's large stable they were to stall their horses, and eventually to their bedrooms in the tower. Arthur had been in a multi-story building only a few times in his life, only churches and inns, and had never before slept above ground level. Dropping his gear by his bed, he went to the window to look out to the sea. This could not be more different from sleeping behind shuttered windows, sword by his hand in case brigands tried to force their way into Ector's manor house.

After he unpacked, Arthur went down to the great hall and out to the castle grounds, inspecting everything he encountered. Finally, he climbed up to the castle walls and walked the full circuit, determining exactly where he would station archers and spearmen to thwart a siege. Having made those determinations, he planned how a siege might defeat his defense, which led, in turn, to refinements in his defensive strategy.

Supper that evening was held in the great hall at a long banquet table but was attended by only a handful of people, all of whom were assigned seats by Maeve on the same side of the table. She sat Kaye, as king-elect, at the center next to Uriens. Maeve sat between Kaye on one side and Arthur on the other. Brenna was placed as far away from Arthur as could be managed. The wizard, as he sometimes did, had simply disappeared.

Maeve kept both Arthur and Kaye engaged in conversation throughout the meal, while Arthur frequently looked beyond Maeve to glance at Brenna, who just as frequently looked in his direction. Arthur as well as Kaye found themselves occasionally hazarding a glance down at Maeve's chest, for she was wearing as revealing a gown as he had ever seen, exposing more of her breasts than it concealed.

When the meal ended, Maeve announced that the visitors, weary from their journey, surely wanted to go immediately to their beds. This pronouncement made it awkward for Arthur to linger behind in an effort to speak to Brenna. However, he did manage to say good night to each person, including Brenna, who whispered to him, "We will have the opportunity to be together before too long."

As he had these last few nights since meeting Brenna, Arthur could not sleep. He would lie in his bed and eventually get up to look out the window to the sea, wondering when he would see her next and if they ever would become lovers. She was not far away, perhaps only down the hall, but entirely out of reach, at least for the moment.

He finally lay down on his bed, his hands behind his head and day-dreamed about Brenna. The door to his room would open quietly. A small body would slip through the narrow opening and close the door behind her. Light footsteps would approach his bed. She would stand still for a moment unlacing the top of her night dress and let it slide to the floor. She would pull back a corner of the bed blanket and crawl in next to him.

His waking dream was interrupted by a gentle tapping at his door. It must be Kaye or Ector. Merlin would have just entered the room. But what if it were Brenna? The tapping was soft, more like a woman's knock than a man's. "Just a moment." He leapt out of bed, quickly dressed and smoothed out his hair with his hands. He went to the door and opened it. There backlit by the torchlight in the hall was the small frame of a woman. Arthur smiled. The woman stepped forward into the light.

It was Maeve.

She must have seen the disappointment in his face because she momentarily lost her smile. She quickly regained her composure. "I wanted to be certain you had whatever you required for your stay at Valphain Castle." She had delivered her words with the exaggerated body movements that he found so disturbing, and these movements were even more troubling at this moment because of the revealing gown she was still wearing from dinner. "I wanted to be certain the bed was *warm* enough for you." She giggled.

On their journey here Brenna warned Arthur that Maeve might attempt to seduce him, just to prove she was capable of it or to spite

Brenna because he preferred Brenna's company to Maeve's. That is how competitive the stepdaughter and stepmother were. But it was far more than his just preferring Brenna's company. Arthur, though he was tournament champion, was unnerved by this woman. Her words, her giggle, even her body movements seemed so insincere he did not know how to evaluate or react to them. And she was too close to him. He worried that she might touch him, perhaps in an intimate a manner. That, he was certain, would be a violation of convention, and he assumed that as a married woman and the wife of his host, her presence, alone, in his bedroom was a violation of his host's hospitality.

The left strap fell off Maeve's shoulder and the top of her gown lowered. He glanced down at her, worried that she would be half naked in another instant. What if someone walked by? Bryso? Or Uriens himself? Or Brenna, who would certainly confront Maeve?

"Thank you for your concern, Maeve. I do have everything I require. I'm certain you are tired after caring for all your guests so you need not be concerned about me." He put his hand on her shoulder, and she turned and moved closer so that her upper body rested in the crook of his arm. He walked into the hall, gently nudging her along with him.

"I know, Arthur, you are tired as well after the tournament and your long ride." She giggled. "I'll check on you tomorrow when you are more rested and more aware. . ." She titled her head toward him. "More aware of your needs."

He nodded, said good night, and closed the door. He worried that he had been impolite and perhaps misunderstood the reason for her visit and her use of the word "needs." But Brenna, who had been battling with her stepmother for years, described Maeve not only as seductive but also as spiteful and vindictive. Arthur wondered if Maeve saw his behavior as rejection and whether he had just made an enemy of her. In any case, he was glad she was out of his room.

He did not think Maeve would possibly return on this night but locked the door anyway.

20) Preparations for War

The noise of carpenters' hammers and saws sounded across the waterfront, as did the occasional shout of a workman. While more than a dozen Saxon vessels were anchored offshore, almost as many had been dragged onto land. Ships, Theil well knew, were the weakest point in Vollo's invasion plan. There were not enough of them to transport the men and supplies he needed, and some of the vessels were hardly seaworthy, which was why they were now beached and being repaired.

King Cergin had given Vollo the use of his summer castle in northwest Germania on the coast as an assembly point for the invasion force. And Vollo had more than made himself comfortable there, occupying the king's own bed chamber. Theil was sure Cergin's generosity had not extended to having the oversized Vollo sleep in his bed and wondered how the king would react to that knowledge. As for Vollo, he was apparently unconcerned about offending the absent king in this manner, but the warlord was also unaware that a spy observed him daily.

Not a day went by that Theil did not expect, to a greater or lesser extent, to be hauled before Vollo and exposed as a spy and assassin. Every time the warlord summoned him, Theil wondered if this would be the day. As Vollo demonstrated with the poor murdered cook, he did not need much provocation nor any proof to crush a man's throat.

Cergin told Theil he would serve his king by serving Vollo, and serving Vollo he did, each day taking on more responsibility as the number of warriors arriving in their camp continued to mount. He had to find appropriate locations for the new arrivals to erect their tents, if they had tents, and check if they were properly armed, and if not, he would have to supply them with what they needed from the castle armory. He also was tasked with supervising the overhaul of the ships and the construction of a storage facility for the food they would transport with them to Britain.

Theil, whose arm was still in a splint, did no labor himself but had been given so much authority over the preparations for war that he was beginning to assume some responsibility for the success of the invasion.

After he examined the progress of the work on the fleet, Theil walked around the castle's exterior, past the many tents of varying size, color and condition that housed their army. Many of the men were professional soldiers; many others had spent much more time on the farm field than the battlefield. Some were warriors of the first rank; others mere rabble. Vollo would use them appropriately with those of lesser value being first to be sacrificed.

Riders approached. Theil squinted against the bright sun to get a better look at them. They did not appear to be new recruits and indeed, were not. They were a small delegation sent by King Cergin. He heard one of the riders ask, "Which one is Theil?" And Theil hurried to meet the man, who introduced himself as Horald.

The emissary dismounted and said in a voice Theil considered far too loud, "You will accompany me to Lord Vollo."

Theil glanced about anxiously. "Given the nature of our business, shouldn't more discretion be exercised?"

Horald dismissed the comment. "I won't ask you to attend my meeting with Vollo."

Walking at a fast pace, Horald led Theil to the castle and told him to wait outside. Theil resented being ordered about a functionary rather than a man of rank, but he did as he was instructed.

Once inside, Horald's demeanor changed from that of a lord to that of a vassal. He slowly approached the intimidating Vollo, who was seated at a table looking down at a map. "King Cergin sends his greetings," said Horald with deference, as he stood before the large warlord. Vollo did not answer, did not look up. "I, too, bring well wishes." Still no response. "The king has sent me to inquire as to the status of your preparations."

Vollo finally looked up at the man and pointedly did not invite him to sit down at one of the two chairs that were opposite his own seat. "If you care to look with your own eyes, you will see the number of warriors here grows daily." Vollo gave Horald the menacing stare for which he was well known. "Unfortunately, the men do not also grow in quality. I will give you the same information I only recently sent to the king by messenger. I need enough bowmen to match the British archers so that my footmen are not cut down before they come within spear or sword point of the enemy. I need more carpenters for the fortifications and towers I need to build at Valphain Castle. And I need more and better ships. See for yourself. I will lose a good portion of my men to the sea with what I have now."

With that comment Vollo returned to his map. Horald realized that he had been dismissed and took his leave with a bow.

Outside he found Theil awaiting him. "The man is unpleasant and self-important," Horald said. "I rode three days for a conversation that lasted less time than it took me to saddle my horse."

Theil could see that being the king's emissary or not, Horald, too, feared Vollo. "Vollo's demeanor is well known, but this isn't a place to talk. He may observe us." Theil motioned toward the waterfront, where they would be out of Vollo's sight.

They had walked only a short distance from the castle, not nearly far enough to satisfy Theil's desire for privacy, when Horald stopped to look him in the eye. "Does your assessment of the situation here match Vollo's?"

"It does if he said we need more skilled men and more and better vessels to transport them."

"That will please the king. He has deliberately withheld ships and men because he is not yet certain that he wants this expedition to launch."

"Withholding men and ships may not be enough. When you sail with Vollo, his thinking and his moods become apparent. He'll launch this invasion with what he has now if forced to. He'll establish a foothold in Britain at whatever the cost to his men and send the few vessels he has back here to transport more troops."

"This isn't news I wish to bring back to the king. He won't take it well, and he may hold the two of us accountable. Has Vollo actually said that he will attack under any circumstances?"

"No, he hasn't, but the man isn't difficult to understand, and the king would be well advised to act upon my assumption."

"Theil!" Vollo was bellowing for him from the castle entrance.

Damn this Horald, thought Theil. This is what comes of carelessness.

Theil left the king's emissary and hurried to Vollo, who appeared, as he often did, on the verge of anger. "What was the nature of that conversation?"

Theil thought being as truthful as possible was the safest approach with Vollo. "He asked if this soldier's assessment of our readiness was the same as your own. He was told yes and was offered the opportunity to see the condition of some of the sailing vessels."

Vollo's expression softened, and he nodded approvingly to Theil, whom he led back into the castle.

A short time later, after he had been dismissed by Vollo, Theil sought out Horald, who was waiting for him at the waterfront, pretending to be inspecting the ships. "Was that anything I need report to the king?" Horald asked.

"Yes." Theil looked back over his shoulder at the castle. "He sends his second in command on a sea journey tomorrow morning."

"You are sailing tomorrow?" Theil nodded. "To Britain?"

"He will not say until morning, perhaps because you are here, perhaps because he knows you are carrying secret messages to the king."

"Nonsense, you are too fearful. However, your assumption that he will invade without additional troops and ships seems correct if he is sending you to Britain." Horald thought for a moment, then said with authority, "The king needs you here. Find an excuse to send someone else on this journey."

Theil's eyes opened wide in disbelief at Horald's suggestion. "Haven't you seen and heard enough of the man to know that you don't refuse him a request let alone an order and that you don't offer him excuses? Besides, Vollo only trusts his second. There is no one else he would send."

"I repeat, the king wants an agent here with Vollo."

"The king will receive precious little information from an agent who can no longer speak. Pardon the bluntness, but the threat from Vollo is far more immediate than any threat from the king."

Horald conceded that Theil was right and relented. He called over one of the two men who had accompanied him on his journey. "This man is called Willem," he told Theil, "and he will stay with you. From this day forward he will be your aide, and he will accompany you on your journey tomorrow."

Theil well understood what this meant. Willem was a spy to spy on the spy. And perhaps Willem had also been told there might come a day when he was to eliminate Theil as Theil had been told to be prepared to eliminate Vollo.

The next morning Vollo gave Theil his instructions. He was to go to an abbey farther along the coast, a day's ride from here, and there he was to wait until a trading vessel arrived. He would be taken first to Britain for a meeting with Vollo's agent there to learn the latest information about what was happening with the British, especially at Valphain Castle and environs. Next, he would be taken to Pictland to negotiate with

King Aingus to have the Pict forces attack the British from the north while Vollo pressed them from the east.

None of this was pleasing to Theil, not the sea journey, not the meeting with a British traitor, and certainly not going into the liar of the barbarous Picts.

Theil, Willem and a third man, who would return to the castle with their horses, left that morning for the abbey. They followed the coast as well as they could and wound their way inland when forced to. By late afternoon a fog moved in from the sea.

They reached the abbey before sunset and were taken in by the monks. After a sparse meal, Theil went to an abbey window, from where he kept watch on the sea. Before long, the mist turned to heavy rain, and the sea became turbulent. He wondered if the storm might prevent the vessel from making a landing. Whatever the cause, no ship came that night, and none came the next morning.

By the afternoon of the second day the weather had cleared, and just before sunset he was able to make out a sail on the horizon. The vessel sped landward and made for a mooring near the abbey, where Theil and Willem went to meet it. From outward appearances it was a trading vessel from Gaul, but trading vessels often also served as pirate ships. This ship was rough and battered; its crew rough and battered as well. They were more likely pirates than traders, and perhaps only a vessel and crew of this sort could serve Vollo's needs.

The ship commander, a craggy-faced, toothless man, called out for Theil. And Theil stepped forward with Willem following close behind. "Only one, the man Theil," said the commander. "Only one makes this voyage." Willem stepped forward and began to protest. But retreated when he found a knife poised under his throat. "Only one. Only Theil makes this voyage."

Theil climbed aboard, and the vessel put back out to sea. It was an easy voyage at first, but as the shore receded behind them, the rain returned. Eventually both the rain and the wind increased in intensity, and large waves began to threaten the ship. Theil hoped the rough nature of the voyage was not a precursor to what would happen when they reached the opposite shore — if they reached the opposite shore.

21) Pairings

While Brenna watched, Arthur loaded an arrow and shot it. He hit the center of the straw target at the far end of the stable. This was Brenna's second archery lesson, the second time they had come to the stable before dawn. It was Brenna's suggestion that they come here so she could shoot without concern for the wind and she could have her lesson before the rest of the castle was awake so she did not have to display her poor archery skills before anyone except Arthur.

But her archery skills were fair, and he thought she had more than archery in mind.

During the first lesson, although their bodies touched far more than was necessary, nothing of consequence happened. Arthur thought that was his fault. He had been waiting for her to be the aggressor.

That might change this morning.

It was her turn to shoot, and he would show her exactly how to hold the bow and draw the arrow. She stood left shoulder pointed to the target. He came up behind her and placed his left hand over her bow hand and his right over her draw hand. Together they pulled back the arrow, and she released. He enjoyed the physical contact, and she seemed to as well. On the next shot, Arthur held her arms the same way, but moved his body closer so that his chest was touching her back and shoulders.

As she drew the bow, the top of her tunic pulled tight, outlining the shape of her breasts in manner he could not resist. Without a thought to the consequences, he moved his hands to her waist and slid them up to cup her breasts.

Brenna let the bow and arrow fall to the ground, turned her face toward him, first kissing and then gently biting his neck. He pulled up the front of her tunic, ran his hands under it and caressed her bare breasts. Never had he felt anything so soft and warm. He had no intention of releasing them.

But Brenna said, "Wait." And she drew away from him.

"Sorry." Arthur thought she had changed her mind.

"No, we cannot be seen." She hurried to the stable door, leaving him standing alone and fully erect. She opened the door a crack. "We may have started too late. The sun is rising, but there's time." She closed the door and latched it, went back to him, wrapped her arms around his neck and kissed him.

Arthur enjoyed the kissing but wanted to feel her soft, warm flesh again. He lifted the back of her tunic and took hold of her buttocks, pulling her closer to him. Brenna lifted up on her toes, trying to climb atop him, attempting to align herself with him as though he could penetrate her through their clothes.

He ran his right hand around her hip to her lower belly, then down through her pubic hair to her genitalia. He gently explored her. Her legs buckled, and she might have fallen to the ground had he not been holding her. "It's very sensitive there," she whispered. "My legs gave out."

He tightened his grip on her with his left hard and touched her sensitive area again. Again her legs failed, and again he had to hold her up. He reached his right arm under her knees, lifted her off the ground and carried her to the pile of hay at the rear of the barn.

Arthur had not planned or anticipated things going this far, but there was no turning back now.

———

Kaye found Maeve in the castle kitchen giving instructions to the cook about what to prepare for the evening meal. He looked anxious as he waited until Maeve was finished with the cook before approaching her. "May I speak to you?" She smiled and gave a playful curtsy. "In private?"

"Follow me." She led him out of the kitchen, across the great hall, and lifting the hem of her dress, up the tower stairs. "Your room is private. You're not afraid to have me in your room are you?"

"No. But what if Uriens saw us? He might not understand."

She dismissed his concern with a wave of her hand. "He's hunting, and besides, Uriens has to worry about what I think not the other way around."

Several chairs in Kaye's bedroom had been arranged as an area where the king-elect could meet with advisors and visitors. Maeve pushed open the door, took a seat and motioned for Kaye to sit next to her, which he did. "You have more courage than your brother."

Kaye appeared puzzled by the comment but let it pass. "How shall I begin?"

She reached across and rested a hand on his thigh. "Speak freely. You will find I am easy to speak with."

He looked at her and forced a smile. "This was Merlin's suggestion, please understand."

She frowned. "Merlin!"

"He believes that you and not Brenna are the reason, well... that the arrangement that he and Uriens discussed has not taken place."

"Between you and Brenna?" Maeve removed her hand from his leg and leaned back in her chair. "Merlin is correct." Kaye raised his eyebrows at her response. "I'm the power behind Uriens and have been for years." She reached out and squeezed his thigh. "I'm the ally you need, not Uriens, and I may relent on Brenna — if you really want her."

"If! Why not? I mean, why wouldn't I want her?"

"Spoiled." Maeve shook her head. "Terribly spoiled. Arrogant. Must always have her own way. She delights in trying to assert that she is better than me. Haven't you observed the attention she pays to Arthur?"

Kaye appeared anxious again. "I have. And you might have noticed that Arthur is very much like Brenna. Arrogant, I mean. I've been in his shadow my entire life until now."

Maeve leaned closer and whispered. "Even now Arthur attempts to cast his shadow over you, at least with Brenna. Move closer." Kaye slid his chair so that his knees were almost touching Maeve's. "You have issues beyond Brenna and Arthur. Some important knights do not support you."

His expression became even more pained. "Merlin assumed as much."

"Be less concerned with Merlin and what he thinks and says. I heard this from Bryso, who told me so the very day we rode back from Londinium. You must plan carefully and everything will be fine. And you will have me to help you." She took his hand and placed it on her knee. He squeezed her leg. "We can be great allies."

⁓

The stable door opened.

Arthur and Brenna were naked hiding behind bales of hay beyond the archery target. They immediately became still, not daring even to breathe. The door closed again, and Arthur hoped that someone had simply taken a peek into the stable. But he heard footsteps moving across the stable, then the braying of one of the horses.

They were caught with no escape until whoever it was left. Brenna pulled her dress across her body, but the movement of the cloth over the hay caused a sound.

Arthur heard a dull thump, a saddle being placed on the back of a horse perhaps, followed by a crash to floor. A voice Arthur recognized shouted a curse. It was Prywycke. Arthur felt greatly relieved knowing that the intruder was his long-time companion, but he was uncertain of what to do because even Prywycke could not be trusted to know this secret. Prywycke might finish saddling the horse and soon be gone. That was the best of all outcomes. But Arthur could not be certain Prywycke would not have some reason to walk behind these bales of hay and find them.

"It's only Prywycke," he whispered, and Brenna held up a finger to silence him. "It's better that I confront him." Prywycke was mumbling to himself, making enough noise that Arthur could risk pulling on his leggings and tunic, and slipping on his boots.

"Straighten your clothes," she said.

"Better not to." Now she understood his plan, and she mussed his hair.

"Is someone back there?"

"Only me." Arthur stood and presented himself to Prywycke.

"You gave me a start. What are you doing back there?"

"Looking for a lost arrow." Arthur held a finger to his lips to quiet Prywycke. He walked over to him and whispered as he pointed back to the bales of hay. "You understand, one of the household maids."

"Oh!" Prywycke both smiled and blushed. "I well understand." He gave Arthur a wink.

"We should give the lady some privacy."

"Of course; yes, of course. I can come back later."

With that, the two men left the barn.

Arthur was suddenly troubled by a deep sense of concern and regret. Despite his vivid dreams, despite their touching during their prior lesson, Arthur never really thought things would go this far. She had given him her virginity, and he felt guilty although not toward her. She was more than willing, in fact, eager. It was Kaye and Ector and most especially Merlin he would have difficulty facing.

Arthur led Prywycke to the tower kitchen, where they took a jug of mead and two goblets, and went to the great hall to sit by the fire.

"Prywycke, I want to ask you a question." Prywycke took a sip of mead and looked expectantly at Arthur. "Suppose something was meant to be yours but didn't come to you. Would you still be entitled to take it?" Prywycke frowned. He opened his mouth to speak but instead frowned again. "Suppose it was a goblet of mead."

"Mead?"

"Yes."

"Suppose a goblet of mead was intended for you but you didn't get it."

"But you don't really mean mead?"

"No, it's just an example of a more general issue. But say it was mead, say the goblet before you was intended for me. Would I be entitled to drink from it?"

"If it was mead, I'd say 'take it'."

"But what if it were not mead but something more important?" He could see from Prywycke's confused expression that he was unlikely to get any useful answer from him unless he specifically mentioned Brenna. Fortunately, Arthur was spared from continuing this ill-advised conversation by the sound of footsteps rushing down the stairs.

It was Kaye followed by Maeve, both looking somewhat disheveled. "Arthur, Prywycke," Kaye shouted. "Come. There is some disturbance in the courtyard."

Arthur and Prywycke hurried after Kaye. On their way out of the tower Arthur passed Brenna, who was entering. They avoided looking at each other.

There were two riders in the courtyard, and they were surrounded by residents of the castle. Merlin was among them.

"What's happening?" asked Kaye, straightening his tunic and running his hand through his hair.

Merlin took him by the arm and motioned Arthur to follow. Prywycke joined them. When they were a far enough distance from the crowd to speak without being overheard, Merlin explained. "Those riders are from a village farther north on the coast. A village near theirs has been raided by Norsemen. They fear an attack on their own village." Merlin looked from Arthur to Kaye. "Our grand plan is like a ship in the calm without wind to move it since Londinium. Uriens hesitates making a final decision. Bryso expresses concern. And nothing moves forward." He poked Kaye in the chest. "These Norse raiders provide an opportunity for you." He poked Arthur. "And for you. Arthur, under the direction of the king-elect will lead a force to defeat these Norsemen."

"We'll need Uriens approval, won't we?" asked Kaye.

Merlin smirked at Kaye. "It *is* usual practice to ask a lord's permission before borrowing his army, yes."

22) The Norsemen

Arthur had put on his chainmail armor and was about to strap on his bracers and greaves when there was a light tap on his bedroom door. It was Brenna. As soon as she stepped into the room and into the light, he could see that she was upset, on the verge of tears.

"Weren't you going to say goodbye to me?"

"Of course, I was." He closed the door and took her into his arms. She rested her head against his chest. "I'm sorry the chainmail is hard and cold." He kissed her forehead, put his hand under her chin and raised her face toward his. "You are not upset because you thought I wasn't going to say goodbye?"

"No." A tear roll down each cheek. "I'm worried that when you face the Norsemen, you will be injured or worse."

Arthur forced a smile. "This is what I was born for and what I've been trained for." He kissed her lips. "I'll be back unharmed. I have a good reason to come back whole."

Brenna opened her mouth to say something but was interrupted by the sound of horns in the courtyard. Arthur turned toward the window. "We are ready to leave so soon!"

"I'll help you finished getting ready."

Brenna assisted him in strapping on his bracers and greaves. Arthur picked up his helmet from his bed, kissed her, and pulled the helmet over his head. He opened the door just enough to see that the hall was empty, looked back at her a last time, and left.

The army was assembled in the courtyard. Every warrior with a horse, some forty of them, mounted up and rode out of Valphain Castle under the leadership of Arthur and Bryso. Everyone else in the castle crowded into the courtyard to wish the riders well, except for two figures who watched from different windows in the castle tower.

One was Brenna. The other was Merlin. He, too, had warned Arthur about the upcoming battle, telling him that he could have no lack of confidence, no indecisiveness, no avoidance of duty. With a victory against the Norsemen, Arthur could begin to redeem himself for failing to keep possession of Caliburn. Merlin did not say so, but his words could have caused Arthur to believe the wizard questioned Arthur's worthiness and would use this excursion as a test.

Before it was decided to send these forty horsemen to meet the invaders, some had argued that foot soldiers should be brought along as well. The ferocity of the Norsemen made them almost mythic creatures, and whenever one of their ships was sighted at sea, those by the shoreline retreated as far inland as they could, leaving behind villages, manor houses and abbeys to be looted. If there was a battle, Norse savagery prevailed, and the British had not delivered a major defeat to these raiders in recent memory, although it was true that the Norsemen attacked mostly villages and villagers, not castles and knights. Adding upwards of a hundred spearmen to their ranks would increase their chances of success, but Merlin convinced them that the Norse raiders would be well gone before anyone on foot could reach them.

The usual Norse vessel carried about two dozen men, a good estimate of the size of the force the British would be facing and giving them a two-to-one advantage over their enemy. Those who thought this was insufficient were the ones who claimed that foot soldiers were needed, and it was Merlin, making his case through Kaye and Arthur, who argued that the time had come to break the grip of fear the Norsemen held on British imagination. The Norse were men and would die on the point of a sword, spear, or arrow as well as any British warrior.

The British force traveled northeast and in late afternoon reached the coast where the Norse raiding party had been sighted. They rode, eyes fixed on the shoreline, searching for a vessel in the water or on the beach, until the sun began to set. The riders paused just inland of a sandy cove; a handful of them dismounted. There was no longer enough light to see a vessel any distance from shore. Several of their company suggested they make camp here and resume their quest in the morning light.

Arthur, sitting astride Snow Storm, did not agree. He was on his own now and had to make decisions without the wizard's help. Arthur shouted to get everyone's attention. "Are the Norsemen resting now? If they aren't, we cannot rest. If they are resting, we can take advantage of the extra time to gain ground on them."

Bryso smiled at Arthur and nodded his approval of his reasoning. "Enough talk. Let's ride on and teach these Norsemen a lesson," shouted Bryso. And they continued their journey in the fading light.

Not long after sunset, Bryso caught a brief glimmer of light in the distance, and their troop came to a halt. While the others remained where they were, Bryso rode ahead to examine the source of the light, and when it appeared as if it might be coming from a campfire, he dismounted, tethered his horse and proceeded on foot. The moon had not yet risen, and the surf beat loudly against the shore, making it unlikely that Bryso would either be seen or heard by the men near the fire. When he got as close as he dared, he knelt on one knee and focused on the campfire. There were four men sitting by its light, possibly Norsemen, possibly not. His eyes searched the water behind them. There it was, a Norse ship. No, there were two of them, two vessels.

Bryso returned to the other riders, who were assembled in a semicircle facing Arthur, and gave his report. "I saw two Norse vessels, not one. Four men are at a campfire guarding their ships. Two ships means there are forty or fifty Norsemen rampaging somewhere through the countryside."

Someone at the rear of the mounted warriors shouted, "They have us outnumbered."

"Outnumber by a mere handful," Arthur said. "We are mounted; they are not. We are better armed. And they don't expect an attack."

Arthur sensed uneasiness in their ranks. Most, it seemed, were not eager to fight the enemy without a large superiority in numbers.

Prywycke suggested they need only attack the four guards left behind and burn the Norse vessels.

"That must be accomplished by stealth," Bryso said. "If we simply ride at them, they will be to their vessels and a distance at sea before we reach them."

"Fine, chase 'em off. Then, we'll be rid of 'em," someone suggested.

A wind began to blow in from the sea. Arthur leaned forward in his saddle and looked from one end of the assembled riders to the other before speaking. "We can chase them off or burn their ships, either way the Norse force would remain essentially complete and would continue to raid elsewhere along the coast. And think of the consequences of burning their ships. A fierce band of Norsemen would be cut off from escape, making them desperate as well as ruthless. How many villages would be pillaged then? And how long before we would have to reassemble to hunt them down?"

The group was silent. Arthur again looked at as many faces as he could. "These suggestions are only slightly better than just riding away."

"Riding away would be cowardly," shouted one man.

Prywycke spoke up. "All my years to finally have a chance to defeat the Norsemen and to not even try. . .I cannot bring myself to do it."

"If we attack, the outcome may be uncertain," said Bryso. "If we ride away, the outcome will be shame and regret, and that is a certainty."

Arthur looked over the group. "Is there any who wants to simply ride away?" No one spoke. "Good. We are all in agreement. Let's use surprise and strategy to defeat the entire Norse raiding party."

Arthur decided to lead the first attack group and took eleven men with him. They rode to where Bryso had earlier tethered his horse, and the group dismounted. Here two of their number remained behind with the horses. Eight other men then removed their chainmail armor and anything else that might make enough noise to alert the Norse guards. They would proceed with only swords, shields and helmets. Arthur and a second man, Drustan, who was a highly skilled archer, would advance with only bow and arrow.

They walked cautiously and quietly along the beach until they were a distance of about five hundred feet from the enemy campfire. There the eight British warriors with swords remained while Arthur and the second archer crawled forward on their bellies until they were approximately one hundred and fifty feet from their targets, as close as they dared come.

Arthur and Drustan stood up, loaded their bows and let fly. Arthur hit his first target. The man fell over and writhed in pain. Drustan hit his first target as well, but the man did not fall. Arthur hit his second target as the man was rising to his feet. The Norseman grabbed his shoulder but continued to move, forcing Arthur to shoot him a second time, dropping him to his knees. Drustan missed his second target not once but twice. The man was only a few feet from one of the vessels when Arthur shot and also missed. The escaping Norsemen managed to climb half way into a boat when he was hit almost simultaneously with arrows shot by Arthur and Drustan, and he fell into the shallow sea.

Two of the Norsemen were still moving on the ground, and the third, only slightly wounded by Drustan's first arrow, withdrew his sword and charged them. But now the other eight British warriors had arrived. They surrounded the one Norseman still able to fight and took him down with their swords, then quickly finished off the remaining three injured Norsemen.

A half-moon had risen when the Norse raiding party, some three dozen strong, arrived on the beach. Each man was loaded with loot as well a sword or battle ax and shield, and one dragged behind him two women by a rope tied to their hands. The Norsemen saw what they might expect to see: four men seated by a fire, their two vessels beached behind them.

The air was filled with whip-like sounds followed by shouts of pain. Several Norsemen dropped to the ground with arrows in their chests and necks; one with an arrow in his belly staggered forward. Another volley of arrows struck them, some deflected off helmets and armor; others did minimal damage, but a few caused fatal wounds. Before the Norsemen could determine the location of the bowmen, another round of arrows flew, felling several more of them.

One of the Norseman shouted and pointed to their own beached vessels, where bowmen stood firing at them. The Norsemen dropped the loot that was weighing them down, raised their weapons and charged the boats. The contingent of British in the vessels, abandoned their bows, took their swords and shields, and leapt onto the beach to meet the advancing Norsemen, but not before they set fire to the Norse vessels.

More Norsemen had survived the onslaught of arrows than Arthur expected, and when the two forces came shield-to-shield and face-to-face, the British were outnumbered. Prywycke and the other half of their force should at any moment coming charging in on horseback to attack the Norsemen from the rear. But the horsemen did not arrive.

The Norsemen were formidable, like battling an army of Brysos, thought Arthur. He pounded and pounded at them with his sword but without much effect, and they gave at least as hard as they got. There would be no quick kills. Arthur did not believe many of the British would outlast their opponents if this fight became a battle of attrition.

The British were being driven back toward the sea. They tightened their ranks to form a defensive line, and Arthur found himself trading sword blows with not one but two Norsemen. Where were the horsemen? The man next to Arthur fell. Before Arthur could assist him, he was finished off by Norse sword.

Bryso and several others charged into Norse ranks, attempting to drive them back. The Norsemen repositioned themselves, and Arthur now faced a giant of a man who was swinging a double-headed ax at him. He caught the first blow with his shield. The force almost cracked his shield in two. The Norseman wound up for a backhanded swing, and Arthur retreated just out of its range. The man swung his ax around and up for an overhead strike. Arthur lunged forward and caught him in the midsection with a sword thrust. The Norseman dropped his ax and grabbed his belly, which ran with blood, but he did not go down. Arthur struck him an overhand blow between his neck and shoulder, and that only brought him down to his knees. It took a third blow to finish him.

The British horsemen finally arrived and attacked from the rear, completely changing the nature of the battle. The British felled a half dozen Norsemen before the enemy realized they were being struck from behind. When some of the Norsemen turned to face the horsemen, Arthur and the others near the shoreline could now take the offensive.

As they pushed forward, Bryso, who was next to Arthur, fell over a body on the ground and landed on his back, his sword arm to one side, his shield arm to the other, leaving him completely vulnerable. Bryso's opponent lifted his sword to strike him. Arthur blocked the blow with his sword, while continuing to use his shield to fend off the attacks of an ax-wielding Norseman he was engaged with. Bryso regained his feet and re-engaged his attacker.

Arthur could now concentrate on the Norseman with the ax and forced him to retreat a few steps. Prywycke appeared behind the man and thrust his sword into the Norseman's back. The man dropped his ax and teetered backwards. Arthur drove his sword into the man's belly. The Norseman fell to the ground.

The British had the enemy surrounded and gradually, over what seemed like a long period of time, whittled their number down to a handful. But still the battle continued. Finally, when not one Norseman remained in fighting condition, the British finished off those who could not survive their wounds, took the others prisoner, and looked after their own wounded. Nine of the British had died; several more would likely not survive their injuries, and everyone else had at least several wounds that required attention.

Nonetheless, it was a major victory. No one could even say when the last time a British force had overwhelmed a Norse raiding party as they had this night.

The British would spend the night here and built campfires on the beach. Tired, battered and hungry, they sat around the fires, nursing their wounds and gobbling down food. The two female hostages had been freed, and the stolen goods arranged in a pile. The five Norsemen prisoners were bound and under guard, and the nine dead British were laid side by side. Prywycke and a handful of men would return the women and loot to their villages, while Arthur and Bryso the next day would lead a triumphant march to Valphain Castle with the prisoners in tow.

Arthur was not with the others by the fires. Instead he had walked down the beach and stood looking blankly out to sea. This victory did not feel as he imagined it would. His brilliant plan almost failed because the barrage of arrows had not done as much damage as he expected and the horsemen were far too slow in joining the battle.

"Arthur." Bryso joined him. Arthur glanced at him from the corner of his eye and looked back out to sea. "The first kill is always difficult," said Bryso barely above a whisper.

Arthur thought about the huge Norsemen who could have easily killed him with a swing of his double-headed ax, the man it took three sword strikes to kill. "The first kill I had no choice. But I was face-to-face with another Norseman when Prywycke stabbed him in the back. He was weaponless and completely defenseless when I finished him with a sword to the belly."

Bryso put a hand on Arthur's shoulder. "That day at the Londinium Tournament, I watched your first match. You unhorsed your opponent and dismounted to help him to his feet. That was exceptional behavior even for a tournament. This was war, and battles are usually won by having two or three of your own warriors surrounding a single enemy. In war there is no fairness in numbers, nor do you ever give an opponent the chance to retrieve a weapon or to get a shield into place or sometimes even allow an enemy to escape."

"I'm also concerned about our own dead."

"Such is the nature of war and being a warrior," said Bryso emphatically. "It always involves the death of some of your own. You must remember instead how many villagers that party of Norsemen killed and how many more they would have killed had they not been stopped. And what would have happened to the two women that you rescued?"

Arthur tilted his head to one side and nodded. "You make valid points. Logically, I understand them, but I still don't feel much better about the killing."

"And think of this. You rescued me. I would not be here now except for you, and for that I will be always in your debt." Arthur had forgotten how he saved Bryso from a fatal blow. "And think of your own words to the men when they wanted to avoid facing the Norsemen. There were alternatives, and you picked the correct one, the only correct one." Bryso's tone softened. "These are always difficult choices to make. Had you not made the decision, someone else would have." Bryso looked back to the campfires. "What if Prywycke or one of the others had made the decision? What if we had burned the Norse vessels and let dozens of them loose to terrorize man, woman and child? Your feelings now are the same that all men experience after their first battle, and the bad feelings will fade for you as they do for everyone else."

Arthur turned toward Bryso and forced a smile. "I know you are correct, but it will take some time for my emotions to accept what my logic understands."

23) Victory's Aftermath

The morning after their victory over the Norsemen, the British troops left the beach where the battle had taken place and headed back to Valphain Castle. Arthur hoped to divert his thoughts with conversation, wanting to talk about anything but the battle. Arthur rode at the head of their column, Bryso next to him. "Much has happened to me in recent days," said Arthur. Bryso nodded his understanding. "And I think I've accommodated well to most of it, but not to the women at the castle and how they behave. I wish I understood them better."

Bryso laughed. "That's the most common complaint of the men who live with them."

His eyes remaining on the road before them, Arthur did not laugh or smile at Bryso's comment. "I would think that with all the training we men go through, we could be taught something about women, how to approach them, why they do what they do."

Bryso appeared skeptical. "Learn about women like learning to spar?"

"In a general sense, yes."

"I would imagine that if you learned to successfully spar with one woman, nothing you learned from that one would be applicable to any other."

"I suppose that's true."

"It is often difficult if to know if there is real intention behind their flirtations and indeed, what is a flirtation and what is not." Bryso studied Arthur's expression. "Are you having a challenge with a woman? Is one acting in seductive manner? Perhaps, more than one?"

Arthur's eyes opened wide at that remark, and he worried that he had said too much. But Bryso could not possibly know that he had been thinking about two women, his secret encounters with Brenna and Maeve's odd behavior the night she came to his room. "In general, I find the women here. . ." He searched for the proper word. "Aggressive."

"Aggressive! Did one crawl under your blanket?" Bryso laughed. "Yes, some women can be, as you say, aggressive, but in all my years, I've never had one crawl into bed with me uninvited."

Arthur held a hand up toward Bryso. "That's not what happened. Please don't say that to anyone."

"Your secrets are safe with me. I may not understand women, Arthur, but I can tell you about life at the castles in this kingdom." He began to whisper although no one was within earshot. "When it comes to sex, people say one thing but do another. They expect perfect behavior, but kings bed servant girls; queens bed the king's advisors; advisors bed the same servant girls as the kings. I've even heard tell of a nobleman who contrived an excuse to leave his wife's bed to be with another woman, and his place in his own bed was taken by the husband of the very woman he was with."

"And that's not an overstatement?"

"A little, perhaps. But the flesh is what it is, and the world is very old. I cannot imagine that anything that has happened to you or might happen to you has not already happened many, many times before."

"You sound as philosophical as Merlin."

"And does he advise you on women?"

Arthur shook his head. "I've always assumed he knows even less about them than I do."

24) A New Concern

News of the war party's approach spread throughout Valphain Castle, and the courtyard filled with people wanting to acknowledge their successful return. Brenna stood on the steps outside the great hall, straining to see over the heads of the crowd, watching as the troop of riders began to pass through the castle gates. Arthur's horse, Snow Storm, stood out even though her view was mostly blocked, and when she saw the animal, rather than smile, she began breathing in labored fashion and tears welled in her eyes.

Close by, also watching the approaching riders as well as observing Brenna, was Merlin. Maeve mentioned to Merlin that he should observe how Brenna and Arthur sit side by side at the banquet table and how they look at each other. Merlin knew that Maeve was jealous of Brenna and discounted the things she said. But now seeing the girl's reaction to Arthur's return caused him to wonder if something more than innocent conversation might be taking place between the two of them.

It was one more concern for the wizard, one more situation to monitor.

Merlin looked again at the returning warriors, and his eyes followed them as Arthur and the other riders filed in. Behind them came a number of dead British soldiers strapped over horses and a handful of bound Norsemen on foot. The sight of Norse prisoners told Merlin they had won an important victory. Arthur had done better than expected.

As the riders continued to pass through the castle gates, the courtyard became nearly as chaotic as a battlefield. Women and children rushed to greet the returning warriors who lived at Valphain or in proximity to the castle. Husbands and fathers dismounted to hug their wives and children. One of the riders who guarded the Norse prisoners hoisted his young son up onto his horse and continued to ride with the boy in the saddle.

Everyone in the castle knew the price of battle, even a victorious one, and servants rushed to tend to the bodies strapped over their horses and to assist the women who were about to learn they were widows.

Merlin watched as a smiling Kaye spoke excitedly to Arthur and Bryso, and soon Kaye sought out the wizard to report on what he had learned. "Merlin, we've had a greater victory than you imagine." Merlin was struck by his use of the word *we*, but then perhaps, as was often true,

Merlin was being too hard on Kaye. "We defeated not a single vessel of Norsemen but rather two."

"And have you noticed that they have Norse prisoners? That is equally important. Gather up Ector and Uriens," said Merlin. "We need to discuss how to exploit this situation." Kaye frowned. Merlin bowed to him. "That is, if it pleases Your Majesty."

Kaye stepped closer to Merlin and whispered. "How do you expect others to treat me as king if you do not?"

"You are not yet king, and if you do not fetch Ector and Uriens, you may not be."

"But not Arthur? You did not say to fetch Arthur as well."

"No, not for this meeting." Kaye smiled.

The four soon gather in Kaye's room. As Kaye, Ector and Uriens sat, Merlin, pacing before them, assessed the aftermath of the victory over the Norsemen. "This situation presents us with an opportunity we must seize now."

"Word of our victory will surely spread throughout Britain," Kaye said.

Merlin leaned toward him and frowned, causing Kaye to draw his head back. "I am not content to simply wait for word to spread. We will spread it. By tomorrow we will dispatch riders to every important lord and knight to tell them how the Norsemen have been defeated. Do you agree, Uriens?"

"Yes, of course." He agreed but did not seem to have been following the conversation.

"And invite them here to see the prisoners," said Ector.

"Yes, yes." Merlin pointed a finger at Ector. "Invite them here. Finally a good idea from you." The remark stung Ector. "It would be good to have them here, if they will come. Let them become accustomed to this being the center of the kingdom. Uriens." Merlin calling his name startled the old knight. "Where do things stand with Brenna? This marriage must come soon to be of much use."

Kaye spoke before Uriens could. "I have news." He leaned forward in his chair and spoke excitedly. "It escaped my mind in the excitement of the return of our warriors. Maeve no longer objects to the marriage."

Uriens appeared surprised by this information.

"You did not know?" asked Merlin. Uriens shook his head. "But it was, as I suspected, Maeve and not Brenna who objected?"

"Yes, but. . ." Uriens spread out his arms. "Be that as it may, Brenna remains an issue. She has not been spoken to, at least not by me." He glanced at Kaye. "My original statement stands as true. The girl is a little head strong — and I suppose I must admit some blame for that. She must be approached a delicate way or she will, indeed, refuse, and I am too tired to fight that battle."

"But you have not yet approached her?" asked Merlin. Uriens nodded. "Because until now you did not have Maeve's approval?" He nodded again. "But you will approach Brenna — when the moment is right? And you will remember all this as well as your tendency to forget things?"

Uriens mumbled. "Remember that I forget. Is that even possible?"

"I hope so. Much depends upon it. Much."

That evening a victory banquet was held in the great hall. Arthur, who had bruises on his ribs and right foreman, and a dull ache in his right shoulder, found himself more resentful of Kaye than he had been before. Kaye happily shared the glory of the victory, speaking about the battle as though he had been there. But he had not lifted a sword or drawn a bow. He had not suffered a single blow nor felt his sword plunge into another men's belly. Arthur also felt a sense of entitlement, a word Merlin had taught him but he had never before understood until now. There must be benefits he should have earned from winning such an important victory, and being able to pursue the woman of his choice was paramount among them, if not to pursue her openly, then in secret, as Bryso explained was common practice.

Brenna and Arthur found each other in the great hall and took seats at the banquet table together. He once might have worried about their proximity being an indiscretion, but he now felt entitled to sit next to whomever he wanted. As the meal began and plates of food were passed around the table and servants filled goblets with mead, Brenna asked him about the battle. Arthur did not want to be overheard, and everything he said he whispered into her ear, and when she spoke, she did likewise with him.

"This victory doesn't feel as I thought it would. I take pride in it but not joy." She leaned back to study his face. "Ten men are dead. One or two more are badly injured and may soon die. I was the leader. It was my battle plan."

"And you won a great victory. Many more might have died without you."

"That's what Bryso said."

"Bryso!" He thought he detected disapproval in her tone.

"I killed three men, perhaps more. I can't be certain because I now understand that in battle it can be difficult to know which blow was the fatal one."

"Arthur, this is just a normal reaction to your first battle."

"Bryso said that as well." She frowned at the name. "Do you hold something against Bryso?"

"He has been like an uncle to me, and I most often treat him as such. But there are times Uriens requires that something particularly distasteful be done. He always turns to Bryso, which I don't hold against him. But he strikes me as being too eager to perform these tasks, and it's this eagerness that disturbs me."

As bold as Brenna was, as much as she wanted to be able to hunt like a man and to learn how to use a sword and mace, Arthur thought she did not fully appreciate the responsibilities of being a warrior and battle lord. "And what about me? I eagerly accepted command of the troop that was dispatched to find the Norsemen. I've been a tool of Merlin's since childhood. Now, I'm a weapon of Kaye's and Uriens's as well."

She shook her head. "No, not just a weapon. You have a heart and a mind unlike the others."

Arthur did not respond to Brenna's comment. Maeve was observing them with interest. "We best end this conversation. We're being watched. The usual place?"

She nodded yes, waited a time, then stood up and left the great hall. After delaying to consume most of his meal, Arthur took his leave of his dinner companions and began to exit the great hall.

Merlin, who had been standing in a corner of the hall observing the scene, approached Arthur as he was about to leave. "A great victory, Arthur. I regret I did not have an opportunity to congratulate you earlier."

For the first time in his life, Arthur, standing toe to toe with the wizard, felt his equal. "You'll be happy to know, Merlin, that my battle experience has matured me." Arthur could not tell if his mentor's expression was one of satisfaction or mock satisfaction. "But the battle was not as I expected; to kill men and have men die under your leadership is the worse feeling I've ever experienced."

"Have I ever said it would be otherwise? But realize that this is only your first battle, and your reaction is to be expected. The maturation process is not complete."

Not complete, thought Arthur. The wizard would never be satisfied with any of his accomplishments. He ignored the comment and left for his rendezvous with Brenna.

Maeve also left the great hall soon after Arthur. She crept up the tower stairs, and as she approached Arthur's room, she removed her shoes and walked barefoot. She crept to his door, carefully laid her hand on the doorknob, and found it loose. In a rapid sequence of movements, she threw open the door, rushed inside and approached the bed. But the bed was empty, and the bed covers undisturbed. Maeve looked on the opposite side of the bed and under it, and finally walked about the entire room.

She hurried to Brenna's bed chamber. Maeve crept to her stepdaughter's door and paused there listening for sounds. She heard none. Once again she found the door unlocked. Once again she threw open the door and burst in. And once again she found an empty bed. She searched the room, her movements more frantic than they had been in Arthur's bed chamber.

Standing in the empty room, she began to think aloud. "Could I be wrong? No. They're not here and not in the great hall. But they're together somewhere else."

In the stable, Arthur and Brenna sat arm in arm on a bale of hay. After the experience with Prywycke almost catching them, they always got dressed immediately after their love making. This behavior, being alone in the stable, would look suspicious to anyone who found them here, but unlike being caught in the act, they could at least attempt to explain it. Brenna had even practiced some of her explanations on him.

They sounded more convincing to her than to him.

Arthur looked down at Brenna, whose head rested on his shoulder, knowing that what he was about to say would disturb the tranquil expression on her face. "There's something bothering me." He hesitated before continuing. "I don't believe that what we are doing is wrong." Now that he had voiced these words, they did not sound as good as when he practiced them earlier.

She lifted her head and frowned at him. "I certainly hope not."

"No, I don't. You know that. Yet, we have to sneak here, and I worry about being caught."

Anger showed in Brenna's face. "Because of Maeve. She would turn it into something evil. And she's the last one to speak." Brenna looked Arthur in the eye. "I believe she is bedding your brother."

"Kaye! That seems impossible. How do you know this?"

"I can sense it. And once I saw them leaving his room. His hair was disheveled, and she was adjusting her dress. She's married to someone else. We are both free. But I'm sure she considers herself justified in whatever she's doing while she condemns us."

There was another issue, as Arthur well knew — Merlin's plan to wed Brenna to Kaye. Brenna did not know of the plan, and he would not be the one to tell her because she would certainly confront Uriens and Maeve and even Merlin. If that happened, it would at least hint at their intimacy if not prove it to the satisfaction of Merlin and Maeve.

Arthur was silent for a few moments, then spoke with some hesitation. "There's something else, but you must promise me never to tell this to anyone, not anyone."

Brenna was puzzled by this remark. "I promise."

"Your solemn promise?"

"Yes, of course."

"I freed Caliburn from the stone, not Kaye." He saw little if any surprise in her face. "I'm surprised that you aren't."

"I know you and I know Kaye, though not nearly so well. I can see which brother would make a king and which would not. I suspected as much when you told me that night at the banquet that you had held Caliburn. Why did you relinquish the sword? Didn't you want to be king? Do you feel the same way now?"

These questions caused Arthur to face his contradictory feelings. "It's too late. I can't undo what has been done. And truthfully I never had any ambition to be a king, never even had such a thought, and even now the only reason I would consider it is that I know I'd make a better king than Kaye. I believe Kaye has managed to deceive himself into thinking that he is not only rightfully king but that he actually pulled the sword from the stone, and that bothers me. But I need to put some of these thoughts out of my mind, at least for a few days." Arthur put his arm around her and pulled her closer. "I just wanted you to know about the Sword in the Stone against the time when that knowledge might be useful."

She pulled back again to look at his face. "And when might that be?"

"I don't know, but you will if the time ever comes."

25) The Abbot

They encountered a series of rolling waves, three and four feet high, causing the ship to dip sharply forward and rise up again. The Gallic sailor Theil trusted least and feared most, Loeiz, a man with a thick scar that ran from the left front side of his throat to the back of his neck, glanced over at him. The voyage from Germania had been more than just unpleasant. Twice they encountered storms, one forceful enough to make Theil ill, providing the sailors on this worn and rotting vessel some amusement at his expense. Loeiz was looking to see if this current turbulence was enough to sicken him. Theil thought the entire crew a thieving and untrustworthy lot and was relieved when Loeiz, seeing that he was undisturbed by the rough sea, looked away.

Theil discretely felt along the side of his tunic to be certain the bag of silver he carried was secure and well concealed. He felt vulnerable because he was not a member of this crew. Even worse, he was a Saxon while they were Celts, even if they were from Gaul and spoke a language different from that of the Celts in Britain. Had the captain and crew not feared Vollo and had they not been well compensated by him, they might have stabbed Theil in his sleep for what little of value he appeared to have on his person. However, if they ever learned about the sack of silver he had just checked, he doubted that fear of retribution from Vollo would prevent them from taking the silver and dropping him to the bottom of the sea.

They were sailing south along the coast of Britain, closely skirting the shoreline. They began to lose the sun at twilight and lit a torch at the bow of the ship so that Vollo's agent, an abbot, Theil was told, could find them in the darkness. They continued down the coast and were not a great distance from Londinium when they saw the torchlight signaling from the shore. The vessel turned and approached the beach. The boat stopped in shallow water near the shore. Theil jumped over the side into two feet of water and walked the remaining distance onto dry land. Taking a few moments to shake what water he could from his boots and leggings, he cautiously proceeded toward the light. He moved close enough to make out the dark figure of a monk, and as he did so, the abbot extinguished his torch and said, "Come no closer."

Theil halted his advance and tried to see the details of the man who stood before him, but all he could make out was the figure of man in a hooded cloak. "You are an abbot?"

"I am *the* abbot. Who is it that asks?"

"Lord Vollo's emissary, Theil."

"Tell Vollo I don't wish to have a different emissary sent each time."

"Voice your complaint to Vollo, himself, when next you see him. You would find his response more than a little interesting."

The abbot laughed. "You know Vollo well enough. You have something for me?" Theil reached into his tunic and withdrew the sack of silver. "Throw it this way." Theil did as he was told, heard the silver pieces tinkle as they hit the ground and in the darkness could make out the figure of the monk bending down to retrieve the sack.

"What news have you?"

The abbot examined inside the sack of silver with his hands, counting the pieces, before answering. "Much has changed. Make certain that Vollo understands this. The British have a king finally. His name is Kaye, and he may not be a king to cause us much worry. That remains to be determined. But he is being advised by the Wizard Merlin, and that's always a concern. And he has a young warlord named Arthur, who may well become a warlord of some consequence. Already, it's said, he slaughtered a party of Norse raiders."

"Is it your belief that the British will unify under this king?" Theil tried but failed to get a better look at the abbot.

"That's a possibility to be considered, and Vollo would be well advised to move sooner than later. There's no advantage in delaying if, indeed, he's serious about this venture and has the wherewithal to accomplish it." Theil, of course, knew that Vollo did not have all the men or ships that he wanted for the invasion, but he would not admit as much to this stranger. "There may be a way to disrupt these new leaders or at least to manage to provoke some dissention among them, easing the burden on Vollo's army."

"And how would that be accomplished?"

"That will be my concern." Theil understood that the abbot had no intention of diminishing his value to the warlord by explaining how someone else might accomplish what he planned to do. "Your concern is to be certain to tell Lord Vollo that I'll pursue an effort of disruption and a plan of deception to further his invasion."

"One more question of you. Vollo instructed me that if your report was substantially different from earlier reports, verification of this new information should be found. Not that Vollo lacks trust in you."

The abbot laughed. "Of course, he lacks trust in me. We are an uneasy alliance, but one that can be very successful. The means of verification should be obvious to you. You are on a Celt trading vessel. Take your wares to Londinium or to Valphain Castle, itself, where the new king resides. See what you can see. Hear what you can hear. And remember to detail to Lord Vollo the accuracy of my report."

It was important not only to verify the accuracy of the abbot's report for Vollo, who would likely decide to invade sooner than he planned, but also for King Cergin, who would likely want to delay the attack or put an end to it altogether.

Theil returned to the vessel, whose captain decided to anchor for the night. They would continue to Valphain Castle the next day.

In the morning they continued to sail south. Theil believed the ship's crew could manage to pass themselves off as traders; they did have some goods to barter, mostly cloth and some metal work, nothing of much value except for some finely crafted German daggers. Theil was also confident he could present himself well enough to escape being detected as a Saxon agent.

A brief journey took them to the closest shore landing near Valphain Castle. They beached their vessel, loaded sacks of their wares onto their backs and walked to the castle. Theil could see immediately why this location had been chosen for a castle. Atop a hill and protected from sea invasion by a steep cliff, Valphain could only be attacked straight on, warriors being forced to charge up hill and confront the castle's massive stone wall. A direct assault would be costly in lives and likely to fail. A long siege was the only alternative, but he doubted Vollo would have the patience for such a siege. And indeed, there was a disadvantage to a siege: the longer a Saxon force surrounded the castle, the more likely the British could gather a large army to attack them from the rear and trap them against the castle walls.

Theil had never before been to Valphain Castle, but others in his group had, and they remarked on the noticeable increase in activity. Theil could see some of it himself. A dozen or more large tents had been erected in proximity to the castle walls, and some wooden cottages were under construction a farther distance out, both indicating that people were being drawn to Valphain. Merchants had set up tents and tables both in the castle courtyard and just outside its gate. There was so much activity that an approaching band of traders from Gaul hardly drew any notice.

No matter that he seemed to blend in with the Gauls, it was still a peculiar feeling for Theil to walk into an enemy stronghold, the very castle that might be under siege by Vollo in a matter of days. It was also peculiar seeing the enemy like this. Except for language and dress, these people were no different from Saxons going about their daily activities, and while this was not a new revelation, to understand it and to observe it were not the same. Indeed, he found this place to his liking. The location by the sea was pleasing; the castle spacious and well maintained, and the people were cheerful as far as he could see in watching them interact with one another. There was no Vollo, always ruthless and now irrational at times, and no King Cergin, who while not as menacing as Vollo, had abducted Theil and might have tortured and killed him had not Theil given the king answers he wanted to hear.

The thought briefly entered Theil's mind that he would like to stay here, leaving the brutality of Vollo and intrigue of Cergin behind him. But he had no way of knowing whether Kaye was any better a leader than these two and little hope that a renegade Saxon would be welcomed among the British. No, put that madness out of your head, he thought, and concentrate on the task that brought you here.

He followed along as the traders in his party spoke to various British merchants and attempted to trade their wares. These negotiations were not in earnest but rather intended to acquire pieces of news and gossip during the conversation. All the while, Theil glanced at the castle's fortifications and took note of how the interior of the castle was laid out.

There was much activity in the courtyard, where a platform was being erected along with tiers of wooden benches in preparation for the coronation. The Gauls learned from a seller of pottery that King Kaye along with Sir Uriens, master of the castle, were at that moment on the platform speaking with the head carpenter. Theil took a good look at the pair and noticed that standing with them was a monk, an abbot, whose function, he was told, it would be to place the crown on the king's head during the coronation ceremony. Theil could not help but wonder if this was the same abbot he had met the night before. This man did not seem as large as Vollo's agent, but it had been so dark during their meeting that he could not say one way or the other.

Theil continued to a back corner of the courtyard where some battle training was in progress. The young man who was demonstrating the technique for the use of a sword was very impressive, and Theil knew immediately that this must be the very same Arthur that the abbot had warned him about. Theil did not need to watch him long to determine that he was a leader as well as a skilled warrior. Arthur was a thoughtful and persuasive teacher, and men looked at him with admiration. While Vollo inspired fear, this man seemed to inspire loyalty and confidence. Theil knew that Arthur was someone who must be taken into account in any Saxon battle plan.

Theil worried that it would appear odd for a trader to be so interested in sparring and did not want to be confronted or even spoken to. Thinking he had seen enough to support the abbot's report, he turned to leave. As he did, his eye caught a beautiful young woman who was studying Arthur's every move. She had pleasing features, perfect skin, and lively eyes. When the woman smiled at something Arthur said, Theil realized that he had become as charmed by the woman as she appeared to be enthralled by Arthur.

26) The Coronation

Brenna, wearing a light blue gown made expressly for the coronation, examined her hair one last time in her mirror. She crossed the bedroom floor and opened the door to leave. Uriens was standing in the hall facing her door. The sight of him startled her. "Father, have you just been standing there?"

He appeared ill. "I want to speak to you before the coronation."

"I can see from your expression this won't be a happy conversation." She stood aside to let him pass into the room and closed the door behind him.

He turned to face her, nervously rubbing his hands together. "This concerns you and Kaye."

"Kaye and me!"

"And you and Arthur."

Brenna pressed her lips together in anger. "You've been speaking with Maeve. You can't believe the things she says."

"I dismiss most of what she tells me." His tone was a mixture of sadness and defeat. "The constant fighting between the two of you. . .it has become too much for me. I see the good — and the bad — in both of you. Whatever your intention, you make Maeve feel old and ugly while I try to increase what little confidence she has."

Brenna dropped her eyes and softened her tone. "I'm sorry if I make her feel old and ugly, but at times she invites trouble. Once she starts, I admit I have difficulty controlling myself."

"She thinks that when you and Arthur sit together at a banquet table that you talk about her and laugh. She also says. . ." Uriens could not say the words.

Brenna turned red with anger. "I can well imagine what she says."

"You need to know that it is not only Maeve who talks."

"But she is the root of all of it."

He held his hands out, palms facing the floor. "Not so loud, please." Uriens looked back at the door and whispered. "Whether she is the root or not, the stories are spreading, and I worry that you will become unmarriageable."

"Unmarriageable!" Her eyes opened wide. "To whom? Kaye! Is that why you mentioned his name?" Uriens did not respond. "You don't deny it. You want to wed me to Kaye." Brenna put her hands on her hips and moved closer to her father, who was more than a head taller. "I'll give you my answer now. No!"

"This is exactly what was afraid of," he said, absentmindedly running a hand through his hair. "But perhaps you don't understand, Brenna, that you would be a queen."

"But married to a man who doesn't deserve to be king. I have little respect for Kaye. He pretends to be what he is not."

"Pretends? Oh, you mean that he has not yet been crowned. But he will be in a few moments, and there are matters involved of great importance, beyond just you and Kaye. Surely you see that?" Horns blew down in the courtyard, causing Uriens to turn toward the window. "Brenna, you must at least consider the possibility. We must at least discuss it."

She pointed toward the window. "Now, as we are being called to the coronation?"

Uriens again looked in the direction of the horns. "I should have come earlier, I know. But Brenna, you cannot make a decision this important after giving it only a few moments thought."

She held up her right hand. "I promise that I will not give you a final answer now at this moment. Is that satisfactory?" He nodded. "Then, we should hurry to the courtyard."

Uriens started for the door, stopped and turned back toward Brenna. "There was something else I needed to tell you." After a long pause, he shrugged his shoulders. "I suppose it wasn't that important or I would have remembered."

The scene in the courtyard of Valphain Castle rivaled the Londinium tournament in pageantry. A stage had been erected at one end, and on the stage was a throne, behind which hung a large banner with the new coat of arms of King Kaye, a golden hawk on a blue background. Seated to the right of the king, a few paces behind Kaye, were Ector and Arthur on one side. Uriens and Brenna, the last to arrive, joined Maeve on the opposite side.

Kaye looked at Uriens and turned the palm of his hand up. Uriens appeared puzzled. Kaye extended his hand as though he expected to be handed something. Uriens finally nodded, and Kaye smiled.

Facing them on three sides of the courtyard were benches for spectators that rose eight levels high. The first two rows were designated for lords and knights and their families. Everyone else crowded in where they could find a seat; many others were forced to observe from atop the castle walls.

Gusts of wind were causing the pennants atop the castle walls and towers to flap loudly. Horns announced the entrance of the abbot and four of his monks. Kaye, dressed in a white tunic with gold trim, stood to face the abbot, while the monks stepped to the side. Kaye knelt before the abbot, who gently struck him with a young oak shoot first on the head, then on each shoulder, whispering a chant in an ancient version of their language that was beyond the understanding of those present. A vassal brought the abbot a silver crown seated on a pillow. The abbot gently lifted the crown, held it high for the spectators to see and placed it on Kaye's head, proclaiming him king.

A shout went up in unison from the crowd. "Long live King Kaye. Long may he reign."

Kaye waved to the crowd as they continued to cheer him.

Merlin, watching him from near the platform, turned to Prywycke, who stood beside him. "Interesting the difference in demeanor between the two brothers, even considering they are of different blood lines. Kaye is like a man who after crossing a stream has little recollection of, and no appreciation for, ever having been on the opposite side."

"A stream?" Prywycke did not understand.

"One might have thought that Kaye had always been king, whereas Arthur has one foot on each side of the stream. He has become a successful warrior and battle leader, yes, but he also remains the boy who dreamed by a pond rather than perform his chores."

"A foot on each side?"

Merlin frowned at him. "Best pay attention to the knighting ceremony, Prywycke."

When the cheering finally subsided, Kaye called his father forward. Ector knelt, and as the king tapped his father gently with his sword on the head and each shoulder, Kaye pronounced him "Sir Ector." Another cheer went up from the onlookers.

Arthur was next to be knighted. He was pleased with the status he was about to be accorded and felt that this moment was the culmination of a lifetime of expectation, more so the expectation of the wizard than his own.

He knelt. Kaye knighted him, and the crowd cheered Arthur's knighting as long and as loudly as they greeted Kaye's crowning.

King Kaye faced the crowd to give them a brief address authored for him during the preceding days by Merlin. It was brief because Kaye said he would be fortunate to get even a few words out before such a large gathering.

"As your king, it is my intention to lead all of you assembled here this day and every man, woman and child in Britain to an age of great prosperity." He was interrupted by cheers and applause. "Prosperity for lord and vassal alike, for farmer and herder, for potter and metal smith, for merchant and trader. That prosperity begins with being able to keep the fruit of our labor rather than have it stolen by Norsemen, Saxons or barbarians from the north." He was interrupted again by cheers and shouts of support. "Prosperity begins with defense. Indeed, without adequate defense we have nothing."

Arthur thought Kaye had managed to make Merlin's words his own. Perhaps, he would grow into the role of king.

Kaye was coming to the conclusion of his short speech. "I ask all of you assembled — and will ask all those not with us on this day — to join in our effort to keep Britain safe. Very soon, I and Sir Uriens will begin a journey to conclude treaties with every major lord and knight not here assembled."

Kaye's eyes scanned the crowd, then he looked over to where Uriens and his family were seated. "I have one more task, one more happy task, to perform this day, and that is to announce to all of you that Brenna, daughter of Uriens and Maeve, has consented to be my queen."

Arthur felt as if he had taken a hammer blow to the head. He thought he might have misheard what Kaye said but could see in Brenna's shocked expression that he had not. Uriens had a look of worry on his face while Maeve smiled. Had they even told Brenna? If they had, she surely would have told him. Did they believe by announcing her wedding at the coronation, they would back her into a position from which there was no escape?

Brenna had become so much of his life, he did not want to give her up and was not sure he could. He thought about her constantly and was happy only when in her presence, especially during their secret lovemaking, when he felt they were away from the world of strife, pain and obligation.

He had to speak to Brenna to find out what she knew and what she planned to do. And he must be discrete about it. All the dignitaries — the new king, the new knights and their families — were expected to be seen at the fair and to mingle with the spectators. It would make more sense to wait until later, but he had to speak to her as soon as he could.

The ceremony concluded and those on the platform and in the stands made their way to the fair that had been assembled outside the castle walls.

Arthur saw Merlin seeking him out.

Taking him by the arm, the wizard led him back toward the platform, where they could speak and not be overheard. "Arthur, I saw your reaction to Kaye's announcement, and your reaction is of concern to me." Arthur was not paying attention. Merlin stepped chin to chin with him. "What has transpired between you and Brenna? Tell me."

Arthur was caught off-guard by his directness. "Are you so naïve as to believe every rumor you hear?"

"I put little credence in rumor. I was the one who taught you the difference between fact and rumor. And that is why I ask you now."

Arthur continued to look the wizard in the eyes but thought the look in his own eyes was giving him away. "Do you think I would act badly with the woman who would become betrothed to the king?"

"When you were a boy, we talked about the difference between logic and truth. Do not give me logic. Give me truth." Merlin had grown angry. "I ask not what you *would do* but what you *have done*."

Arthur grew angry as well, less because of the present situation than the years of being goaded and scolded by Merlin. "My entire life I've had to answer to you. I'm a grown man and a knight of the realm, and I'm no longer compelled to give account of myself to you."

With those words Arthur walked away, and Merlin shouted after him. "Whatever you have done, it must cease now that Kaye is king."

Arthur walked to the fair and was greeted by people who congratulated him on his knighthood, and all the while he glanced over people's shoulders in search of Brenna. He finally caught sight of her. She was with her father and stepmother, and he kept a distance. He discretely followed them as they sampled some food and watched the same juggler who had performed at the tournament. Brenna was finally able to separate herself from Uriens and Maeve by lingering behind to watch a contortionist.

Arthur moved next to her and without making eye contact, said, "Did you know of this announcement?"

"No." Brenna continued to look straight ahead at the contortionist. "My father spoke to me about Kaye just before the coronation. I refused to marry Kaye but said that I wouldn't give my final answer today just to end the conversation."

Arthur looked about the crowd to see if anyone was observing them. "Perhaps, we need to stay apart for a time."

"Don't yield now." Her voice was low but her tone intense. "Circumstances and time are not in our favor. The more this wedding is planned, the more difficult it will be to undo. I will put an end to it one way or another, and soon. I promise." Brenna searched the crowd. "I best go to Uriens and Maeve." She finally looked at Arthur. "Until later."

The fair continued throughout the afternoon and early evening. That night the great hall was again the site of a banquet, this one in honor of the newly crowned king. The hall was filled nearly to capacity, and Maeve took the time to search every corner of the hall until she was sure that both Brenna and Arthur were not in attendance. Maeve found Uriens and pulled him aside so they could speak in private. "Arthur and Brenna are missing."

He sighed. "Surely after today that is merely happenstance. She can't be that reckless."

"We have given her a chance to right this situation. . ."

He interrupted. "But are you even certain they are together?"

"Of course, I am. We — you and I — will lose out if they are caught because Kaye is now king. Merlin no longer requires your support nor does Kaye require your daughter as queen."

"Oh, Maeve, I don't believe that is true. Merlin will stand by his bargain."

"I won't take that risk. Those two, Brenna and Arthur, they need a serious fright, and I know exactly how to give them one."

Uriens shook his head. "This is all so confusing. I don't see how you can be so certain that they're together."

Ignoring his comment, Maeve looked back to the crowd in the Great Hall. "I need someone I can trust."

"Trust? I trust Bryso above all others." Maeve turned to leave. "Wait. Where are you going? What is it that you plan to do?"

Leaving Uriens behind, she went in search of Bryso but could not find him. Instead she took a male servant from the kitchen, and as they were leaving the tower, instructed him to take a torch from the hall wall.

Moving at a quick pace, she led him the through the sparse crowd that lingered in the courtyard, directly to the stable and pushed open one of its two doors. "Look there." She pointed to the stacks of hay near the archery target.

Holding the torch before him, the servant walked to where she had directed. He held the torch high and moved it from side to side. Seeing nothing, he called back to her. "There is nothing here. What was supposed to be here?"

Without answering, she hurried to where the man was and looked for herself but saw nothing.

27) Trapped

Rather than go down to the banquet for Kaye, Arthur stood at the window of his tower chamber staring blankly out to the sea. Being confronted by Merlin had shaken him, and he was undergoing a change of heart, not in how he felt about Brenna but rather about whether he should act upon his feelings for her. As young boy he attempted to deceive Merlin about unimportant things such as chores, but on this day he had deceived his mentor for the first time on an important matter.

Attempted to deceive, Arthur corrected himself, for Merlin was unusually perceptive and often seemed to know exactly what was in Arthur's mind. Merlin probably knew the answer to his question before he asked it.

It had been easy for Arthur to justify what he and Brenna were doing. He loved her. Their sexual encounters had become a compulsion. Even the manner in which they had to meet in secret and take risks added excitement and bound them closer together. And secret liaisons were not uncommon at Valphain Castle. He had come to believe Brenna's claim that Kaye and Maeve were themselves involved in one. And there was the matter of the sword, Caliburn. He had freed it from the stone, not Kaye. He was *entitled* to Brenna. Or so he told himself.

On this day, the day he achieved knighthood, he thought back to his combat training, to when Gerens no longer wanted to fight and Arthur thrashed him all the more for it, to how he never once backed down from Marrek despite the beatings he had taken. He had been uncompromising then. He had integrity. Perhaps that was why he was able to draw Caliburn. Could he do so again, now that he was planning to meet his lover in secret, in a dirt floor cellar under one of the castle towers?

And he had been careless and indiscrete, which was bad for any warrior and worse for a battle lord. Merlin heard enough to question him on the matter. Maeve clearly suspected them. He and Brenna were the subjects of common rumor.

It had to end.

Before they were caught.

Tonight he would tell her. He did not know what words he would use or how she would react, whether she would agree, whether she had reached the same conclusion on her own, whether the fiery Brenna would become defiant and say that rumor should not dictate their behavior.

As soon as it was dark, Arthur left for their meeting place. He walked to the west tower, which was a distance from the main gate. Valphain Castle had been built over a spring that was accessed from a cellar built under the west tower. The spring, once the castle's source of water during a siege, had long ago run dry and the hidden cellar under the tower was long forgotten, except by Brenna, who played there as a child. Arthur usually had no difficulty entering the tower unseen at night, but this night, two men, drunk from overindulging at the day's coronation and fair, were standing before the tower arguing about the most promising areas to hunt. From the nature of their debate and how unsteadily they stood, it was obvious that they were not fully possessed of their senses. Arthur thought he could simply walk by them largely unnoticed, but now that he was determined to be cautious, he decided to wait them out.'

The argument turned personal. The shorter of the two men began to thump his companion on the chest. "You know nothing of hunting."

"If you wish to keep a full set of fingers, you will not again thrust one into my chest."

'What have I been reduced to?' thought Arthur. 'Unable to simply walk into a tower for fear of being caught, hiding in the dark because of these two men who were likely too drunk to know exactly where they were.'

Finally the drunken men moved on, still continuing to argue. Arthur, pausing only to check a final time that no one else was in the vicinity, hurried to the thick wooden door at the base of the tower and slipped inside. It was too dark to see, and he placed one hand on the stone wall to feel his way around to the back of the staircase to a small opening behind it. The walls and steps leading down to this cellar were stone, and he continued to find his way by keeping one hand on the stone wall. At the end of the long flight of stairs, he saw the light of a candle, meaning that Brenna had arrived ahead of him. She waited on the earthen floor that had once been the bed of the spring. It was a small area, slightly larger than what was needed to accommodate two adults lying down. They had covered it over with several layers of blankets, added pillows as well, and surrounded it with a half dozen candles, only one of which was now lit.

Had anyone happened upon this place, they would have no doubt about how it was being used.

She was seated crossed-legged, her clothes bundled around her, indicating to him that she had reached the same conclusion he had.

———

Maeve returned to the Great Hall. As she worked her way toward Uriens, she nodded hello to some of the guests but did not stop to speak to any of them.

"Did you find Brenna?" asked Uriens.

"I did not."

Uriens was worried. "Do you suppose she is in trouble of some sort?"

Maeve smirked. "Not the sort of trouble you mean. She isn't lost. She's hiding."

"She is angry with me, I know. . . We talked before the coronation. . .Kaye just announced the marriage. . .We — Brenna and I — never really spoke." Uriens shook his head. "And she is not in her room?"

"I didn't look in her room."

Uriens smiled. "Well, of course. Such a fuss you made, and she is probably in her room."

Uriens went up to Brenna's room and paused outside her door composing himself. "Brenna, it is me." He knocked on the door. "Brenna." He knocked again. "I understand if you are angry or upset, but I can explain." He knocked several more times and pushed open the door. The room was empty.

———

Brenna pulled her gown down over her head and wrapped a blanket around her shoulders. Arthur fixed his tunic, which had gotten turned inside out, and slipped it on. He stood up to put on his leggings and sat back down next to her. "That was unplanned."

"That was excellent, planned or not." She reached her arms around his neck and kissed his cheek.

"When we agreed to not to see each other like this, I thought we should give each other a farewell."

She struggled in the dim candle light to see his expression. "And now how do you feel about not seeing each other?"

"I don't know."

"I don't either."

"One thing is for certain, that we shouldn't see each other for a time, not like this. Let the interest in us and the rumors die down. And let's see what happens with Kaye."

Brenna playfully slapped the back of his hand. "I told you: nothing will ever happen with Kaye."

"I was thinking that if we resume. . ."

She leaned over and kissed his cheek again. "If?"

"If we resume, we will need to be more careful, much more careful." Arthur turned his head toward the cellar steps. Brenna was about to speak, but he held up a finger to silence her. She heard it as well, a voice that carried faintly from outside the door above them. Arthur hoped the two drunks had returned.

The tower door was pulled open. Arthur quickly put out the candle, more concerned with its smell than its light, and the two remained still. Someone, perhaps more than one person, entered the tower. Footsteps could be heard climbing the stairs. It sounded as though a single person was moving up the tower steps, but there could also be a second person at the tower door or just outside it. They listened carefully, but there was no more talking or any hint of what this person or these persons wanted in the tower.

It was not long before the footsteps came back down the steps. If finding Arthur and Brenna was the reason for this visit and the searcher knew about the stairs down to the dry spring, they would shortly be discovered in compromising circumstances. But they had not been completely abandoned by luck. The footsteps appeared to be moving away, and the tower door was then closed.

They sat silently for a while to be certain no one had stayed behind or planned to return to the tower. They quickly finished dressing and hurried up the stairs. Thinking they had just escaped a dire situation, Arthur tried to open the door and found that it was locked from the outside. He tried forcing it open but could not. With no weapon or tool, he tried striking the heavy wooden door with his arm, then with his boot. He would break an arm or foot before he damaged this door.

Neither had to say a word. They were trapped. Arthur, followed closely by Brenna, rushed up the stairs to the archer portals, which faced the exterior of the castle. The portals were too narrow for a person to pass through, and even if they were not, it was a drop of more than forty feet to the ground below, enough to break the legs of a jumper or worse.

It was getting late. Soon he and Brenna would surely be missed at the banquet if they were not already. Someone might come looking for them, perhaps even here in the tower. Arthur rushed down the steps and again tried to open the tower door without success. Their best hope was to catch someone's attention riding by the west tower, although there were likely to be few riders this late in the evening, and he hurried back up to the archer portal.

Merlin had once told Arthur that sometimes, but not often, when a person is most desperate, something a little magical occurs. Their magic appeared in the form of a solitary horseman; the rider, it turned out, was none other than Bryso, the man who would have died at the hand of a Norseman had it not been for Arthur. If Arthur could have wished for anyone to ride by, it would have been Bryso. Arthur called out to him. Bryso halted his horse, looked about but could not locate the voice. Arthur shouted down at him, "Above you."

Bryso looked up toward the voice. "Is that you, Arthur?" Bryso rode toward the tower. "I thought you would be busy enjoying the banquet."

Arthur lowered his voice now that Bryso was directly below him. "I'm locked in the tower. Can you come around and open the door?" Before Bryso could ask how that had happened, Arthur said, "It's a story better whispered than shouted."

Bryso went around to the castle gate, identified himself to the night guard, and was admitted to the courtyard. He rode to the west tower, slid off his horse and opened the tower door, which had been bolted from the outside. Arthur hurried out to meet him, shutting but not bolting the door behind him. "Can I count on you for a small favor?" He grabbed Bryso by the arm and led him away from the door.

"Anything. You know I'm in your debt."

"No one need know about this incident at the tower, about my getting locked in."

Bryso gave Arthur a knowing wink, and the two men, Bryso trailing his horse, walked away, allowing Brenna to slip out of the west tower.

Brenna hurried to the main tower and entered through the kitchen, where her favorite servant, a rotund woman named Finola, was helping prepare supper. "Sir Uriens has been searching for you," Finola said to her as she rushed by. "He's all bothered."

"I know, I know." Brenna ran up to her room to change her clothes, which had become soiled with dirt. When she finally arrived in the great hall, many of those assembled turned in her direction. She forced a smile but could not hold it long.

Arthur, thinking it best to put some distance between Brenna's arrival and his own, came a while later. His absence must have been discussed because he thought his arrival was being noted by many of the people in the great hall, making him feel uncomfortable. Think what you will, he told himself, not one of you has any proof.

28) Aingus, King of the Barbarous Picts

The voyage to Pictland was another lengthy one. They sailed north along the coast of Britain and turned west into a long and narrow inland bay. Near the end of the bay, positioned with a lake behind it, was the castle of King Aingus. Theil was surprised by the beauty of the terrain. There were open vistas, blue water, and low hills in the distance. The castle was more than he expected but much less than those in either Britain or Germania. The structures were of wood rather than stone, and the defensive wall was an earthen embankment. There was a moat that had been dug around the exterior of the wall. Primitive, thought Theil, but well designed. Anyone wanting to take this castle would not find it an easy task.

Traders did not often visit Aingus' kingdom, Theil was told by one of his shipmates, and the men working the fields by the sea paused in their labor as the trading vessel, now being rowed in the absence of wind, moved past them and toward the castle. Theil and a Gaul named Morcant, perhaps the most verbal member of the crew, were put ashore while the captain remained with his vessel, a safe distance away in the water, presumably willing to leave Theil and Morcant in Aingus' hands if escape became necessary. They were met by four men armed with swords and axes, who looked at them with suspicion as Theil explained he was here as an emissary of Saxon King Cergin and wanted to speak to King Aingus.

They were led across the moat bridge, through an opening in the earthen embankment and into the castle. Aingus was waiting in a small throne room, bare except for crossed axes and crossed swords hung along the walls. Aingus was a heavy-set, balding man with a light brown mustache that hung over his entire mouth and had an angry expression in his eyes. He sat in a chair, a throne of sorts, and was flanked by two large warriors, both with long unkempt hair and beards. Theil bowed before Aingus and introduced himself. "King Cergin of Germania and the great warlord Vollo send this messenger, Theil, to bring you good wishes."

Aingus seemed unimpressed. "And what proof have you that you are an emissary of these two men?" Theil handed over a silver medallion carrying Vollo's seal. Aingus studied it and pointedly held on to it. "What have you from King Cergin?"

Theil had not anticipated this and hesitated momentarily, deciding he should attempt to shoulder the blame himself. "Apologies, Sire." Theil bowed. "The king would gladly have sent a medallion but was not asked for one. The fault lies with this messenger."

"Arrogant Saxons." Theil did not know if Aingus was speaking to him or to his own guards. "Does King Cergin think I am any less of a king than he?"

"No, Sire, nothing could be less true. King Aingus is well known and well respected throughout Germania."

Aingus nodded in acceptance of this praise. "Get this man a chair." He pointed to Theil, then, gestured toward Morcant. "And who is this?"

Theil answered for Morcant. "He is a crewman on the vessel that came from Britain to your kingdom."

"If he has no business here, he can wait outside." The king shooed the man off as though waving away an insect. Aingus turned to Theil, who sat down before him. "Tell me what business the Saxon king has with me."

One of the guards turned an ear toward the conversation, and Theil glanced at him briefly before addressing himself to Aingus. "King Cergin offers an alliance."

"An alliance!" Aingus leaned closer to Theil and said with great emphasis, "This much you must understand and report back to your warlord and your king. I am unbound. I and I alone command this kingdom. I consult with no man, ask permission of no man and ask forgiveness from no man."

"To be sure. This is well understood, and the alliance is in no way intended to alter that."

"Good." Aingus relaxed back is his chair.

Aingus' reaction caused Theil to momentarily lose the sequence of the argument he intended to make. "It would be of mutual benefit," he said after a brief pause.

"For my benefit! Am I to believe that your king sends you across the sea for my benefit?" Aingus laughed. "If it was not intended to benefit your King Cergin, you would not be here."

"Certainly it benefits King Cergin, but as I did not explain well enough, the alliance would be mutually beneficial, to King Cergin as well as to yourself, King Aingus."

Aingus stared at Theil. "Explain."

"As King Aingus well knows the Britains have been in disarray for many years, but finally they are ready to crown a king." From Aingus' expression, Theil thought he had not known about the changing situation in the south. "Kaye is the name of the man who will become king if he is not already, and his brother, Arthur, may well become a powerful warlord. Who can be certain what threats may be posed by these two?"

Aingus slammed his hand down on the arm of his chair. "You are not here to tell me that I need to fear an attack from the British and can be saved by an alliance with Saxons?"

That was part of the argument Vollo instructed him to make, but Vollo had underestimated Aingus, who seemed to be trying to unnerve Theil with his strong reactions to almost everything that Theil said. Theil bowed from the shoulders as a sign of respect to the Pict king. "We are aware that the Picts are well able to defend themselves in the unlikely event of a British attack. That is the lesser issue. The greater issue is that we Saxons would like a settlement on the east coast of Britain, perhaps near Valphain Castle." The intention was more Vollo's than Cergin's, but Theil would not admit that. "In Germania at this very moment men are being recruited and ships prepared for an invasion. Indeed, ships may already be under sail."

Aingus finally appeared to be taking him seriously. "You attack from the east and I from the north."

Theil nodded to Aingus. "The timing is perfect. Kaye's fledgling army would be divided in two, assuring both Your Majesty and the Saxons of victories. And this would not be an alliance, but rather a simple agreement as to the nature and timing of military movements."

Aingus had questions about what Theil had seen at Valphain Castle, which Theil described accurately, and about the nature of the Saxons war preparations, which he greatly exaggerated. The Pict king sat thoughtfully for a while and finally said to Theil, "You do not know how I conduct the affairs of my kingdom, but I am not a man to strike a bargain with a stranger. So, you will stay with us a time while I consider this proposal."

Theil smiled and nodded his acceptance of this offer, understanding fully that he was a prisoner.

The king ordered one of his two retainers to find a place for his guest to sleep, and as soon as Theil was out of earshot, ordered the second retainer to find the seaman from Gaul and bring him here.

Morcant was found, brought before Aingus and sat in the same chair Theil had occupied. The king wanted to know how much of Theil's story Morcant could verify. Having been among the trading party that visited Valphain Castle, Morcant gave much the same account of Kaye and Arthur and the increased activity there as Theil had. But since his vessel had picked up Theil at an isolated abbey in Germania, he had no opportunity to observe the state of the Saxon forces.

"Listen carefully." Aingus spoke to Morcant in a menacing tone. "My orders are always carried out exactly as I say them. You are to return to your vessel and to tell your captain that the Saxon will stay with me for several days, maybe longer. Your vessel is to remain here in wait for him. It's very important to me that the Saxon complete his mission. And your vessel will be safe at its anchoring. If you require anything, food, drink, anything, you are to ask me for it. But you are not to leave. Understand?"

"Yes." Morcant bowed his head. "I understand."

That evening Theil was brought to the supper Aingus and his men were enjoying in their great hall. Never had Theil seen anything as raucous, and he was no novice when it came to such gatherings. He had never witnessed men drink so much mead so quickly or eat so much food in such a slovenly manner. He had come to think the Pict reputation for barbarism came as much from their dining habits as their approach to warfare. Several times friendly tests of arm strength led nearly to fights, and one time such a contest did, with the two participants wrestling each other to the floor and straining mightily to gain some advantage. Everyone, and most especially Aingus himself, enjoyed the battle. It was allowed to continue until one man pulled a knife from his boot, and only then were the two pulled apart.

Theil decided to drink very little to keep a clear head among these wild men.

Aingus announced that their guest should not only learn about one of their best games but should also participate in it as well. The game, he explained, was a test of balance and skill with a knife. Two contestants would stand facing each other barefoot, their feet shoulder length apart. Each man would toss a knife into the floor next to his right foot and would have to extend his foot to where the blade stuck in the wood. The same procedure followed on the left foot and so on. As their legs moved farther apart, it became more difficult to both maintain their balance and to throw their knives accurately. The harrowing part of the contest came when their legs were spread almost as far as they could reach. If the knife point stuck several inches too far, the game was ended as the thrower lost his balance and toppled over. A few inches in the wrong direction, and a man could lose a toe or put a knife blade through the center of his foot.

The entire assemblage of Picts gathered around the playing area. Theil, whose newly healed arm was still weak, faced off against the Pict who had earlier pulled a knife from his boot during a fight. The only advantage Theil had in this game was that his opponent had drunk far more than he had. Theil made the first throw and slid his right foot out to where his knife in the floor. His opponent did the same. Next they threw left. A dozen throws by each man followed, and each had his feet extended more than three feet apart. Theil made a throw that landed too far and had to extend his right foot about another four inches, stretching him almost as far as he could go. On his next throw, he did much worse. The blade fell too close to his left foot and sliced a small piece of his toe off. Theil thought he was being evaluated by how well he played this game. He grimaced but did not cry out, which appeared to earn him respect from the Picts. Fortunately, he had missed the bone.

"Invalid throw," Aingus said. "Each throw must be farther out than the last. Throw again."

Theil, with his toe spilling blood onto the floor, threw again, and had to extend his aching left foot another two inches. On his next throw, his opponent tossed his knife too far, and as he stretched out — the mead playing some part in his unsteadiness — he began to teeter, waving his arms in an effort to find his balance and finally falling forward onto his hands and knees.

Theil won and was congratulated by Aingus, who put an arm around him and said, "I like this man." The king had him take a seat next to his own at the banquet table and handed him a goblet of mead. Theil took it, poured a little over his bloody toe, saluted the assembled Picts and downed the mead in a single gulp, to the delight of Aingus and the cheers of some of the others.

The next morning Aingus took Theil, his toe bandaged and throbbing with pain, hunting, and as they rode, Aingus asked him about Germania. Theil responded with vivid descriptions of his home. The king asked him about his family, and the two men learned they had something common. Both had lost sons in battle.

"I have many brave and skilled warriors," Aingus said, as they rode side by side, "but few that know much about anything. You come from Germania and are better acquainted with Britain than any of them. I would like to have someone with experiences of other lands to consult. I may even ask your King Cergin to make you his permanent emissary to me."

That idea did not appeal to Theil. Staying here any length of time might mean dying in a brawl or a knife fight during a Pict banquet. "There is an issue with that idea." Aingus was puzzled and studied Theil's face for an answer. Theil pointed down at his feet, "These ten toes may not be sufficient to play your knife game."

Aingus laughed.

When they returned from hunting, Theil endured another Pict evening of eating and drinking. There was no knife play or bloodletting this time, but he was coaxed to drink far more than he normally did. The next morning when he was summoned to meet with Aingus, his head hurt more than his aching toe.

Aingus, sitting in the same chair and flanked by the same two warriors as during their first meeting, motioned for Theil to be seated. "You can tell your King Cergin and your warlord..." He struggled for the name.

"Vollo."

"Yes, Vollo. You can tell them that I agree to their proposal. I see no need to call it an alliance or anything more than each army acting independently but coordinated in time." Aingus's response caused Theil to smile. "I will need to know when the Saxons will attack."

"Of course, Sire. The ships may well be on their way. Word will be sent to you."

Aingus nodded in agreement. "Before you go, I have a gift for you." He held out his hand, and the warrior to his right placed a sheathed knife in it. Aingus smiled and handed it over to Theil. "In compensation for the piece of toe you lost."

"Thank you." Theil examined the intricate carvings on the handle, then drew the knife its sheath and examined the blade. "Excellent. It is a gift worthy of your generosity and hospitality."

After Aingus instructed one of his warriors to escort Theil to the Gallic vessel, he sent for two of his field commanders, Cinaed and Ailleg, and waited impatiently for them. Cinaed was the first to arrive. The king motioned him to sit down in the same seat that Theil had occupied.

"Take two men, Cinaed, and ride to Valphain Castle to King Kaye, if, in fact, he is already king. Stop first at Hadrian's Wall to tell any Britains on watch there of your mission and ask for an escort so that you will safely reach their king." Ailleg now arrived and was motioned to a chair. "You, Cinaed, will tell this Kaye that the Saxons will invade within a dozen days or perhaps less. Tell Kaye the Saxons tried to enlist my aid in this effort but that I refused. As an indication of the truth of this story, give Kaye this." Aingus reached under his tunic and produced the silver medallion marked with Vollo's seal. "Explain that Vollo, whose seal this is, is the warlord that the Saxon king has appointed to lead this attack."

Aingus turned to Ailleg. "Start preparing the army for a long march and a long campaign. We must be ready within a dozen days. Those arrogant but foolish Saxons expect us to attack first, to weaken Kaye's forces and weaken ourselves in the process, so that their invasion would meet less opposition. But I've turned things around. The Saxons will attack first and ease the way for us to march south."

───

As their vessel left Pictland, Theil, still plagued by an aching head and a badly cut toe, was pleased at the success of his mission. He had obtained good information from the abbot and succeeded in getting Aingus to agree to an alliance even if the Pict king did not want to call it that. The problem he faced when he returned to Germania was to convey what he knew to Cergin as well as Vollo and to do so without further risk to his life.

When they reached the mouth of the bay, Theil was surprised that the vessel turned south again instead of heading east across the open sea and asked Morcant the reason for this deviation. "The abbot," Morcant said. "Before we return home, we're to check if he has another message for us. If he does, he ties a white cloth to a tree that sits atop a large rock situated so that it can be easily spotted from the water. If the cloth is present, we're to wait until he arrives."

After sailing for several days, they reached the rock and tree that Morcant had described. They saw the white cloth. They would have to anchor and wait for the abbot, however long it took.

29) Banishment

Arthur could see from Prywycke's expression that something was troubling the man. His old companion told Arthur that King Kaye had summoned him, and Arthur knew immediately that he was the source of Prywycke's discomfort and that the issue must involve Brenna. Arthur reminded himself that no one had proof. Even Prywycke, who nearly caught them in the stable, and Bryso, who had to free Arthur from the west tower, had not seen the woman he was with. And he could count on the discretion of these two men more than any others.

Just deny it. They can prove nothing.

Prywycke silently escorted him as far as the door to Kaye's chamber and left him in the hall. Arthur took a breath and pushed open the door. Inside with Kaye were Ector and Merlin. All three were somber. He would have expected Merlin and Kaye to be angry. They were not.

"Sit down, Arthur." Kaye gestured to a chair opposite him. Ector and Merlin each stood on one side of the king. "It's pointless for me to add any preface to what I have to say. So, I'll come directly to the purpose of this meeting." Kaye hesitated, looking at Ector and Merlin before continuing. "Everyone knows of your dalliance with Brenna. I know you don't have nearly the respect for me that I have for you, but I never expected that you would insult me in this way. You have known from the start that we were trying to arrange a marriage with Brenna."

Arthur might have better defended himself if Kaye had been angry. Until this moment, Arthur had only seen himself as violating convention, but he had wounded his brother as well. "Brenna and Maeve have long battled. Maeve spreads rumors."

"It goes well beyond that. The two of you are seen together far more than is natural. People see you at the banquet table and how you look at each other and touch each other." Kaye finally showed some anger. "Everyone observed that the two of you were late to dinner last night and knew you were together."

Arthur was about to say that he and Brenna were merely good friends when Ector interrupted. "You should know, Arthur, that the two of you were seen at the west tower."

The events of the previous night ran through his mind. Someone might have seen them enter or leave the tower separately, but no one had seen them together. He was certain of it.

Merlin entered the conversation. "Many times have I told you, Arthur, that logic and truth are not one and the same. But in this situation, logic and the ways of the flesh tell the story. You cannot deny what has been happening between the two of you. And in a situation such as this, what people think is as important as what they know."

Kaye now looked sympathetically at his brother. "We could bring witnesses, more than a handful, who could say they observed the behavior between you and Brenna. The little things they would say would mount up. But witnesses would only further embarrass you and embarrass me. And Brenna's reputation would be none the better from such an exercise."

Arthur sat silently, his eyes down. This was a battle he no longer had the stomach to fight. It was a battle already lost. Even he would think his defense sounded hollow. The time had come to take a thrashing and try later to recover.

"Look at me, Arthur," said Merlin, and Arthur did so. "No man lives without making mistakes. Your mistake happens to be large, untimely and public, but you are also a hero to the people here. It does no one good to allow you to further shame yourself." He paused to let Arthur consider these words. "We have a proposition for you. You are familiar, of course, with Hadrian's Wall." This, as Arthur well knew, was a defensive wall built by the Romans to keep out the Picts and other northern tribes. Stretching across the whole of the countryside, it had been long abandoned. "You can take a handful of men, travel north, garrison the wall, and stay there until you are recalled however long that might be. If you agree, nothing further will be made of the matter with Brenna."

Under other circumstances, Arthur would have had many questions: How many warriors would he have? How many men, if any, were there now? How would they be supplied? How would they communicate? How could he be expected to garrison a fortification that was many leagues in length without thousands of men? How had the Romans accomplished that task? But he understood they were merely giving him an assignment to send him away from Valphain and were unconcerned about how well Hadrian's Wall would be defended. It was an assignment without worth, but he was willing to accept it if only to be able to leave this room with even a small portion of his dignity.

Arthur was resigned to his fate. "When would I depart?"

"Soon. In the morning."

Arthur nodded his acceptance, slowly rose from his chair, and without looking at the other three, left the room.

Merlin caught up with him in the hall before he had gone far. Arthur turned back toward him, unable to look his mentor in the eye. "Hadrian's Wall is no place for a promising knight and warlord to be, Arthur. Although it is not exactly banishment, it is the equivalent. Still, you have been given a reprieve. Keep that fact in mind against the day when you may be able to grant a reprieve to someone who has made a mistake against you. And remember this as well, that you can find opportunity in the most unusual of places."

Arthur knew that Merlin was trying to offer him some hope, but he was not thinking about opportunity. His attention was solely on avoiding further humiliation, gathering his belongings and riding out of Valphain in the morning. Without responding to the wizard's comment, he left Merlin to perform one last difficult task before leaving, saying goodbye to Brenna.

It did not take long to find Brenna. She was searching for him, and they met in the great hall. She smiled. "I have good news." He could not imagine what that might be. She took him to the kitchen to speak in private.

Finola, the servant, was there. She wiped her hands on her apron. "I'll leave you two alone and see that you aren't disturbed."

Even before Finola left the kitchen, Brenna began her story. "Uriens and Maeve confronted me. They said that we were caught in the tower although I know we were not actually caught and denied everything. Whoever told them told Kaye as well, and now that he is king he is likely to change his mind about the wedding bargain. That should have made Maeve happy. Anything to my detriment usually does. But she appeared sad, and I have not yet determined why." Brenna lost her smile when she saw that the expression in his face had not changed. "You don't seem to grasp what this means."

"And you don't know what this morning has meant for me. I have, in essence, been banished to Hadrian's Wall."

Her expression became stern. "Refuse to go."

He shook his head. "I have just experienced a humiliation beyond any I ever expected or ever hope to experience again. It demonstrated to me how far things have gone astray."

She suddenly was on the verge of tears. "Because of me?

"Because of circumstances."

"But you blame me?"

"No, we were equal partners in this, and that was the best part of it." Arthur paused searching for the correct words. "I feel as though my heart has been cut out."

"I was in your heart. Have I been cut out with it?"

"No, that will never happen." He wanted to reach out and hug her, to reassure her, but could not. He was too upset himself to be able to console anyone else. And perhaps he did hold her partially responsible.

Her eyes locked on his. "What of the things you said last night, that we only need to be apart for a time — time to think?"

He wanted to say that he did not want to leave her, but the words would not come. "It's as if I have been wounded by a sword and need to heal."

"It's your pride."

"Yes, and respect for myself and the respect of others." He did not want to encounter one other person, answer one question about what had happened or why he was leaving or see one smile or look of pity for his fall.

"What about Caliburn?" she said hopefully. "Tell people that it was you and not Kaye..."

He interrupted her. "It's too late for that. Even Merlin is no longer on my side. No one would believe me, and if they did, it would only cause harm. I've caused enough harm."

"Then, if you insist on going to Hadrian's Wall, take me with you."

"Take you!" Arthur's voice had been louder than he intended. He lowered it to a whisper, but his tone was emphatic. "The reason they are sending me to the wall is to separate us. How could I take you with me? I could be banished altogether. And even if I could take you with me, what would you do there? The place has been long abandoned and is surrounded by desolation. I'm not certain what I'll be doing there except inviting an attack from some wandering band of Picts."

She stared at him for a moment. He had seen sadness and anger, heartbreak and hope in her face all in the space of a few moments. Now she appeared disappointed — with him. "You are correct, Arthur. You need time to recover. Your thoughts are troubled, and this is not the time or manner in which to make a decision. You know where my room is. If you wish to talk tonight, no matter how late, come to me."

It was not in him to yield even on this. "I will send word to you from Hadrian's Wall."

Arthur turned and left Brenna without looking back. He exited the kitchen and started to cross the great hall. There was Maeve standing in conversation with Finola. Eyes straight ahead, he walked briskly toward the tower stairs, but despite his resolve to ignore Maeve, he glanced at her. Maeve looked at him, seemingly upset. She opened her mouth as if to speak but did not. Arthur could not know what was in her mind, but he thought her sad look might mean that she was sorry he was leaving and sorry for the part she had played in his banishment.

If this were the case, he was in no humor to forgive her.

That afternoon Arthur met the men who would constitute his garrison. There were a dozen of them, none appearing as if they would be of great use in a battle, and several sufficiently frail or aged that he wondered if they would survive the long march to the wall.

The next morning, just before sunrise, Arthur's small band of men assembled to begin their journey. Arthur, on Snow Storm, was in the lead. He was followed by three horse-drawn, two-wheeled carts, each horse with a rider, each cart loaded with supplies, mostly food but also spare weapons and enough firewood to last a few days in case there was none at Hadrian's Wall. At the rear were nine foot soldiers. Except for the night watch, not a person observed them exit the main gate.

How quickly circumstances change. Only a few days ago he had ridden before a cheering crowd at the Londinium tournament holding his battle hammer aloft in a victory salute. Now he was going to the barren frontier.

Arthur looked back at Valphain Castle as the first rays of the sun lit a corner of its tower. Most of the castle was still asleep. They were warm in their beds, sleeping untroubled, while he faced the cold morning and his own regret.

Book Three

30) Upside Down

Allum looked up from the fading fire and addressed himself to the story teller. "Everything is upside down in this story. Arthur and Merlin are at odds. Arthur is a knight, not a king, and he is banished. And are you saying that Kaye was actually crowned king?"

The Old One threw up his hands in exasperation. "I describe Kaye's coronation and its aftermath, and you ask me if Kaye became king. Is it your hearing that is deficient?"

Allum did not back down. "I ask the question because history doesn't speak of a King Kaye."

The Old One leaned forward in his seat and scowled at Allum. "That is because history is told by such as you two who tell stories about white eagles circling overhead during coronations and dropping serpents into the laps of unsuspecting abbots."

"It wasn't at the coronation," Donal said. "It was when Calibur was pulled from the stone."

"That does not alter my point. And the sword was Caliburn-b-u-r-n."

"To please you, we shall accept that there was a King Kaye."

"Pleasing me has no bearing on what is true and what is not, does it?"

Allum gestured at the fire. "Is there more firewood?"

"You should accept that there was a King Kaye exactly because there was one." The Old One pointed to the corridor leaning out of the great hall. "The firewood you will find in the kitchen. In that direction. You and your partner can bring back a good quantity of it."

The pair walked to the kitchen to where the firewood had been stacked, and when they were out of earshot of the Old One, Allum asked Donal, "You don't believe that Kaye became king, do you?"

Donal nodded yes. "No one could make up such a story and add so much detail if it weren't true."

"He might be able to." Allum motioned toward the great hall to indicate the Old One. "He has sat here for endless time with nothing better to do but concoct stories for such as us."

Donal began to load wood into his arms. "It's difficult to know what is true. You, yourself, Allum said that people speak of such things as ogres and elves that don't exist. Couldn't there be people who existed but aren't spoken of?"

"Of course, there could be — but I don't think they were kings."

"Whether you believe his story or not, there's no advantage in you challengin' the old man."

"Donal, you make a good argument for once. I'll pretend to believe every word that he utters."

Allum and Donal, each with arms full of wood, returned to the great hall and set down their loads by the hearth. Allum added logs to the hearth. The wood began to crackle and plumes of fire began to rise.

Donal warmed his hands over the renewed flame. "Tell us, Old One, who was it that caught Arthur and Brenna in the west tower? Was it Maeve or someone else?"

The Old One looked from Donal to Allum. "Who was it, indeed? But more important things were happening with the Saxons. And the Picts."

31) Hadrian's Wall

The journey to Hadrian's Wall proceeded slowly, delayed by the pace of a few of the older foot soldiers. The sad little garrison, as Arthur thought of them, paused frequently for extended rests, made their camp well before sunset, and was able to cover less territory each passing day.

Arthur, riding at the head of the group, was usually lost in thought and memory, and on occasion, self-pity. When they stopped for meals, Arthur sat alone and ate little or nothing. When they bedded down for the night, he slept fitfully or not at all. Several days it rained, and when it did, the showers were usually heavy, soaking through their clothing and muddying the road before them. And each time Arthur considered the weather a perfect complement to the circumstances in which he found himself.

As they neared Hadrian's Wall, their party encountered four horsemen on the trail riding toward them, and Arthur recognized one rider as Sir Balan, Arthur's worthy opponent from the tournament in Londinium. Balan hailed Arthur, who rode ahead of his troop, stopping when his horse and Balan's were almost nose to nose.

"You are far from your home, friend." Balan smiled at him. "What takes you to the north country?"

"We are riding to Hadrian's Wall. I didn't expect to encounter anyone I knew on the journey but am pleased to see you, Balan."

"To Hadrian's Wall?"

"And why, Balan, are you in the north country?"

Balan glanced over Arthur's shoulder at the odd little band of men behind him. "Surely you are not intending to garrison Hadrian's Wall with a handful of men."

"No, it's a scouting expedition of sorts. The news has likely not reached this far, but Kaye has taken the throne, and there are many things that must be done."

"At Hadrian's Wall?" Balan leaned forward in his saddle and softened his voice. "So, your brother wishes to have Valphain Castle to himself for a time."

"Yes, have the castle to himself for a time. And I-I thought it best to get away. But why are you this far north?"

"My castle is in that direction." He gestured toward the sea. "My brother's is inland, not a great distance away. I was visiting him." Balan again glanced at the strange entourage with Arthur. "Is Kaye considering having sentries along the wall? Even that would take hundreds of men."

"I have no conception of how many men it would take, and indeed, I have never seen the wall or any of its towers. As I said, this is a scouting expedition — of sorts."

Balan pointed to the road and in the air traced its path north with his finger. "This road leads to a tower in the wall, once a passageway for traders. This tower is a place you could make your base while you are there. Will you be there at least a few days?"

"At least a few."

Balan spurred his horse. "I shall come visit you in a few days' time."

"That would be very enjoyable." Arthur watched him ride off and thought Balan was unlikely ever to visit.

After another two days' journey they saw Hadrian's Wall ahead of them, an impressive structure because of its size but clearly long devoid of human habitation and care. They continued to the tower described by Balan, and while the men unloaded their three carts outside the structure, Arthur inspected its interior. The doors, walls, floors and the few pieces of furniture that remained were covered with a mixture of dust and dirt that to the touch darkened Arthur's fingers. In some ways, he thought, this was worse than camping outdoors. Before they moved their gear in, the rooms in the tower they planned to use would need cleaning, and they would have to improvise cleaning implements. Some window shutters needed repair, and they dared not use any of the fireplaces until they knew their chimneys were clear. Except for the battered furniture, there was no fire wood.

Their most immediate tasks would be adding to the small supply of firewood they had, cleaning the cistern, and filling it from the closest stream or pond.

It was a full day's work to prepare the tower to accommodate a dozen men. Performing some constructive labor began to buoy Arthur's spirits. He had eaten little since that fateful meeting with Kaye and had lost enough weight that his clothes fit him loosely. That night he joined the others by the fire and ate a full meal for the first time in days. Eating made him feel better, and he thought refusing himself food during the journey had added significantly to his morose outlook.

After supper he went to the room he had selected atop the tower to serve as his bed chamber. He should have been tired, and although physically taxed from the day's work, he found himself unable to sleep, staring out a window where the right shutter hung by a single hinge. Out there in the black night was the mysterious north country, home to the Picts and other Celtic tribes that periodically warred with the British. Out there might be adventure, and if so, he welcomed it, anything to prod him out of his state of melancholia and self-pity.

As he had every night and every day since his banishment, Arthur thought about what he might have done differently. He could not help falling in love with Brenna. That happened very suddenly, almost the moment he saw her at the fair. And he did not regret any of the time he spent with her. Would he have been more discrete? With absolutely certainty. He regretted being caught far more than he regretted the indiscretions. He also thought about Caliburn. He would not be here now in this situation had he held onto the sword. But he could not have foreseen the series of events that followed giving it to Kaye.

The next morning Arthur, after a fitful sleep, walked the wall both east and west, but on foot he could cover only a very small portion of it. Balan was correct, the wall was so long it would take a thousand men or more to garrison it. But a smaller group of men could be stationed along its length to warn of an approaching army. And perhaps a few well-equipped men could even delay such an enemy on its march south.

Arthur saddled up Snow Storm that afternoon and rode out the gate and to the west along the wall. The next day he rode east and the following day north toward Pictland. These rides became a daily practice, and Arthur even rode north at night. As a boy he had heard stories about the dangers of this place, but it was peaceful now.

He was returning from a ride when he saw a figure atop the wall looking out at him. It was Balan. True to his word, he had come for a visit. Arthur tethered his horse and went up to greet Balan. The two knights — Arthur had to remind himself he was still a knight even if he had been banished to this desolate place — strolled causally along the wall, discussing whether it could be defended by anything less than a full army.

"Deception," said Balan. "That's the most you can accomplish. Deception." He gestured up and down the length of the wall. "I would station a man — very visibly — every five or six hundred feet. Let the

Picts or any other invaders speculate as to how many men remain out of sight behind these walls. At night light fires in the same locations. A line of fires seen from a distance might discourage an army with the intention of moving south. At the very least, it will give them pause."

Balan's expression turned serious. He motioned for Arthur to look behind him. There on the north side of the wall were three approaching horsemen. They were Picts.

32) The Traitor

Theil was still asleep. Morcant called his name once, and when Theil did not respond, he shook his shoulder. Theil slowly opened his eyes. "The abbot has finally arrived."

The wait for the abbot had been a long one, and Theil hoped the information the abbot had would be worth the delay and the discomfort. The crew took to their oars and pulled the ship toward land. Theil squinted against the morning sun to search the shore for the abbot. He was standing a few dozen feet from the water, and behind him only partially concealed by a tree was his horse, a shield hanging from its saddle, which indicated that the abbot was, in fact, a warrior, perhaps even a knight.

The ship came to a halt a distance from the shore. Morcant stuck his oar straight down into the water and pronounced that it was less than two feet deep. Theil climbed overboard and made his way toward land. He stepped into a hole, sank waist deep and found his way back to shallower water. He reached the shore and let out a few curses. The water was cold; the air was chilly; and it felt miserable to be wet up to his rib cage.

As he approached the man waiting for him, the abbot pulled his hood farther down over his face so that he could not be recognized, not that Theil could recognize any Britain other than the warlord Arthur and the beautiful young woman who seemed so taken with him.

"I have both news and a plan." The abbot pointed to Theil. "I take a great risk in doing all this. And it is important that you make Vollo appreciate all that I have done and continue to do for him."

"Understood." Theil's first thought was that despite whatever contributions the abbot had made, Vollo would never fully trust an ally who turned traitor to his own people. Vollo would have no respect for the man; neither did Theil. Then, he remembered that he had tried to kill his own battle leader and was now a spy against him in the service of the king. What would the abbot have called him?

"The important information I have for Lord Vollo is that I've seen to it that this Arthur is no longer a threat. He has extraordinary battle skills. But that wasn't my main concern. He's an excellent battle strategist and leader of men. He might have grown to be very powerful."

"You killed him?"

"No, but he is disgraced and exiled and is no longer a concern."

This seemed too easily done, and Vollo would be sure to question Theil about it. "How was this accomplished?"

"There was a woman." Theil immediately knew the woman he meant, the one that so fascinated Theil, himself. "She was promised to the king. Arthur took her and needed only to be exposed."

The abbot reached into his tunic and withdrew a map. He motioned Theil closer and pointed out where along the coast Vollo's forces should land and how they should proceed after their landing.

Theil listened carefully to the plan and thought it a good one. As he turned to leave and was considering how best to keep the map dry as he returned to the ship, the abbot shouted after him, "Remember I need you to explain all this in accurate detail."

The man in the monk's robe watched as Theil waded back to ship and was helped up and over the side. The Gauls again took to their oars, and the vessel moved back to sea.

The abbot pulled off his monk's robe. Bryso returned to his horse and stored the robe behind his saddle.

33) A Warning

The three Pict riders stopped a short distance from the wall and shouted up to Arthur and Balan, who were looking down at them. "We are sent by King Aingus with an important message for his brother, King Kaye. We seek safe passage to Valphain Castle in order that we are able to convey that message."

Balan shouted down to them. "Tell us the message. We will convey it for you, and you won't have to concern yourself about safe passage."

"The message is from king to king, and I am instructed to deliver it to King Kaye's ears only."

Balan and Arthur stepped back from the edge of the wall to confer.

"Most unusual," said Balan.

Arthur wrapped his hand around the handle of the sword in his scabbard. "Unusual that a party of Picts comes claiming friendship or that they already know about King Kaye?"

"Both. I hadn't heard about Kaye until you told me. How did the Picts know?"

"If this is a trick of some kind, it depends on deceiving Kaye." Arthur frowned. "I worry that might not be too difficult a task."

"Yes, of course, Kaye is only a novice king," said Balan thoughtfully. "But he has advisors, hasn't he? Merlin is not so easy to deceive."

"He has Merlin and also Bryso. But Kaye is easily influenced and might listen to anyone, including Uriens' wife, Maeve." Arthur moved closer to the edge of the wall and again looked down at the three riders, who were awaiting a response. "I suppose there is no way of knowing whether their mission is genuine or a trick unless we take them to Kaye."

Balan seemed unconcerned about escorting them to Valphain Castle. "No, no other way. We will have to play this out — carefully."

Balan told the three Picts to drop their weapons to the ground, and they would be allowed to pass through the gate.

"We will have our weapons returned?"

"Of course," said Balan, "if your mission is as you describe it."

It was decided that Balan's men would escort the unarmed Picts to Kaye while Balan rode to his castle and returned here with a few dozen of his own warriors to shore up their defense in case the Picts planned an attack. Arthur would remain at Hadrian's Wall, and as soon as the others left, he stationed his pathetic army of less than a dozen men at six hundred-foot intervals along the wall and instructed them to remain visible from the north. The men took firewood with them to light fires at sunset, fires large enough for the Picts to see at a distance.

Once they were in position, Arthur mounted Snow Storm and rode north toward Pictland looking for any sign of an advancing army.

Kaye was walking in the courtyard with Maeve when a sentry rushed up to him with the news that three Pictish emissaries were at the castle gate with a message from King Aingus. "Picts here!" Kaye turned from the sentry to Maeve. "What could the message be?"

"Don't be concerned," said Maeve. "They probably bring greetings to the new king."

Kaye shook his head. "Unlikely, not from what Merlin told me about the Picts. And where is Merlin?"

This question he addressed to the sentry, but Maeve answered. "I haven't seen him in days, and we're well rid of him for a while."

"And Ector and Uriens? Where are they?"

Again Maeve answered. "You know full well, Kaye, that they are off seeking an alliance with Dumure."

"Find Bryso and Prywycke," he told the sentry. "Bring them to the great hall. Bring the Picts there as well. But not immediately. I need to prepare for them."

The great hall was perfectly arranged when the Pictish delegation was finally admitted. Kaye, in crown and white tunic, sat in his makeshift throne before the hearth, which was lit with a small fire. Prywycke stood dutifully at his right shoulder, the usual position of a chief advisor. A half dozen armed warriors stood on either side.

Bryso had not been found.

The three Picts entered flanked by four of Balan's warriors who had escorted them from Hadrian's Wall. The Picts bowed to Kaye, and their leader stepped forward.

"I am Cinaed, and I bring you greetings and well wishes from your brother King Aingus."

Kaye nodded his acceptance of the greeting. "And on your return you will extend to my brother King Aingus my greetings and well wishes."

Cinaed bowed in acknowledgment of request. "It is a matter of the greatest urgency that has brought us here. In recent days King Aingus was visited by an emissary of the Saxon King Cergin and his warlord Vollo. The Saxons plan to invade. And soon. They aim to take Valphain Castle, itself, to make as their base."

Fear was evident in Kaye's eyes. He was momentarily speechless, and it was Prywycke who asked the obvious question. "And why would the Saxons tell this to a Pict king?"

Cinaed glanced at Prywycke but addressed his response to Kaye. "They offered King Aingus an alliance. They invited us to attack from the north to draw your army away from the coast, leaving it vulnerable to them."

"I've long been a warrior and am skeptical of any claim made by a Pict," Prywycke said. "Why do you come all this way to inform us of the Saxon plan?"

Cinaed smiled. "Pict and Brit, we are all Celts, and while we have had our skirmishes, we have not tried to conquer you, and you have not tried to conquer us. Would the same be true of the Saxons, who have already said they intend to make Valphain home?" He looked from Kaye to Prywycke and back to Kaye again. "And you don't know King Aingus as I do. He is no one's tool, nor is he a fool. No Saxon king could deceive him into throwing his men into a battle for the purpose of making it easier for a Saxon invasion fleet to land."

"I thank you for your warning," said Kaye, "and thank King Aingus as well." He looked to Prywycke. "But as my counselor has said, we British and Picts do not have a history of trust between us."

Cinaed reached into his tunic, withdrew a silver medallion and handed it to Kaye. "This bears the seal of the Saxon Vollo. It was given to King Aingus as proof the bearer was the emissary of Vollo and Cergin. King Aingus now gives it to you as proof of their visit."

Kaye took the medallion and studied it closely. Without looking up from it, he instructed several guards to take the visitors to the kitchen to be fed.

When the Picts were gone, Prywycke leaned over Kaye's shoulder to look at the medallion. "Kaye, I don't know why the Picts would give us this information."

"The medallion looks genuine." Kaye looked up at Prywycke. "I believe the Picts are telling the truth, that Vollo's representative did visit

Aingus. In any case, we have no choice but to prepare for a Saxon invasion, whether it comes or not. Don't you agree?"

"Risky to do otherwise."

One of the British warriors who had escorted the Picts returned to the great hall and bowed before Kaye. "I was instructed by Arthur to tell you that, whatever the Pict emissary had to say, the king should send warriors to strengthen the defenses at Hadrian's Wall in case the Picts are preparing an attack."

Kaye turned red with anger. "How could he reach that conclusion without even knowing what the Picts had to tell us? Does he think I have men to spare?" He grew calmer and softened his voice. "Tell Arthur I will give consideration to that request in light of what the Picts have just told us, but I may well need every available man to defend Valphain Castle and not a battered old wall in the far north."

Bryso entered the hall.

"There you are. We've been searching for you." Kaye dismissed Balan's warrior and hurriedly told Bryso what had transpired during the visit of the Pict delegation. Bryso listened carefully but said nothing. Kaye studied Bryso's face a few moments and asked for his opinion.

"I must agree with Prywycke," said Bryso. "The Picts are never to be trusted. Why would they care if British and Saxon forces would try to destroy one another? What advantage do they receive in preventing such a battle? No, we cannot leave the north undefended."

Kaye's expression became pained. "We must defend the north as well?"

"Yes," said Bryso emphatically. "What better strategy than to launch an attack from the north while having all our attention on the east? But we can't we dismiss the possibility of a Saxon invasion either. There may be some truth to what the Picts told you. My recommendation would be to begin to gather as large an army as we can and to prepare ourselves to fight on two battlefields, east and north." Kaye listened quietly and attentively. "I, myself, will gather some warriors and take responsibility for having the northeast coast scouted for Saxon vessels from this day on."

Bryso turned to Prywycke and asked if he could speak to Kaye privately. Prywycke raised his eyebrows at this request but left the room. As soon as he was gone, Bryso whispered to Kaye in the manner of a man hatching a conspiracy. "My concern is for you and for our kingdom.

You know that. And certainly the well-being of the two are intertwined. Many have said — and I ask your pardon for repeating this — that Arthur is the cause of your success. They saw Arthur win the Londinium tournament and know that he, not you, defeated the Norsemen. And they wonder why you have sent him away."

Bryso paused to let Kaye consider his words. They seemed to be draining his confidence.

"There are even those who say that Arthur would make a better king or that they only follow King Kaye because Arthur is his warlord. Will they continue to do so now that Arthur is at Hadrian's Wall?

"I have watched you these many days, Kaye, and know what you are capable of. You are equal to Arthur in some ways and superior in others. He reacts. You take measured steps. But his success has come in a public arena. Yours has not. And that is your one disadvantage. Let Arthur command a small army in the north, where no one observes him and nothing of any consequence is at stake. It is you who must win a victory here against the Saxons. Such a victory would ensure the future of your kingship and help unify the kingdom behind you."

As Bryso spoke, a faint smile appeared on Kaye's lips. His confidence had been inflamed. "Bryso, your words are greatly appreciated. We have much to do. You say you'll have the coast scouted?" Bryso nodded. "Can you also devise a battle plan, perhaps with two or three alternatives, for countering a Saxon invasion by sea?"

"As we speak I'm already considering possible alternatives."

"I am in your debt. A final request. When you leave, could you send Prywycke to me?"

Bryso left. Prywycke arrived and was instructed by the king to organize messengers to bring the news of possible Saxon and Pict invasions to Ector and Uriens and to the nobles and knights who needed to contribute fighting men to their defense. As Prywycke left, Kaye shouted after him. "And find Merlin."

Kaye went in search of Maeve, found her in her room, and told her of the warning from the Pict king. He also repeated most of what was said by Bryso.

"I've told you this before, and I think you never heed me," said Maeve. "Merlin came close to ruining you. He built up Arthur's confidence at the expense of yours. Why you should ever listen to the addled old man, I cannot understand. But despite his worse efforts, see how things have unfolded now. You are a king while Arthur was defeated by a young and head-strong woman."

34) The Saxon Fleet

They had finally arrived at their destination in Germania, and Theil was amazed to find the sea near their landing destination full of ships. Most were standard two-masted Saxon warships, with a few being twice the length of the smaller ones. Others were vessels originally used for fishing or trading, and there was even a captured Norse longboat. Theil stopped counting at fifty. Because there were no ships on the beach being repaired, as there were when Theil began his journey, he assumed the entire fleet was fully seaworthy.

His ship had to thread its way through these vessels toward the beach, past boats where men were storing supplies, checking sails, working on wooden seats and oars, and standing watch.

On land, near the castle that served as Vollo's headquarters, there were far more men engaged in a greater variety of activities. He estimated there were more than a thousand of them and perhaps as many as two thousand. There were blacksmiths sharpening swords and spears, archers and spearmen engaged in target shooting and throwing drills, and men sparring with swords and battleaxes, while others watched and cheered them on. Men were chopping and stacking wood, mending tunics and boots, and inventorying supplies and weapons. And in a dozen locations around the encampment cooks stirred large caldrons of stew that sat over open fires.

The warlord had been busy.

Theil, his belongings in a sack hung over his shoulder, was one of the first to climb out of the vessel as it reached shore. He had gotten only a few dozen feet towards the castle when he encountered the man he least wanted to see, Horald, the emissary of King Cergin. Horald expected Theil to stop to speak to him, but Theil walked past him and continued toward the castle.

"Wait, I want to speak to you." Horald hurried to catch up with Theil, who walked at a fast pace. "Have you forgotten who I am?"

Theil continued walking, forcing Horald to keep up with him. "Your presence raises suspicion and risk. Vollo will have his report before you have yours."

"I command that you stop." Horald was indignant.

"Command all you wish." Theil was indifferent to him. "Vollo has his report first." He turned toward Horald. "Many days at sea causes a man to crave a hot meal. Be at a cook's caldron later, and you shall have your report." Theil continued on, leaving Horald behind.

When he reached the castle, Theil found the entrance guarded by two warriors, one armed with a sword, the other with a mace. They blocked his passage. "Lord Vollo awaits my report."

The man with the mace was unimpressed. "Lord Vollo wants no visitors until after the midday meal."

"Tell him Theil has returned."

But the man refused, such was Vollo's power of intimidation. Theil had no choice but to find a place to sit and wait. He grew both impatient and hungry, and it felt to him as though much of the day had passed when he heard footsteps approaching from inside the castle. He turned to see Vollo accompanied by two more guards in the castle doorway. Theil stood to greet him.

"You are here!" Vollo was annoyed at what appeared to be Theil's laxity. "Why haven't you reported to me sooner?"

Theil gestured toward the two guards, and the one with the mace said hesitantly, "Lord Vollo, you said no visitors until. . ."

"Fool. Isn't there a man here who can think?" The guard lowered his eyes as the warlord glared at him. Vollo turned toward Theil. "You have more sense than any ten of these others. Come." He motioned toward the castle's interior. "I'm eager to hear what you have to tell me."

Vollo led him inside to the great hall. He sat behind a large table and motioned for Theil to sit opposite him. "Well?" was all he said.

"The British have a new and unproven king named Kaye. Their best warlord is banished — the work of the abbot. He wants to be certain you know that. And King Aingus agrees to an alliance."

Vollo smiled. "All good news"

Theil withdrew the map the abbot had given him and turned it so that it faced Vollo. "The abbot has also devised a battle plan that is well thought out." Leaning closer to the table, he explained the abbot's plan and pointed out the relevant locations on the map.

Vollo sat for a few moments thinking over all he had heard and studying the map. He finally slammed his hand down on the table and smiled. "This plan and what you have told me about the situation in Britain give us substantial advantages." Theil was relieved that Vollo was pleased. "Theil, you have always been the one man I could rely upon, and you've done well on this mission as you have on others. You'll be my second-in-command of the invasion force."

This was not news that Theil welcomed. Continued proximity to the warlord was not something he desired, nor was being part of the invasion force. His best hope had been to become lost among the thousands of soldiers Vollo had assembled. Such was not to be the case.

"As you have doubtlessly seen, Theil, preparations have proceeded here at a fast pace. I knew you would bring me good news, but this is even better than I expected. There now is no possible reason for delay. First, I must send word to King Aingus so he will put his Pictish army in the field. Take some rest, Theil. I will need you at your best."

Theil left the castle. Having become excessively cautious, he looked back to be certain that neither Vollo nor any of his guards was following him, and only then did he seek out Horald, who had been waiting impatiently for him. Before the annoyed Horald could say a word, Theil spoke. "It is Vollo's guards who caused the delay." Theil approached a cook, asked for and was given a bowl of stew. He found a place to sit and eat a distance from the other men. Horald sat next to him.

"Things have here changed greatly." Theil ate a spoonful of hot stew.

"King Cergin has given Vollo what he requested," said Horald. "Vollo has grown too powerful. He has promised these men the wealth of the kingdom of Britain, and the story of his return from the dead is told throughout Germania. Men flock to him." Horald gestured to the encampment to prove his point. "For Cergin it became less dangerous to support Vollo than to oppose him."

That comment caused Theil to stop eating while he considered how Cergin might finally decide to deal with Vollo. "This much is certain, Horald. Britain is ripe for the taking, and Vollo has a good plan and several advantages." He gave the king's emissary the same report he gave Vollo.

Horald was not as certain of the invasion's success as Vollo was and raised an objection. "Too much depends on this traitor, this abbot."

"True, but Vollo trusts no one. There must be a contingency plan of one sort or another."

"Perhaps, the great Vollo will undo himself." Horald moved closer to Theil and whispered in a barely audible voice, "If he gets that far, if he actually passes through the gates of Valphain Castle, your instructions are to finish him." Stew spilled out of the spoon half raised to Theil's mouth back into the bowl as he looked at Horald's expression to be certain he was serious. He was. The king had invested in the success of his warlord's plan and would reward that success with a death sentence. Theil did not understand why this task had fallen to him. As difficult as killing Vollo might have been before, the warlord was now surrounded by guards.

"One soldier can only do so much, can only arouse so much suspicion."

"There is no one else." Horald smiled. "Vollo seems to trust you. And no one else."

Theil hoped for at least a short rest, that the invasion might be delayed, but that afternoon he saw the first piece of the invasion plan put into motion when the crew of the first ship to depart arrived on the beach. They looked British but were Saxons in British clothing that Vollo had collected on his prior raids. They boarded their ship, a trading vessel, raised their sails and sailed off for the open sea. Dressed as they were and occupying that particular vessel, they could come ashore in Britain without anyone suspecting who they were. Theil assumed their task was to prepare for the arrival of the others, as well as to send information back to Vollo that all in Britain was as the abbot had said.

It was not until three days later that the pace of activity in the encampment increased and became more structured. Supplies were taken from the storage areas and arranged on the beach. One by one the vessels started pulling into shore to receive their allotments of food, spare weapons, and other material. The work of provisioning the vessels continued until nightfall and resumed the next morning. On the following day crews were assigned to each vessel, and after Vollo, with Theil as his aide, took command of one of the large war ships, the fleet left Germania.

The first ship to leave Germania slowly moved along the British shoreline. Guided by Morcant, who was familiar with coast of Britain, they searched for the beach outlined on a map Vollo had given them. They stopped before the entrance to a bay that was nearly a perfect half circle and argued over whether the rock formation on the beach matched the one on the map. Finally, they decided it did not and continued their voyage south.

The next bay they reached was much closer in appearance to the drawing they had. It had four large rock formations, but their size and location were not a precise match with the map. After another discussion, it was decided to land a small shore party.

Four men with shovels went over the side to dig behind two of the larger rocks. The first crew dug up nothing but sand; the second found what they were seeking, a cache of weapons, armor, food stuffs, and other items buried from an earlier raid on a British village. The remainder of the crew now came ashore and loaded the unearthed stores onto the ship. When they finished, they set off for the location where they would establish their base.

The ship traveled a few more leagues south until it reached their designated landing place. The vessel put onto the beach. A handful of men dressed in British armor and armed with British weapons were the first ashore. While two stood guard on the beach, the others disappeared into a dense forest. Eventually they found a small clearing, where they began to establish a base that would be well hidden from both the beach and the north-south path that traversed the woods. The others back at their vessel began ferrying their supplies from the ship to their camp, and when the vessel was fully unloaded, they put out to sea again to find another cache of buried supplies and to meet with a man who would be dressed in a monk's robe.

35) Lady in the Mist

As he had the last several days, Arthur rode alone north of Hadrian's Wall searching for signs of a Pictish army. He had come to enjoy these rides: the solitude and the stark beauty of the open landscape that was so different from the thick forests of Britain. He was no longer constantly berating himself about his indiscretions with Brenna and had become more accustomed to his new life — during the days at least.

But his nights in the abandoned tower remained cold and lonely, passing slowly and without joy.

On these rides he never went so far north that he could not return to the tower before sunset. On this day, however, he was riding farther into Pictland than he had before despite the overcast sky and air that was heavy with moisture. There was a lake in the distance, and he decided to reach its shore. The lake was long and narrow, stretching from the southeast to the northwest. Its water was calm, much calmer than the sea, and a mist hung in the air just above its surface. At the lake's far west end was a line of mountains, their peaks hidden in fog. He would have liked to have ridden closer to the mountains for a better look, but he thought an invading Pictish army was more likely to come from the opposite direction, from the eastern end of the lake. So, he turned Snow Storm in that direction as the mist started to move inland from the lake.

He had gone a fair distance and the end of the lake appeared to be within reach when the mist became a fog, and the fog quickly became so dense that he could no longer see the lake or more than a few feet before him. He turned his horse around and began to return to the tower, but now the fog was so thick he could not see the ground beneath Snow Storm's hooves.

Snow Storm's head and shoulders dropped. Arthur was thrown forward in his saddle. The horse slid down a slope and splashed into shallow water. Snow Storm reared up and neighed. Arthur patted the horse's neck and spoke softly to him. There must have been a bend in the lake that he had forgotten, and they rode straight into it. Arthur calmed the horse and turned him back toward the shore. Snow Storm had difficulty getting a firm footing on the muddy incline but managed to climb back up onto land.

He thought it fortunate that his mount had not broken a leg. It was too risky to proceed farther, and he decided to rest his horse and himself until the fog lifted or at least thinned sufficiently for them to see where they were going.

He unsaddled Snow Storm and laid down on the ground, his head propped up on the saddle. His intention was to relax and stretch his legs after riding all day, but having slept so little for days on end, he gradually slipped into sleep.

Arthur sensed a presence. He opened his eyes but saw nothing. Still he felt the presence and was able to sense its direction. He sat up and looked toward the lake. There was a woman dressed all in white coming toward him out of the fog. She was young and beautiful, but her face was expressionless and her eyes blank. No, he was wrong. He could see now that her unusual appearance was not because she was moving through the fog. She was made of mist. He could see through her body in places where the mist was thin. The breeze kept her entire body in flux.

Despite eyes that never moved or seemed to focus, she pointed to him and beckoned him to come to her. Arthur felt his body involuntarily stand up and move toward her. The mist that formed her body continued to move and swirl; only the eyes remained fixed. He approached to within a few of her, and she held out her empty hands, one above the other. Somehow he knew to watch her hands, and in them the mist began to form a sword, which, like the woman, was hollow and in flux. Her eyes never moved, never looked at him, as she extended the sword toward him. In her outstretched hands the sword slowly began to solidify, the hilt turning red, the blade silver.

She held it out waiting for him to take it. He hesitated and finally reached out for the sword.

The feel of his hand closing forcefully upon itself woke him. There was no sword, no lady standing before him made of white mist. He was still lying with his head on a saddle, his horse tethered only a few feet away. He was breathing unevenly, his body quivering slightly, such was the impact this vision had on him. It was dream, yes, but not one to be easily dismissed. There were other worlds, Merlin had told him, and the beings in those worlds sometimes walked in dreams. The wizard once told him of a magical creature called the Lady of the Lake. He was near a lake. The woman had been inside the mist if not made of it. He would have to ask Merlin if he had dreamed of the Lady of the Lake.

Arthur heard voices. His imagination, he thought at first. But the voices were real. The sounds were carrying across the lake in the cold air.

He got up and walked to the water's edge. The dense fog had become a mist once again, and there was still some light in the sky. Across the lake he saw dozens and dozens of campfires. It could be nothing other than a Pictish army campaigning. How long they had been there and how he had not heard them before, he did not know. The important thing was that they had not seen him.

A light flashed into Arthur's eyes. A ray from the setting sun had lit something in the water just off shore. It was a sword! And like Caliburn in the stone, it was point down in the water with its hilt and the upper half its blade visible above the water.

Without taking his eyes from the sword, he carefully moved down the embankment and into the water. He walked out to where the lake was almost knee deep, grabbed the sword by its red hilt and pulled it out of the lake bed. Like the sword in the stone, he could feel energy in it. It felt alive

Arthur rode through the night. He had put the sword from the lake in his scabbard and tied his old sword to the rear of his saddle. Frequently, he would feel the handle of the new sword to be certain it was real. The feeling of energy was gone, but this sword had a distinctive enough handle that he could not confuse it with any other.

At dawn, Arthur paused to give Snow Storm a rest. He withdrew the sword and examined it in the light. A word had been etched into the cross piece of the hilt. He could make it out now. Excalibur. He would have to ask Merlin what the word meant.

He arrived back at the tower in late morning. As he approached, he was delighted to see several dozen guards visible along the wall. Undoubtedly these were Balan's men added to his own. One of the guards atop the wall announced Arthur's arrival, and the main gate swung open. Balan was there to greet him.

They had much information to exchange. Arthur spoke about the Pictish encampment, hundreds and hundreds of warriors strong judging by the number of fires. Balan told him of the three Pictish emissaries, the nature of their mission to warn Kaye of the Saxon invasion, and Kaye's intention to send a small force to shore up the defense here.

"The Picts arrived this morning from Valphain expecting to continue on to King Aingus to report on the success of their deception," Balan said. "But because you did not return last evening, I decided to detain them here. It's fortunate that I did, now that we know they have an army in the field."

Their three Pictish guests were now captives, and Balan sent some men who were experienced in dealing with prisoners to learn what they could about the Picts plans, the size and nature of their force, and anything about Aingus that might help in outmaneuvering him. By one means or another, Balan assured Arthur, they would obtain whatever useful information there was to be had from the three Picts.

Arthur now had a second concern — the Saxons. The obvious assumption was that the Saxon invasion Kaye had been warned about was a Pictish lie to divert Kaye's forces from the north to the east. But if there was one thing Merlin had taught Arthur, it was to challenge the obvious. The less apparent possibility was that the Saxon invasion plans were real, that the Picts and Saxons had agreed on a coordinated attack, but that the Picts had warned Kaye so that the British and Saxon armies would face each other first.

That meant the defense of the kingdom might rest primarily in Kaye's hands.

The hard truth was that Kaye had in a remarkably short time learned to present himself as king, but in reality he was a leader with no experience and no natural gift for strategic military planning. If Kaye's shortcomings led to part of Britain falling to the Saxons, it would be Arthur's fault because he had allowed his weak older brother to lay claim to Caliburn.

Even that claim Kaye had done passively. He never once said he pulled the sword from the stone; he simply never admitted that he had not.

Balan was about to leave him to check on their prisoners when Arthur called him back. "Balan, I haven't been completely truthful with you in my concerns about the defense against the Saxon invasion." Balan listened attentively. "I am a good strategist; Kaye is not. He has always seen Merlin as my mentor, not his and might not heed the wizard's advice. Uriens has grown somewhat addled with age, and although Bryso is a great warrior, I know nothing of his leadership in battle. I worry that Kaye will have too little help to plan an adequate defense."

"If you want to return to Valphain Castle, Arthur, I'll command things here."

"There are too few of us here as it is. No, I am thinking that we need to end the Pictish threat here as quickly as possible so that all effort can be focused on the Saxons. Or need at least to delay them. The Picts can't possibly expect us to take the offensive."

"Offensive?" Balan shook his head in disbelief. "Surely you mean after Kaye's reinforcements arrive."

"No, and I know that sounds mad. But you have already shown, Balan, how we can disrupt them and make them reconsider their invasion."

"How?"

"By deception. By stationing our few men along long stretches of the wall you concealed our number." Arthur's enthusiasm for his plan was growing. "By attacking at night we could again conceal our number. A handful of our horsemen could ride into the Pictish camp tonight and inflict whatever damage we could while the enemy slept. They would be surprised and confused in the dark and are certain to overestimate the size of our total force. They would be forced to reevaluate whether we would be an easy target."

Balan, appearing skeptical, mulled over the idea. "It might have some effect, true, but only a temporary one. But it could delay them until Kaye's men arrive — if those men arrive soon. The trouble is your idea is very likely suicidal."

"Not necessarily, not if we strike quickly and leave quickly, not if we ride out before they can mount their own horses." Arthur smiled. "And consider this: we have the clothing, armor, weapons, and horses of the three prisoners. We could ride to the very center of their encampment and raise no suspicion until we began to use our weapons."

"True." Balan raised his eyebrows. "But, as I said, the difficulty will be riding back out again."

"I assure you, Balan, it is not my intention to make a pointless self-sacrifice, but I see a way to deal a major blow to the Picts and am willing to take a risk to accomplish it. There are risks worth taking, Balan, and things worse than death."

Later that day, as Balan promised, his men did find some useful information that caused Arthur to modify his plan. Aingus was an absolute tyrant, and there was no strong second-in-command. The Pictish army numbered about three hundred and fifty strong, the vast majority on foot. The men camped out in the open except for Aingus, himself, who slept in a white tent at the center of the camp. Kill Aingus, and it would likely take the Picts days or longer to reorganize.

Arthur wanted to move quickly. He, Balan, and one of Balan's best warriors dressed in the clothing and armor of the three Pictish prisoners. These disguises were ill-fitting, but that was unlikely to be noticed in the dark. Riding the Picts' horses, the three left that afternoon for the enemy encampment. A dozen other mounted warriors rode with them.

Fate provided them with assistance that evening in the form of a mist that was followed by a rain storm. By the time they reached the lake where Arthur saw the Pictish encampment, the rain came down in such volume that visibility was only a few dozen feet and the rain drops descended with such force they could shut a man's eyelids. The rain also doused the Pictish campfires, and their side of the lake was in darkness. Arthur and his party rode around the eastern end of the lake and to the north shore. When they were within a thousand feet of the enemy camp, all the riders but Arthur stopped.

He rode ahead into the enemy camp.

36) Kaye's Gamble

Kaye and Maeve climbed to the top of the castle wall to watch the army arriving behind Ector and Uriens. The troops stretched down the approach to the castle and well into the forest. Merlin was also with them.

"Those are more warriors than I knew existed in the whole of Britain," said Kaye, smiling broadly. "I must admit I've been worried about the Saxons since learning of their invasion plan."

"You needn't tell me. I've seen it in your face and the manner in which you've been pacing in the great hall."

Warriors continued to file out of the woods. "There was good reason to be concerned — until now."

The new soldiers began to set up camp outside the castle walls, and as they were settling in Kaye convened a war council that met in the great hall. His most trusted advisors — Ector, Uriens, and Prywycke — were there: all but Bryso, who was away patrolling the coast. Despite the advice of Maeve, he included Merlin in the group.

It was the wizard who was first to speak. "Our first task is to decide how best to divide our forces to meet attacks from two enemies, each coming from a different direction."

Kaye stared at Merlin. "Yes, of course, that is exactly what I was about to say."

"Well then, get on with it."

Kaye continued to stare at Merlin, opening his mouth as if to speak but said nothing. He took a breath and said, "Defending this castle is most important, are we all agreed? I can dispatch a hundred men, perhaps two hundred, to Hadrian's Wall. The Picts would have to fight a long campaign south to threaten us here."

"There are many villages between here and the wall," said Merlin. "Would you concede them? Do not forget this castle is near impregnable. Half the men we have here now would be adequate to defend it. Why not use our forces in the most effective manner to protect as many as possible?"

"No, I will not leave Valphain poorly defended." He looked to Uriens for approval and received it. "We can always send more men north."

"You can always bring more men back from the north."

"May I say something?" They all turned toward Ector. "Without knowing the size of either opposing army, we, all of us, are only guessing."

Merlin pointed a finger at Kaye. "Let us agree to an initial division of forces with the understanding that it can be modified later as needed."

Kaye looked to Uriens, then Ector and finally to Prywycke, and saw no objections. "Agreed. But the initial division will be as I have said, a few hundred men to the north."

"The next issue is who will command here," said Merlin.

Kaye did not hesitate to answer. "Bryso."

Merlin rose and slowly walked around the chairs of the other four. "If your concern, Kaye, is primarily with the Saxons and defending this castle, shouldn't you have the best battle leader here?"

"Oh no!" Kaye turned his head to follow Merlin's movement. "I won't bring Arthur here. He has won only one battle, the one against a handful of Norsemen." He looked to Uriens. "Isn't that true? Whereas Bryso has been in many battles. And, Merlin, there is the matter of our agreement. We agreed, you and I, that I would be lenient on Arthur if he left and stayed away — at least for more than the score of days he has been gone."

No one, not even Prywycke, argued in favor of Arthur's return. An offense was an offense, a punishment a punishment. Merlin let them all have their say before speaking again. "You all know that I sometimes glimpse the future."

Kaye had grown agitated. "So you claim." It was the most daring remark he had ever made to Merlin.

The wizard was taken aback by Kaye's insolence but only momentarily. "Do you think I would have spent all these years grooming Arthur if I did not know that he was vital to our future?"

Kaye gave an ironic laugh. "Where is he now and where I am?"

"By happenstance. An accidental king." Uriens was confused by Merlin's remark and turned for clarification to Ector, who looked away.

Kaye stood up to stare Merlin level in the eyes. "Arthur will remain where he is. I am the king, and that is my final word."

"Be wary of my final word. I will not continue to argue with you, but instead will accompany the warriors going to Hadrian's Wall and bring back Arthur."

Kaye flushed red. "I forbid it."

"Kings have no authority over wizards." Merlin turned and walked toward the courtyard.

Kaye watched him leaving, hurried after him and caught up to him before he exited the great hall. "I am king, Merlin. I will not have you speak to me like that."

Merlin turned back, gave Kaye his most intense stare, causing Kaye to retreat a step, and whispered so that only Kaye could hear. "You would no longer be king if everyone knew who really pulled the sword from the stone." He stuck a finger in Kaye's face. "Give me more trouble, and you will learn why wizards can ignore kings." Merlin softened his tone. "I leave you with almost two thousand men and thick castle walls, Kaye. You should be able to hold on to Valphain Castle for the few days I will be gone." Merlin wrapped his cloak around his shoulders, turned, and left the tower.

The next morning two hundred men, including only a few dozen horsemen, left Valphain Castle for Hadrian's Wall. Bryso, returning to the castle on horseback, was close enough to Valphain to see this group exit through the main gate and smiled when he saw that Merlin was leading the group.

Bryso waited until Merlin and his troop disappeared into the forest. He rode into the castle courtyard, recruited a youth to stable his horse, and went straight to see Kaye, who stood before the hearth in the great hall, staring into the flames. Bryso feigned a sense of urgency as he approached the king. "I have news. A Saxon fleet has been sighted along the northern coast."

Kaye turned to face him. He first raised his eyebrows in surprise and quickly lowered them into a frown. "A large fleet?"

"Perhaps a dozen vessels were seen. There are most likely more." Bryso motioned toward the courtyard. "I see our ranks have swollen. We are ready, then, to take the offensive." Kaye was surprised by that comment. "You look confused."

"I am. I thought the plan was to defend the castle."

"I never suggested that we take a siege. I said you must win a victory. Being defensive, taking a siege may be easy — at first. After a time, a castle becomes a dungeon. I know. I have been trapped in more than one siege. And a castle can become worse than a dungeon when the food supplies dwindle and are finally gone. Even now, how much additional food is needed to feed this new army?"

Kaye did not know.

"Understand that defending the castle is one strategy," said Bryso, "but a strategy that worsens with time. If there is a chance to attack, to surprise the enemy, defeat him quickly, that is a better strategy."

Kate bit his lips. "Merlin's last words to me concerned the safety of these walls."

"Merlin! Is it he who convinces you to sit and take a siege? Haven't you, yourself, said that Merlin advances Arthur at your expense?"

"I will not be convinced of anything by Merlin."

Although there was no one within earshot, Bryso looked from side to side, leaned closer to Kaye and began to whisper. "We have more than enough time to attack the Saxon landing, surprise them and cut them down on the beach as they leave their vessels. If they suffer enough losses in coming ashore, they may decide to return to Germania. At the very least, we would weaken their forces, perhaps enough to render a siege of this castle ineffective.

"This is how it would unfold. When we attack, many, if not most, of the Saxons would still shipboard and unable to fight. Others would be caught climbing out of their vessels, their arms loaded with supplies instead of weapons. They would suddenly be surrounded by our warriors swooping in on horseback and driving them back into the sea.

"And there is always the option that we could fall back to Valphain if necessary."

Kaye walked to a chair and sat down. Bryso stood over him waiting for a response. "We can always fall back?" asked Kaye, without looking up.

"Yes, we can always fall back and be in the same situation we would be in had we decided to take a siege from the start."

"I must admit, Bryso, I hadn't considered how it would be to suffer through a long siege. I don't relish the idea of being trapped inside this castle by a hostile army and having to look out at it every day, withstanding attack after attack. And Maeve only recently mentioned the difficulty in feeding this large army even without siege conditions."

"If a siege lasted long enough, Kaye, we would be forced to leave the castle, take the offensive and battle the Saxons in the open. Or worse still, we would have to assault the temporary fortifications the Saxons are certain to erect outside the castle. At that point, what good are these castle walls to us?"

"All this makes sense. Still I am hesitant to take such a step."

"And do you believe you are not making a decision by staying here? Once the Saxons are ashore, you'll lose this option."

Kaye looked up at Bryso. "But how would we know where they plan to land? And when?"

"If I were in command of the Saxons, I would pick a beach close to the castle, secluded and large enough to accommodate my ships and men. And I know exactly such a place."

Kaye was puzzled by Bryso's certainty. "But they could land elsewhere, couldn't they?"

"Of course, they could, but they are sailing within sight of the shore. That's how my scouts were able to spot them. We should be able to follow their progress. We can attack them on whatever beach they land, and if necessary, we could always abandon the plan and return to the castle. But if we wish to attack them on the beach, we must move quickly."

"How quickly?

"Now."

That afternoon they left in search of the enemy. Kaye and Bryso rode in the lead of several dozen horsemen who had assembled in the courtyard, leaving behind a small force to defend the castle. Cheering their exit were women, children, and men too old or feeble to fight. The spectators stood waving on the castle walls and watching from the tower windows. Among them were Maeve, who had encouraged Kaye to pursue this plan of attack, and Brenna, who had complained to her father that all this was transpiring without Arthur's or Merlin's knowledge and approval.

As they exited through the castle's main gate, more horsemen fell into line behind them, and after the horsemen came hundreds of foot soldiers, both spearmen and archers. They moved down the hill from Valphain, turned inland and continued north into the forest.

The woods gradually became denser until they traveled a forest path that could accommodate only two riders abreast and in places only one. Their army stretching out in a long narrow file behind them, Bryso continued to review his strategy with Kaye, whose confidence grew from Bryso's certainty that their plan was flawless.

They continued to ride, and the nature of the forest changed little. The trees were so tightly packed in places that a horse could barely squeeze between them. In some cases, the trees were surrounded by bushes or linked together by vines. The narrow forest path was the only way to travel at even a moderate pace. Eventually the forest began to thin, and that is when Bryso told Kaye that they were nearing their destination. A shout from Bryso brought the long column to halt as they reached the edge of the woods and could see the semicircular beach a little more than a thousand feet away.

The beach was exactly as Bryso described, secluded and within a day's march of Valphain; there was enough space to land dozens of vessels. But the horizon was clear; not a ship or a sail was in sight.

Bryso studied Kaye's pained expression and smiled. "It's common before a battle, any battle but especially the first, to be both eager and anxious."

"I must admit, I was relieved to see that the sea wasn't full of Saxon ships. But it's also true that a long wait would be no better. It would be much like withstanding siege."

"I don't anticipate we'll have to wait long." Bryso swept his arm around the perimeter of the beach. "This is my thinking. We surround the beach with men. Horsemen and archers alternating in the front line, well hidden in the woods. Spearmen behind them. We need to allow enough of the Saxons to reach the beach from their boats, or we'll simply drive them off undiminished."

"When you say enough, how many Saxons will be allowed to disembark? We certainly don't want to risk having to face the whole Saxon force on this beach."

"Several hundred, at least. Maybe more. It depends on how many men they have. The attack would begin with a volley from our archers against the Saxons on the beach. Our horsemen would then ride in from all directions. They would be supported by about half our spearmen, the other half holding a defensive line at the edge of the wood." Bryso pointed to the water. "The archers would then turn their attention to the vessels close enough to shore that an arrow strike would fell their crewmen."

While Kaye kept watch on the horizon, the remaining daylight was spent positioning their forces around the beach in the manner Bryso had described. When they were finished, they had a meal and settled in for their watch. The sun set, and still the sea was clear. Their entire force remained on alert into the evening, but as it grew late, the men began to sleep in shifts. Kaye, who had grown accustomed to the comforts of the castle, rested uneasily on the ground and remained awake during the first watch until finally falling asleep.

Kaye had slept only a short time when was awakened by Bryso, who was kneeling beside him. "They are here."

Kaye quickly got to his feet and was led by Bryso to the edge of the beach. Out at sea he could see the light from torches burning aboard ships. There were dozens and dozens of fires, dozens and dozens of vessels. "You said a dozen, Bryso, a dozen vessels had been spotted. That would seem a far larger Saxon force than we anticipated.

"I said more than a dozen ships. And I said there could be more than that. And there are." Bryso's tone betrayed no lack of confidence. "Suppose we were trapping a snake. The snake sticks its head out of his hole in the ground, and we cut it off." He made a chopping motion with his right hand. "How much of the snake remains in the hole doesn't matter. That's exactly what we'll do. Sever the head of the Saxon snake."

All the sleeping British troops were awakened and instructed to take their positions surrounding the beach. Kaye remained by Bryso, his eyes fixed on the dozens of fires at sea. "Bryso, why do they not come ashore? I would think they would want the cover of darkness."

"I would think the same unless they want to rest before coming ashore or are concerned about the nature of the tides or striking rocks in the darkness."

"Of course, that's their reasoning. They want a clear path to the beach."

Their watch continued deep into the night. The Saxons vessels never moved.

37) Raid on the Pict Camp

Dressed as a Pictish warrior, atop a Pictish horse, Arthur rode alone in the night toward the enemy camp. As far as he could see ahead of him in all directions, Picts lay on the ground, indistinct forms sleeping under their blankets while the rain poured down with such volume and force that a campfire was not possible. It was as if he were approaching a sleeping dragon that at any moment could rise up showing its true form and devour him.

Never had his mind been so alert, never his body so tense for action, and when the thought of the impossible nature of this task entered his mind, he banished it. There was no turning back. He could not disappoint Balan, even though Balan tried to persuade Arthur not to attempt this mission.

The Pictish warriors slept on the ground in the mud, covered in blankets, not a single head extending out and exposed to the weather. They slept singly or in groups of two, three, or more. At least, that is how Arthur saw them because he had to find enough space between them to ride his horse. One bad step and he could be exposed despite the Pictish armor he was wearing.

He had not anticipated that they would be grouped so closely together as to make passage between them this difficult. His focus had to remain directly in front of his horse's front hooves, and he could scarcely look up or to the side to see if anyone was stirring. He was entering an intricate maze in which there might be no correct path to his goal.

His goal was to find the tent of King Aingus, kill him in the hope of leaving the Picts leaderless, and without raising an alarm, ride back to Balan and the others, who waited a short distance away from the camp.

Arthur reached the first line of sleeping Picts and carefully rode between them. The clatter of the rain masked the sound of his horse. He moved to the right, where there was a path between two sleepers on one side and three on the other. That he was able to pass by without disturbing them was encouraging, but this small victory was more than outweighed by the fact that he would have to successfully perform this feat dozens of times, and failing even once could be fatal.

Even worse than being killed, he could be captured. Balan had warned him that it was far better to die fighting than to be taken prisoner by the Picts, especially if he succeeded in killing their king.

Arthur continued his slow progress, weaving right, then left, then further left. Directly ahead was a line of sleepers so close together that there appeared to be no way to pass through them. Arthur turned to his right looking for an opening. As he slowly rode, he continued to hear Balan's warning that the way out would be far more difficult than the way in. Finally, he found a path to take him back toward the center of the camp and was heartened by the sight Aingus' white tent about two hundred feet ahead.

Arthur's horse snorted once and a second time. He instinctively reined the animal to a stop. The second snort caused one Pict a few feet away to stir under his blanket. Another nearby Pict rolled over from one side to the other, rearranging his blanket over his head. Arthur and the horse remained motionless while he waited to see if either man had been awakened. He watched them carefully, and when neither moved again, he resumed advancing toward the white tent.

Aingus's tent was just ahead, and Arthur was surprised to see an open space around it. He thought there might have been sentries, asleep if not awake, but the Picts apparently preferred having some distance between themselves and their tyrannical king.

When he was almost to the tent, he began to think about the manner of his retreat. No, concentrate on the task immediately ahead and worry about escape after. And that task required an important decision to be made. The only way he could be certain to reach Aingus was to dismount and enter the tent on foot, but his only means of escape was riding over and through the sleeping Picts and if necessary, outracing them to edge of their camp. He could not risk being caught on foot, could not risk dismounting and having to remount or having the horse wander off.

Arthur rode directly to the entrance of the king's tent, having come this far unnoticed through half the Pictish army. Instead of using his new sword, he withdrew his battle hammer from his belt, leaned over the right side of his horse and used the weapon to lift the tent flap. The cold, moist wind must have awakened Aingus. As Arthur rode inside the tent, he heard the man in the tent shouting at him. What he was saying, Arthur could not understand, but in what little light there was from a small oil lamp, he could see that the man rising from a cot was bald and large bellied, fitting Aingus's description. Arthur spurred the horse forward, lifted back his arm and delivered a hammer blow to the man's head, sending him screaming over backwards into the cot. The cot fell, dropping Aingus to the floor with the inverted cot turning over on top of him.

The oil lamp also toppled over; its flame was extinguished.

Arthur thought he delivered a fatal blow and was surprised that Aingus was able to cry out. He should dismount to be certain Aingus was dead, but the scream had probably awakened the nearest Picts. The tent was now in total darkness. Aingus's body was hidden beneath the cot. Arthur would have to climb down from his horse, remove the cot and locate Aingus in the dark. That would take too long. And if Aingus was still able to move and had the strength to resist or to grab onto Arthur's arm, he would never get out of the tent alive.

Arthur turned the horse back to the tent entrance, fumbled trying to pull back the flap with his hammer and finally got back outside into the rain. A few men were stirring, but no one was getting up or reaching for a weapon. He might have tried slowly weaving his way back out of the camp the way he entered it, but Arthur had neither the patience nor the nerve for that. He kicked his horse forward and began to shout, hoping the sleeping Picts would roll out of the way of a galloping horse and clear a path for him.

He rode over and around men who still lay on the ground and at one point had to force his horse to jump a sleeper. He had gotten several hundred feet when the commotion caused the Picts to start sitting up and turning over onto their hands and knees, and when they saw a horse bearing down on them, they scurried out of the way.

Arthur thought that he was now about half way through the camp, half way to safety.

A few of the Picts, realizing that something was wrong in the camp, were rising to their feet. They stepped out of the path of the oncoming horse but tried to grab at Arthur as he rode by. A few more had weapons in hand or were reaching for them. Arthur began swinging his hammer, right and left, felling anyone that came within striking distance. He was so busy fending off Picts that he lost sight of the end of their camp and was no longer certain he was even heading in the right direction.

A large man ran directly at Arthur's horse, waving his arms wildly and shouting. The horse reared up, almost throwing Arthur off its back. Arthur managed to stay mounted, but the man now had hold of his horse by the bridle. Arthur was surrounded. He whipped his hammer in circles over his head and down at the Picts, both right and left in a desperate attempt to hold them off, but he thought he could not possibly fight off so many men.

From the opposite direction, Balan and the other British warriors waded into the mass of Picts. Mounted, armed and armored, they were more than a match for the Picts who stood unprotected around Arthur and fought with only swords or knives and in some cases with their bare hands. The British cleared a path to Arthur and attacked the Picts who had him surrounded. They quickly freed Arthur from his trap, but now the entire Pictish camp was awake and running toward them. The British regrouped around Arthur and raced toward the edge of the Pictish camp, moving like a scythe cutting down any Pict who approached them.

Soon they were free of the camp, leaving the Picts on foot behind them. When they were a safe distance away, they stopped to rest. Remaining mounted, the rain still pouring down, they formed a circle. Arthur, who was breathing heavily, bowed to Balan and the others, thanking them for coming to his rescue.

"I never thought you would make it out alive." Balan seemed to have enjoyed their adventure.

"Neither did I," said Arthur. "During the whole ride in I could hear in my mind your warning that the escape would be impossible. On the gallop out, I had no time to think."

"And did you reach Aingus's tent?"

"Yes." Arthur was still trying to catch his breath. "I got inside and struck him a good blow. Whether he survived or not, I couldn't tell. I thought I shouldn't indulge in Pictish hospitality too much longer."

Balan laughed. "I doubt they will invite you back. But perhaps they haven't learned their lesson well enough." He looked back in the direction of the Pict camp. "I propose we wait here to see if we are followed."

They did not have a long wait. Every Pict with a horse, about fifty of them, had mounted up and was in pursuit of them. The British had spread out, concealed by both darkness and rain. They allowed the Picts to ride past them and attacked from behind. Arthur caught up to one Pict and felled him with a hammer blow to the back of the head. The shout of the first man caused the Pict ahead of him and on the left to look back at Arthur. Arthur maneuvered his horse against the Pict rider and delivered a hammer blow that the Pict caught on his shield. The Pict retaliated with a blow from a flail that Arthur deflected with his shield. Arthur swung his hammer, the Pict his flail. The flail chain wrapped around the neck of Arthur's hammer, and it was pulled from his hand. Arthur lifted his shield against the Pict with his left hand and withdrew his new sword with his right. The Pict must have thought Arthur weaponless. He raised his flail for another strike leaving his midsection exposed. Arthur delivered a sword thrust to the man's belly. As he pulled back the sword, the Pict fell from his horse.

On the initial British attack, nine Picts were killed, wounded or simply unhorsed. The Picts turned to face them, but in the rain and darkness there was no way to tell if they were facing twenty enemy riders or a hundred. The Pict ranks broke. Most retreated back toward their camp. The few who stayed to fight were quickly surrounded and finished off.

The triumphant British returned to Hadrian's Wall, and although it was the middle of the night, they had a banquet to celebrate their victory. The best banquet they could mount here was not as good as the worst they had had at Valphain Castle, but Arthur ate and drank as he had not in many days, happy to simply to be alive and to have taken a major step in what he hoped might be his redemption.

~~~

At the Pict camp, the wounded were being tended to where they lay in the mud. The dead had been carried to the back of the camp to be cremated as soon as it was dry enough. A defensive line was set up on the eastern edge of the camp, where the British had attacked, and sentries were posted on the remainder of the perimeter. The Picts were further disheartened when only a little more than half of their horsemen returned with news that they had been beaten back by a British army.

In the king's tent, two oil lamps had been lit, and four of Aingus's lieutenants stood over him. The left side of his face had been bashed in, and he lay unconscious, occasionally moaning. His men had washed and bandaged his wounds but did not know what else to do for him. When one man suggested that some mead might ease his pain, a second objected that Aingus, not being awake, would surely choke on it. A third man whispered let him choke.

~~~

The next morning, when the rain finally stopped and ground began to dry out, Merlin and the warriors from Valphain Castle arrived at Hadrian's Wall. Arthur, who went out to receive the wizard, was uncertain how his mentor would greet him, uncertain whether Merlin was still angry over the affair with Brenna and whether he had lost all faith in his pupil. But Merlin appeared more than happy to see Arthur and embraced him, which Arthur never remembered happening before.

Balan joined them and even before Merlin could tether his horse, Balan began talking excitedly about the heroic act Arthur had performed. "Young Arthur, here in the blackest night and worst rain I've ever witnessed, simply rode — rode alone, mind you — right into the Pictish camp, right past a thousand sleeping Pictish warriors."

Merlin raised his thick white eyebrows at this news. "Arthur, is this true?"

"It's true, although the number of Picts was closer to three or four hundred than a thousand."

" 'By your leave,' he says to these murderous barbarians, 'Clear a path. I'm on my way to the center of your encampment.'"

"I was dressed as a Pict and riding a Pictish horse. It was dark and raining hard."

"The lad is too modest." Balan made a waving motion with his hand. "After weaving his way through the sleeping Pictish contingent, he rode directly to the tent of King Aingus, which was at the center of the entire Pictish army."

Arthur thought Balan's version of what happened was far more heroic than it actually was. Balan did not describe — nor did he know — that Arthur considered turning back when he reached the edge of the Pictish camp or that he rode his horse ever so carefully among the sleeping Picts, fearful he would wake even one. Nor did Balan say or know that when his horse snorted twice and two Pictish warriors stirred in their sleep, Arthur remained motionless for a time, unsure of whether his heart was still beating.

"Into Aingus's very tent he goes."

Rode in, not walked in, as I should have, thought Arthur.

"Arthur wakes the sleeping King Aingus and bashes him in the skull. 'Thank you for your hospitality, your majesty,' he says, 'but I can stay no longer.'"

Merlin looked from Balan to Arthur. "Then, Aingus is dead."

Arthur lowered his eyes. This was the part of the story that concerned him. "I can't be certain. I struck him in the head, and he must have sustained an injury of some consequence although I can't say for certain it was a fatal blow."

The wizard mulled over this information. "Even if Aingus is only injured, this is a setback for the Picts. An army often reflects the courage of its leader. A leader with a bashed skull can hardly set an example for his men, can he now?"

Balan left to see to the accommodation of the newly arrived troops.

Arthur accompanied the wizard as he went to tend to his horse. "Merlin, there is something I want to ask you. I had a dream — a very vivid dream — about a lady made of mist."

Merlin, a look of great interest on his face, stopped walking and turned toward Arthur. "The Lady of the Lake. She is a water spirit and can appear in lakes, streams, and pools of water, even snow and mist as you describe."

"But she was a dream?"

"Of course, she is a dream. She lives in the world of dreams."

"She led me to this." Arthur withdrew the sword, and Merlin examined it carefully. Arthur pointed to the cross piece of its hilt. "What does this word mean?"

"Excalibur. It is the name of the sword."

"And does the name have any meaning?"

"Any meaning?" Merlin stared at Arthur for a few moments. "No, no meaning, not as yet."

Before midday, every man who had arrived from Valphain Castle that morning had heard Balan's story in one manner or another. In some versions there were as many as three thousand Picts, in others Arthur bashed his way into the camp and back out again, in still others the Picts had left for home that very night.

Later that afternoon, the Picts themselves arrived in the form of two Pictish riders who appeared in the distance and slowly approached Hadrian's Wall. Careful to stay out of arrow range, they rode east along the wall, observing sentry after sentry as far as they rode. They reversed direction and did the same in the west.

Then they headed back to their encampment.

Balan dispatched one of his men to follow them from a safe distance. The scout watched from across the lake as the Picts on the opposite shore broke camp and marched north toward their home.

38) Head of the Snake

Just before dawn the fires on the Saxon vessels began to die out one at a time. To the British hidden in the woods surrounding the beach, this did not seem unusual because the sun would be rising soon. They had spent a long and uncomfortable night, their weapons at the ready in case of movement by the Saxon fleet toward the shore. They took turns napping, sometimes finding a suitable place to stretch out; just as often the best they could do was to sit on the ground and lean their backs against a tree.

The Saxon ships were far enough offshore that in the morning light only the bare outlines of the vessels could be distinguished. There were, as the many small fires indicated the night before, a significant number of ships, four or five dozen of them, a sizeable invasion force.

Now that the sun was rising over the sea, the British were prepared for the Saxons to move toward the shore at any moment. The men limbered backs and legs that had grown stiff overnight, inspected their weapons, and ate whatever food they had handy, mostly salted meat and stale bread. They stood or knelt at their posts with the spears, swords, and bows in their hands, their eyes fixed on the enemy ships.

Kaye, who stood next to Prywycke behind a tree, looked out from between its branches at the Saxon fleet. "This waiting," said Kaye. "The strain of it must be worse than battle itself."

"Always is."

"I wish they would either attack or sail away."

"Appears your wish is granted." Prywycke pointed to the most distant Saxon vessels, which were moving farther out to sea.

"Are you certain they are pulling away?"

Several of ships turned south. "Certain."

Kaye, followed by Prywycke, went quickly in search of Bryso, who had been inspecting their battle formation. "Bryso, what are the Saxons doing? Should we be relieved or concerned?"

"It's unclear." Bryso shrugged his shoulders. "Perhaps they knew we were here."

"How? We remain well hidden even now in the daylight."

"They might have gotten a scout ashore somewhere else along the coast and spotted us. More likely, they only anchored here for the night and plan to land south of Valphain Castle, something we were unlikely to expect."

"That seems not to concern you?"

"No, whatever the reason the Saxons did not land here, we always had a contingency plan. We'll fall back to Valphain Castle, and all we have lost is a night spent in the forest instead of resting comfortably in our beds."

Bryso and Prywycke began shouting orders, calling their men out of hiding and telling them to pack up their gear. There was a substantial amount of complaining among the men for having spent a hard and mostly sleepless night out here only to have the Saxons sail away. Now they were leaving without even having a decent morning meal.

They left the beach in the same order in which they had arrived from Valphain Castle, Kaye and Bryso at the head of the column of horsemen, the foot soldiers at the rear. The army moved into the forest and onto the narrow trail that led back to Valphain. They traveled only as fast as the footmen could walk, and on this day the footmen moved slowly. They continued without taking a rest for most of the morning and traveled a good distance.

They were in a densely wooded area where they could travel no more than two abreast. Kaye heard a scream. He turned to see a spear being pulled from the side of the rider directly behind him. As the man, gushing blood, fell from his horse, two Saxons attacked the rider behind Bryso, pulling him down from his mount and stabbing him with their swords.

Bryso grabbed the reins of Kaye's horse and galloped ahead, pulling Kaye with him.

Foot soldiers leaped out from behind trees and bushes to attack the riders at the front of the British column. With two and three Saxons attacking each rider, they were able to pull the British from their horses before the riders could even draw their swords. Saxon bowmen were unleashing their arrows from the cover of the woods on other parts of the column, and the forest path was suddenly being covered with dead and dying British and dead and dying horses.

Once Bryso and Kaye rode by them, the Saxon frontline quickly placed a wooden barricade across the path blocking the British column off from their king. Stakes were hammered into the ground to secure the barricade, and it was flanked by bowmen.

Saxon warriors continued to fight on the British side of the barricade, finishing off the wounded and gathering up every loose horse. The
lead part of the British column was in confusion and disarray. They were
hampered by the woods on either side of them and by the crowding of
their own warriors behind them. There was no room to maneuver their
horses; Saxons appeared out of the forest, struck, and disappeared back
into the woods. The remainder of the British force, strung out in a long,
narrow column, had effectively been contained and could not enter the
battle.

Behind the Saxon line, two men pulled Kaye down from his horse;
one took Kaye's sword from its scabbard. Bryso also was down from his
mount. Kaye observed that Bryso was standing unguarded and that he
still had his weapon. A Saxon commander appeared, and Bryso, still
armed, was permitted to approach him.

"Well done," said Theil.

"Where is Vollo?"

"Still shipboard."

The two men walked to Kaye, whose expression was a mixture of
fear and confusion. "Do as instructed," said Theil, "and you will survive.
And remember this as well, never say no to Lord Vollo or show him the
smallest measure of insolence or disrespect."

Bryso moved face-to-face with Kaye. "Don't appear so surprised,
Kaye. When given the opportunity to join the winning side, you will
take it also. You were overly confident, you and your brother. It was easy
enough to rid myself of him and easy enough to lure you out of the safety
of the castle." He looked at Theil and laughed. "He's like a fawn trapped
by a hunter." Bryso turned back to Kaye. "Still confused? The Saxons
landed days ago and have been preparing this trap ever since. The ships
you saw, the ones we spent the night watching, contain only the crew
required to sail them."

Behind them the sounds of battle grew louder as the British tried
to break through the Saxon barricade to rescue their king. They were
unsuccessful, and it was Prywycke who finally ordered the horsemen to
disperse into the forest and to attack the Saxons from both sides of the
path they had blocked.

The first group of advancing British horsemen rode straight into
Saxon traps. Horses were tripped by ropes strung between trees and
impaled on spikes that had been hammered into the ground, their riders

thrown. The British who were able to advance beyond these traps rushed into more spikes while other horses were felled by stepping into holes that had been covered with tree branches and leaves.

Saxon foot soldiers rushed out of their hiding places to attack the horsemen on the ground.

The riders who survived the traps found the woods too tight for them to effectively maneuver their horses and were at a disadvantage to the footmen who surrounded them.

The most experienced British warriors now shouted for a retreat and a regrouping. There was no reason to throw themselves against the Saxons now. The very head of their column, including the king, was gone and beyond rescue. They could not determine how large an enemy force they faced but did know the Saxons were dug in and well defended. They fell back about five hundred feet and deployed a defensive line of foot soldiers on both sides of the forest road while Prywycke and several other battle leaders met to discuss what they should do next.

They had been outmaneuvered and tricked into spending the night watching an invasion fleet that had already gotten its troops ashore and in position to ambush them in the forest. They decided the Saxons might have more tricks in store for them, and they should remain in a defensive posture for a while to see what else the enemy might do.

And so they waited, an unnatural thing for fighting men to do under such circumstances.

Theil, having escorted Kaye and Bryso to the rear of the Saxon formation, hurried to the battle line. He could hear some movement on the British side, a good hundred or more feet away, both from men on foot as well as from horses. Nothing happened for a time. Finally, the British advanced. The Saxons let them come within fifty feet, then twenty-five.

The order was given; Saxon archers fired on them.

The British shot back, but both sides were so well protected by the forest that little damage was done.

More of the British force was joining the rear of their battle formation. They began to spread out farther to both the east and west and eventually outflanked the Saxons, forming battle lines on three sides of the enemy. As the British flanks moved in on the Saxons, they engaged in hand-to-hand combat. But every time the British seemed to be making headway, the Saxons fell back. They could gain no advantage, and the Saxons seemed to seek none.

The battle was halted at sunset because neither group could see well enough in the dark to distinguish its own warriors from the enemy.

39) The Night Watch

Finola, the rotund kitchen maid, knocked on Brenna's bed chamber door and called to her. Carrying a tray of food, she pushed open the door and found Brenna staring out the window. Finola said she had noticed that Brenna had not been eating, placed the tray down on the bed and invited her to eat. But Brenna did not look back from the window. The maid attempted to draw her into a conversation about how empty the castle felt since the men left to fight the Saxons. Brenna still did not respond. Finola tried once more to engage her. "You miss him? You miss Arthur."

Brenna turned to face Finola. "You know?"

"I have known you since the day you were born. I can look at you and know exactly how you feel."

Brenna walked to the bed and sat down, careful not to disturb the tray Finola had laid there. "I think of him every morning when I rise, every evening when I go to sleep, and every time I am awake in my bed in the middle of the night." Brenna's eyes became teary. "I feel abandoned by him, and I'm a little angry as well as very sad. He could have attempted to resist Kaye's effort to send him to Hadrian's Wall, but he didn't."

Finola sat next to her and gently placed a hand on her shoulder. "But everyone knew about the two of you, and the talk of the castle was that Arthur was nearly banished. Perhaps, he was banished and had no choice. And forgive me for saying this, but I could feel the strain this put between you and your father and stepmother."

"Maeve and I haven't gotten along for years. It has little to do with Arthur." Brenna turned toward Finola. "I'll find a way to bring him back from Hadrian's Wall. If Uriens knew what I know, Arthur would be returned and that arrogant Kaye put in his proper place."

Finola held her hands up as if to stop Brenna. "Please, you have had sufficient trouble and heartache. I've seen you more than once bracing yourself against a wall or a chair as though you had lost your breath. That's the result of this strain. Young as you are, it does you no good. Let things rest as they are and afford yourself some time for thought — and rest."

They spoke for a while longer. Finola finally left after making her promise she would eat. Brenna never touched the food; instead she attempted to sleep. However, sleep did not come, and eventually Brenna got out of bed, dressed in warm clothes and headed toward the balcony atop the tower to look out at the sea.

***

There were four men on watch that night at Valphain Castle, twice the usual number because of the sighting of the Saxon fleet. They stood atop the castle wall, two on either side of the main gate. A small force of warriors remained behind to defend the castle, but the walls were impenetrable, the wooden gates almost so, and to scale the walls would require tall ladders that invaders would have to carry uphill. The attackers would be easy targets for archers and a few loads of rock dropped on them from above.

Two of the night watch looked out over the dark sea; a third had his eyes closed and was drifting to sleep standing on his feet; the fourth was focused on the forest, where he had seen a light, no more than a speck of a flame between the trees. There it was again. He nudged the drowsy man next to him, who opened his eyes, asked, "What?"

"A light, out there in the forest." The guard pointed to where he had last seen the light.

"I see nothing."

"Keep looking."

He saw it as well. Someone was approaching. "Shall we alert the others?"

"Let's see who it is first. It's more likely one of our own returning home than anyone else."

The light was a torch held in the hand of one of seven riders who approached from the woods. It was too dark to see who they were, but there was something about them, their slow pace perhaps or the fact that one of their number was hunched over, that made them appear as though they had suffered a defeat of one sort or another.

As they neared the castle, the rider holding the torch waved it from side to side. "He is signaling us," said the guard who first noticed the light. "That rider appears to be Bryso."

And when the riders came closer, the guard saw that it was indeed Bryso, and the man next to him hunched forward in his saddle appeared to be King Kaye.

"The king is wounded. It's I, Bryso; open the gate."

All four guards rushed down to open the gates and let the riders inside. One of them noticed that the king's hands were bound and that a cloth had been tied across his mouth, but before the guard could give an alarm, Bryso struck him down with a single sword blow to the neck. Two other guards were brought down by sword thrusts. The fourth blocked an attack with his arm, suffering a wound that almost severed it. He cried out and ran for the castle tower but was cut down from behind by a Saxon rider.

One of the other Saxons took the torch from Bryso, climbed to the top of the wall, and used it to signal the rest of their party in the woods.

Vollo, sitting on a horse at the edge of the woods, saw the signal. He turned to Theil, who was next to him. "The gates of Valphain Castle are open to us." The warlord silently gave the signal to move forward and led hundreds of his warriors, all of them on foot except Theil, up the hill to the castle and entered it through its gates.

As Saxons began to fill the courtyard, they divided into two groups. One led by Bryso rushed to the buildings behind the main tower to make prisoners of the British warriors who were sleeping there. Another group, led by Theil, went to the main tower to capture whatever lords and ladies remained in the castle.

As Brenna climbed the stairs to the tower balcony, she heard the sounds of activity emanating from the courtyard below. And when she reached the balcony and peered down over the side, she saw hundreds of men rushing about the castle grounds. At first, it appeared that their army had returned, but they would not have been moving at the frantic speed of these men. The castle was under attack. The enemy was inside the gates. There were far more of them than British warriors still in the castle, and some of the enemy warriors were hurrying into the tower itself.

Brenna started back down the stairs and had not gotten far when she heard footsteps rushing up the steps below her. It was too late. She was caught. She went back up to the balcony and concealed herself, as best she could, against the stone door frame.

Footsteps were approaching, and she could see the light from a torch. Pressed against the outside frame of the arch connecting the tower steps to the balcony, she would not be seen by anyone who merely stood in the archway and looked out. However, if the person coming up the stairs, almost certainly a Saxon, took even a single step out onto the balcony, she would be caught.

Brenna took off a stocking. She gathered up a few pieces of stone that had been chipped from the balcony floor, put them into the foot of the stocking and wound them tight into a weapon. The footsteps stopped just inside the archway. A torch was extended out far enough for Brenna to see it. The tip of torch remained suspended in air for a few moments. Someone was looking about the balcony but had not stepped out onto it.

The torch was withdrawn, and its light faded.

40) A New Lord of the Tower

Theil paused at the top step leading to the tower balcony. It appeared empty. He started to head back down the stairs, but his sense of thoroughness caused him to turn around and walk out onto the balcony to be certain.

He was struck by a blow on the left shoulder, harder than a human fist but not nearly so hard as a mace or hammer. It was a painful strike but caused no damage. He rushed out onto the balcony, raised his sword over his head to slash at his attacker but paused when he saw in the torchlight who the attacker was. It was a woman, and he recognized her as the young lady he admired when he visited this castle with the traders from Gaul. She was the one who appeared so interested in the warlord Arthur.

Theil's pause gave the woman sufficient time to strike another blow, which he fended off with his forearm. He could see that she was frightened, and the fact that he was larger and more powerful than she and armed with a sword might not be enough to stop her from attacking him again. He dropped his sword and torch, and grabbed her arms. She kicked him. He turned her around, wrapped both arms around her and lifted her off the ground. She kicked him with her heels.

"You are safe," he said. And she kicked him a third time. "Far better with Theil than to be captured by the others." She began to calm herself and stopped kicking. "You are the girl who watched Arthur."

"You know Arthur?"

"No."

"Then, why help me?" She was breathing heavily and tired from struggling.

"No reason or perhaps many reasons." He could not tell her that he was fascinated by her; she would start kicking him again. "You can take your chances with the others or allow Theil to help you." She stopped resisting. He put her down and released the hold he had on her. She started to lose her balance and braced herself against a wall. "Are you injured?"

"Just give me a moment."

He waited until she stood erect and turned to face him. "If you live in the tower, you are likely a person of some importance. If so, that may count against you with Lord Vollo. What is in his mind, no one can say. But it will be safer for you to pose as one of the castle's servants."

It took some convincing, but Theil was able to persuade the woman to pretend to be a kitchen maid. As Saxons searched all the rooms in the tower, he led her by the arm down to the kitchen, where they encountered the maid Finola. The woman appeared upset at the sight of Brenna in the hands of a Saxon warrior, but her concerns were allayed when Theil handed Brenna over to her. "Dress her as a servant," he said, "and make certain that she always appears and acts as one. Watch over her."

He started to leave but turned back. "Your name?"

"Brenna."

He bowed to her. "Theil."

The tower of Valphain Castle was taken over by the Saxons. Every room, every storage area, every hallway, every staircase was searched, and the tower residents, except the servants, were herded into a few rooms. All the weapons were collected, and Saxon guards were stationed everywhere including the kitchen. The invaders inquired about certain people by name: Uriens, Ector, Maeve, and Brenna. And Merlin. They were told the wizard had gone north, and they could not find Brenna. But Uriens, Ector, and Maeve were found and taken to a tower bedroom. Their Saxon captors shut the door behind them, and one stood sentry outside.

Ector went to the bedroom window to look down at the activity in the courtyard. Saxons were lining up British prisoners. He could only shake his head at the sight of it.

Uriens sat on the bed with his head in his hands. Maeve, sobbing, sat next to him, and he put his arm around her to console her. "Will they kill us?" she asked, and the question caused Ector to turn back from the window.

"They have no reason to kill us," said Uriens.

"Give me to their soldiers?"

"Even Saxons must respect nobility."

Ector walked to the center of the room. "If I could venture a guess, I don't think they would have confined us here if they meant to do us harm."

"Yes, Ector is correct, Maeve. Listen to him," Uriens said unconvincingly, but he quickly lost his composure. Uriens dropped his head into his hands again. "I can't believe the castle is lost. In five generations never an occupation. One or two sieges, yes, but never this. I wish I had not lived to see this day."

"Don't say that." Maeve began to sob again.

The door opened, drawing the attention of all three. Kaye was pushed into the room, and the door shut again.

"Kaye, son." Ector rushed to hug him. "Are you hurt? What has happened?"

Kaye looked at Uriens. "It was Bryso."

"Bryso?" Uriens was confused.

"He led us into a trap."

"Who did?"

"Bryso."

"I trust him more than. . ."

"You aren't listening, Uriens! Bryso led us into a trap!"

Uriens looked to Maeve for an explanation.

Kaye addressed himself to Ector. "He led us out to meet the Saxons, said we could overwhelm them on the beach. But they were already in the forest. The attack was so sudden there was no time to react or to think." Kaye now shouted at Uriens as if it were his fault. "And it was all Bryso's doing. They let him keep his sword. They greeted him as a friend."

Uriens looked up at Kaye from the bed. "I don't understand. You are king, but you are speaking of Bryso as though he were."

Uriens' words struck Kaye with force. "You are correct." His voice lowered to a whisper. "I am king."

The door opened, and a guard entered, causing Maeve to draw closer to Uriens. "Lord Vollo calls for King Kaye to be brought to him."

Ector grabbed Kaye's arm. "I will ask to go with you."

He gently removed his father's hand. "I am king and will act like one." Disheveled and dusty from his night in the woods and his long ride back to the castle, Kaye paused to dust himself off, straighten his tunic, and flatten his hair with the palm of his hand. He followed the guard out of the bedroom.

Vollo sat in the great hall at the banquet table, flanked by a guard on either side, Theil standing at his right shoulder. Vollo was drinking mead, a servant by his shoulder ready to fill the goblet when it was empty. The sight of him caused Kaye's legs to become unsteady.

Vollo motioned for Kaye to sit beside him. Kaye remained standing. "Sit," shouted Vollo, and Kaye sat. A goblet was placed before him and filled with mead. "Drink." Vollo gestured toward the goblet. "It has been a difficult day for all of us."

"Thank you." Kaye, cautiously looking around the hall, sipped from the goblet.

Vollo took a long swallow of mead. "Not every battle has a pleasing ending. Experience teaches you that. Today could have gone much worse for you and the British. We could have crushed your entire army. As it is, you have suffered minimal loses. But we have your castle. And we have you."

Food prepared by Vollo's own cook and served by his servants was placed before the two men. "Eat. A man cannot think when his belly is hollow. We Saxons are a civilized race."

Kaye forced himself to take several bites of roasted meat.

"We both well understand what happens next," said Vollo. "The rest of your army will arrive here, most probably tomorrow, and lay siege to the castle." Vollo laughed. "I needn't tell you how difficult it would have been for my army to storm this fortress or engage in a long siege. And we came prepared with sufficient supplies to last many, many days." Vollo gently slapped Kaye shoulder, almost as a sign of affection. "We can be allies. I have treated you and your people well, and will continue to do so. The barbarous Picts, who also have intentions regarding Valphain Castle and all of Britain, would have hung your corpse from the main gate by now."

That remark caused Kaye to pause in his eating.

"You can prevent more lives from being lost." Vollo pointed a finger at Kaye. "You are responsible for what transpired today in the forest. Our plan depended upon deceiving you. But you can atone for that. You can allow your army to throw itself against these castle walls and be slaughtered. Or you can forge an alliance with me. You must know that a Saxon presence in Britain is inevitable. You can and will prevent the siege. You will tell your men to lay down their arms. Why should there be more blood than necessary? Well? Speak!"

Kaye took a breath and looked Vollo in the eye. "Yes, stop the bloodshed and death. A siege would cause many more British deaths, that's true. It would also cost Saxon lives."

"Don't forget Bryso." Vollo leaned closer to him and whispered. "Where there is one traitor there might be others. Who can you trust, Kaye?" Vollo laughed. "You can trust me as well as any of your own." He slammed his fist down on the table. "Now, which is it? Alliance with me or risk the alternative?"

"An easy choice, Lord Vollo. You have the castle, and I don't wish see my men dying against its walls trying to reclaim it."

"And you don't wish to be hung from the main gate?"

"No."

Vollo laughed and took another swallow of mead.

41) A Saxon Roommate

Before Vollo's fleet sailed from Germania, Horald told Theil to kill the warlord if he managed to enter Valphain Castle. Now there sat Vollo in the castle's great hall, eating and drinking his fill. But he had taken the castle by trickery, not by force. The British army had not yet been defeated. Even if Theil wanted to assassinate the warlord, it was too soon.

More than that, he no longer had the stomach to murder a man, even Vollo.

Vollo noticed Theil standing at the entrance to the great hall and motioned him to the banquet table. As Theil sat, Vollo instructed the servants to bring him food and drink. "Thank you, no, Lord Vollo." Theil put his hand to his belly. "The midday meal was substantial."

"Well, I'll continue to eat, and I'll most likely drink enough mead for the two of us." Vollo drained a goblet and held it out for a servant to refill. His eyes were watery, his lips moist. Vollo placed goblet on the table and waved his arm around the great hall. "What you do think of this castle?"

Theil gazed around the great hall. "It does not have the grandeur of Cergin's throne room."

"No grandeur? No, I suppose not." Vollo tore himself a piece of bread.

"The location is very good, however."

"The location? You mean overlooking the sea?"

"Yes."

"I suppose if that suits your taste."

Theil rarely heard Vollo discuss such trivialities. He slurred some of his words, and Theil thought he must be drunk.

Vollo looked at him with a pained expression in his eyes that Theil had never before seen. "Theil, you think I'm hard on the men. I know you do. I remember on our last voyage how you tried to persuade me they needed rest. You were right. So, now I wish to begin with the battle leaders. I want you to be certain they are well cared for." Vollo rested a hand on Theil's forearm. "Bed them in the tower and let them have the servant and peasant women. You, Theil, you take the best room and the best woman."

Theil forced a smile. "Thank you, Lord Vollo. It shall be done."

Before Theil attended to that task, he needed to protect the woman Brenna, whom he had convinced to disguise herself as a servant. That had been difficult enough. Now he would have to persuade her that she must pretend to be his woman for her own safety.

He hurried to the kitchen, where he found Brenna dressed in maid's attire, her hair mussed, her face dirty. None of this hid her beauty. He walked straight to her and took hold of her upper arm. "Come along." He whispered, "This is for your protection."

As Finola watched with suspicion and alarm, Theil marched Brenna out of the kitchen, through the great hall and to the tower stairs. "What are you doing?" Brenna's voice was a mix of anger and concern, and she tried to pull her arm free.

"I will explain when we are alone."

"Alone!" She tried to shake loose of his hold, but he held tight and pulled her up the steps.

He found an empty bedroom on the third floor away from the quarters on the second floor, one of which Vollo had made his own. The guard in the third floor hallway smiled at them, and Theil realized that Brenna's expression and her periodic efforts to break his hold on her arm aided in the deception. She appeared to be a woman being dragged to a bedroom against her will, and indeed, she was.

Theil told the guard in the hall that this room and this woman would be his and that no one was to enter the room unless Theil, himself, gave permission. He opened the door, and as he attempted to usher Brenna inside, she pushed back. He shoved her into the room. He closed the door behind them, turned toward Brenna, and found himself facing the point of a kitchen carving knife. "Touch me, and I'll cut your belly open." There was determination in her voice, and he had no doubt she would use the knife.

Theil held up his hands. "This is to prevent you from being touched by others. All the British servant women are being given to our warriors."

"And you are the one who made me appear as a servant. This was your plan all along." There was no fear in her expression now, only anger.

Theil held his palms up in a pleading gesture. "A soldier in a conquering army can take a woman hostage by force. Deception is unnecessary. If you have doubts, go down to the great hall now and tell Vollo that you are Brenna. Or go back to the kitchen and wait for one of the others to drag you off to his bed or blanket."

Her expression softened a little, but she continued to hold the point of the knife at him. "Why have you singled me out? Why are you so concerned about me and no one else? Because I am Uriens's daughter?"

"No, that is not the reason." Theil hesitated searching for words that were both vague and convincing. "Suppose there was someone in your life, a young person, that you wanted to help but were not able to. And that person. . .that person died. It might make you feel better, a little better, if you are able to save someone else."

Despite his vagueness, she seemed to understand and lowered the knife. "So, we must share a room?"

"There is no alternative."

"And this person who was lost, it was your daughter?"

"My son." Theil was hardly able to get the words out.

Brenna studied his face. "I suppose we have to wait here a time to fool the guard." He nodded yes. "Then, let's at least sit and be comfortable." Brenna, placing the knife next to her, sat at the head of the bed and Theil sat a safe distance away near the foot. "Do you want to speak about it? Often it helps."

He shook his head. "No, except that it was a horrible death in a fire." She reached over and placed a comforting hand on his shoulder for a moment. "Brenna, you have entrusted an unknown Saxon with your life and well-being. So, my well-being and life can be entrusted to you. You can understand my anger at the one who caused this death — Vollo and his mad ambition. What sits before you is not a typical Saxon warrior but a man, alone, caught between the ambition of Vollo and Cergin." Brenna appeared confused by this last remark. "It's a story for another time," he said.

42) Return from Hadrian's Wall

Merlin thought his special vision must be failing him. Something as significant as encountering a large British battle formation in the forest was an event he should have foreseen but did not anticipate. That the army was here was one concern. That it was facing south toward home instead of north was another. He, Arthur, Balan and the others who were returning from Hadrian's Wall were met by Prywycke and quickly told about the Saxon ambush, the number of British dead and wounded, and the assumption that Kaye and Bryso, whose bodies had not been found, must have been taken captive.

It was less Merlin's vision than his sense of logic that enabled him to conclude why Kaye had been taken hostage and why no Saxons had been spotted in days.

Merlin convened a three-man war council of Arthur, Balan, and himself. Prywycke came along uninvited. The four sat cross-legged beneath a tree as Merlin began the discussion. "It appears the Saxons were in good position to continue the battle here, but they have apparently withdrawn, taking Kaye with them. What does that suggest to you?" He addressed the question to the group but meant it for Arthur.

Merlin could see in Arthur's troubled expression that he had found the answer. "They are in Valphain Castle. Somehow they used Kaye to gain entrance."

"Prywycke," said Merlin, "dispatch a rider to confirm this."

Arthur stood up. "I'll go myself."

Merlin motioned for Prywycke to leave and beckoned Arthur to be seated. "You cannot ride into Valphain Castle the way you did the Pictish camp, eliminate the Saxon leader and have their entire army withdraw."

"That wasn't my plan." Arthur continued to stand. "But if an entire Saxon army gained entrance by stealth, so can one man."

"To what end? To rescue one woman? Much more is at stake than that, and Brenna's fate is tied to that of all the others. At the moment we need you here, Arthur."

The bluntness of Merlin's remark appeared to sting Arthur, and he did not argue the point. Still, he refused to sit down.

"I need not tell you that Valphain Castle will be very difficult to take by storm." Merlin looked around at the others. "To even begin an attack would require the construction of siege engines."

"Are you suggesting a siege instead?" asked Balan.

Arthur answered. "There's no time for a siege. It has to be an assault."

"We could build siege towers," said Balan. "The towers, of course, would have to be tall enough to put our warriors at a height equal to the Saxons on the castle walls, and they would be difficult to carry up the sharp incline of the terrain leading to the castle walls. Towers are the most obvious approach but may not succeed and would likely be costly in lives, win or lose."

There was no response to Balan's assessment. "Arthur!" Merlin was annoyed with his pupil, who was as distracted now as he was as a boy during his lessons. "We would appreciate your assistance."

Arthur sat down, was quiet for a few moments and began to address the problem in the logical manner that Merlin had taught him. "There are only two ways into the castle, over the wall or through it."

Merlin raised an eyebrow. "Only two?"

"Balan is, of course, correct. The terrain is too steep for towers. With no good way over the wall — certainly we shouldn't try to climb it with ladders — we'll have to go through the wall at its weakest point, which, of course, is the main gate"

"And how are gates usually stormed?"

"Merlin, this isn't one of your lessons."

"Answer, Arthur. You more than anyone else wants to take back the castle."

Arthur responded in the manner of a student doing a recitation. "Men rush the gates with shields held over their heads for protection, and usually with arrows, stones, and buckets of flaming oil raining down on them. It's a very costly approach, too costly. Shields are not sufficient." Arthur suddenly appeared hopeful. He looked from Merlin to Balan. "However, we could build a huge shield, fifty feet or longer, a wooden structure with a roof and two sides, one thick enough to protect us from arrows and stones."

"Wood burns."

"Yes, Merlin, but even a burning roof will afford us protection if we move fast enough. The difficult part will be moving it, although because of its much lower height, it would be easier to move than towers. We could build handles inside the walls for men to carry it and hang a battering ram at the front. We would make it long enough to protect a hundred warriors. We would carry it to the front gates of Valphain Castle and batter them in."

It was not what Merlin had in mind, but he could make this idea fit in with his plan. The wizard slapped his palms down on his thighs. "That is exactly what we shall do, build such a shield. It will require almost as many craftsmen as warriors — tree cutters, carpenters, and miners."

There was much to be done, and they would begin their preparations immediately, but the tension in Arthur's body, who stood up again, caused Merlin to believe he was still considering riding to the castle on his own. He asked Balan for a private moment to speak to Arthur. "Sit," Merlin said. "Please." And Arthur sat. "You understand this is the only way?"

"Yes." Arthur shook his head. "But the consequences of what has happened already. . ."

"Understand, Arthur, that Brenna is either safe or has suffered whatever harm was to come to her shortly after the Saxons took the castle."

"That gives me great comfort to think that she may be dead or servicing the entire Saxon army as we sit here and talk! That argues for me attacking now."

"She is resourceful. You know that. She may have concealed herself. But you were not there to protect her when the Saxons came. You cannot change that now by riding back to Valphain to be slaughtered by the enemy."

He hung his head. "It's my fault for not being there."

"More so my fault because I was the last to leave Kaye — though I cautioned him not to leave the castle." Merlin placed a hand on Arthur's shoulder and gently rocked him as though trying to shake him back to his senses. "This is no time for regret or recrimination. This is the time to act and to lead. There are many other people in Valphain Castle as well as Brenna. The only means of rescuing her is to rescue all of them." He pointed to the British army. "You also have their well-being to consider. And the time has come — finally — for you to live up to your responsibilities."

The wizard had the army assemble, and Merlin presented Arthur to the hundreds of warriors within earshot. Arthur stood facing them. The wizard told Arthur generally what he should say to the troops, but he had trouble finding the precise words. The silence caused the men to pay even closer attention. Finally Arthur looked over the group and spoke in a loud voice so that as many as possible could hear him. "We — the Wizard Merlin and I — believe that Kaye has been captured. He can no longer lead you and should never have been your leader. For that I take responsibility and responsibility for all that has transpired since. I pulled Caliburn from the stone." This comment elicited a reaction from nearly every man present. Arthur held up his arms to silence them. "In the confusion of that moment or perhaps it was in the confusion of youth, I let Kaye have the sword. Despite that failing, I have won one battle over Norsemen and a second over the Picts. If you will accept me as your leader, I promise you a third victory over the Saxons."

The men cheered. Arthur was surprised. Merlin was not. Word of Arthur's ride into the Pictish camp and his near single-handed defeat of an entire army made him the obvious choice to lead the British.

They packed up their gear and moved carefully through the forest where the Saxons had built their traps and fortifications. They continued to Valphain Castle and took to the woods surrounding it, where they remained out of sight.

Meanwhile, riders were sent to recruit the craftsmen they needed and to gather food supplies, which were already nearly depleted. The assault on Valphain Castle, Merlin calculated, must take place within a score of days and would better be brought to a conclusion in less than a dozen or their army would likely be fighting with empty stomachs.

When the craftsmen arrived, they quickly set about felling trees, the sounds of their chopping along with the hammering and sawing of the carpenters alerted the Saxons to their presence and the watch on the castle wall was doubled. When this stage of their preparations was complete, Arthur led the march out of the woods and into plain sight of the castle walls. He was flanked by Merlin and Balan. All three paused well out of arrow range as the army behind them divided into two columns and moved left and right. Horsemen came first in normal fashion. Next came spearmen and bowmen, and finally the craftsmen, carrying the tree limbs and trunks that had been chopped down earlier.

Saxons began to line the castle wall to watch the British advance.

As the army spread out in a long formation facing the castle, craftsmen and foot soldiers alike began digging holes and inserting the ends of sharpened tree limbs and trunks into them to create a protective stockade, not a continuous barricade to protect their entire army but enough to give them cover and to funnel any Saxon attack into narrow spaces.

The Saxons had stripped the huts that had been built on the grounds in front the castle of all useful items but had left the huts themselves. British warriors under the cover of their archers rushed to the huts and shacks to disassemble them and bring back their wooden walls, which would be put to good use.

A large man with long white hair appeared on the wall near the castle's main gate and caught the wizard's attention. "He must be their leader, Vollo," said Merlin. Arthur was staring at the Saxon. "Arthur, if you are considering riding within bow range and trying to take him down with an arrow, realize that you would be the one felled by a volley of arrows."

Arthur said nothing. He merely frowned, convincing Merlin that he had considered such a maneuver.

Theil sought out Bryso, who had not joined the group on the wall to watch the British army advance. Theil, greatly troubled by his own sense of disloyalty, was interested in studying Bryso because the man seemed content — no, more than that he seemed *pleased* — with his treachery against Kaye and Uriens. Was there something Bryso knew or believed that might give Theil some peace of mind? No, that was a thought born of desperation. They were just two different men.

"Vollo is calling for us," said Theil. "I believe he wants us to go out to negotiate with the British."

Bryso gave a sarcastic laugh. "Then, I was correct to stay out of their sight. I can still pretend to them that I am a prisoner here. I assume that is what he wishes."

"Most likely."

Theil and Bryso went to the courtyard, where Vollo was standing before a gathering of his battle leaders. The warlord was issuing orders, and when he finished with the others, he turned to Theil and Bryso. The pair, with Bryso posing as a hostage, was to deliver the news of the British-Saxon alliance to the leadership of the British army and to instruct them in the name of King Kaye to lay down their weapons.

Vollo, who often spoke of the British as leaderless and inept, seemed optimistic that the British might acquiesce; Theil was not.

The gates to Valphain Castle opened, and out walked Theil and Bryso while two dozen Saxon archers covered them from the wall. The two men proceeded about twenty feet toward the British battle line and paused until they were certain the British had seen them. A solitary figure emerged from the British formation to face them. Both Theil and Bryso recognized the figure as Arthur.

"His presence will make our mission more difficult," said Bryso. They resumed advancing to a point midway between the two armies. "If this mission fails, I hope Vollo doesn't blame us."

Theil looked at Bryso from the corner of his eye and remained silent.

When the three men were about ten feet apart, they stopped and stood with Theil and Bryso facing Arthur. Bryso greeted Arthur, introduced Theil, and came immediately to the purpose of their meeting. "Although I'm a captive, I've been sent along with Lord Vollo's lieutenant because you know that you can trust me and know that I bring you the true words of King Kaye."

"Why can't Kaye speak for himself?"

"He could, indeed." Bryso motioned back toward the castle. "But that would require you to speak to him in the castle."

"We come to tell you of an alliance your king has made with Lord Vollo, and he orders your army to put away their arms" said Theil.

"But your ally, Saxon, can't leave his own castle."

"Nonetheless, your king has given a command."

Arthur directed his response to Theil. "A king in captivity is not a king. His commands no longer carry any force. We welcome an alliance but only after the Saxons leave Valphain Castle and surrender their arms."

"We? Surrender! We have your castle and your king."

And so it went, neither side yielding.

Theil and Bryso walked back to the castle, paused for the large wooden gates to be opened, and went inside. Vollo was standing in the courtyard waiting for them. He did not look happy and must have been able to determine the nature of their discussion with the British from their facial expressions. Theil gave his report that the British had not agreed to lay down their arms or to an alliance. He thought that Bryso made Vollo's humor worse when he started speaking about the return of Arthur and how the British now had a formidable leader.

Bryso then made a suggestion. "We could have another meeting with Arthur and use the opportunity to eliminate him."

"Kill him!" Vollo raised his eyebrows at that idea. "And have they no other leaders whatsoever? Arthur is very young, you said." Bryso nodded yes. "He committed an offense serious enough to be banished, you said." Bryso nodded again. "Can't we use him to our advantage? What kind of man is Arthur?"

"A great warrior and good strategist. But quick to anger."

Vollo listened with great interest. "And what was the cause of his banishment?"

"It involved a woman. She was a temptation he couldn't ignore. The woman was Brenna, Uriens's daughter."

"And this is the same woman who has not yet been found. Finding her, Theil, will be your task, your most important task." Theil tried to conceal his concern. Bryso would recognize Brenna if he saw her and would certainly expose her. "Our goal should be to provoke Arthur into attacking before the British preparations are completed, and this Brenna is the key, whether she is found or not. He will come if she is in danger. Bryso and Theil, you will attempt another negotiation, and Bryso, you will inform Arthur that I have designs on taking this girl as a wife, or mistress."

43) Assault

Theil never witnessed Vollo express interest in any particular woman. He was certain that the warlord's mention of Brenna was, as he had said, only a ploy to provoke a premature attack from Arthur. Nonetheless, Brenna was very attractive, and Vollo could be tempted to act out the threat he planned to make to the British battle leader. As soon as his meeting with Vollo ended, Theil found Brenna in the castle kitchen and gave her a warning to make herself even less conspicuous than she had already.

And above all else, not to allow Bryso to see her.

Later that same day, after inspecting their defenses and conferring with the night watch as he did daily, Theil returned to the tower and saw Vollo in the great hall, alone and drinking mead. Vollo's behavior had changed, and Theil was uncertain of its significance. As long as he had been with the warlord, Vollo had spent most of his nights poring over maps and battle plans, plotting raids and invasions, detailing supplies and the number and nature of the vessels needed in his invasion fleet. Since they captured Valphain Castle, Vollo could more often be found sitting over a goblet of mead, head down, a blank expression in his eyes. Perhaps, thought Theil, Vollo preferred the quest over the fruits of victory, or perhaps, he found Valphain Castle not to his liking. And Theil could not discount the lasting impact the poison may have had on him.

Vollo seemed not to notice him. Theil continued on to the kitchen, where Brenna was working with the servant Finola. Brenna smiled when she saw him approaching. "All is well. You needn't keep checking on me. I can look after myself." She leaned closer to him and whispered. "I'm more concerned about you. If you keep checking on me, Vollo will become suspicious."

"Your concern is appreciated, Brenna. But you are more at risk. Please confine yourself to the kitchen and the bedroom."

"I watch her carefully, Master Theil," said Finola.

Theil looked back toward the great hall. "Vollo is drinking a great deal tonight."

"At times, Master Theil, I can hardly keep his cup filled."

"I will continue to direct the search for you, Brenna, outside the tower, but remain cautious. "

Theil left the kitchen. A short time later, Brenna announced her intention to go to the bedchamber that she had been sharing with Theil. However, Finola insisted that she be allowed to check the great hall first. The short, heavy-set woman hobbled out of the kitchen and into the passage leading to the great hall. She returned with a look of concern on her face. "Master Vollo still sits there and drinks."

"I'll be fine. Vollo and all the other Saxons take me for a servant."

"Please, wait a little longer."

Twice more Finola checked the great hall, and each time she reported that Vollo appeared drunker than he had previously. The frustration was apparent on Brenna's face. "Since these accursed Saxons took over the castle, I've been made to live like a fearful animal. I simply want to go to my bedchamber, and that is exactly what I'll do, Vollo or no Vollo."

"Please, Mistress Brenna..."

Brenna put her hand on the older woman's arm and smiled at her. "I'll be safe."

Brenna left the kitchen and began to cross the great hall toward the tower stairs on the other side. She had taken only a few steps when she looked at Vollo from the corner of her eye. He was staring at her. Several more times she glanced at him, each time his stare was unchanged. When she reached the base of the stairs, she lifted the hem of her long dress and began to hurry up to the third floor.

Behind her, Vollo pushed his chair back from the banquet table and stood up.

Her footsteps fell softly on the wooden stairs. Below her much heavier feet began the climb. Her pace quickened.

She reached the bedchamber, closed the door behind her and quickly looked about the room. Her eyes settled on a wardrobe. She hurried to it and began to push it to the door with great difficulty. It moved only a few feet and jammed on a rug that had bunched up. She rushed to the other side of the wardrobe and with great effort pulled the edge of the rug out from under it and out of the way.

There were footsteps down the hall. A door to another chamber was flung open.

She managed to push the wardrobe up against the door and remained leaning against it.

The door to her chamber was pushed open a few inches until it smashed against the wardrobe. The door was pushed several more times, and each time, the door, the wardrobe and Brenna were shoved back farther. Vollo's left arm and shoulder reached through. She abandoned the door and ran to the other side of the bed.

Vollo finished opening the door, stepped into the room and stared at her, a wild look in his eyes. He hesitated a moment and came around the foot of the bed. Brenna crawled across the bed toward the door and managed to regain her feet on the other side. He caught her by the shoulder of her dress and tore it down past her waist, exposing her bare flesh. She slipped out his grasp, but he caught her again by the arm, pulled her back toward him and threw her back against the bed. She reached under her pillow, withdrew the kitchen knife she had used to threaten Theil and held it up to Vollo's face. He slapped the knife out her hand, sending it across the room, and held her by her right arm.

With her free hand Brenna dug her fingernails into his right eye.

Vollo screamed and reached to his eye, blood running out between his fingers and down his cheek.

Brenna ran out of the chamber, lifted the strap of her torn dress over her shoulder and continued down the stairs. She went straight to the kitchen. When Finola saw her coming, she threw her hands to her mouth.

"Hide me."

Finola in panic looked left and right. "Where?"

Brenna's eyes quickly searched the kitchen. "No, he would find me here and kill me. I must escape from the castle." Brenna ran out the back entrance of the kitchen and out into the night.

Coming down the tower stairs, running through the castle, and into the courtyard, Vollo was a frightful sight as he shouted, his eye swollen and bloodied. The Saxon army was quickly put on alert for a small, young woman with a torn dress.

When the news reached Theil, he knew the woman who attacked Vollo was Brenna, and his first thought was that she was as good as dead and beyond help. He hurried to the kitchen in the hope that Finola could tell him what happened and where Brenna might be. He found Finola, but the woman was crying so hysterically she could tell him little more than Brenna had run away and Vollo was going to kill her.

Theil well understood the difference between bravery and a self-sacrifice that could not possibly result in any good outcome. Every warrior must understand as much. Such was the case with Brenna. She was beyond help and beyond hope. Vollo might be lenient with a woman who only tried to defend herself, but that was doubtful. Theil could not help but remember the fate of the cook who was thrown overboard. If Theil intervened, he, as the warlord's trusted second-in-command, would suffer a fate similar to Brenna's.

Sadly, he could not help her.

Theil remembered Vollo's threat to Kaye, to hang his corpse at the castle gate. He could not live every day seeing Brenna's body abused in that manner.

Theil rushed out to the courtyard. The castle grounds were full of activity. Fortunately it was a moonless night, which might afford Brenna some cover. The first place Theil checked was the main gate. It was closed and well-guarded. He doubted she had managed to escape to the British forces. He circled to the rear of the castle tower, past men who were searching the back buildings, and there he found her. Two warriors had hold of her, each by one of her arms. She appeared dazed. Even in the dark he could see she was bleeding from the mouth, and the upper left side of her body and hip were naked to the cold air.

But Theil hesitated for a moment and crossed a bridge from which there would be no returning. "Do you not know this woman is a British noble woman and must be accorded some civility no matter what her offense?" Theil's rank and the authority in his voice caused the two warriors to defer to him. "Give custody of her to me." Theil took Brenna by the arm and softened his tone. "You shall be credited with her capture when she is given to Lord Vollo."

He wrapped Brenna in his cloak and led her away, hoping the two warriors behind them would not intervene. They did not. He whispered to Brenna to try to walk normally so that she would be less noticeable. "We must find a place to conceal you."

"I know such a place if we can reach it." She spoke softly and her eyes were blank as though she were in a dream state.

He avoided other Saxon warriors when he could, and when he could not, he told them he was taking the woman to Vollo. Given her ordeal, Brenna was understandably a little confused and twice took them in the wrong direction. Finally and almost miraculously, they reached the west tower without being apprehended. In the dark, they were able to enter the tower unnoticed. She led him down the stairs to the place where she and Arthur had made love. It was cold, and she was shaking. She may have felt safe now, but Theil knew they were trapped here. This was their prison, perhaps their tomb.

Theil sat her down on the earthen floor.

"We'll be safe here," she said, appearing more alert.

"Not without food and water." He stood.

"Where are you going?" She reached out for his tunic sleeve but could not reach it.

"Your servant Finola. She must occasionally supply us with food and water or we will not last more than a few days and certainly not until the British are able to retake the castle. If they can retake the castle."

Brenna stood, still unsteady on her feet, and grabbed him by the arm. "I won't let you go. It's far too risky."

"The risk has already been taken."

He gently removed her hand and climbed the steps to the door of the west tower. He cracked it open a few inches and looked outside. He was able to slip out unseen. Theil walked across the courtyard, passing several men. He hoped that no one yet knew that he had failed to deliver Brenna to Vollo. Perhaps, they did not, and that was why he was able to reach the kitchen entrance without being challenged.

Inside Finola was seated on a chair, staring at the floor and sobbing. She stood up the instant she saw Theil. "Is she safe?"

"For now. Do you know the west tower?"

"Of course."

"There is a dangerous task that must be performed, and it is understandable if you refuse to perform it, but unless you can supply her — supply us — with food and water every few days, we will not survive in hiding."

"I would give my life for Brenna. I will do it beginning tonight."

"Begin tomorrow. It is too dangerous tonight."

Theil left the kitchen by the back door. He immediately came face-to-face with one of the men who had caught Brenna. Judging from the man's expression, he either knew of Theil's treachery or was about to deduce it. They were close enough for Theil to use the dagger that hung from the left side of his belt. In one motion he withdrew it and plunged it to the man's belly. He twisted the blade to keep the man from screaming, withdrew it and watched him drop to the ground.

With this act he lost whatever slight hope he had that he could again be accepted among the Saxons. His own people would kill him on sight as would the British. He had only one ally left in the world: Brenna. Brenna and her servant Finola, if she held to her promise to bring them food and water.

44) Trouble in the British Ranks

A lone horseman rode out of the main gate of Valphain Castle. Arthur watched the rider's approach and was joined by Merlin, who stood by his right shoulder. It was Bryso. Without taking his eyes from Bryso, Merlin leaned toward Arthur's ear. "Do you wonder how Bryso is able to wander in and out of the castle so easily?"

Arthur looked at Merlin. "Are you questioning Bryso's loyalty to Uriens? Of course, they send Bryso. Who else would the Saxons send? Certainly not Kaye."

"And do you wonder why Bryso, as well as Kaye, was captured?"

Arthur turned back toward the approaching rider. "Yes, that has occurred to me, and now that I think of it, there was one situation in which I trusted Bryso and may have been wrong in doing so." Arthur was thinking of the night Bryso had freed him from the west tower.

"More harm has come from too much trust than from too little trust," said Merlin. "And do you think that Kaye, on his own, would have devised a plan to trap the Saxons on a beach? And have you considered how the Saxons knew where our army was?"

Arthur gritted his teeth. "A case can be made against Bryso when you raise all those questions. I'll have to struggle to be civil to him."

"Then, struggle. Much is at stake."

Bryso smiled when he saw the two men who were observing his approach, and Arthur thought Bryso looked none the worse for having been a captive. Bryso dismounted, greeted Merlin, and hugged Arthur. Others, including Prywycke and Balan, came to meet him, and Bryso said again and again he was happy to see them all. "I've been sent to persuade you to abandon your weapons and join with the Saxons." Bryso shook his head. "A fool's errand, I'm well aware. But I must appear to make an effort before I return."

"Bryso, won't you stay with us rather than go back to the castle?" asked Prywycke.

"I fear they would punish Kaye if I don't return. Although, in truth, my treatment by the Saxons is better than I expected. That does not include, however, being well fed by them."

A small group walked Bryso toward some stools at the center of the camp where they could sit and eat and speak. There was much they

wanted to ask Bryso about the size and composition of the Saxon army
and any special defensive measures they had taken in Valphain Castle.

As the group continued to walk through the camp, they passed
Arthur's giant shield, a wooden structure that was thirty feet long, ten
feet wide and seven feet high. It was still being built. There were also
many siege ladders; crudely built, they each had a single vertical pole
with steps nailed to it. Bryso seemed to take all this in with interest,
which Arthur noticed.

Arthur fell to the rear of the group and grabbed Prywycke by the
arm. "Keep an eye on Bryso." Prywycke looked confused. "Keep an eye
on him. Follow him if he moves away from the group and above all keep
him away from the digging." Prywycke still appeared somewhat puzzled
but nodded his agreement.

By Bryso's estimation, the Saxons had no more than a few hundred
men and had added nothing to improve the castle's defenses that he had
seen. The only factor preventing the British from overrunning the rela-
tively small band of Saxons was the castle wall. Arthur took note of all
this information but could hardly contain his desire to learn of Brenna's whereabouts and condition. When Bryso was finished eating and
answering questions, Arthur asked for a private word with him.

They walked a short distance from the others. Bryso looked back
at the group to be certain they were out of earshot and whispered to
Arthur. "There is something I must tell you, Arthur, and it will be difficult for you to hear."

"Is Brenna hurt?"

Bryso held up a hand as if to allay Arthur's concern. "No, but. . ." He
looked from side to side. "Kaye has agreed to an alliance. I've told you
as much already. Uriens has also been forced to voice support for Vollo.
To seal what he believes is an alliance with Uriens, Vollo plans to wed
Brenna."

Images of the large and vile Vollo touching Brenna came into
Arthur's mind, and he tried to block them. "We can move on the castle
soon, almost at once. Is there time to prevent this?"

"Before the wedding? Yes, but not much. And who can say whether
he will take her before then?"

Arthur left Bryso with the others, taking care to remind Prywycke
to keep watch on him. He went off alone to think. He reviewed the castle assault plan in his mind, considered the readiness of his army and

consulted with Merlin, whose initial response was that he wanted to wait several more days before attacking Valphain. The two walked to *the digging*, as Arthur referred to it. Concealed under Arthur's large assault shield was a hole in the ground. It was the entrance to a tunnel that had been continuously dug during day and night. Miners, augmented by carpenters and others, had hollowed out a tunnel that was in places more than six feet high and twelve feet wide, and was braced with a rib cage of wood in the manner that mines were constructed.

Arthur took a torch and led Merlin inside to inspect the progress that had been made as workmen continued to extend the tunnel and install wooden beams to shore it up. When they finished the inspection and began to leave the tunnel, they debated their readiness. Merlin wanted two more days; he relented and said one. Arthur insisted the success of the plan would not depend on another five or ten feet of tunnel. And food stores were running out, which, of course, argued for quick action. He wanted to attack the next morning.

As they were exiting the tunnel, they saw Bryso and Prywycke coming in the opposite direction. Arthur attempted to conceal his anger, but it was apparent in the tone of his voice. "I told you, Prywycke, to keep Bryso away from here!"

Prywycke turned red. "I thought you said to show him the digging."

Arthur was too aggravated to explain. "Away! Both of you!" Bryso appeared perplexed. "And you, Bryso, will have to remain here with us."

Bryso was outraged. "Is this some matter of trust? It can't be. I was fighting for Britain when you were too small to lift a sword."

Even if Bryso's outrage was both genuine and justified, Arthur would not back down. "It's a matter of caution. The Saxons have ways of gaining information from any man. I can't let you return to them."

"Torture!" Bryso stepped closer to Arthur and looked him in the eye. "The Saxons could gouge out my eyes and chop off my hands, and I wouldn't reveal the existence of the tunnel."

"You are more certain of that than you should be. No man can say how he would react to torture if the torture is severe enough. You will stay with us."

As Arthur led them away from the tunnel, Bryso continued his protest. "And Kaye, your brother, what if they punish him for this?"

Arthur had not considered Kaye. He certainly did not want to be the cause of his brother being tortured or killed, and he already felt responsible for Kaye's capture, for Kaye becoming a king by accident, and for the fall of the castle. But more was at stake than Kaye. "Whatever the Saxons intend to do to Kaye will happen no later than the moment we attack. Your return to the castle gains him no benefit."

For the remainder of that morning and through the afternoon, Arthur hastened the pace of their assault preparations with the intention of attacking Valphain the following morning. That evening, while their warriors sat in small groups at campfires eating their supper, Arthur and Merlin continued to confer on their battle plans. They were interrupted by Balan, who brought disturbing news. There was dissention among the troops.

One name came to Arthur's mind, Bryso. He went in search of Bryso and found him standing over a handful of men who were seated at a campfire. Arthur and came up behind him unseen through a cluster trees.

"He underestimates the number of Saxons," said Bryso, "and his plan is to catch them off guard is to use a tunnel. I have just come from Valphain, as you well know. I have seen the number of Saxons on the castle grounds. It is impossible to tunnel into the castle unseen, and you will be cut down as you attempt to climb out of it. And all this risk he takes for a single woman, a woman who has been bedding with a Saxon battle leader."

Arthur's rage was instantaneous and uncontrollable. He grabbed Bryso, a sizeable man, from behind and slammed him face first into the nearest tree. He threw Bryso, whose nose and mouth were bleeding, to the ground, put his foot on his chest and held his sword to Bryso's throat. "You said Brenna was to wed Vollo. Now you say she is bedding someone else. Which is the truth? Or are neither true?" Bryso, breathing heavily, his eyes open wide in panic, did not answer. "You told me the Saxons were few in number; now you say there are many and I have underestimated their number. Which is the lie?"

"Arthur." Merlin had found them. "Steady, be steady."

Why the wizard would urge temperance with this man, Arthur did not know.

"Don't be concerned, Merlin, I won't kill Bryso for these lies." These words caused Bryso, whose face was dripping blood, to breathe a little easier. Arthur continued in a loud voice to ensure all present heard his accusation clearly. "But I might run him through if I had proof that he was responsible for the Saxon ambush, as both Merlin and I believe to be the case."

Arthur stared down at Bryso. "Perhaps, you no longer wish to live as one of us, Bryso, but tomorrow you will have the chance to die as one of us. You will ride beside me at the head of the army. If your heart is still with us, that should please you. If your heart is with the Saxons, they will not respond kindly to seeing you leading the charge against them. In either case, you will be fighting with us and against them."

45) A Final Pause

The Old One had paused in his story. He sat by the hearth, the fire casting plumes of light and shadow across his face. He did not move.

"What happens next?" asked Allum.

The Old One did not answer.

"I thought you didn't believe this story," said Donal.

"I haven't said that I do but won't say that I don't." He addressed himself to the Old One again. "What happens next?"

Still no answer.

Donal leaned forward in his seat for a closer look at the Old One. "I think he's dead."

"Dead!"

The two got up from their stools, slowly approached the storyteller, and stood over him and looked for signs of life. There were none.

"Do we have to bury him or can we just leave him where he is?"

One of the Old One's eyes opened. "Why do the pair of you hover me like birds over carrion?"

"The story. We wanted you to finish it."

"I did. Last night."

"It still is night."

The Old One looked about the hall and shooed Allum and Donal back their seats. "How can I be expected to tell a story with the two of you perched over me?"

The two hunters returned there stools, and when they were seated, the Old One cleared his throat. "Each year a tournament was held in Londinium. . ."

"We are well past that part."

The Old One frowned. "So we are. So we are."

46) Merlin's Magic

The rising sun cast a grayish light through the snow that had begun to fall overnight and reflected off the shields and armor of the British army that was arrayed in a line facing Valphain Castle. In the center of the formation was Arthur's newly completed wooden shield, large enough to provide protection to sixty warriors. Hundreds of foot soldiers carrying spears and several dozen of them holding ladders flanked the shield on either side. Archers stood behind them; back farther still were the horsemen, and at the center of horsemen were Arthur, Bryso, and Balan.

Bryso, his face bruised from the confrontation with Arthur the day before, looked back and forth between their formation and the castle, where only a few Saxons stood watching them. "Why not attack now while so few of them are even awake?"

"We're not ready." Arthur did not want Bryso to understand the nature of their attack even though there was nothing he could do now to compromise it.

The top of the castle wall quickly filled with Saxons, two hundred or more of them, most with bows and arrows in their hands, a few with spears or swords. Arthur hoped that Vollo himself would appear, and he was not disappointed. Vollo's massive size and long, white hair could be recognized at a distance. As the Saxon warlord looked out at the deployment of British warriors, Arthur wondered what Vollo might be thinking about the British intentions and strategy. That they should have attacked before first light? That they erred in giving the Saxons time to assemble? That they were planning to throw themselves against the castle walls with the crude ladders they carried? Had he noticed the giant shield? Would he guess its purpose and reinforce the main gate?

Arthur nodded to Balan. It was the signal for him to keep a watch on Bryso. Arthur rode to the tunnel entrance, where Merlin awaited him. He dismounted, and as soon as he was face to face with the wizard, he asked, "You're certain this will succeed?"

Merlin frowned at him. "You ask this now? It is somewhat late to be changing your mind."

"I just want to reaffirm that this trick has worked in the past."

"Yes. . .so I have heard."

The words *so I have heard* echoed through Arthur's mind. "You haven't done this before?"

"Of course not. When would I have had the opportunity?" He pointed to the tunnel entrance. "Shall we inspect our construction?" Merlin handed him a torch. "Be very careful with the flame."

They worked their way through the tunnel to the point where its straight line reached an end and turned at right angles both to the left and right. It had not been Merlin's intention to tunnel into the castle but rather to tunnel under the castle walls. Here at the cross section of the tunnel, the wooden ribcage they had constructed appeared to have a stone ceiling. In actuality, the stones above their heads were the base of the castle's exterior wall, which was no longer resting on solid earth but rather on the wooden support beams they had erected. Each vertical support beam had been coated with oil and wrapped in straw at the bottom.

The pair inspected the construction. Merlin held his torch higher to better see Arthur's face. "Are you ready?"

Arthur held his breath. He wanted to mentally review their plans but could not organize his thoughts. They had come this far, he finally decided; there was no turning back. "Ready."

As they left the tunnel, four men with torches went to the farthest ends of the tunnel and began lighting fires at the base of the support beams.

Arthur returned to his place in the battle formation and fixed a stare on the castle walls. He withdrew his sword, Excalibur, from its scabbard and held it aloft. Sunlight ran up its blade.

He ordered the horsemen to move to the front rank. Bryso gave him a curious look. Arthur was certain Bryso was not the only one wondering what the purpose of this maneuver was. No army threw horsemen against a castle wall. In assaults on castles foot soldiers, supported by bowman, would attempt to climb the wall first, and if successful, they would open the gates for the mounted warriors.

Arthur ordered them to move forward a little farther so that they were just beyond the range of the Saxon arrows. The distance, however, did not prevent some of the enemy bowmen from unleashing arrows through the falling snow. They fell well short. The Saxons began to jeer at them, daring them to attack. But the British did not move.

A crack appeared at the base of the castle wall. Smoke began to seep from it and then from several other smaller cracks in the wall. A portion of the wall sagged, causing the Saxons atop it to shift their weight to keep their balance. The wall emitted groaning and cracking sounds as the Saxons looked about trying to understand what was happening. A two hundred foot section of the wall collapsed, the lower stones falling into the tunnel below and the upper ones falling in all directions, dropping Saxon warriors with them and throwing them on both sides of what had been a wall.

Arthur led the British charge, the horsemen quickly covering the distance to the wall, the foot soldiers running behind them. Scores of Saxons did not survive the wall's collapse or survive it in fighting condition. Those who struggled to stand back up were easy targets for the British horsemen. Arthur, wielding his new sword, which seemed to move with unusual speed, took down one Saxon to his right who had just gotten to his feet and a second who was about to load an arrow into his bow. A foot soldier came at him from the left. He caught a spear jab on his shield, then a second jab. He raised his sword above his head and brought it down on the wooden shaft of the spear, hoping to deflect it but managed to break it in half. A second overhand strike to the spearman's neck took him down.

Carefully threading their horses through the fallen stones, Arthur and a few other British horsemen led the advance into the castle courtyard, where they were met and outnumbered by Saxon foot soldiers. An arrow glanced off Arthur's helmet, and one caught Bryso, who was on Arthur's left, in the leg. Both men were surrounded by Saxons, and they whipped their swords in circles, hoping to fend off their attackers until help arrived. An arrow struck Snow Storm's leather saddle, just missing Arthur's leg and causing the horse to rear up. The frantic movements of the horse caused the Saxons to back off a few steps, which gave Arthur the time and space to take down one of his opponents with a forward sword swing, and a second Saxon with a backhand.

There were war cries behind them. The British foot soldiers were joining the battle and would soon substantially outnumber the remaining Saxons. Arthur's goal was to reach the main tower, where he assumed Brenna and the other hostages were being held, and to free them before they came to harm — if they were as yet unharmed. But he noticed that Bryso was in trouble, still surrounded by Saxon foot soldiers. One of them came at Bryso from his blind side and thrust a spear into his right shoulder. Bryso dropped his sword and doubled over in pain. Arthur rode to his defense, killing the spearman and driving the other attackers back. British foot soldiers joined the encounter and occupied Bryso's attackers as he sat on his horse, head down, hand over his shoulder where he was pouring blood.

Although Bryso was likely a traitor, Arthur had offered him the chance to die as one of his own people and Bryso had taken that opportunity. Arthur dismounted and retrieved Bryso's fallen sword. Whether Bryso had the clarity of mind to know who was handing him the sword, Arthur did not know, but he reached out a bloody left hand and took it. It was the second time Arthur had saved his life.

Arthur remounted and surveyed the battleground. Vollo, a bandage over one eye, had survived the fall of the wall and stood like a tower among the British foot soldiers, wielding a mace, and seemingly downing a man with every swing. Arthur spurred Snow Storm and rode directly at Vollo, sword held aloft. Vollo saw his approach and turned to face him. He dropped his mace and grabbed a spear that lay next to one of the men he had just killed. He braced for the attack as Arthur rode down on him. Vollo dropped to one knee, braced the butt of the spear against the ground and jammed the point into Snow Storm's chest. The horse, mortally wounded, fell, tossing Arthur over his head. The collision with the horse knocked Vollo backwards.

It took a few moments before Arthur, who struck his head on the ground, was able to work through his muddled thinking and hazy vision to remember where he was and to see what was happening. He lifted himself to his hands and knees and saw Vollo already back on his feet, retrieving the mace he had dropped. Excalibur! It had fallen from Arthur's hand when he was thrown from the horse. He was not sure where it was. As he stood up, his eyes moved from Vollo, who was approaching him, to the ground around him, searching for the sword. There it was, a distance away, far enough that he would have to take on Vollo barehanded.

A rider raced toward them. Arthur hoped it was Balan or one of the other knights. It was Bryso, a sword in his left arm, his right dangling uselessly at his side. Arthur stood weaponless with Vollo on his right and Bryso approaching.

Vollo also saw Bryso's approach and turned to face him. That confused Arthur at first, but he remembered that Vollo would have seen

Bryso riding with the British in their charge. The large Saxon moved into Bryso's line of charge, sidestepped the horse, and struck Bryso a mace blow, knocking him from his mount. Vollo stood over Bryso and struck him a fatal blow. In his anger he struck the dead man several more times.

Arthur managed to get to Excalibur, and the extra moments Vollo spent on Bryso gave him time to reach the warlord. When the Saxon turned to search for him, he found Arthur facing him a few feet away. Arthur plunged his sword into Vollo's belly, and as he withdrew it, he expected the Saxon to fall. He did not. Vollo took a breath and seemed to be gathering his strength. He began to raise his mace. Arthur struck him blow between the right shoulder and neck. Vollo dropped the mace but remained standing. Wondering whether the man had more than mortal strength or was protected by a spell, Arthur delivered another blow to his neck. And Vollo finally went down.

He stood over the fallen Saxon, waiting for him to try to stand. But he did not move.

Leaving the dead warlord, Arthur hurried to the main tower and entered. It appeared to be unguarded. His fear was that once the castle's defenses had been breached, the Saxons would either use their hostages as shields or kill them. They could not have expected Merlin's trick and must have been preoccupied defending the breach in the wall, unconcerned about their hostages. He went up the stairs and threw open the door to the first bed chamber. It was empty as were all the others along this corridor. He went up to the third floor, and the first door he tried would not open. He pushed against it and thought it must be barricaded from the inside. He called out to those inside and identified himself.

Almost instantly he heard the sounds of heavy objects being pulled back from behind the door. When it was pulled open from inside, he saw Ector, who smiled and embraced him. Arthur was happy to see him and relieved that he was uninjured, but he had expected Brenna to be here and was disappointed she was not.

As Arthur stepped into the bedchamber, a broadly smiling Kaye was next to greet him. He, too, embraced Arthur. He whispered into Arthur's ear. "I'm truly sorry for all that happened. You will be restored to your former position. That's a promise."

Arthur took his brother by the shoulders and held him at arm's length so that he could look him in the eye. "All that was a mistake." Kaye smiled. "No, I don't mean my being sent to Hadrian's Wall, but the mistake that happened that day in the wood at Londinium. That's over now." Kaye's first reaction, judging from his expression, was denial and resistance. "You lost this castle to the Saxons, and if Bryso is to be believed in this once instance, you agreed to an alliance with Vollo. What is more important, you were never entitled to the sword."

"This isn't a decision to be made by you and me alone. Others must decide."

"The army already has."

Arthur moved to Uriens, who sat on the bed looking older and weaker than when Arthur had last seen him. "Sir Uriens, your castle has been returned to you, and I apologize for any anguish I've caused you." There also was Maeve, who smiled anxiously at him. He did not yet have it within him to forgive Maeve for whatever part she had played in exposing his romance with Brenna. He ignored her to ask where Brenna was.

It was Ector who answered. "We have not seen her since the Saxons came, but the servant who brings us food, Finola, said that she was being protected by a Saxon battle leader."

Those words wounded him more than any of the blows he had taken during the day's battle, for he knew instantly that Bryso's claim about Brenna was true. It was sadly ironic, he thought, that a man who seemed to consistently lie was telling the truth in this one instance. Arthur left them to continue his search of the tower, only now with a new worry. He might find Brenna with another man.

She was not in the tower, but he knew where else to check, their hiding place in the west tower. He went down to the courtyard, where the British were rounding up the remaining Saxons, disarming them and putting them under guard. He found Prywycke and asked him to follow him to the west tower. When they reached the tower, Arthur said that he would not go inside but told Prywycke where to look, what he could expect to find and that if, in fact, there was a Saxon with Brenna, he was to be given safe conduct out of Valphain Castle.

While Prywycke opened the wooden door and entered the tower, Arthur stood off to the side, out of sight.

When the tower door opened again, he watched from a distance as Prywycke led Brenna and a Saxon out. She was wearing a cloak that must have belonged to the Saxon, who walked with his two arms wrapped around her. The manner in which she leaned against him confirmed what he already knew.

Arthur remained motionless. He felt hollow inside. He had expected this but seeing the confirmation of her infidelity would haunt him the rest of his days.

Merlin was approaching. The wizard had an uncanny ability to know where Arthur was. He motioned toward Brenna. "Do you not wish to speak to her?" Arthur shook his head. "You are certain?"

His face was expressionless, and he could not speak for a time. "What would I say to her, Merlin?" he said angrily. "I wish great happiness to you and your new lover? I risked everything I had for you — my dignity, my future, and you became the mistress of a Saxon?" He stared at Merlin, who did not attempt to contradict him. Arthur's tone softened. "I thought I had a bond with Brenna that transcended everything else, transcended becoming king, being loyal to my brother, acting honorably. That she could be with another man so soon can only mean that I was wrong about the nature of that bond. It is not the loss of her that puts a lance through my heart but more so the realization that I never had her, not really. Perhaps, it's in Brenna's nature that men fall so deeply in love with her that they take great risks to be with her. I did." Arthur motioned to the Saxon as he was led away with Brenna. "That Saxon risked everything for her as well."

"And later will you regret not speaking to her now?"

"No, but I'll regret every day that things between us are not as they were. I will never overcome this."

"You will. There will be another woman."

"More visions of the future, Merlin?"

"No, just the nature of your being a man." Merlin rested a hand on Arthur's shoulder. "In her defense, you were away. He was here. She was alone, frightened and in danger. You cannot know the fear she experienced."

"I understand." He took a deep breath. "I'm at fault as well. But I am bitter that she led me down a path that she was so quick to abandon."

"It was a path you gladly walked." Merlin looked back at Brenna, who was almost out of sight. "I sensed just now in seeing her that she is not well. And I mean more than whatever ills she suffered at the hands of the Saxons."

Arthur still felt deep concern for her. "But you could be wrong about her being ill?

"Yes. As you should know by now, my *vision* is not always correct." Merlin turned to take a last look at Brenna but she was gone. "You were seduced by Brenna's beauty and charm as your brother was seduced by the power and prestige of the sword. You have both lost something. You both will have to set a new course."

Merlin turned and began to walk away. Arthur followed. They went to the front of the courtyard, where the wall was in shambles and what was left of the Saxon army sat captive outside where the castle gates once stood. "Yesterday morning," said Arthur, "I was more certain of Brenna than I was of winning this battle. I never expected it to end like this, to win the battle and to lose her."

"You may not understand this now, Arthur, but one day you will. When you allowed Kaye to claim Caliburn that morning in the forest, you strayed from the path destiny laid out for you. Brenna was merely a circumstance to force you back onto it."

Arthur stopped walking to look Merlin in the eye. "Are you saying all this had to happen, that it was preordained?"

Merlin shook his head. "No, not exactly. This particular destiny was always out there for you like the Sword in the Stone resting at the end of a forest path. It was never certain that you would reach for the sword or that circumstances would permit you to draw it." Merlin shook his head again. "I just never foresaw that you might draw Caliburn and release it to Kaye."

"And all this turmoil and agony was to meant to get the sword back into my hands."

The wizard nodded. "That appears to be the case."

"Then, it was a very painful journey. I wish destiny had used another device, anything but this."

"So your heart has been broken by a woman. It won't be the last time. And you have won a battle. There will be more." Merlin pointed to the sky. "You spoke of this day ending, but the morning sun only now appears. Are you certain there are no Saxons free and armed? Have you sent scouts to see if there is another Saxon army hiding in the woods? To watch for another Saxon fleet off the coast? To monitor Hadrian's Wall to see if the Picts have regrouped and are heading south?"

"No, not one of those things," said Arthur sarcastically, although he knew Merlin was only trying to prod him out of his melancholia.

They locked eyes for a few moments before Merlin spoke. "Even so, you haven't done too badly." Merlin turned and began to leave him.

Arthur was going to ask the wizard where he was going but decided he did not need to know. And Merlin was right about one thing: Arthur had more to do, much more. How ironic, he thought. There was a time when Arthur would lose himself in thought to avoid his responsibilities. Now to avoid the thought of Brenna and this day's disappointment, he would lose himself in his responsibilities.